THE BLACK TEMPEST

First Edition
First Printing, 2017

Book design by Christopher Loke
Cover design by Christopher Loke
Cover images by Docbaney/Pixabay; artverall/Pixabay; pixmartin/Pixabay; RondellMelling/Pixabay

Jolly Fish Press, an imprint of North Star Editions, Inc.

Library of Congress Cataloging-in-Publication Data (Pending)
ISBN 978-1-63163-106-1

Jolly Fish Press
North Star Editions, Inc.
2297 Waters Drive
Mendota Heights, MN 55120
www.jollyfishpress.com

Printed in the United States of America

To Future You,
For all the amazing things you're about to do.

THE BLACK TEMPEST

THE TIME SHIFTERS BOOK TWO

RYAN DALTON

CHAPTER 1

October, AD 641

Light pulsed from the great machine as it awoke. A silvery-white glow illuminated the surrounding trees, chasing away the deep dark of night.

As the ground rumbled beneath Tyrathorn's feet, he allowed himself to marvel at the machine. The Empyrean Bridge remained his people's greatest achievement. Now, in their most desperate hour, he would use it to save everyone.

Footsteps approached from behind, and his first lieutenant appeared at his side. She pushed back the deep hood of her cloak, letting the snow fall in her hair. Her armor gleamed underneath, bathed in a faint red glow.

"Holding yourself ready, yet I have already dispatched the guards." He gestured to the bodies around them. "Do you not trust our plan?"

"It's the enemy I do not trust. They grow more clever, and their forces grow more dangerous." She turned to face him, her expression grave. "We're losing, Thorn. If this fails—if the enemy uncovers it before we're ready—it's over."

"I do not intend to—" Tyrathorn cut off, whipping around

to stare into the trees. A *shift* in the flow of Time had occurred nearby.

Mentally he reached through the nexus in his armored chest plate and tapped into the Time stream. Temporal energy flowed through the device and into him, sharpening his senses, lending him power.

His lieutenant drew her weapon and put her back to his. "Where?"

While his eyes scanned the tree line, his true sense cast out farther, waiting for another disturbance in Time. It had barely been a ripple, like a toe dipped in a lake. Which could mean nothing—Time did not always flow like silk, after all—or it could mean an enemy Chronauri had discovered them.

Tyrathorn willed his power outward. A blue glow passed through the fine chain mail covering his body, then rippled across grayish-silver armor plates. The cold night air whipped around him as he braced for an assault.

None came.

They stood like statues in the falling snow, ready to strike. But after a long stretch of silence, Tyrathorn began to question himself. Had he really felt the *shift*, or were his nerves making him jump at shadows?

His companion turned to him with a questioning eye. Resigned, he nodded and released the power he'd been holding. The glow faded from his armor. Together they ascended the ramp to a wide platform, where a control panel waited.

The Empyrean Bridge sat atop the platform—three hovering rings of polished metal and stone, each forty feet across. Behind them stood four cylindrical metal pylons, glowing with that silver-white inner light, constantly feeding power to the rings.

Tyrathorn tapped a series of commands and two rings moved

aside while the third floated toward the center. The machine hummed, pylons glowing brighter as the ring began to spin on its axis. Faster it spun, until within moments it became a blur.

"Tell me your first order," he said.

"Wait four and a half minutes, then follow you through the portal."

"And your second?"

She cocked an eyebrow. "Win."

A hint of a grin touched his lips. So much spirit, and unlike so many others, she understood him. This was why she was his most trusted. Why she was the only family he would ever need. He offered a hand and she accepted it, armor clinking against armor as they shook.

"See you when it's time to save the world."

Her eyes caught fire. "No matter what."

With a *boom* that rattled the trees, the ring became a swirling vortex of red energy. Tyrathorn approached it tentatively. In two minutes it would stabilize, ready to send him where he needed to be. And when.

On his third step he felt the *shift* again, only much closer now. An instant later, weapons clanged and his lieutenant shouted in alarm. *No! It's not ready!* Spinning, Tyrathorn reached for the power through his nexus and readied his weapon.

He wasn't fast enough.

Red bursts of energy rocked the air, a storm of light and sound that temporarily blinded him. Shockwaves drove him back a step, then another, shattering the weapon in his hands. His lieutenant cried out for him to run, just go, leave her. More weapons clattered and he heard running footsteps.

"No!" she yelled.

Her body smacked into his, and then there was only pain. It

lanced into his side like fire, exploded behind his eyes as something bashed against his temple. In blind agony, he faltered as her limbs tangled with his. They tumbled backward through the portal.

The world flashed white.

CHAPTER 2

Present Day
Six months after the defeat of Lucius Carmichael

"I've got you now, Gilbert. You're dead. *Dead!*"

Valentine stared down her opponent, holding a mask of confidence. Glancing at what she held in her hand, she wondered, would it be enough to survive? Everything depended on what she did next.

Squaring her shoulders, she tossed her remaining chips on the pile. "All in."

"Ooooooh!" Fred elbowed Winter. "She just threw down the gauntlet, yo!"

Winter mock glared at Valentine. They were the only two who hadn't folded this hand of Texas Hold 'Em, and it was obvious that Winter tasted victory. She elbowed Fred back.

"Do you even know what a gauntlet is, party boy?"

Fred shrugged. "Some'n to do with personal hygiene? I don't know, dawg."

At Valentine's left, Malcolm leaned subtly in her direction and stole a glance at her cards. Then, pretending to stretch, he leaned the other way to do the same with Winter. The petite girl whipped her long black-and-purple hair and arched an eyebrow at him.

"You must be joking, Mal. Stop spying for the enemy!"

"Excuse me, Miss Tao, but I was clearly trying to *cheat*. At least accuse me of the right crime."

"It isn't over yet," John said. His fingers brushed the back of Valentine's arm. "Don't count my girl out."

As always, the calm of his voice flowed over her like a deep, warm river. She favored him with an affectionate smile. The quick moment between them seemed to stretch on until her heart could barely hold the—

Winter put a hand to her mouth and blew a raspberry. "Thanks for the advice, Captain Romance." She matched Valentine's bet. "Like I said before . . . gotcha."

With dramatic flair, she tossed her cards down to reveal a flush. Valentine's heart sank amid the *oohs* of the others. Her bluff called, she laid down a two-pair hand.

Winter offered a high-five. "Nice bluffing, Val. You almost made me fold."

"What about you?" Valentine said. "That whole overconfident routine made me think *you* were bluffing."

"Double bluff," Malcolm said. "Nice."

"I accept your praise for my brilliance," Winter said, raking the chips toward her already sizable pile.

Valentine marveled as the group laughed together, quietly watching each of them. It was six months to the day since Lucius and his doomsday machine had been defeated. And look how far they'd come.

Fred's arms were out of the casts, and Winter's hearing had returned to normal. Despite battling an enemy that would gladly have taken their lives, those near-death memories hadn't beaten them. They'd kept all of their spirit, and then some.

John's psychologist visits had worked wonders in mending the fractures in his heart. Facing a supervillain from the future, falling through a rift in Time, then facing that same villain again, only to lose old friends in the process—it could easily have broken a weaker person. But here he was, mended.

Lucius had forced Valentine and Malcolm to face their own demons, too, which had turned out to be a blessing. It still wasn't easy moving on—the pain of losing their mother would always linger—but slowly they were learning to embrace the life ahead of them. In recent weeks Valentine had realized she felt like her old self again, and Malcolm had confided similar feelings.

Things were *good*. She drank in the banter of her friends, relishing the cozy comfort of it all. This was home now. It also didn't hurt that tomorrow was Saturday, which meant they could sleep late, *and* that they only had one more week of freshman year.

Fred dealt the next hand. "A'ight, peeps, we gotta step up our game or Winter's gonna be winning all summer."

"Oh, right, it's almost summer." Malcolm zipped up his hoodie. "I keep forgetting."

Valentine glanced out the window to see snowflakes. For the fourth night in a row, snow blanketed the countryside. The deeper cold had delayed for months, likely due to Lucius tampering with the sky, and now *real* winter frolicked as if it had been set free.

"Speaking of that, any more reporters sniffin' around?" Fred asked. "Weird weather might bring 'em back."

Malcolm shook his head. "We got pretty good at pretending to be clueless."

"And the weathermen say it won't last long," John offered. "Our strangeness may be wearing off."

In truth, it had been fun having a secret like in spy movies. After international news crews descended on Emmett's Bluff, someone figured out that the crater across the street—the crater that had been Lucius's house with no doors—sat at the very center of the twelve giant energy beams that had rocked the town. So, of course, they tried scoring interviews with everyone nearby. Valentine and Malcolm made a game of all the silly misdirections they could give.

Ever since, Emmett's Bluff had gained a reputation as Home of the Strange, and they were now a destination for alien and conspiracy theorists. Some came just to see where the beams had punched holes in the town, though the government had long since covered the craters.

No one had even come close to figuring out the truth. Which wasn't surprising, since the truth was stranger than any of their theories.

"They'll definitely be back if they hear about the ice pillars," Winter said.

Valentine blinked. *What?*

Malcolm leaned forward. "Uh, what ice pillars?"

"You haven't heard? But they've been happening . . ." She trailed off as John and Fred shook their heads—they hadn't heard, either. A light went on behind Winter's eyes. "Oh! Sorry, I forgot it came from a contact I have for the school paper. He works for the *actual* paper. They're sitting on the story until they can figure out an angle."

The group waited for her to elaborate, but Winter seemed satisfied with her answer.

"And that story is . . ." Valentine prompted.

"Oh. For a couple months, these big ice pillars have been popping up in town—about ten so far, I think. No one knows because the mayor has his people crush them as soon they're found. Guess he doesn't want a panic."

"What'd it look like?" Malcolm asked.

"Weird. Like a big, round column, except it's sort of twisty like the threads on a screw. Like twenty feet tall and totally solid, except there are chunks missing at the base."

The group fell quiet. Maybe it was bad memories for Valentine, but she found herself wondering, were these just aftershocks from a villain they had already vanquished? Or were they something more?

"Guys," Winter said. "It's no big deal. No one's been hurt. It's just *ice*—it'll melt."

That seemed to placate Fred and John. Not Valentine, though, and one glance at Malcolm showed that he felt the same. With effort, she pushed the worry away. *We already had our fight and we won. So just relax.*

Maybe she was on edge because of what was coming later tonight. They all knew it needed to be done, but still, it brought back memories.

All day, Valentine had been flashing back to her fight with Lucius. Trading hit after hit, ripping away his control of that pocket watch, absorbing some kind of . . . something . . . an energy she'd never felt before. An energy that was still there, even now. She could almost reach out and—

She shook herself. "We can go soon, right?"

"Have to wait for Dad to get home and go to bed," Malcolm said. "Then we'll go."

Just then, the front door squeaked open, followed by footsteps. And whistling.

"Speak of the devil," Valentine said with a bemused smile. "Wow, he's whistling a pop song from this decade."

Neil Gilbert strolled into the kitchen, looking like he'd stepped out of the "Dad Edition" of *GQ Magazine*. New sport coat over jeans, dark-rimmed glasses, even his light brown hair was swept back in a casually stylish way. He stopped at the sight of them.

"Now, I could've sworn I only had two kids," he said, then approached with a wide grin. "Hey there, teenagers!"

Everyone said hi. Their dad stopped between Valentine and Malcolm, resting a hand on each of their shoulders. The twins smiled up at him, and Valentine placed her hand over his.

"You didn't lose the house yet, did you?" he asked, surveying the table. "It's where I keep all my stuff."

"We'd have to be playing with real money," Malcolm said. "We did lose the car, though."

"And our college funds," Valentine added. *Is he actually wearing cologne?* "How was the interview?"

He gave a thumbs-up. "Great stuff. Should give the new book a nice plug."

"You've had more interviews than normal," she said.

"Yeah, I suppose. This book's important, though, so it's getting some extra push. That's the life of a tortured artist, kids." He chuckled and moved to the stairs. "Alright, bed's calling my name. Don't stay up too late, now." Pausing on the third step, he pointed back at the group. "I'm just kidding—it's the weekend! I order you to stay up far too late."

He practically floated up the stairs, whistling all the way.

"Whoa," Fred said. "Someone replaced your dad with a happy dude."

Malcolm shrugged. "It started a few months ago. He's practically his old self."

"So, that's how he was, before . . ." Winter made an awkward face, "you know."

Before our mom died, Valentine finished in her head. *No one likes saying it.*

"It's like he's waking back up," she said. Under the table, she reached for John's hand and relished the thrill as their fingers intertwined. "I think maybe he sees we're happy, so he can actually start living again."

"And good for him," John said, tracing his thumb over her palm. "Everyone's earned good days."

"True that." Fred picked up his cards. "A'ight, let's see who's gonna lose to me before we go do our thing."

Reaching into his pocket, Malcolm withdrew Walter's Silver Star and held it over the edge. "You had more honor than ten men, Walter. We'll miss you every day."

The others quietly said their own goodbyes. When they finished, Malcolm let the medal fall into the crater. With a faint thump, it disappeared into the snow and buried itself among the remains of the house. Winter nudged him and nodded, a *thank you* for what he'd said. Together, the companions gazed into the abyss.

"So," Fred said. "Same time next year?"

They agreed without hesitation. Then, knowing that Walter would roll his eyes at them for standing in the cold to talk about him, Malcolm turned back toward the street. The others followed suit.

A *BOOM* shook the air behind them. The ground rumbled

and a rushing wind gusted from inside the crater. Whipping around, Malcolm and the group faced the crater again.

A second *BOOM* vibrated through their bones. In his mind Malcolm felt something intangible *shift* and then rip. Inside the crater, the air twisted open and bright light poured out of the aperture. Something solid shot out and dropped to the ground, and the light disappeared in a blink.

Returning to the edge, Malcolm peered into the crater. Between the remains of the house, he caught sight of a small mound that hadn't been there before. The mound moved and groaned.

"Someone's in there!" Valentine said.

Malcolm, Valentine, and John slid down the embankment and scrambled across the dips and rises in the crater. Dodging past remnants of the house that jutted from the ground, they halted above the prone figure of a tall, armored man covered in thick frost. In a ten-foot circle around his body, the snow had frozen into a solid sheet of ice.

"What on earth . . . ?"

Hesitantly, Malcolm removed the man's helmet. Shoulder-length black hair spilled out to frame a young face, lean and olive-complexioned. His right temple was heavily bruised, and blood seeped from a jagged gash at the edge of his scalp.

"He's young," John said. "Eighteen or twenty, maybe."

"Mal, look at this." Valentine touched the plates of ornate silver armor, etched with fine scrollwork in a flowing, wavy pattern. Underneath was a layer of dark gray chain mail—a mesh finer than any Malcolm had seen.

"Where's this guy from?" she said.

"Where?" John said. "Or *when?*"

"I've never seen armor like this before." Malcolm leaned in for a closer look. "Whoa, this guy's hurt!"

A wide gash split the armor's right flank. Valentine parted the layers and winced in sympathy. A deep slash had cleaved the man's side open, leaving a seared red wound. Oddly, while the rest of him was covered in frost, Malcolm could feel the wound radiating heat.

"Call an ambulance!" he said.

Fred pulled out his phone. "On it."

"Should we move him?" Valentine asked.

"It could hurt him," John said.

The armored man's chest heaved with guttural hacking. His eyes fluttered open and locked onto Malcolm in terror. He lunged forward and grabbed Malcolm's arms.

"He's coming! He's—" he cut off with a grimace and sucked in a breath. "The Black Tempest is coming! No stopping him, you've all got to *run*. Run!"

Spasming, he slumped to the ground and his eyes rolled back. His breathing grew more labored and the small bit of color in his cheeks drained away.

"Does he mean Lucius?" Valentine's eyes darted around warily.

Malcolm shook his head vehemently. "No way. Lucius is out of the game. We made sure of it." He glanced up at the sky. "He's talking about someone else. Maybe someone wherever he's from."

Malcolm forced himself to relax and slide out of arm's reach. After fighting Lucius Carmichael, the instinct to defend himself with force had not yet faded, and he didn't want to hurt an al-ready-injured man. Sitting in the snow, he tried to digest what he'd just heard. Valentine's brow was furrowed, and he knew she was pondering the same thing.

"A year ago, I'd have said he's delirious and doesn't know what he's saying," she said. "But now?"

"Yeah," Malcolm said. "And we've seen too much to think he's just crazy."

"So, if it's true, who's coming and why should we run?"

"I don't know. But if it *is* true," he looked pointedly at Valentine. "We'd better get ready."

"Yes . . . but ready for what?" John said, his voice filled with dread as if he already knew the answer.

Valentine reached for his hand, but her eyes were on Malcolm. He could see it in her expression—she knew. She just didn't want to believe.

Malcolm knew exactly how she felt. "I won't say it, Val. We've already fought two Time-traveling bad guys, and we won. We're done."

He stood, pacing back and forth. The others stood with him and brushed the snow off their clothes.

"If anything does happen," John said, "just know that I'm with you for—"

A faint scrape was their only warning. A gray blur burst from the shadows. Leaping over the fallen man, the blur lashed out with impossible speed.

Before he could react, Malcolm found himself flat on his back, the wind knocked from him and an ache spreading across his chest. A heartbeat later, Valentine and John joined him on the cold ground.

Their attacker loomed over them, and Malcolm gaped. What had seemed to be a blur was actually a black-haired girl about his age, clad in more silver-gray armor. Her eyes locked with his, ice blue and brimming with fury.

Malcolm grunted as she dug her knee into his chest. With a snarl she aimed the point of a long dagger at his throat. The blade radiated red light and the air around it sizzled and popped. "Stay down," she commanded. "And stay away from him, *kuputsa*. He's my—"

Valentine's foot connected with her head. Seizing the moment, Malcolm punched her square in the face and rolled away, stumbling to his feet. He watched in wonder as the girl shook it off and stood, visually sizing them up.

"Wow," Valentine said. "You hit a girl."

Malcolm shrugged. "I don't think the rules apply when she has a knife at your throat."

Hurried footsteps approached. Winter and Fred arrived from the crater's edge, fists up. Fred wore his serious face while Winter pointed at their attacker.

"Come on, Hunger Games," she taunted. "Make a move!"

The armored girl seemed taken aback, perhaps reevaluating her odds against five. To Malcolm's chagrin, she whipped off her cloak and a second dagger appeared in her other hand. She loosed a guttural roar, as if summoning something from deep inside. Her armor and weapons blazed with red light, the air around her crackling in a halo of energy.

Malcolm gasped as something inside him stirred. He could feel—could almost see—her pulling the energy from deep inside herself, bending and channeling it. He fell back a step. *What is going on?*

"Are you feeling that?" Valentine whispered.

He could only nod.

Sheathed in waves of red light, the girl reminded Malcolm of a coal inside a dying fire. As he stared in awe, she raised her blades and took a threatening step toward them.

"Asha?"

The voice had come from the injured warrior. The girl stopped dead in her tracks and angled toward him.

"Tyrathorn? I'm here to—"

Impossibly, he managed to sit up and focus on the girl.

"Asha, don't . . . please . . ."

The burst of strength faded quickly. Swaying, he clutched his wounded temple and seemed to search for words. Malcolm could see his eyes glazing over.

"Tyrathorn?" he said. "Am I . . . who is Tyrathorn? Who is Asha? Who is . . . are you? Where . . . ? The Black Tempest. He is coming. I have seen it!"

Her eyes went wide, as if she'd seen a ghost. The tips of her daggers dipped. For the first time she looked uncertain.

"Run, girl," the warrior pleaded. "Please. Do not let him find you." He sucked in a breath and broke into a coughing fit. "I will fight him for . . . for as long as I . . ."

He toppled over, going limp.

Scrambling toward Tyrathorn, Asha fell to her knees and cradled his head and shoulders in her lap. As she rocked from side to side, the light faded from her armor.

She whispered in his ear too softly to be overheard. Then her attention returned to Malcolm, radiant blue eyes piercing him.

"Please," she said. "Help my brother."

CHAPTER 3

"Hunger Games?" Fred asked.

Winter shrugged. "First thing that came to mind, warrior girl and everything. I was going for effect."

"But Katniss used a bow, didn't she?"

She arched an eyebrow. "Don't tell me you actually read a book."

"Well, see, they make these new things called movies . . ."

Seven of them sprawled across benches in the hospital's waiting room, the long day finally catching up with them. Oma Grace and Clive Jessop sat dozing in the corner. Malcolm chuckled at their snoring.

Especially Clive. He didn't look or move like someone well over a century old, but the man slept like the dead and snored like a chainsaw. He leaned against Oma Grace with the casual intimacy of a friendship that had itself spanned over a century.

Malcolm turned to Valentine. "You're sure the clothes will fit her?"

She pressed against John while he stroked her wavy red hair. "I think we're around the same size, but it was hard to tell with that armor."

"It's preferable to her walking around armed," John observed. "With that look on her face, people would have called the police."

"Probably more comfortable, too," Malcolm said. "Maybe she—"

He cut off as, across the hall, the bathroom door swung open. A young, fair-complexioned girl stepped out in jeans and a *Doctor Who* t-shirt, her black hair in a ponytail. For a split second, Malcolm didn't recognize Asha. The only thing that remained was her hardened expression.

She does have nice lips, though, he thought. *Wait, what?*

She approached gingerly, eyes darting to every corner, taking in every detail, never resting. She chose a seat facing the doorway and set a duffel bag between her feet.

Awkward silence filled the room, like it was a tangible thing that might smother the first one to talk. Malcolm felt a kick and Valentine inclined her head toward Asha with a look of expectation.

He sighed. *Okay, then.* "Uh, so . . ."

Asha faced him and he forgot all the words he knew. Those ice blue eyes seemed to flash, as if filled with electricity.

"We, uh, told the doctors that you guys had a LARPing accident."

Her head tilted. "What's a larping?"

"Oh, right, you probably don't . . . well, it's where people dress up in armor and swords and *pretend* to fight."

"Battle training?"

He cleared his throat. "Not really, no. Um, no one actually does the sword-and-armor thing anymore. Not for real."

She stared into space, as if considering, then turned her

stare on him again. "Of course. With all the years we visit, I forget. Continue."

Malcolm glanced at his friends in a silent plea for backup, which yielded no results.

"That's all I've got. You already know your brother's in surgery. They'll tell us when it's done." He paused to gather his thoughts. "So . . . you *are* both time travelers, right?"

She nodded as if that should be obvious.

"When are you from?"

"We're . . . not allowed to say. Only the—"

High-pitched tones blared from the nurse's station. Asha sprang to her feet, duffel unzipped and a blade in her hand.

"Whoa!" Malcolm leapt in front of her. "Easy. It's probably just for a patient. Sometimes their heart monitors slip off. Relax."

For an instant she had the wild look of a cornered predator, and Malcolm wondered if she'd simply go through him. Then she blinked and sat down. Her beautiful yet ridiculously long dagger disappeared back into the bag. Staring after it, Malcolm knew he should stay on topic, but couldn't help himself.

"That's a *qama,* right? A Cossack dagger?" Sitting, he tapped his foot against the bag. "The design is similar, at least. The blade is thinner, and I don't recognize the markings all over—"

Someone cleared their throat, and Malcolm saw that Clive and Oma Grace had woken. "Focus, please, young man," Oma Grace said as they scooted their chairs closer.

"Maybe start with why they're here," Clive said. He offered his friendliest smile, which bounced off Asha with no effect.

"Right." Malcolm looked to Asha. "So, what he said."

She examined the floor and bit her bottom lip, as if considering her course. Malcolm couldn't imagine how overwhelming this must be for her. How would he decide where to begin, much less which details to share with strangers?

After a moment, Asha nodded to herself. Straightening in her chair, she pushed back her shoulders and tilted her chin higher. The change was small, but it transformed her from Lost Warrior to Lost Royalty.

"I am Ashandara Corvonian of Everwatch, daughter of Eternal King Jerrik and Meliora, Queen of the Infinite. My brother and I are High Protectors of the Ember Guard, and we have come because our war could no longer be contained to our kingdom. It has arrived here."

These were the most words she had spoken at once, by far. Enough that Malcolm caught her subtle accent now. It was soft, almost lyrical, like a slightly musical version of Israeli. Or maybe Persian with a hint of British? Or maybe none of the above.

"Why?" Valentine interjected. "Why here and now?"

"I do not know. Our enemy, the Black Tempest, has fixed his eye on seizing control of my kingdom. He means to bend its power to his own will, instead of toward the good of all." She shook her head. "Though he would say the opposite—that his cause is just. But how can you trust one who hides behind a mask?"

"Tell that to Batman," Malcolm muttered.

"Who is Bat Man?" Asha asked, tensing. "Is he an enemy?"

Winter plucked a decorative conch shell from a side table and held it to her ear. "What's that? Uh-huh . . . yeah, okay, I'll tell him." She pointed at Malcolm. "The ocean says you're a nerd."

The group snickered and Malcolm felt his cheeks warming. He shook his head to indicate to Asha that his remark meant nothing, then gestured for her to continue.

"Hold on," Winter jumped in again. "So, some random people are fighting because they can't agree on politics, and now we're going to pay the price. That about it?"

"It's not so simple," Asha returned.

Winter rolled her eyes. "It never is."

Asha's stare drove into her. "This conflict began in my kingdom, but the outcome will echo across the timeline. The key battlefront had to be somewhere. As it happens, that is here and now." She eyed them all curiously. "No denial? No disbelief? You don't react as . . . as I have seen before."

Malcolm gave a wry grin. "We're not exactly strangers to this."

"I got a feeling there's more, though," Clive nodded at Asha. "Keep goin', Miss."

Asha hesitated, as if choosing her words carefully. "There are those that would corrupt the course of events, twisting the timeline to their own desires. The timeline is strong—it can absorb and compensate for some of this . . . but not all. Cracks are forming in the fabric of our universe, and as more of them appear, the rules that help contain those people are beginning to fail. And so chaos has grown.

"Others saw this and dedicated themselves to defending the timeline. That's why Everwatch was founded. My order, the Ember Guard, are the kingdom's elite force. When a corruption in Time is discovered, we find its root and set things right."

"How are you able to do that?" Valentine asked.

Asha moved to answer, then hesitated again. Malcolm noted how she'd done this several times and wondered how much she was choosing to hold back.

"Over the years, we have . . . developed tools. Some are large and powerful, others more subtle. In addition, every Ember Guard must be a Chronauri of Second-*sev* or higher."

Chronauri . . .

Malcolm's whole being vibrated like a gong, struck by the mallet of that strange word. Valentine gasped and clutched her chest, and he knew she'd felt it, too. The elusive power called to him again, whispering just beyond his reach, tugging at the deepest places inside him.

Chronauri . . .

"Whoa." Fred stared at the twins. "Spooky. Y'all just did the exact same thing."

"At the exact same time," Oma Grace said, her face pinched with worry. "Are you all right?"

Malcolm's mind swam through thick fog, detached from his body. Distantly he noticed the concerned looks that passed around the room. Asha examined them with narrowed eyes, which could signal anger or suspicion or a dozen other emotions.

A hand pierced the fog to rest on his shoulder, and an ebony face filled his clouded vision. Clive drew a finger-sized gadget from his shirt pocket, its tiny yellow light blinking, and waved it from Malcolm's chin to forehead. After three passes it chirped and the light turned blue.

"Just dazed. Though who knows what from?" He eyed Asha. "You say anything mighta done this?"

Before she could speak, the surgeon walked in.

CLIVE's oversized truck bounced over the railroad tracks, snapping Valentine's mind back to the present. Ever since they'd left the hospital, she'd welcomed anything to spark a physical reaction. Cold pinpricks of snowflakes on her face, the crunch of gravel under her feet—they reached through the murky film wrapped around her mind, pulling her back into her body.

Where is John? she thought in alarm. Oh, right. Fred had called his driver to retrieve himself, John, and Winter from the hospital.

Back in the waiting room, the surgeon had been awestruck. According to her, Tyrathorn should be dead. The wound on his flank had cleaved through multiple organs, and whatever blow he'd sustained to the head had cracked his skull. Asha had stiffened at that.

But Tyrathorn's body had practically put itself back together as the doctors worked. He had done more than just survive—he was healing faster than they had ever seen.

However, the wounds were grave enough that they wanted him sedated for another day. So there was no point in anyone staying. They were to use the few remaining hours of night to get some rest, doctor's orders.

Though her brain had felt clogged with cotton, Valentine had noticed the dangerous look on Asha's face. She'd been prepared to draw blades and cut her way to her brother's bedside. Fortunately, Oma Grace had intervened with her usual sage words and the warrior had calmed.

Wait, what's happening right now? Oh, Oma Grace was talking.

"—will need a cover story, both of you," she was saying. "The twins' father is unaware of our activities, and we prefer to keep it that way. Isn't that right, my girl?"

She reached back to pat Valentine's knee. Valentine slowly realized she should speak. "Yeah, he, um . . . probably wouldn't take the truth very well."

With that, the last of her detachment melted away, leaving her fully in her own skin. She breathed a sigh of relief.

"And Dad's finally himself again," Malcolm said. "Don't want to mess with that."

Oma Grace smiled at Asha. "So, my girl, we'll simply say you're having family difficulties. He's a good man—he won't ask further."

Asha just nodded. Valentine could see a subtly stunned, almost lost expression playing across her face. Her heart went out to the girl. Crashing through a tear in the universe, rushing her brother to the hospital, then suddenly being in the company of strangers—it had to be a massive shock.

That didn't include what terrible thing must have happened to them before arriving. She was strong—that much was obvious—but even the strong needed support.

Her mind wandered toward John, as it usually did in idle moments. His quick glances, the little brushes of his fingers. They'd each experienced their share of the strange, and giving her heart to someone who truly understood her had been the best choice she'd ever made.

On returning home, they did their best ninja impression by sneaking through the darkened house as quietly as possible. Malcolm tripped over his own sneakers, which he'd left by the stairs after promising to take them up to his room. Valentine stifled her laughter, and Oma Grace added insult to injury by whispering a lecture on responsibility.

Asha made as much sound as a feather landing on cotton. Moving on the balls of her feet, she dodged effortlessly around every shadow despite never having been there before. While her body wasn't visibly tense, she radiated hyper-awareness. Or maybe readiness was a better description. Like a soldier in a strange land, she adopted a passive veneer while tightly coiled underneath.

Valentine couldn't help wondering where this girl had been, what she had seen. What would give such old eyes to someone so young?

"Have you been here before?" Valentine asked. "I mean, to this part of the timeline."

Asha pursed her lips, glancing away. ". . . No."

"Ah. That makes sense."

"What makes sense?"

"Why you watch everything like it might bite you." Asha started to bristle, and Valentine quickly smiled. "I'm just teasing. You can relax here. Just give me a few minutes to straighten up, and then you can stay in my room."

Asha looked taken aback. "You're giving me your room?"

"You're a guest, and you've had a terrible day. Of course I am."

Her expression almost did relax, though not quite. "That's . . . generous. But I won't impose. The couch will be fine."

"Are you sure? It's no problem."

She shook her head. "I'll be fine."

Valentine acquiesced and left to fetch sleeping clothes and bedding. She threw the items together as quickly as possible, reluctant to leave Asha alone. After all, the only ally she had was miles away, sedated.

She crept back down the stairs, careful to avoid any creaks that might wake their father. Halfway down, just before the wall ended and the banister began, she caught Malcolm's hushed voice and stopped to listen.

"That's the remote control for the TV."

"And this?" Asha asked.

"Control for the ceiling fan."

"Oh."

Valentine peeked around the corner as Asha reached for something.

"And this?"

"That's a snow globe."

"What does it control?"

Malcolm chuckled. "Nothing. It just looks pretty. Here."

He placed his hands over the object and jiggled, kicking up the fake snow so it would spin around the miniature castle.

Asha's eyes widened, her expression softening. "Ooohhh . . ."

She likes it? Valentine marveled. Hours ago she was ready to slice them to pieces, and now she was enchanted by a snow globe.

Asha seemed to realize the same thing. Shaking herself, she pushed the bauble into Malcolm's hands and backed away. Her mental armor reappeared and she stood straight as an arrow.

"Thank you for your aid," she said in a formal tone.

To Valentine's surprise, Malcolm seemed unfazed. He just smiled and said good night, then moved to the stairs. Which reminded Valentine that she'd just been eavesdropping. She started down the stairs again, stifling a giggle as Malcolm pushed past her on his way up.

Soon she had Asha sorted, then showed her the downstairs bathroom where she could freshen up. It wasn't home, whatever home was to a Time-traveling battle princess, but it would do for now.

Valentine gave the living room one last scan, noting that Asha had set the duffel bag within arm's reach. For the first time, it occurred to her that the girl might actually be afraid.

"Hey, can I ask you something?" she said on impulse. "Why are you trusting us?"

Asha considered. "I was unsure at first. I . . . don't know the Black Tempest's identity. But I do know his allies. I've come to learn their nature, and you do not match it." She paused, regarding Valentine. "You are . . . good people, I think. That can't be faked forever."

Valentine smiled. "Thank you."

"Also, if any of you pose a threat later, I can just kill you then."

Valentine's smile melted. "Oh. Okay, nice talk. Good night!"

She fled upstairs to her room. Letting out a long sigh, she plopped onto her bed and deflated. Instead of falling asleep, though, she pondered what Asha had shared. Like it or not, her presence was proof that something was happening in this town. Again. If Asha was right and a new threat was on its way, then . . .

Then Malcolm was right and they had to be ready. Because who else was there? Sitting up, she eyed the silver object on her desk, glinting in the moonlight. That familiar hunger, that bone-deep need, caught fire inside her again. It clawed at her, beckoning her toward the desk. She'd managed to keep the project to herself for weeks now. But would she be able to much longer?

Setting her jaw, she moved to the desk and got to work again. They *would* be ready. They'd already defeated one Time-traveling supervillain, after all. What could this new guy possibly do?

CHAPTER 4

Ol' Bottle Joe wasn't a fool, no sir. Plenty o' friends said he was, back when he'd told 'em his grand plan to hitch rides out to the Midwest. *Ain't no one gonna pick up no vagrant on the highway, Joe.*

But ol' Bottle Joe knew the secret. Homeless or not, a big toothy smile, real and genuine, got you far. A smile that said ain't no harm meant, Joe's a nice man just lookin' for a bit of help. That same smile'd kept him fed and warm for years. So what if Bottle Joe didn't have no address? He did alright turning in all sorts of bottles to be recycled. And if the day's haul was a bit light, well, ol' Bottle Joe had that smile in his back pocket.

One day he waved a big *so long* to freezing Boston, slapped on that smile and rode it all the way to Emmett's Bluff. Less bottles, but nicer people and no one kicked him. He loved every inch of this place and ain't no one gon' change his mind.

Bottle Joe walked the streets more often now, 'specially after sundown. See, his town got hurt 'bout six months ago. Then, after them lights tore holes in his town, folk rolled in with big plans. People tryin' to help, building new pretty things to replace the ones got ripped up. Well, this was his town, too, and call Ol' Bottle Joe a stark fool if he didn't do his bit to help.

So he walked, collected nice bottles, and whenever folk needed help Ol' Bottle Joe was there. People'd got to know him, and now they smile when they see him. Just today he'd helped a young girl find her li'l cat, and he'd located a rich man's wallet. Got a handshake and even a few bucks to say thanks. Nice man.

Duplass Boulevard was his favorite. Half old buildings and half new ones. History next to future, and right downtown. Perfect for Ol' Bottle Joe to keep people safe and—

"Excuse me," a woman called. "Can you help me, please?"

Bottle Joe stopped at the mouth of an alley. Daydreamin' again, hadn't noticed the pretty lady standin' there. No, pretty didn't cut it. Downright gorgeous, 'specially in that fancy black dress.

"Ain't you cold, ma'am?" he said, tugging at his graying beard.

She glanced down at herself. Almost looked like she blushed. Moved a sparkly li'l purse from hand to hand. Gotta try not to stare, not make her feel afraid. Ol' Bottle Joe only helps.

"What's the trouble?"

"In here. Please help."

She pointed toward the back of the alley. Lots of shadows, boxes stacked between snow piles. She moved back there, not waiting.

"Someone hurt?"

"So much more important, sir. Don't worry, I can pay you."

He stood straighter and followed. Lady'd called him *sir*.

"You wanna pay, that's nice, but Ol' Bottle Joe helps no matter what."

She reached the alley's end and turned, smilin' real wide. True Hollywood smile, made the Bottle Joe Brand smile look like a dim bulb.

"You're sweet. Your friends said you would be."

He scratched his head. "Friends?"

"They're in your line of work. In fact, they helped me, too." Her head cocked to the side. Them pretty eyes took on a bit o' mischief. "Johnny Pert? WashMan? Gonzo?"

Other homeless folk, she meant. "You mistaken, ma'am. Ain't seen none o' them in weeks."

"Oh, I'm certain."

"Well, uh, what'd they help you find?"

She rummaged around in that sparkly purse. "Not find something, Mister Joe," she said as her hand came back out with a little round metal thing. "Test something."

Bottle Joe chuckled. "Makeup? Hope it's my shade!"

Her smile went sorta tight. Didn't look Hollywood no more.

"This is called a nexus," she said. "My people use them for something special. This one, though, is even *more* special—modified to perform a very important task. Would you like to try it?"

Bottle Joe felt uneasy, but weren't sure exactly why. "What I gotta do?"

"Just stand there and smile, my love."

He took a step back. "I ain't so sure—"

She pressed some'n on that thing and it came to life! Legs popped out and li'l blue lights started flashing. Then it flew straight at Bottle Joe!

It thumped against his chest, li'l legs diggin' into his coat and latchin' on tight! Bottle Joe stumbled back, slapping at the creature or machine or whatever the crazy thing was. Pull, rip, tear, still it weren't enough, and the scary thing kept its hold.

Panicked, he flung himself away from that crazy lady and her crazy dress, slippin' on snow and crashin' through boxes.

His breath got knocked away, but he managed to stand, tried to run for his life, but the lady stood blockin' the only way out.

The thing on his chest beeped, lights flashed, and a blast o' cold stunned Ol' Bottle Joe all the way down to his bones. He gasped. She just stared at him, watchin' like he were some science project!

He managed to get some breath. "What'd you do to me?"

The cold got worse. That li'l thing beeped again and the air around him started swirlin' like a whirlpool, colder every second. His skin frosted over, stingin' like crazy, messin' with his vision.

"Please, I ain't done nothin'. Only ever helped!" He moved too slow, words comin' out thick and labored. Tears froze on his cheek. "Stop, lady, please! I'm a nice man!"

The lady just watched, and even crazier, she smiled.

Ol' Bottle Joe called out one last, desperate cry and then all the world flashed and turned to shiny crystals and he couldn't move no more. His mind just floated, barely there. Like he weren't no one or nowhere anymore.

Am I dead?

CHAPTER 5

The sun was rising. Hunched over his desk, Malcolm barely noticed the first faint rays as they filtered through the blinds. Once again, he'd barely slept a wink.

Pieces of the pocket watch lay spread out before him—the same silver, antique watch that had been at the center of Lucius Carmichael's plot. The focusing jewel on the cover had been shattered, but the internal workings had remained as functional as ever.

Malcolm had dismantled it anyway. Before, it had been a device for traveling through Time, but that wasn't enough now. He needed more.

So the pocket watch had to become something else—something beyond just a Time machine. It lay in pieces across his desk, mingling with the innards of other small electronics he'd cannibalized.

For many weeks he'd spent his nights this way, piecing the new device together bit by bit, driven by a strange need and guided by an unknown instinct. *What am I even building?*

He shoved the thought away. It didn't matter right now. What did matter was that it was nearly complete—somehow he knew it.

That need drove him more than anything, deep as an ocean, relentless as a hurricane. Each day the pressure grew. And tonight, after that strange name "Chronauri" had crashed through his mind, the need had threatened to swallow him whole.

So under a small work lamp, Malcolm toiled feverishly with tiny tools to finish his device. With every piece he completed, the power that flowed just beyond his senses drew closer. It beckoned to him as if it needed him, too.

Sweat painted his brow. *I'm so close, I can feel it!*

His hands worked faster than his mind could manage. Desperate and hungry, he surrendered to the unbidden knowledge that seemed to move his fingers for him.

A spring here, a cog here, a crystal here, delicate wiring to connect this spinning thing to that glowing thing, counterbalance those two points, keep going just a few more don't stop *almost there I CAN ALMOST TOUCH IT!*

Malcolm gasped and flung the tools onto the desk. *There.*

Snapping the lid shut on what used to be a watch, he clutched it tightly to his chest. *Please please please please.* Eyes closed, he mentally reached out to probe this new device. As he pressed on it with his thoughts, something inside it opened like a doorway.

Pure energy crashed through it.

Flooding every cell in his body, it sang to him just like it had from inside Lucius's machine. When it had saved his life. It called to Malcolm, he called to it, and without knowing why, he felt whole again.

He could even perceive the source now. It was the energy of Time, and all around him it raced by in a torrent, driving the universe forward.

Before, there had been an impenetrable wall between it and

Malcolm. Now this new device somehow acted like a doorway in that wall. Just by willing it to happen, he could open the door, reach through, and absorb some of that energy.

He savored the thrill once more, letting it linger for a long moment. Then he forced himself to take control again and push back toward rationality. *What does this mean? Why did I crave it so much?*

What am I? At that, his exhilaration faded.

Before he could search for an answer, a wave of dizziness swept over him. His insides rumbled and that newfound instinct shouted a warning. There was something happening, but not with him.

He could feel it nearby—a bending, twisting, *shifting* sensation in the flow of Time. Gripping the chair's armrests, he forced his mind to focus, pushing through the clutter of sensory overload toward . . . whatever it was.

He'd been right. Something was drawing in massive amounts of Time, as if a hole had been blasted in the ocean floor and water was rushing to fill it. No, not like a hole, more like a . . .

He sat bolt upright.

Like a doorway. And it's coming from—

Suddenly he knew the source. Leaping from his chair, he ran to his bedroom door and flung it open. Across the hall, Valentine threw open her own door. Malcolm gaped as they came face-to-face in the hall.

A red glow was rippling across her skin.

"Mal, what are you doing?" she whisper-shouted.

"What am I doing?" he whisper-shouted back. "I feel what *you're* doing!"

"Oh, man, I knew it. I knew you were hiding something! You built something out of the watch, didn't you?"

"How would you even guess that unless you did something, too? I see the caduceus in your hand."

She tried hiding it behind her back, but Malcolm had caught a glimpse. Valentine held the caduceus—the device Miss Marcus had used to manipulate unsuspecting victims with her voice. Valentine must have built it into something new, as Malcolm had with the watch.

Faced with the accusation now, she couldn't deny it. He saw it in her eyes.

"Oh, and by the way," he added. "You're glowing! Like, literally."

"So are you! Stop it right now. If someone sees, I'm pretty sure they'll want to know why you're glowing blue."

"Oh, stop on command? Let me just get the instruction manual for Time—" Malcolm stopped short. "Wait, blue? You're glowing red."

Valentine froze, and her outrage crumbled into fear. She bit her lip. "Holy crap, Mal. We're messing with Time somehow, and we're glowing. What are we?"

He worked to soften his voice. She wasn't the enemy. "Are you okay?"

"Honestly . . . I feel amazing. But even that's scary."

"Yeah. We'll figure it out, Val. Togeth—"

A crash echoed up the stairwell. The twins whirled toward the sound, just catching a muffled cry for help.

"That sounds like Dad!" Valentine said.

In unison they sprinted down the hall. Reaching the stairs, they charged down the steps, hit the landing, and skidded around the corner into the living room.

And burst into laughter.

"Oh, good, you two have met," Valentine said.

Neil Gilbert lay face down on the floor with his cheek buried in the carpet. Perched on his back, Asha twisted his arms into a submission hold. She glared up at them, eyes red from recent sleep.

"Who is this?" she demanded.

"Yeah, who is this?" their dad echoed.

Malcolm tried and failed to put on a serious face. "Um, Asha, meet Neil Gilbert. Dad, meet our friend Asha. She's kind of intense."

Asha hesitated. ". . . Your father?"

Her faced turned to what must be her version of mortified, which was to say she looked slightly less likely to kill them all. She released her hold and stepped back while he stood.

"I apologize, sir," she said with a formal tone, standing straight. "You startled me while I slept."

She regarded the twins fully now, and her eyes bulged. Malcolm tensed, expecting an outburst, but in the next blink the look was gone.

Neil forced a chuckle. "Uh, that's okay." He scrubbed fingers through unkempt hair. "Don't take this the wrong way, but why are you here?"

Oma Grace slipped into the room and wrapped her arm around Neil's.

"Not to worry. I'll explain everything." Oma Grace turned to the twins. "Perhaps our guest would like a shower."

Valentine nodded, exchanging a curious glance with Malcolm. He knew they both wondered the same thing. *Don't they see the glow?* Asha had—that much was obvious. Which meant she might be able to answer some questions.

Steam drifted from underneath the bathroom door. Standing beside his bed, Malcolm examined every inch of the small silver object in his hand. The caduceus had been one of Lucius's devices for deep hypnotic suggestion. *Mind control.* After Miss Marcus had used it to betray her friends, then lost her mind, it had fallen into Valentine's possession.

Only now he barely recognized it. As he'd done with the pocket watch, Valentine had reconfigured the device using components from other technology. Driven by her own need, her own instinct, she'd used it to draw energy from Time itself.

"This must have taken you weeks."

"Yeah," she said.

"Why didn't you tell me?"

Leaning back in his desk chair, Valentine pursed her lips. "When I first touched that power, it was when I fought Lucius in Fred's house. Remember what I told you—how he used Mom against me, tried to make a bargain?"

Malcolm nodded.

"When he did that, it felt like she was dying all over again. I got so mad, I grabbed the watch from him and just . . . I don't know, took control somehow. I felt all that power rushing through me, but right then I didn't question it. I just used it to hurt him." She paused, blowing out a weary breath. "It's a moment I'd like to forget. So, when everything was over and I started craving that power again, I felt . . . ashamed. How could I justify wanting something like that?"

"Wow, I never thought about that," Malcolm said. "For me it was so different. It helped me save Fred when Ulrich shot at him. Then, when I fought Lucius, it saved my life."

Valentine eyed him. "Yours couldn't have been easy to build, either. Why did you hide it?"

"Because if it went wrong and killed me, and it was something you knew about, you'd think it was your fault for not stopping me." He shrugged. "I didn't want you to have that burden."

Malcolm prepared to hear a lecture on trusting her, which he probably deserved. Instead, she smiled.

"You know, you're a pretty good guy."

He grinned. "Yeah, I'm pretty awesome. Must be why I get so many chicks."

Valentine giggled. "Well, don't forget how suave you are."

"That, too. They dig it when guys talk about history books."

Her expression changed. "You know, you have had chances with girls around here. I know you get lonely."

Malcolm caught the implied question. Now it was his turn to search for words. How could he explain why he'd caught those girls' signals and turned the other way? Why he'd chosen solitude? Would it even make sense if he said it out loud?

"Well . . . I mean . . ."

The bathroom door opened, ejecting a wave of steam. Asha appeared like a hunter through a fogbound forest. Her eyes roved, searching for threats out of habit. When she spotted the twins, she stepped through Malcolm's doorway.

She wore a pair of his sister's jeans and a gray cotton shirt. Long black hair clung to her neck and forehead, still wet. When her eyes managed to stay still, Malcolm noticed, they were actually quite—*wait, stop, don't even finish that thought. Just don't.*

"Feeling better?" Valentine asked.

Holding up a finger, Asha swung the door closed and fixed the twins with a hard stare. "Who are you really?"

"Um," Valentine said. "What do you mean?"

"I saw you both," Asha snapped. "I saw your corona."

"Corona?" Malcolm said.

She waved her hands around his body. "The glow."

He sat up straighter. "I thought you noticed. But our family didn't, did they?"

"How could they unless they're Chronauri?"

That word again.

"You are not with the Black Tempest," Asha continued. "So, what do you really want?"

Valentine frowned. "You fell into our laps and told us some great evil was coming. What we want is to keep our town safe, just like we did before."

Asha moved to retort, then bit back her words. She studied the floor and took a succession of slow, deep breaths.

"I'm sorry. You're not my enemy, I see that. But until my brother's memory returns, I'm the only Ember Guard here. I cannot let them get around me."

Ember Guard. Black Tempest. Chronauri. Malcolm made sure the bed was behind him before letting his knees weaken. He sank onto the mattress, awash in panic and excitement and dread and a cocktail of other emotions.

"Jeez, Val," he said. "We're actually a thing. We're . . ."

"We're Chronauri," she finished. To his surprise, she gave a relieved smile. "All these months, I thought we were alone. But we're not."

Though he understood, Malcolm didn't share her relief. To him it felt like being marooned on an alien planet, knowing nothing about how to survive. His eyes flicked to Asha. *Is that how she's feeling right now?*

Despite his fears, an opportunity was presenting itself. Each of them had knowledge the other needed. Though they barely knew each other, there was no choice but to start acting like allies.

He drew the modified pocket watch from his pocket and tossed it to Asha. She plucked the device from the air and stared at the case, momentarily mystified. Thumbing the release button, she peered down into its inner workings, and finally the light bulb went on. She stared at Malcolm, astonished.

"Who taught you how to build a nexus?"

AFTER Neil left for his favorite writing spot, the twins and Asha moved to the living room. Asha volunteered to share what she knew first. Oma Grace brought them breakfast and listened, eyes tight with concern.

As she heard the tale, Valentine's head practically spun. It was almost too crazy to believe. She clutched her . . . nexus, Asha had called it . . . between her hands, finding comfort in its presence.

For two years the Black Tempest had threatened Everwatch, but his effect had been small at first. Most who lived in the kingdom had come because they believed in its mission, and were not easily shaken from that.

Yet, somehow he managed to form a ragtag group of rogue Chronauri under his banner—a group that continually grew in size and strength. No one could figure out where they were coming from. The king and queen chose to ignore them, however, believing that the lack of serious victories would cause the rebellion to flicker and die.

They had greatly underestimated the Black Tempest.

According to Asha, some levels of Chronauri could absorb Time energy and use it to *shift* how the timeline flowed around them. This power manifested mostly in variations of speeding Time up or slowing it down.

Part of what separated those levels was how much Time they

could wield. An extremely rare Fifth-*sev* Chronauri, the Black Tempest's power was exceeded only by his drive and ingenuity.

He had apparently been a prodigy in slowing Time, and he'd focused that talent into unparalleled control over the elements of winter—ice, snow, bitter cold, Arctic winds. More than just a warrior, he was an artist. His signature became a suit of black ice armor, as stunningly ornate as it was deadly, and thus his moniker was born.

Eventually he built a force large enough to cause real worry, but still no one could determine how. Where had these new allies come from, and how had he been able to gather so many?

His movements against Everwatch became more effective, yet the king and queen only ever used enough force to defend the city. For some reason mysterious to all, they were never willing to crush the rebellion.

Asha's words dripped with bitterness. "They would barely let the Ember Guard fight. It shamed us. Finally, I decided it was enough. If my parents would be fools, I would finish this for them."

"Just you against all of them?" Valentine said. *Is this girl that good?*

Asha paused. "My brother as well, and first we needed information. So I snuck into the enemy's camp, overheard his War Council, and that changed everything." She drew in a slow breath, as if preparing for a dive into deep water. "First, I learned how his force kept growing. The soldiers who guard the Empyrean Bridge—he threatened their families' lives, and secretly used the Bridge to scour the timeline for criminals with Chronauri abilities."

"Empyrean Bridge?" Malcolm asked.

"The machine we use for Time travel." She shuddered.

"If I had waited one more day, I would have missed their plan and all might have been lost. When I heard, I knew that I . . . *we* . . . had to stop the real war before it began, save Everwatch ourselves. Because who else was there?"

Valentine gave a sympathetic smile. "We know how that feels."

"And that's why you're here," Malcolm said.

Asha nodded. "I . . . and my brother . . . intended to use the Bridge to get here first. Prepare for the Black Tempest and defeat him on arrival. But one of his agents ambushed us, and we fell through the vortex before it was ready. Now I believe we may be too late."

"You still know his plan, though," Malcolm said.

"I didn't hear everything, but this location is key. I believe they will use your town as a staging ground to assault Everwatch. They have grand plans, and those plans do not include your home surviving."

"But, if they want your city," Valentine said, "why is Emmett's Bluff in danger at all?"

Asha looked grim. ". . . I don't know."

Valentine's heart sank. "Great. So there's a villain out there with a vendetta against some secret kingdom, and we're going to pay the price." She looked to Malcolm in despair. "It's Lucius all over again."

"No, it's worse. We're not facing a scientist now—it's a warlord."

Asha's eyes flitted between them. "Scientist?"

"Long story," Malcolm said. "Right now we need to figure out what to do next, and I have no clue where to start."

"There!" Oma Grace pointed to the TV, which was muted and tuned to local news. "Kids, look. What is that?"

Valentine went still as a stone. Malcolm fumbled for the remote and turned up the volume.

". . . may have been appearing for the past two months," the anchorwoman said. "Sources say they only appeared in very small numbers before, and authorities had them destroyed in secret. But after last night, they are impossible to hide now."

Ice pillars.

Photos of at least a dozen cluttered the screen. Huge, twisty things with random chunks missing, they resembled old gnarled trees that had cropped up overnight.

"You wanted a place to start," Oma Grace said. "I believe we've found it."

"You did say the Black Tempest had cold powers," Valentine said to Asha.

Her face had gone still as stone. Swallowing hard, she seemed to search for her voice again. Valentine wondered if this was what fear looked like on a hardened warrior.

"I need to see . . . my brother," Asha said. "Can you take me there, please?"

"I'll check if he can have visitors yet," Oma Grace said. Standing, she moved toward the kitchen.

Valentine's heart went out to the girl. The ice pillars may have confirmed that her enemy was already there. It also meant that her brother was unguarded. As soon as he was able to move, they had to get him to a safer place. In the meantime, she had more questions.

"Asha," she said, leaning forward in anticipation. "What is a Chronauri?"

"And how did this happen to us?" Malcolm added

"You were born with it."

Scanning the room, Asha stood to retrieve an empty paper

towel roll and the snow globe. She indicated the cardboard tube first.

"Imagine this cylinder is the boundary of our universe, if it were infinitely long," she began. "Everything inside—dust, air particles, microscopic life—imagine these are the elements that make up our universe. Stars, planets, people, everything. Now, if I set this down and leave it, what will happen to the things inside?"

"Um . . . not much, I guess," Valentine said.

Malcolm scratched his head. "Yeah, they'd float for a while, then settle to the bottom."

"Yes. But what if I did this?" Placing her mouth at one end of the tube, Asha gently blew into it with a hollow *whoosh* sound. "What happened to them now?"

"Your breath pushed them forward," Malcolm said.

Asha nodded, looking pleased. Valentine waited for more explanation, but the girl's face seemed to say that all had been revealed. Malcolm raised his eyebrows, and Valentine was glad she wasn't the only one still lost.

"And that means . . ." she prompted.

"Oh. I forget this is all new to you." Asha shook her head. "I'm sorry. My breath is like Time. It's the energy that drives the universe forward. Without it, everything just . . . stops. Time is the reason nonliving things decay. As it flows through them, they erode like stones in a stream."

"Would it flow through living things, too?" Malcolm said.

"No. Every living thing is born with an internal store of Time. Somewhere inside you, in a state that no machine could interpret, is your true heart. Its Time energy will sustain you throughout your life. But its storage capacity is limited, and as we get older the energy depletes and its flow becomes slower. When it can no longer fully sustain us, we age, we break down, we die."

"So, everyone has an absolute time limit," Valentine said, feeling a twinge of sadness. Of course everyone knew their life was finite, but to hear it described as something so inevitable somehow made it more real.

"A person may extend their life by being healthy, or injury may take their life regardless of how much Time remains," Asha explained. "But for a normal person, yes, the Time they have is all they will have."

"So we all have a Time battery, sort of," Malcolm said.

"You said normal people," Valentine said, somehow already knowing the answer. "It doesn't apply to everyone, does it?"

"No."

"It doesn't apply to Chronauri," Valentine continued. "Because they . . . we . . . are different?"

Asha stared at the nexus in Valentine's hand.

"How?" she said in disbelief. "How did you build that when you know so little? When there's been no one to teach you?"

"I take it these are important," Malcolm said, pulling his own nexus from his pocket.

"In my home, those are more than just tools," Asha said. "Creating our first nexus is a milestone in our lives. It's a symbol of the faith that Everwatch and the Ember Guard have in us. Only those they trust with this power are ever taught how to build one."

"What happens when someone figures it out by themselves?" Valentine said. "It must happen occasionally."

Asha hesitated. "I . . . No. I've never heard of it happening."

The revelation pressed down on Valentine like a physical weight. She suddenly found it hard to breathe. What sort of craziness had they stumbled into?

"But we both did it," Malcolm said, his voice subdued. "And we didn't even know what we were building. What does that mean?"

Before Asha could answer, Oma Grace returned with a stricken expression.

"My dear, we must get you to the hospital," she said. "There's a problem with your brother."

CHAPTER 6

The double doors burst open. Malcolm trailed behind Asha, with Valentine on his left and Fred on his right. The sounds and antiseptic smells of a hospital always stirred up unpleasant memories. He pushed them back and focused on now. Asha stalked like a wolf on the hunt, peering into the huge observation room windows as they walked down the hallway.

Valentine tucked her phone away with a *tsk*. "She's still not picking up."

Malcolm had overheard her talking to John earlier—he was stuck helping his adoptive parents—but Winter had continued to elude her.

"Been textin' her all day, girl hasn't responded," Fred lamented.

His driver had practically set a speed record in arriving at their house after the twins had called him. Malcolm's biggest surprise had been that Oma Grace wasn't coming with them.

"I've finished my fight, dear boy," she had said when Malcolm asked why. "All these years, I'd forgotten how it felt not to prepare for war. But it's time I admit that I'm an old woman. Now, don't think that means I won't be here for you, silly. But perhaps I should help from the background now. After all, someone has to keep your father clueless about what's really going on around here."

Then she'd smiled and hugged him fiercely and done her grandmotherly duty by commanding him to be careful. Her retirement from . . . well, whatever this was . . . left a bittersweet taste in Malcolm's mouth, but she'd seemed happy.

He caught up to Asha. "It's pretty quiet. Maybe they exaggerated—"

A white-coated body burst through an observation window, crashing to the ground amidst a hail of safety glass. Ear-piercing alarms blared from the nurses' station.

"I SAID NO MORE!"

"Oh," Malcolm said. "Well, never mind."

Asha broke into a run and he stayed on her heels. The doctor who'd just taken his maiden flight stumbled to his feet as they blew past him. Rounding the corner, they burst through the door.

Tyrathorn lay in the hospital bed, both legs and one arm strapped down. His right wrist still wore the frayed end of a broken restraint. Swinging a folding chair like a weapon, he warded away three nurses and a security guard.

"Thorn, stop!" Asha yelled.

She leapt on top of her brother. Pressing one hand on his chest, she used the other to grip his wrist and twist. With a hiss, he dropped the chair and swung at her. She wrenched his arm low and pinned it down with her knee.

"Thorn, look at me!"

Sweaty and wild-eyed, he thrashed beneath her. "Not again!"

With a frustrated huff, Asha drew back and slapped him hard across the face. One of the nurses yelled an objection.

She slapped him again. Then, clutching her brother's face, she forced his eyes to meet hers.

"Stop it. I'm your sister!"

Locked onto her now, Tyrathorn blinked . . . then deflated, all the fight draining from him.

"Asha?" he said weakly. "Please . . . don't make me sleep again."

In the end, it was Fred who saved the day. The staff had been livid, despite Tyrathorn's pleadings that sedation brought on terrible nightmares of a dark enemy. They'd felt real and he could not bear them.

Still, hurling one of their staff through a window had not been the best way to negotiate. That doctor had argued for locking him away for psychiatric evaluation. Malcolm had noticed Asha's posture change, preparing to fight her way clear with her brother.

With tension building to a head, Fred had requested to see the administrator. After a private conversation, the staff had suddenly become convinced that their patient was well enough to be discharged. Just like that, it was over.

"Fred, how?" Valentine said, incredulous. "How did you do this?"

He shrugged, oozing nonchalance from his waiting room chair. "Same way I got him in here with no ID or insurance. No biggie."

Malcolm faltered. "What do you mean?"

Fred chuckled. "Seriously, dude? You can't just bring in a half-dead guy without someone askin' questions. So I gave 'em, uh, incentive not to ask any."

"What does that mean?" Asha asked, her leg bouncing with

raw nerves. She wouldn't be able to relax until they got her brother out of here.

Valentine gaped. "It means he bribed them."

"Whoa, whoa," Fred protested, though the sly grin gave him away. "I tipped them for doin' such a great job. Feel me? And I was already gonna offer a fat donation. Just picked today to do it. Total coincidence, man."

"How are you able to do that?" Asha said.

"What? Oh right, you're new here. I'm, like, super rich." He leaned back in his chair. "Got my own money, and my dad'll donate if I ask him."

Malcolm could only shake his head. "Nicely done, Fred."

Asha stood and placed herself squarely in front of Fred's chair. Staring down at him, her strikingly blue eyes flashed. His grin faded and he radiated an uncertainty that Malcolm shared.

She moved and Fred flinched, then dipped his head in embarrassment. She had only offered her hand. With a tight smile, he accepted it and shook.

"Thank you," she said. "I will not forget this."

He waved her gratitude away. "Please, girl. Ain't no thing."

Soon they heard the squeak of a wheelchair. Tyrathorn appeared in the doorway, pushed along by an orderly who fled as soon as he'd crossed the threshold. Before the doctors could change their minds, they escaped into the cloudy afternoon.

"WHERE to now?" Fred asked after they loaded into his limousine. "Back to your place?"

Malcolm shook his head. "We've got work to do. Let's go by Clive's first, then to . . . uh, we never actually talked about where Tyrathorn was staying. I guess with us."

Fred tapped the intercom button on his console. "Yo, Jeeves, we're headin' to Clive's auto shop now. Cool?"

A muffled sigh came through the speakers. "Yes, sir," the driver said, and the vehicle rumbled into traffic. Malcolm regarded his friend with amusement.

"What?" Fred said.

"Jeeves?"

Fred chuckled. "Yeah, not his name. Dude ain't even British. But for what my dad pays him, he can handle a nickname."

"I think he may hate you a little," Valentine said with a grin.

Fred shrugged and turned to Tyrathorn. "You could crash with me. My house is dope, man, you'll dig it."

The dark-haired man eyed Fred as if he'd only understood every third word. Which maybe he had. Fred tended to be a walking outdated slang machine.

"I'm unsure if Asha and I should separate," Tyrathorn said. "If the enemy discovers one of us, the other should be there to defend."

"Although," Valentine said, pondering, "if he knew you were here, wouldn't he have attacked by now?"

Malcolm turned to Asha. "What do you think?"

Surprise flashed across her face, then disappeared.

"I . . . am not sure. We never discovered all that his people were capable of." She eyed her brother with what looked like a cross between hope and trepidation. "Thorn? How much do you remember?"

Dismayed, he shook his head, black hair brushing across his shoulders. "Not enough. When I sleep, I get flashes. Some feel like memories, some . . . I do not know. But I remember his rage. I remember black ice gleaming as he cut down my friends. I—" He shook his head. "Ashandara, I am terrified of this man."

Asha's jaw tightened. Gingerly, she placed an awkward hand on his arm. "Memories or not, we'll find his servants and destroy them."

"Totally," Fred chimed in. "This ain't our first rodeo."

"It is not just memories of him, sister." Tyrathorn squeezed his eyes shut. "My memory is filled with holes. Childhood, early teen years—I remember them clearly. But as the years progress, less and less of it is clear. I barely remember turning nineteen this year."

Asha went pale. "Thorn . . . this year, you turned twenty-two."

Oh, that can't be good, Malcolm thought. He cleared his throat. "Um, well, you went through a huge trauma. I'm sure you'll get everything back soon. Maybe after we see Clive we should drop you two off to rest."

"And investigate those ice pillars without me?" Asha shook her head. "Not a chance."

"Ice pillars?" Tyrathorn asked.

As Valentine began to explain, he suddenly grimaced and clutched his head. Hissing in pain, he shut his eyes and rocked back and forth. Malcolm tensed, ready to act if the wounded warrior lashed out again.

Tyrathorn muttered under his breath, a constant flow of unconnected thoughts. "Cold so cold Black Tempest ice ice ice ice rescue partner power the chances family winter ice ground zero frost hammer ice always ice so cold . . ."

The group held its collective breath as their new friend lost his mind. Was this what remembering something looked like for Tyrathorn?

Only Asha seemed unshaken. She pulled him around to face her. "Frost Hammer? Thorn, what are you remembering?"

"What's a frost hammer?" Valentine asked.

"*The* Frost Hammer," Asha corrected without taking her eyes off Tyrathorn. He seemed to be settling down now, the random words fading. "The Black Tempest's closest ally, his most trusted enforcer. Her power is second only to his; her brutality is second to none."

"Oh. She's Darth Vader," Malcolm observed, an instant before realizing it would mean nothing to Asha. He noted her questioning glance and shook his head. "Never mind. So, Thorn still needs a place to rest."

By then, Tyrathorn had calmed enough to register what they were saying. His eyes—electric blue just like his sister's—took on a sharp edge.

"No. Stopping the Black Tempest is my mission. I will investigate with you."

"It's why we came here," Asha added, with an uncertain glance at her brother. "Right?"

He paused before responding, then nodded. "Of course."

Though Malcolm didn't doubt the warrior's sincerity, that pause had given away how little he remembered. Malcolm would wager that Tyrathorn had absolutely no memory of their reason for coming here. But who was Malcolm to turn away willing allies?

CHAPTER 7

Though every bay door was closed to keep out the chill, a symphony of mechanical *clanks* and *whirs* vibrated through the red brick building. As they exited the car, Malcolm heard thunder in the distance and struggled not to brace for an attack. He led the group inside.

Every time he walked onto the shop floor, he remembered the very first time. When he'd been blown away by seeing an auto restoration shop that looked more like NASA. When he'd realized that vintage and exotic cars filled every rack, shipped to the mechanical genius Clive Jessop from around the world. When he'd been introduced to the man himself by Walter Crane—his friend. The friend he would never see again.

The memories felt strongest here. It was partly why he'd spent so many happy hours here over the past six months, enjoying Clive's company, rarely reminiscing about their old friend but always knowing. The only person who visited more was John.

Clive was buried in the engine bay of some old classic that had seen better years. By the time it rolled out, though, it would be showroom ready. Stepping closer, Malcolm cleared his throat.

Clive glanced around and caught a glimpse of Asha. With

a shake of his head, he turned back to the engine. "Mind waitin' in the office, Miss? Spectators ain't allowed in here."

"Yeah?" Malcolm asked. "What's the policy on really, really old guys?"

The clanking in the engine bay stopped. "Ain't you see the sign? Only really handsome old guys allowed, and really ugly young ones."

Malcolm laughed. "Get over here. I'll show you ugly."

Clive faced them fully now. Grinning as wide as the Grand Canyon, he pulled Malcolm into a quick embrace.

"What brings you here? Got new friends?" He eyed Asha and Tyrathorn, his expression saying he knew exactly who they were.

"New customers," Malcolm said. "Here to do some hunting. Think we could look around your . . . other . . . shop?"

Clive nodded knowingly. "I may have just the thing. Gimme five minutes?"

They waited behind the shop, which was where the real show began. The huge yard was enclosed by brick walls and packed with row upon row of classic vehicles—everything from World War II military transports to 70s-era Ferraris—all Clive's personal projects in various states of restoration.

Soon Clive emerged, wiping his hands on a cloth, and led them to the very back of the lot. The clouds were growing darker. Soon they would be grateful for being inside.

Past all the cars sat another red brick building with only one bay door—a smaller replica of Clive's gigantic shop. As they approached, the door hummed open to reveal a space much different than had originally been there. Malcolm remembered the bachelor's clubhouse fondly, with its big TV and leather sofas and poker table. Over the last six months, they had all disappeared.

Rows of rectangular tables had replaced them, covered in tools and gadgets. One whole wall boasted stacks of containers of varying size, from plastic to concrete to steel. Work stools were scattered between the tables and along the kitchen counter. *Goodbye, secret clubhouse. Hello, secret laboratory.*

Pausing at a random spot on the wall, Clive leaned closer and blinked twice. A shimmering beam scanned his face, left to right, then top to bottom. With a beep and a click, the "brick" swung open to reveal a small hidden compartment.

He reached inside and withdrew a pair of silver spectacles. Despite having come from an enemy, they'd proven irreplaceable. Lucius had designed them to analyze any technology and display holographic data to the wearer. But, while *he* had used them to build a doomsday Time machine, Clive and John were using them to create all sorts of wonders.

Sliding them on, Clive clapped his hands. "Now, let's get to work."

They followed him across the room to sit at the one empty table, big and round. Meanwhile, Clive approached the wall of containers.

"Go secure," he commanded.

A series of tones trilled. The bay door slid shut and engaged a thick security crossbar. The windows disappeared behind steel covers.

"Now, then. What're we up against?"

"Think Lucius, but meaner and battle-trained," Malcolm said. "Also, crazy ice powers and Time manipulation."

"He'll have allies," Asha said. "At least a dozen, probably more."

Clive took a moment to process that. "Well. Okay. Access vaults A11, G4, and X23." The doors to three containers popped open with a hiss, and Clive moved to collect his toys.

"Dude," Fred whispered, gesturing around the room. "What is going on?"

"Yeah," Valentine said, incredulous. "I knew he could build things, but this?"

They hadn't been here since Lucius. From that day on, Clive and John had been busier than ever. They'd accomplished things no one would have thought possible for a small-town mechanic and a teenage boy.

"The spectacles," Malcolm reminded them. "Remember?"

"Yeah, we know," Fred said. "Blink twice and they show you how any technology works."

"And how to build it," Valentine finished. "But six months ago he only had a few little gadgets."

Malcolm reflected. "Well, I guess he and John wanted to be more prepared. So if this happened again, we could . . . you know, do better."

That hit home. He could see on their faces that they understood. Clive had lost a friend, too, and he never wanted it to happen again. Not that way.

Asha leaned forward. "I'm very lost."

"As am I," Tyrathorn said.

The twins suppressed chuckles. Fred didn't bother to hide his.

"Sorry," Malcolm said. "Lot of history here."

Valentine rested her hand on Asha's arm. "Six months ago, we faced our first bad Time traveler. He left behind a few useful things, including those glasses."

Tyrathorn frowned. "Another Time traveler? Are you certain?"

"Crazy, right?" Fred said. "Big jerk from the future, tried to vaporize our town just to get himself home."

Tyrathorn shared a look with Asha. "Two incursions in six months?"

She agreed. "The odds are astronomical."

"Yeah, it's hard to—" Malcolm stopped. His eyes narrowed. "Are you saying it's not a coincidence?"

"Your enemy. He was from the future?" Asha said.

Malcolm nodded.

"How far?"

"Centuries."

"Hmm." Asha glanced again at Tyrathorn.

He rubbed his temples. "It is difficult to remember all my training. This is not a coincidence, surely, but that does not have to imply a connection. Which may mean . . ." he searched for words ". . . that . . ."

"That there may be something about this place," Asha finished. "Something that's drawing them here."

Malcolm sat stunned. If they were right, he shuddered at what it could mean.

"Dude," Fred said. "That is so messed up."

"Are you saying this may keep happening?" Valentine asked.

"We can't know for sure," Asha said. "Not without Everwatch technology."

"If we were home, it might be possible to determine the cause." Tyrathorn pressed his hands to the table. "Until then, we have this threat to face. And I will not fail my people."

Asha watched her brother, a torrent of emotions rushing across her face, just under the surface. Malcolm couldn't begin to decipher them after knowing her for only a day. He couldn't even tell if Tyrathorn's words were making her happy or sad. *Or angry, maybe. Curious? Determined? Ebullient? Tempestuous? Other big words?* He gave up.

One expression, though, he had seen for sure. In fact, he'd seen it on several occasions before. He just wasn't sure what to make of it. Whenever Asha looked at her brother, her tough exterior weakened. Underneath it he saw uncertainty, maybe even fear. But maybe that would go away once he fully healed.

"Got a few things y'all might enjoy," Clive said.

Looking proud, he took the remaining chair and set a handful of strange objects on the table. Small masses of cobbled-together tech. Metal, glass, wires, maybe even porcelain—the materials were as random as the objects themselves. He started by sliding a familiar object to the center of the table—a black metal ring.

"You'll remember the Accelerator rings, of course. I managed to improve their output. Speed, strength, and healing boosts are all doubled."

"Doubled?" Fred exclaimed. "Aw, snap, son. We're gonna be unstoppable!"

Malcolm grinned at his friend's spirit but kept his own doubts private. The rings were largely responsible for them surviving Lucius in the first place, and every little bit would help. But if their new allies were right, would even double be enough now?

Clive poked at two donut-shaped coils. Three inches across, a dozen varieties of wire and metal tubing twisted together into circles. The coils were joined together by magnets.

"Skippers—short range teleporters. Keep one on you, throw the other. When you slap the one you kept, you'll transport to where its partner is."

Next he picked up what looked like brass knuckles with a tiny satellite dish welded to the front. With an excited grin, he stepped back and pressed a button on the device. It activated with a *snap-hiss* sound, and a transparent shimmering barrier appeared in front of Clive.

"Here's a fun one. Throw somethin' at me."

Tyrathorn picked up a pen and flicked his wrist. The pen sliced through the air as if fired from a bow, hit the barrier, and bounced away. Malcolm stared back and forth between them, unsure whether to be more impressed at Clive's device or the warrior's deadly hand.

"Ha-ha!" Clive pumped his fist in triumph as the barrier deactivated. "Personal shield. Lasts 'bout twenty seconds. Takes a full day to recharge, but it might just save your life."

"Clive," Valentine said, marveling, "how did you figure all this out?"

"Wish I could take all the credit, but your boyfriend's a proper genius." Clive's smile fell as he traded the shield device for a Chapstick-sized black tube. "Now, this one you might not like."

He pressed the red button on top. Shadows in the room began to twist and distort, stretching from corners and beneath tables. Malcolm gripped the table, his heart racing as the shadows wrapped around Clive in a cloak of pure darkness. Valentine and Fred went stiff.

"Our enemy used this to hide, and to intimidate us," Clive's voice emanated from the darkness. "Now we can return the favor."

Mercifully, the shadows unfolded and slipped back to their natural places. Malcolm deflated and leaned against the table, shaking.

"Good lord," Fred breathed. "Maybe warn us first. Jeez."

"Sorry, but it's an advantage we might need. It's just a tool, son. Takes a person to make it evil."

"Cloaking may provide a tactical advantage," Asha observed. She was right, Malcolm knew. So what if it brought back bad memories? Wasn't the town's safety worth it? Meeting Asha's eyes, he nodded. She mirrored the motion back to him, her lips quirking up in a smile.

In response, the tiniest little spark burst in his chest. Startled, he pulled his gaze away from her. She was a warrior, he was on his own path, and it was as simple as that.

But . . . wasn't there more to each of them than that?

"Now, I saved the best for last."

Clive gestured to a clear glass orb the size of a Ping-Pong ball. At its center, no bigger than a fingernail, a red orb pulsed with faint light. Curious, Malcolm reached for it, but stopped short when Clive covered it with his palm.

"Before you run off with one, you gotta know how dangerous it is." Picking it up, he slid his stool to an open space farther away from them. "Glass is real strong, won't break just anytime. When you wanna use it, squeeze thrice, like so." He pumped his fist three times. "Activates the core and makes the shell breakable. Then give it a toss."

Stepping back, Clive lobbed the glass and hit the stool dead center. The clear shell shattered and the center exploded, unleashing a spherical storm of whirling red light three feet in diameter.

Malcolm stared wide-eyed. In the center of the storm, the stool changed.

In two seconds, its smooth finish disappeared. In three, the wood began to disintegrate. In four, it collapsed into dust. After five seconds, the storm abated, leaving a dust pile of what used to be the stool.

Valentine and Fred gasped. Asha and Tyrathorn looked mildly surprised, but neither shocked nor afraid nor impressed. *What kind of tech does Everwatch have?* Malcolm wondered.

"It just . . ." Valentine grasped for words. "I mean, how?"

"I call it a Time grenade. That red center is temporal energy, concentrated into a single point. Whatever's caught inside the blast, it ages a thousand years in five seconds. Enemy wants to mess with Time? Well, now so can we."

Malcolm and Valentine eyed each other. He knew what had just entered her mind. *There's another way to manipulate Time . . . and we may be the key.* Whatever they could do, they needed to learn how to control it fast.

"How'd you figure this out?" Fred asked Clive.

"Trial and error, mostly," Clive said. "At first, we wanted to try it with gravitational force. But if we'd gotten the balance wrong, the grenade woulda collapsed into a black hole. Too dangerous in the end."

"You know, Clive," Malcolm said, "any government or corporation on Earth would kill for just one of these."

He grinned. "Guess we better stay outta the news, then."

"That may be harder these days," Valentine said. "Everyone's watching this town."

"We'll just have to be smarter," Clive said. "Meantime, soon I'll have enough of these for all of us. They'll—"

As he looked at Malcolm, Clive's words died on his tongue. His eyes, bright and happy just a moment ago, darted feverishly from left to right. *He's reading something,* Malcolm thought. *But what could I have—?*

With a start, Malcolm came halfway out of his chair,

remembering the nexus in his pocket. Clive's hand clamped down on his shoulder, holding him there.

"Son," he said. "What are you carrying?"

CHAPTER 8

They told him everything.

Halfway through the story, Clive sank into a chair and stared into space. When they finished, he sat in silence for a long moment, then asked a single question.

"Does Grace know?"

The twins admitted that she didn't. *Why did we keep it from her?* Malcolm wondered. He didn't have an answer. Maybe because of fear. Fear of what it could mean, what it could change.

"She needs to know," Clive said. "Whole town's at stake again, plus some other place with even more people." He nodded toward Asha and Tyrathorn. "You both know 'bout this? You can help?"

"We are Chronauri as well," Tyrathorn said. "As much as I can remember, I will teach them."

"How'd y'all learn to make this, anyway?" Clive asked the twins. "A nexus, you called it?"

"I would like to know as well," Tyrathorn said. "That knowledge is closely guarded. Who taught you?"

What surprised Malcolm the most was how unsurprised Tyrathorn seemed about the objects.

"Did you tell him?" he asked Asha.

Asha shook her head.

"She told me nothing. Somehow, though, I am not surprised. Perhaps without knowing it, I felt the power in you both." Tyrathorn squinted at Malcolm, as if trying to see inside him. "However, it still does not explain who taught you."

In unison, the twins shrugged.

"No one taught us," Malcolm said.

"We just did it," Valentine added. "Felt like instinct."

Asha and Tyrathorn exchanged a significant look. Malcolm felt that overwhelming weight return.

"Is that . . . bad?"

"It is *impossible,*" Tyrathorn said.

"Asha said that, too," Valentine replied.

"Building a nexus is a rite of passage—one that takes instruction and practice. Even *with* guidance, I have never heard of a Chronauri completing one on their first try." Tyrathorn studied the twins. "Do not fear honesty. We are allies. If you are protecting someone . . ."

Malcolm bristled. "Hey, we're not lying."

"There was just this *need,*" Valentine explained. "I felt Time and had to get to it, so I started building. Whenever I finished a piece, I just kind of knew the next step."

"Me, too," Malcolm said. "Almost like something was pulling me along. I can't really explain it, but it's the truth."

The two sets of siblings eyed each other now, uncertain where to go from there. After a tense silence, Tyrathorn shook his head.

"I cannot fathom this. That does *not* mean I do not believe you," he added quickly. "There is simply no explanation for it. Unless . . ."

He looked to Asha again.

She shook her head. "You remember correctly. I've never heard of it either."

"One more mystery," Fred said. "Like we ain't got enough of those. Right?"

"We'll add it to the pile," Clive said. "If an explanation comes along, so be it. Meantime we got bigger things to deal with. Leave your nexus with me, both of you. I'll learn what I can, see if I can make improvements."

Malcolm almost protested, but the determined set of Clive's jaw stopped him. One night apart wouldn't hurt anything. It surprised him, though, how attached he'd already become to his nexus.

With that, Clive dismissed them. He had work to do and so did they. Seeing them to the door, he bade farewell and closed it behind them. A final clank let Malcolm know he'd locked himself inside.

The clouds had grown oppressively low and dark. Thunder rolled overhead. By nightfall they'd either get a snowstorm or freezing rain.

Malcolm pulled his coat tighter, flinching as a bolt of lightning raced across the clouds. Valentine jumped, then her cheeks colored in embarrassment.

"Are your storms so bad?" Tyrathorn asked with a bemused grin. "You seem afraid the lightning will attack you."

"Hah," Valentine said. "Remind us to tell you a story sometime."

As they walked between antique vehicles, Malcolm found himself next to Asha. She had a distinct way of moving—light on her feet, yet radiating power. A dancer's grace, a fighter's strength.

Trailing behind, Fred left Winter another message. She still wasn't answering her phone. Ahead, Valentine and Tyrathorn were already discussing something Malcolm couldn't hear, so he searched for something to say to his companion. She surprised him by speaking first.

"He cares for you very much."

"I'd trust Clive with my life. Same goes for the rest of these jokers. They're family." He glanced sidelong at her. "But you know what that's like, probably more than we do."

Instead of looking proud, her expression turned wistful. Almost sad.

"I would die for the Ember Guard, to the last man or woman. They all know that."

She started to add more, then stopped, avoiding his eyes.

"Hey," he said. When she didn't look, he bumped against her. "Oops."

With an exaggerated eye-roll, she finally met his gaze.

"I know we're not the team you want—a bunch of untrained amateurs," he said. "But I promise, whatever happens, we'll never quit on you."

Malcolm hadn't learned yet what Asha's expressions meant. This one brightened just a little, though. She gave a tentative smile.

"You may have the skills of an amateur, Malcolm Gilbert," she said, "but you don't have the heart of one."

Did she just give me a compliment? He smiled back.

"Well, as for the untrained part," he said, "we need to change that, and fast."

STRANGE *world we live in.* Clive slumped in his chair, allowing himself a moment to feel overwhelmed. *And it just got stranger.*

Time, he understood. He'd had experience with it. But

people who could wield that power with their will, like it was just another tool? That was something else entirely.

He sighed, prodding the twins' devices. They'd built these all by themselves under the cover of night, bless 'em. Good kids, smart kids, but still kids. In their haste they mighta overlooked something, mighta cut corners or used inferior components.

He sat forward, his eye catching one connection inside Malcolm's nexus. *Like right there. The boy used a quartz crystal, when I'll bet he shoulda used a sapphire.* Fatigue melted away as Clive's internal fire reignited. Leaping from his chair, he turned in search of his tools.

The back corner of the room burst with blue light. A crack like thunder shook the building, knocking Clive off his feet as waves of icy wind swept through the air.

Had this new enemy found him? He lunged toward the round table, just managing to slip on a black Accelerator ring and grab the personal shield before the rift in Time closed.

The corner plunged back into shadows. Clive waited a tense moment for something to happen. Then one of those shadows moved. Putting up his fists, he prepared to go down swinging.

Clive stepped into the light.

Gaping, Clive stared at himself. With a nasty cut on his forehead, clothes torn and dirty and coated in frost, *Clive* limped toward Clive until they stood on opposite sides of the table. Despite his battered appearance, he was grinning.

"So, that secret new project? It works just like you hoped."

So this was no trick. Only Clive knew about that particular device. He lowered his fists.

"I can see that. Good to know." He swallowed. "So, what's the future like?"

"Pretty cold," *Clive* said. "And pretty bad."

Clive nodded, understanding. If *he* was still him, there was only one reason he'd use that device. "We gonna do somethin' about it?"

"S'why I'm here." Moving to the lab tables, *Clive* grabbed a sheet of drafting paper and laid it out flat, pencil in hand. "Now listen close, or we're gonna lose everything."

CHAPTER 9

Valentine twisted a lock of wavy red hair between her fingers, trying and failing to hide her frustration. They'd visited five pillars since leaving Clive, and each had been swarmed by gawkers looking to score photos for their blogs.

Stretching, she allowed herself a moment to enjoy the soft leather of Fred's limousine. Though she hated to admit it, having a rich friend could be fun. Three months ago, after everyone had healed, he'd bought out an entire movie theater to celebrate. Even now, that memory made her smile.

"So, let's recap." Malcolm opened a town map. The ice pillars on the news were circled in blue, and those they'd visually confirmed were circled again in red. "What have we learned?"

"That tourists suck?" Valentine offered.

"They *totally* suck!" Fred said.

"The shapes of the missing pieces were inconsistent," Asha said. "I don't know if they're random, but they're also not uniform."

Examining all the markings at once, Valentine finally identified what had been nagging at her since the beginning. Excitedly, she drummed her fingers on the map.

"Mal, look at the pattern. What do you see?"

Her brother turned the map this way and that, shaking his head. "I can't find any pattern."

"Exactly!"

"I'm not following, Val."

"What does science tell us? That sometimes the absence of a result is still a result. So, if there's no discernible pattern, what could it mean?"

His eyes lit up. "That the locations don't matter. These were probably just convenient spots to do . . . whatever they're doing."

"Yes. I mean, look at what's surrounding each place."

He studied the map again. "They're all near populated areas, but far away enough to be hidden."

"So they wanted easy access to public areas, but they didn't want attention. Not while it was happening."

"What are you comparing against?" Tyrathorn asked.

"Lucius's Time machine was powerful, but really unstable. He dug tunnels under the town as vents for all the excess energy." As Valentine spoke, she marked twelve locations in a circular pattern. "The vents opened in these spots. He used this specific pattern, and that gave us clues. Helped us figure him out."

"Now we're seeing the opposite," Malcolm said. "So we're guessing the ice pillar locations aren't special."

"I see," Tyrathorn said. "Because they are likely not part of the grand plan, we should not expect more to happen there."

Valentine nodded. "If they were, they'd probably be organized. And protected."

"I wonder, then," Asha said. All eyes fell on her, and for a split second she seemed to regret speaking up. It was gone in a blink, though, and she pushed forward. "If these are random, how do we know they've all been found?"

The car fell silent. Valentine wanted to kick herself, feeling like a fool. *Never assume you know all the facts!*

"Wow, good point." Malcolm flashed an eager grin. "Maybe we should go hunting."

"Yes!" Fred pumped his fist and smacked the intercom button. "Punch it, Jeeves, we got places to be!"

It took two more hours. Poring over the map, guessing possible locations, getting it wrong and doubling back to try somewhere new. Valentine suspected "Jeeves" must want to strangle them by now.

"Doesn't he ever get suspicious?" she had asked Fred after the first hour. "Or wonder what we're doing?"

"Probably." Fred had given a careless shrug. "We pay him enough to forget what he sees. Plus, he signed a nondisclosure thing. He keeps his mouth shut, he gets a cushy retirement."

She could only shake her head. Sometimes rich people were strange.

As daylight faded, they found it. The last hidden ice pillar—the only one not overrun by conspiracy theorists.

In a labyrinth of alleys between old buildings and half-built new ones, two monstrous ice pillars towered side by side. Their twisted shapes climbed the walls and branched out at the top, intermingling like the archway to a crystalline forest. Like the others, each was missing huge chunks of ice at its base, as if the center had been hollowed out.

Valentine couldn't help but marvel. Though they were harbingers of the Black Tempest, the pillars were beautiful in an otherworldly sort of way—a far cry from the crude structures Lucius had built.

That memory shook her from her stupor. *Stop staring and*

get to work! She broke from the group and aimed for the left pillar. "Let's take pictures."

Her words broke the spell for the rest of them. Asha joined her while Malcolm and Fred moved toward the right pillar, snapping photos with their phones.

"Yes," Asha said. "My brother will want to see them. He won't be happy about missing this, but he needs rest."

Tyrathorn's pain and fatigue had become more apparent as the day had worn on. Whatever stalwart front he put up, his wounds were far from completely healed. On the way here, he had finally succumbed to sleep.

Valentine's phone flashed for each picture. "Looks like the others. Similar size and shape, big chunks missing. See anything else?"

Asha glanced back and forth between both pillars. "The missing pieces—their shapes don't match, but the overall sizes are similar."

"Hmm." Valentine stepped closer and peered inside. "The outside is super smooth and clear, but inside it's cloudy. Almost like it was melted and refrozen."

"Same over here," Malcolm called. "Maybe I'm crazy, but the two sides of this empty part . . . they almost seem symmetrical."

Something about that struck Valentine, ringing true. There was only one way to tell for sure. She stepped inside the pillar. Mentally she traced a line down the middle of the ice and split the structure into equal halves.

The two halves matched. From this perspective, the whole space began to take on a real shape—a form that tickled the back of Valentine's mind, begging for recognition.

"The shape seems almost . . . humanoid?" she mused. "Except way bigger."

"Dude, this is crazy," Fred said.

"We've seen crazy before," Malcolm said. "Not sure about the humanoid shape. Mine must be different."

Valentine glanced at Asha. "Have you seen this before?"

She shook her head slowly, as if in a dream. "I've never seen anything that can do . . . this."

Should that comfort or worry me? Valentine stepped back into the open air. Shortly after, Malcolm exited his pillar.

"So, something was inside these things, right?" Fred asked. "But now it's gone."

"Could be," Valentine replied. "What might have been inside them?"

"I'm going to guess something evil," Malcolm said.

Valentine's eyes drifted across the ice. *If they can do this, what else can they do? When we track them down, will we face more than we bargained for?*

"Maybe we should—"

She cut off, a strange feeling hitting her senses. A . . . *shift* of some sort—that was the only word she could think to describe it. Something in the Time stream was moving, changing, and it was coming closer. She caught Malcolm's eye and saw the same alarm.

"What is that?" he said.

Asha looked between them, puzzled. Then her expression darkened. Grabbing them, she turned away from the pillars.

"We have to go."

"But, what—?" Valentine said.

"NOW!"

With a thunderous boom, a red vortex burst open between the ice pillars. A humanoid shape appeared at the horizon of the vortex. Its hand stretched toward them.

Valentine's feet left the pavement. The alley spun, and pain exploded through her as she crashed to the ground. Wait, no . . . not the ground. She was pinned to the wall!

Seized by some unseen force, her friends smacked against the wall beside her. She struggled against whatever force gripped them, but it held as strong as steel.

The power of Time glowed in Valentine's senses. She reached for it, eager for its strength. Her will bounced off an invisible wall and her heart sank. *Clive has my nexus, and we left all his gadgets in the car! Stupid stupid stupid!*

The figure emerged fully from the vortex, hooded cloak billowing in the wind. *The Black Tempest found us!*

As he stepped forward, Valentine heard the heavy clank of armored boots. Behind him the vortex swelled, and three more cloaked figures appeared. As a unit they stalked forward to confront Valentine and her friends.

"So clever. At least, you think you are."

Wait. That voice belongs to a woman. As if to verify her thought, the leader's cloak parted to reveal ornate black metal armor over a lithe and curvy frame. *Who is this?*

Even if she had known the woman, it would have been impossible to identify her. She wore a full helmet that applied some sort of filter to her voice. Its intended effect curved away from Valentine, and probably Malcolm, but to each side she could see Fred and Asha trembling.

"Your schemes mean nothing."

The woman stretched out her hand again. Like heat rising from hot pavement, distortion waves rippled from her palm. Valentine gasped as the pressure holding them constricted like a vise, squeezing until her breaths came ragged and shallow.

"They will shatter against us as wood shatters on steel."

"Then why come here? Why bother confronting us?"

Valentine recoiled, realizing the words had flown from her own mouth.

"A courtesy. Our master wishes for all adversaries to receive one warning. One chance. This is yours."

Between the folds of her cloak, red energy flowed from a device in her chest plate. It traced down her left arm to collect in her palm, until she held a glowing orb.

Whipping around, she hurled it at the wall behind her. With a *boom-whoosh,* an explosion vaporized a ten-foot stretch of brick. Valentine shut her eyes as masonry pelted her.

"Should you test us again, you will be crushed and forgotten."

On cue, the other cloaked figures leapt into action. One unleashed gouts of flame from his hands to spiral high into the air. Another extended her arms and two whips sprang from her sleeves, links of metal and leather coursing with electrical energy.

Valentine yelped as arrows sank into the wall beside her head. She watched then, as the third figure produced a bow and loosed arrow after arrow. As the arrows flew, she felt a *shift* and they disappeared in a flash.

They're leaping seconds back in Time, striking before he even fires them! How are we supposed to fight that?

The woman approached now, challenging them one by one.

"Should you interfere . . ." She stopped in front of Asha. ". . . it will matter not who you are . . ."

Then the twins. ". . . what you believe is your destiny . . ."

Fred came last.

". . . or what paltry threat you present."

With a wave of her hand, his coat ripped to shreds. Two small crossbows floated up from his belt, locked and loaded with steel-tipped bolts. She made a small gesture and the crossbows flew into splinters.

"In the end you will founder, you will fall, and your bodies will grow cold."

With that, they turned and marched back toward the vortex, the terrifying woman bringing up the rear. One by one her minions crossed through the light and disappeared. Just short of its horizon, she turned back.

"To remember us by."

Valentine heard a snap, and beside her Malcolm screamed.

CHAPTER 10

"**W**hat is going on?" Fred shouted. "Who was that? How did she do that?"

The limo rumbled over train tracks, zooming away from the alley.

"The Frost Hammer," Asha said, visibly shaken. "She wields Time in ways I cannot explain. Ways I have never seen from a Chronauri. And that voice . . ."

"If she knows we are here," Tyrathorn said, "the Black Tempest must know as well."

Malcolm's head lay in Valentine's lap. She wiped his sweaty brow. Though he shivered and clutched a broken left arm, his face was a mask of defiance. This would only double his resolve.

"They could have killed us," she said. "But I don't buy her line about giving us a warning."

"Agreed," Asha said. "The Frost Hammer does not have a reputation for mercy, nor does . . . her master. There must be another reason—one they don't want us to know."

Valentine shook her head, stunned at how effortlessly the enemy had overwhelmed them. She wasn't even the leader. What would facing the Black Tempest be like?

"If only I had been there—" Tyrathorn began.

"You're wounded, and they had every advantage," Asha said. "We were not ready."

"We still ain't. We need major upgrades." Fred stared out the window, a haunted pall hanging over him. "When that woman talked . . . never been that scared in my life. Wasn't natural."

Malcolm turned toward the Corvonians. "You have to start training us."

Valentine nodded. "Once Mal heals, we'll do whatever it takes."

"Val," Malcolm said through chattering teeth, "we can't wait that long. Get to Clive's. I need my nexus."

"You need rest. Then we'll worry about—"

"Val, please."

Sighing, Valentine looked to Fred. He gave a resigned shrug and asked the driver to change course.

With that, everyone deflated into their seats. Their first clash with the enemy, and it had been an embarrassing defeat.

"By the way," Valentine said. "Crossbows? Really?"

Fred held up his hands. "Hey, y'all got your own ways. How am I supposed to help? You didn't like the gun last time, either."

"Oh, you mean the one Ulrich shot you with?"

"Low blow, girl."

When they pulled up in Fred's limo, Clive was waiting for them outside the shop, a nexus in each hand. Relief washed over Malcolm at seeing his.

"Whatever you do with 'em, hopefully they'll be more stable now. I tightened a few things, gave you some better quality materials. Replaced all your wiring with silver-plated copper. Silver's more ductile than copper, and it's less resistive."

Malcolm squinted. "Ductile?

"It can be drawn out into a thin wire," Valentine said.

"True. It's one reason you see electromagnets using copper." Clive eyed Malcolm with concern. "Y'all need anything else?"

"Thanks," Valentine said. "But our dad called a minute ago. He wants us home."

"You gon' be able to hide that arm, son?"

Gritting his teeth, Malcolm sat up. Waves of agony and nausea swept through him with every motion. He hefted the nexus in his hand.

"I have something else in mind. That's why I need this."

Clive nodded. "Be safe. I'll be in touch soon. We got things to do."

He stepped back and the limo rolled onto the street. Malcolm stared down at the device. In his mind he relived that moment months ago, tumbling inside the heart of Lucius's machine, run through by a shard of glass and knowing he was about to die.

Then something had rejuvenated him. A mysterious energy.

The limo clattered over a pothole. Malcolm grunted at the flash of pain in his arm, then looked up and realized all eyes were on him. Up until now, he hadn't known how to explain what was in his head. So he just started talking.

"I should be dead, after what Lucius did to me." Lifting his shirt, he showed them the scar on his chest. "But he made a mistake—he threw me into his machine, where I absorbed Time. It saved my life—healed me. Maybe it can again."

"He is right," Tyrathorn said. "The more you touch Time, the more it sustains you. That is how I . . ."

Their voices faded into the background. Closing his eyes, Malcolm concentrated on the energy that flowed just beyond sight. On the presence of the nexus. In his mind it glowed bright around the edges, like a door holding back an ocean of light.

He willed the door open. Slowly, just a crack at first, then a little more. A trickle of Time flowed toward him, reaching out as if for a long-lost friend. He opened the door further.

Time poured into him. Malcolm gasped and then sighed as cool, refreshing life and vastness and vitality filled his cells. He took a moment to relish the feeling—a strand of the universe had bent to his will. Then, with a steadying breath, he beckoned more to him.

"By Eternity!" he heard someone say. Asha, maybe.

"If I did not believe before . . ." That might have been Tyrathorn.

A torrent rushed into him. Prepared for it now, he caught the light and bent it back into himself, willing it to fold around him, to course through every cell. The world fell away as he wrapped himself in a cocoon of Time.

Seconds passed. Forever passed. Malcolm felt the moments between moments, impossibly tiny curves and pools in the flow of a vast and endless river. The universe called and he answered, swelling to drink in more of its radiance.

"Hhhheeee ccccaaaannnnoooottt ccccoooonnnntttttiiiinn-nnuuuueee tttthhhhiiiissss wwwwaaaayyyy . . . !"

Malcolm felt Valentine's hands on him. Her warmth inter-mingled with the coolness enveloping him. He felt the pressure of her will on Time.

"Mmmmaaaallll, lllleeeetttt ggggoooo . . ."

Something in Malcolm wanted to resist, to shove her away. The beautiful power felt too good. *She is your sister. You trust her.*

That did it. Opening himself to Valentine, he embraced the touch of her will, letting go of the cool glow and reaching up for the warmer one she offered.

"Iiisss iiittt wwwooorrrkkkiiinnnggg???"

"Hhheee iiissss cccoooommmmiiiinnnggg bbbaaaccckkk tttoo uuss nnoooww, III bbeelliieevvee, and there! It is over."

Valentine, Asha, and Tyrathorn collapsed back into their seats, breathing deep sighs of relief. Wearily, as if they'd fought a hard battle, the Corvonians eyed Malcolm with guarded expressions. Valentine rested her head on his shoulder and closed her eyes.

"Welcome back," she said.

"What happened?"

"You were wrapped in light and everything slowed down. I mean *really* slowed down, but in a weird way. It was like I moved super slow, but I could tell it was happening. And then . . ."

She gestured around them, and Malcolm's eyes widened in shock. The entire cab glistened with a thick layer of frost. His friends shivered as if they'd been caught in a blizzard. Words caught in his throat as he struggled to pick which question to ask first.

Tyrathorn held up a reassuring hand. "When we train, I will endeavor to explain how this happened."

"Sorry. I thought I could control it." Malcolm hung his head, embarrassed. "How far did it . . ."

"Just within the car, I believe," Tyrathorn said. He rubbed his arms. "Though in here . . ."

"Every blink felt like a year," Asha said.

Behind her eyes, Malcolm thought he could see something now—equal parts wonder and . . . fear. But why would she fear what happened, and why did she keep glancing between him and Tyrathorn? She must see things like this every day. Right?

"Yo, dawg," Fred said, his voice a reverent whisper. "That's *legit* the coolest thing I've ever seen."

Malcolm laughed and the rest followed, draining the tension from the car. *Good.* He didn't want to be afraid of himself.

"Your corona was blue," Tyrathorn observed. He turned to Valentine. "Is yours as well?"

"Mal said mine was red."

"Interesting."

"What does it mean?" Malcolm asked.

"It suggests your nature. Your ability will be to slow the flow of Time, while your sister's will be to increase it. Past and future, ice and fire."

Those distinctions did run through their personalities. Malcolm was obsessed with history, while Valentine always looked to technology and the future. He preferred to read, she preferred to *do*. That those distinctions would carry through to this made a crazy kind of sense. Why wouldn't someone wield Time with the whole of who they were?

"Can we only do that?" he said.

"It depends on your *sev*. If you are Third-*sev,* then yes. In Everwatch, one must be at least Third-*sev* to join the Ember Guard."

"Second-*sev,*" Asha said.

"Second-*sev* for what?"

She raised her eyebrows. "To join the Ember Guard."

Tyrathorn frowned. "But . . . I remember it . . ." He squinted, as if wracking his brain for a memory he could trust. "That is why you did not get in. That is why . . ."

Malcolm sat up. *Wait, she's not one of them?*

"Thorn," Asha said slowly, enunciating every word. "The limit has always been Second-*sev.*"

"But, our father—"

"Our father wanted his daughter to have a throne, not a sword. That is why he blocked my entry."

Tyrathorn rubbed his temples. "I cannot tell what memories are true."

"We'll find our way through. You don't need every memory to win this war."

"What if I do? What if I know a key detail but cannot remember it?" He sighed. "How can I defeat an enemy when I cannot trust my own mind?"

She hesitated, looking unsure, then laid her hand on his. "You trust *me*."

Tyrathorn gazed at her hand, and placed his other hand on top. Then, as if a thought had struck, he turned fully toward her.

"Our father blocked your entry. Past tense. Do you mean . . . ?"

Asha smiled.

"So, you—"

She nodded. "I made it in, Thorn."

Pure joy lit up his face. Grabbing his sister, he embraced her with an elation that Malcolm would never have expected. When she grunted and pretended to gasp for air, Tyrathorn released her and held her at arm's length.

"You are my sister twice now," he said. "*My heart, my sword will ever blaze . . .*"

"*For all of Time, for all my days,*" Asha finished.

They clasped hands, less a handshake and more a sign of fraternal bond. A sharing of something beyond blood. For a moment, they truly seemed like soldiers.

"Asha's talked about *sevs*," Valentine said. "You'll teach us what they mean?"

Tyrathorn nodded. "Of course. It seems we will both have to."

Malcolm stretched, suddenly tired. Then realization popped in his brain. "Val, look!" Holding up his left arm, he laughed as he waved it around.

"Dude, no way!" Fred reached over and squeezed it. "Whoa."

He marveled at his arm the whole way home, which seemed to amuse the Corvonians. They shared little grins whenever Malcolm poked at it. The bone was still tender, but it was whole again.

Soon after, Fred was calling goodbyes through the limo's sunroof. Standing in their driveway, the twins waved as he disappeared onto the main road. Then Malcolm made a grand gesture toward the front door.

"Prince Thorn, welcome to our castle."

Tyrathorn laughed as they mounted the front step. Malcolm opened the door and sniffed, expecting to be greeted by the smell of something delicious in the oven.

Nothing.

Oma's not cooking? She usually tried some crazy new dish on Saturdays. Then a new scent wafted close, barely there but unmistakable. *No one here wears perfume like that,* he mused. Then who—?

A feminine giggle echoed from the kitchen. Male and female voices murmured, the words too muted to be caught. Valentine closed the front door and the noises in the kitchen changed. Chairs scraped, murmurings came faster, and the crystal of wine glasses clinked against the sink.

"Hello?" Malcolm called.

"In here, son," their dad called.

Rounding the corner, Malcolm stepped into another world. It looked just like their kitchen, but it wasn't. Something had changed.

Their father stood there, a smile painted over tense jaw muscles. He ran a hand through his hair—a trademark nervous tic.

He wasn't alone.

Whoa. Malcolm's eyebrows climbed. A beautiful woman stood next to his father, dressed like she was expecting an evening out. Athletic, tall-ish in high heels and a black cocktail dress, she looked ready to walk a red carpet.

On seeing them, her expression blossomed into a dazzling smile. Dark brown hair swished as she stood straighter.

"Hello," she said.

"Kids, this is Callie de la Vega," Neil said, sliding his arm around her waist. "My girlfriend."

CHAPTER 11

Dinner at Redendo's. Their dad had insisted.

"Everyone likes Italian!" he had said.

Perfect for soothing edgy nerves with comfort food as everyone got to know each other. Malcolm hadn't known whether he should invite their other company, but the Corvonians had picked up on the vibe and volunteered to look after themselves.

Of course that's what was going on, Malcolm thought as they drove to the south side of Emmett's Bluff. New clothes, big smiles, going out for so many "interviews." He grinned, shaking his head. *How did I not see it before?*

"It's so wonderful to finally meet you both," Callie said, smiling back at them from the front passenger seat.

Against her light mocha skin, the smile glowed as if she were posing for photos at a movie premiere. In her dress and heels, with every hair perfectly in place, she was an embodiment of glamour that contrasted sharply with his father. Writers weren't known for glitz.

Malcolm cleared his throat and gave his best smile. "Nice to meet you, too . . . um . . ." His eyes widened in horror. *Already forgot her name. Nice going.*

"Callie. Don't worry, you just heard it. I've been hearing your names for months."

Malcolm saw her eyes flicker toward Valentine, who stared blankly into space. As subtly as he could, Malcolm nudged her.

"Oh," she said. But her attention flew right past Callie. "Um, where did you say we're going, Dad?"

"Italian, sweetie."

"You both must be excited for summer," Callie said. "Do you have plans?"

Images flashed through Malcolm's mind. *Ice pillars. Time portals. Cloaked enemies.*

"Uh . . . yeah, we'll probably have our hands full."

He glanced at Valentine. She was staring at Callie now, unblinking and intense, as if she'd caught the woman stealing something from her. He nudged her harder.

She barely managed to nod. "Mm-hm, big plans."

Her phone was in her lap. Malcolm knew because she picked it up every eight seconds, probably wishing she could text John. Her boyfriend still shied away from owning a phone. Despite his genius, John's habits from growing up in the early 1900s were still fading slowly. Carrying a phone everywhere just didn't appeal to him yet.

Valentine was no help here and was clearly more upset about their dad's girlfriend than the mortal danger they'd faced earlier. To be fair, though, it was weird and would probably feel that way for a while. He'd seen enough classmates deal with this to know that.

Most of them got angry, too. He wondered if he would experience that. Right now he wasn't angry, just awkward. *Is that normal?*

If he was being honest, a corner of his mind clung to his

mother's memory a little tighter now, determined to honor her. But even though he was young, he'd learned something about being lonely. About how hard it was.

I chose that for myself, though. No attachment, because . . . he shied away from that train of thought.

Loneliness sucked, no matter the reason. But it must suck extra for someone like their dad, who was happy and then had his wife taken by disease. Didn't he deserve someone who would make him happy again? Could Valentine not reason her way through that?

For tonight, at least, he'd have to be nice for them both. "So, Callie, where do . . . I mean, what are, uh . . ." *Should've thought of a question before I opened my mouth.* "Work? You job somewhere?" *Smooth, genius.*

Callie brightened. "I'm a journalist, actually. Freelance for lots of magazines. I always liked your dad's books and wished I could interview him, so one day I decided to reach out. We started talking, and . . ."

"Oh." Malcolm kicked his dad's seat playfully. "So you actually were going for interviews."

Neil chuckled. "At first. After Callie called, I walked into the café and right past her. No way did I think such a fox would be there for me. Turns out she was just that crazy."

Callie's eyes rested on Neil's face as he spoke, lips quirked up in an affectionate smile. Her fingers brushed his forearm.

When they weren't touching him, they traced the lines of her silver bracelet. It wrapped around her left wrist in shiny bands, twisting and folding back on itself in such an intricate pattern that Malcolm couldn't determine where the clasp was. Three small red gems punctuated the design.

Callie caught him watching, sending a jolt through him.

His cheeks reddened, and she gave her own embarrassed smile. Her hands moved to rest in her lap.

"Nervous habit," she admitted.

So she was nervous, and willing to admit it. Malcolm decided right then that he liked Callie de la Vega. He liked that underneath her Hollywood looks, she hid a desperation to make a connection with them. It meant she cared about his dad.

When they ordered dessert, real conversations were happening and only occasionally was there an awkward silence. It was nice. Callie was nice.

The only hitch was Valentine. Malcolm couldn't tell if she was trying to be antisocial or just caught up in her own head, but she was a major buzzkill.

Difficult to engage, staring off and giving three-word answers. Not pouting, just . . . not there. Even when they pulled into the garage and said their goodbyes, Callie kept trying to engage her to no avail.

He wondered if Callie would try to hug him. They'd had a nice evening, but a hug this soon might bring back the weirdness and—oh, good, she offered a handshake. He accepted gratefully.

Valentine shook her hand mechanically and said goodbye. Not good night. Goodbye.

Neil asked for a minute, so Malcolm grasped Valentine's arm and led her into the house. As soon as the door closed, he whirled on her.

"Nice going back there."

She blinked. "What?"

"Look, I know this is crazy, but you can't just check out like that."

"What? Was I . . . I didn't mean to." She looked run-through, as if she'd just woken up to learn she'd committed a crime in her sleep. "I just . . ."

Their dad came through the door alone. Turning his back to them, he closed the door slowly. His shoulders heaved with a sigh, and after a moment he faced them. Valentine stiffened.

But he just looked weary. Dipping his head low, he spoke toward the floor, barely above a whisper.

"Valentine, I know this was unexpected. Maybe I should have talked about her from the beginning instead of springing her on you. I just . . ." he sighed again. "I just hope next time you'll be able to make a little more of an effort." With that, he kissed her on the cheek and patted Malcolm's shoulder. "Love you both. Good night."

They stood there until his bedroom door clicked shut. Valentine shook her head.

"I tried, Mal. I didn't mean to be rude. I just never expected this. And . . ." She hesitated, as if reluctant to say the rest. "Yes, this is hard for obvious reasons. But isn't it also a little convenient? We have a new enemy, his partner is a woman, and this new woman shows up on our doorstep. She's even wearing that weird bracelet that didn't match her outfit. Tell me it's a coincidence."

Malcolm looked askance at his sister. "So, you're saying . . . ?"

"I'm saying that woman is the Frost Hammer."

He scoffed. "Come on, Val, they've been dating for months. That doesn't match up."

"Maybe she's a patient villain."

To Malcolm, the very idea was ridiculous. Not everyone in the world was caught up in their weird lives.

Before he could respond, there was a knock at the front door.

They eyed each other confusedly. Who would knock this late at night? They approached the entryway, each gripping their nexus and preparing for a fight. Malcolm twisted the knob, tensed, and flung the door open.

Winter stood there, holding an overstuffed suitcase. At a glance, Malcolm knew something was seriously wrong. Her clothes were rumpled and mismatched, her hair askew, and tears streaked her reddened face.

"Say yes to this," she pleaded, her voice thick and trembling. "Can I stay with you for a while?"

"Of course you can," Valentine said.

Dropping the bag, Winter fell through the doorway and melted into Valentine's arms. Clutching her like a lifeline, she broke into desperate sobs.

CHAPTER 12

Pitch black in the forest. A clearing hidden among the trees. Weak campfire. Battered soldiers, exhausted, reaching toward the glow for a small bit of warmth.

A soldier peers upward. Stars obscured by black clouds.

So tired. The edges of his vision are wavy and black. But tomorrow, home. They will share what they discovered, and this war will change.

The paltry flame shrinks. He rubs his chest under his armor. It's getting colder—have to risk it. Another wood ration appears among the burning embers. The wood doesn't catch fire.

It catches frost.

The silvery sheen spreads across the wood, chasing the fire away. The soldier is on his feet, sword and shield in his hands. They are discovered.

"To the trees!"

Armor clinks as his brothers shake from their frozen stupor.

Six hooded figures burst into the clearing. The night erupts in ice and fire and pain and screams and death. The soldier's heart pumps blood and terror. He finds an enemy, moves to strike. He can't move. Looks down.

Feet frozen to the ground.

Blinks. Silence falls. His friends lie still, steam ejecting from their open mouths. Last breaths. Ice crawls over them, burying, consuming.

The trees rustle. A seventh figure appears. The soldier recoils, topples onto his back.

Black armor sculpted from ice. Jagged, razor sharp, and beautiful. He leaves a frozen path behind him. The Black Tempest stops above the soldier.

The soldier's mind jumps. Sees through his enemy's eyes. The Black Tempest regards the tiny, shivering man. Whimpering, weak. But every enemy is worth his attention.

His mind jumps and he floats overhead. He wants to scream at the soldier. Get free and run! Everwatch must know what he saw! The soldier only cowers.

The Black Tempest speaks. The soldier cries out, claws at the ground, struggles to crawl away. Ice lances from the Black Tempest's palm. Pierces armor. Skin. Flesh. Bone. Heart. Armor again. Then frozen ground. The soldier writhes, pinned to the earth.

His mind jumps. Soldier's body again. Ice boils from the wound, covers him like his brothers and sisters. He cries, begs for mercy. Tears freeze on his face. Why? Why him?

Ice squeezes his heart, spreads into his lungs. He gasps. Can't—

Tyrathorn snapped awake.

Scanning the darkness for an enemy, he reached for the armor by his side. Must have lost his weapons before falling through the portal, but the nexus in his chest plate would protect him.

Once you remember how to use it properly.

Oh. That's right. Reality flooded back to his waking mind.

He was not lying dead on frozen ground, but on a foam mat on the floor of Malcolm Gilbert's chamber. Throbbing aches crept across his torso and temple, the half-healed wounds unhappy with his sudden movements. He sat up, breathing hard, a sheen of sweat coating his battle-hardened frame.

A muffled, bleak sound reached him through the closed door. Someone was crying. It must be the girl of Eastern lineage. She'd arrived Saturday night and spent the entire next day in Valentine's room with the women gathered around her. He hoped she would find peace.

His thoughts turned back to the dream—yet another dream of *him*. They always left him breathless and terrified.

This one had left him shivering, too, but he couldn't quite remember why. Already the images were fading. He grabbed for them in desperation, struggling to lock them down before they could slip away. If he faced them, perhaps they would go away.

But like mist, they dissipated. Sighing in frustration, Tyrathorn fell back against his pillow and thumped his fist on the floor.

MONDAY mornings usually sucked.

But this was the last Monday of freshman year, and sophomore just sounded so much better.

Valentine's feet flew over the spongy track. A wide curve loomed ahead and she mentally powered up to take it at speed. Soon after their near deaths at Lucius Carmichael's hands, she'd taken up dance again, and the benefits were showing.

"Hey, come on," Malcolm panted at her side, sweat matting his shaggy brown hair. "Some of us are mortal."

She giggled and slowed down. Not too much, though. *Let*

him sweat. Her brother stayed in good shape, but he hadn't spent the last six months dancing every day.

"Better?"

"Sorta."

"If we're going to face another bad guy, it might help to be able to run."

"Yeah, in the other direction." Malcolm grinned, hooking a thumb behind them. "At least I'm not back there."

Valentine glanced back. They were more than half a track-length ahead of the next runner. In a few minutes, they might even lap the slowest.

As if on cue, an amplified voice rang out from the bleachers. "*Come on, get the lead out!*" Coach Boomer yelled through his megaphone. "*I've seen kindergartners run faster than that. What are you, preschoolers? Pick it up, little babies!*"

Valentine chuckled. Then she noticed Malcolm examining her and stuck out her tongue. "Can I take your order?"

"Just wondering how you're handling Winter's thing. You spent all yesterday with her."

"You were around, too. So were John and Fred."

"Yeah, but you took on the most. I thought she'd never stop crying."

Once more, Valentine suppressed the ball of emotion writhing in her stomach. She'd managed to bury it this morning so she could get Winter moving, but there it remained. Never before had she seen a friend's life crumble so fast.

"I still can't believe it. I mean, it's crazy, right?"

"Yeah. I don't know what I'd do."

After Walter's funeral, Winter had arrived home to find her family life in flames. Her mother, it turned out, had been cheating on her father. Recently he'd hired a private investigator, who uncovered evidence—and not just recent stuff, but evidence that went back years. For much of Winter's life, her happy family had been a lie.

"I got home and they were screaming," she told them. "Throwing things, saying the most awful stuff. I had no clue what to do, Val. So I locked myself in my room and hid under the covers. Hoped tomorrow would be better." But it hadn't been. "When I got up, the kitchen was destroyed and my . . . dad . . . was just sitting there in all the wreckage. Sometime during the night, my mom had packed up and left. She ran, and she took Summer with her. No note or anything, just gone!"

She'd spent the rest of the day vacillating between tears and fury. What could Valentine do except be there for her? And where could Winter go from here?

"I just feel so helpless," Valentine said. "I've fought a super-villain from the future and lived to tell about it. But I can't fix my friend." She felt tears welling and forced them back. "What am I supposed to do?"

"Just be there, I guess."

Until a better plan came along, that one would have to do.

Showered and changed, the twins weaved through the packed hallways. There was one stop to make before they hurried to their next class, and it was important.

"There she is." Valentine reached back to pull Malcolm along.

Winter stood at her locker, staring blankly at the books inside. Her backpack sat between her feet, ignored as she stood like a statue. What terrible memory was playing in her mind right now?

Fred stood beside her. He'd spent all Sunday trying to make

his friend smile, whispering little jokes, being clumsy on purpose. None of it had worked. Now he wore a forced grin, and relief painted his features as they approached.

"Hey," the twins said in unison, then glanced at each other.

"Ha, twins," Fred said.

Sidling closer to Winter, Valentine moved to put an arm around her shoulders.

"Please don't," Winter said, recoiling.

Valentine nodded. "Okay. Do you need anything?"

Closing her eyes, Winter sighed, then forced herself to trade out books. Every motion seemed a monumental effort, as if heavy weights were attached to her arms and legs. She zipped the bag closed while her friends looked on helplessly. When she spoke, her voice barely registered above the crowd.

"How about a brand new life?"

She melted into the crowd, trudging to her next class, where she would resume staring into space. Fred sagged against the lockers.

"I got no clue what to do," he said. "She's my oldest friend, y'know?"

"I think you're already doing it," Valentine offered.

"Hope so." Fred snatched his bag from the floor. "Anyway, see ya."

Malcolm plucked at Valentine's sleeve. "We've got to move, too. You know how Madame LaChance is."

Valentine rolled her eyes for two reasons, and followed. The first was her French teacher's hatred for all things about the English language. The second . . .

"I know why you like to be early."

He flashed a knowing grin. For a boy in Emmett's Bluff, there were fringe benefits to enrolling in French. They became apparent to everyone who stepped into the classroom, as the twins did now.

"*Asseyez-vous rapidement, s'il vous plaît,*" Madame Sabine LaChance called from her desk as the bell rang. She flipped her hair, full lips teasing with a mischievous smile. "*Nous avons beaucoup de choses à faire, mes beautés.*"

My lovelies. Or something close to that, anyway. It was her pet name for them all. She'd maintained that charming yet unattainable demeanor all year. Now she stood up, marker in hand. Sunlight streamed in from the window behind her, wreathing her long chestnut brown hair in a golden glow.

And now she has a halo. Valentine shook her head, expecting to see drool hitting desks at any moment. *We should've taken German.*

High heels clicked as LaChance swayed toward the whiteboard. Today, the 24-year-old bombshell sported stiletto heels and a ridiculously tight sweater with a plunging V-neck. V-necks seemed to be the woman's favorite, as they allowed for her go-to move. *Tilt head, bite lip, smile as a lock of hair falls into your cleavage. Classic.*

The only crack in her demeanor was the vitriol she held for English. Valentine had only ever heard her speak French, even to other teachers.

It would be easier to take if she were a bad teacher, but she wasn't. The twins would leave her class with a good grasp of basic French. Even now, during their last week, she wanted her students to soak up knowledge.

It should be interesting. It was to Malcolm, of course, but right now all Valentine felt was tired. The past few days had upended everyone's lives again. Six months' rest, that's all they'd gotten before the next crisis.

Her thoughts wandered away from class, through all that had been, all that might be coming. Would everyone in this room be so relaxed if they realized how close they'd been to dying six months ago? In the coming days, would she hold their lives in her hands again?

Her fingers crept into her pocket and brushed the object resting there. After what happened in the alley, she would never be caught without her nexus again. The Corvonians would teach her to channel her power. Her skill would grow and keep the people she loved safe.

Valentine's unfocused gaze rested on the clock above the whiteboard as it ticked away. She gripped the nexus fully now, savoring the warmth of power. Her thoughts floated free, wandering closer and closer to the doorway between her and Time. Energy stirred beyond it as if reacting to her presence.

Tick . . . . . tick . . . . . tick

She wanted it. Needed it. The door cracked open and a trickle came through, pure exhilaration giving its light to her. The second hand moved inevitably forward. Her body watched the clock while her mind nudged the door open wider.

Tick . . . . tick . . . . tick

Time flowed into her now, burning like a familiar flame, begging to be wielded. Distantly she felt someone's hand squeeze her arm. It didn't matter.

Tick . . . tick . . . tick

With the barest push, the doorway flew open. Time rushed through, its radiance pouring into every fiber of her being. She embraced it, bending and wrapping it around the core of her will.

Tick . . tick . . tick

The hand on her arm squeezed harder. Madame LaChance's

movements began to race, a jerky unnaturalness to her pace. The rest of the class mirrored her, every movement like a video on fast forward. *What is happening?*

Tick.tick.tick.tick.tick

She could see it now. The red glow, like a warm blanket around her. The raw energy of the universe pouring off her in waves, *shifting* the flow of Time in the classroom, pushing it faster and faster and faster and faster *tickticktickticktickticktick* it's still going *oh god I can't stop it how do I stop it* and something foreign wrapped around her will a presence of blue a tide of cool relief and "Val-Val-Val-*Val*-VAL!"

Valentine shoved the power away. Her control unraveled and the energy burst outward. The window shattered. A shockwave flung books and students and desks through the air to drop haphazardly back to the floor.

The flow of Time crashed back to normal and Valentine gasped, utter terror gripping her as she observed the carnage. Even the overhead lights were busted.

Malcolm grabbed her and pulled them both to the floor. She yelped, then yelped again as he kicked both their desks over on top of them.

"Punch yourself in the face," he whispered.

"What?!"

"You want to be the only one with no injuries? Do it!"

He led by example, drawing back and socking himself in the temple. Which couldn't have been easy—the brain was hardwired to protect itself.

Trembling, still trying to process what had just happened, Valentine shoved aside her instincts for self-preservation. With her jaw clenched, she drew back and punched it as hard as she could. Even after the beatings she'd taken last year, it still hurt like crazy.

Malcolm nodded. "You back with me now?"

She nodded, knowing her expression must still be hollow. Malcolm's eyes narrowed, but he let it go.

She didn't want him to. She needed to talk, needed to figure out what she'd done. *Why was my mistake so much worse than his?* She moved to speak, but he held up a hand.

"I know. We'll talk later. Right now we have to get everyone out."

"Why?"

"Because the room is on fire."

CHAPTER 13

Firemen stood outside the broken window, spraying a heavy stream of water inside. Steam and smoke billowed out as if a volcano had suddenly appeared inside their classroom. *Which actually seems plausible for this town,* Valentine thought.

Not that anyone would be shocked by it anymore. The people of Emmett's Bluff were growing accustomed to the Strange.

Even now, as students and teachers milled around the parking lot, no one watched the spectacle. They just huddled in their coats, listened to the story of a shockwave knocking everyone over and setting a bookshelf on fire, and said, *Huh, weird, so what are you doing this summer?*

Valentine couldn't stop trembling. Gathered in a circle with her, Malcolm, Winter, and Fred worked to appear as nonchalant as everyone else.

"Holy crap, girl," Fred said in a hushed tone. "What happened?"

She searched herself for an answer. How could she describe the storm of power and emotion so they would understand?

"I'll take a guess," Malcolm said.

She smiled gratefully.

"I felt something . . . I don't know, *shift* . . ." he said. "I think it was Val bending the flow of Time. Just a little at first, then more. It got bad when she started glowing red."

"A *shift*. Hmm," Valentine said, brow furrowed in thought. "Yeah, that's how I thought of it, too."

Winter had been staring at the ground, blank as a mannequin, but now her head snapped up. "What does that mean?"

"Okay, picture a river," Malcolm said. "All the water's basically flowing in the same direction, right? So, what happens if you build a little channel to divert some of it? The water you catch will *shift* to flow in a new direction."

"That is how it feels," Valentine agreed. "It's like we're catching a little part of the river and changing its direction. The crazy part is we can feel when someone else does it, too."

"And you were glowing," Fred said. "Anyone see?"

"I think we're the only ones who can see it. People like us." Valentine stopped short. "Wow. *People like us*."

"I think she did sort of what I did in the limo," Malcolm said. "Pulled in too much, tried to control it, but it got away from her. Time started to seriously speed up. That's when I tried to help."

"So, that was you I felt."

"Yeah. Then you let go, but instead of just fading away, all that energy burst out. Remember how I accidentally froze everything? It's like the opposite happened for you."

"Whoa. Wish I coulda seen that, dawg." Fred shrugged when they stared at him. "What? Ain't nobody hurt, they got to see something crazy, and we all got outta class. If I had that power, I'd be usin' it every day."

"You do have a power," Winter murmured. "You can dork harder than anyone."

The two of them shared a look—the kind only old friends

could have with each other. Then Fred wrapped his arm around Winter and she leaned into the embrace, resting her head on his shoulder.

Valentine wanted to speak but held back, fearful of bursting the moment. A glimmer of the Winter they knew had just peeked through. It was a relief to know she was still in there somewhere, broken but not gone.

Fred stood straighter. "Hottie alert, incoming."

Madame LaChance hobbled in their direction, looking as if she'd gone through a tumble dryer. Hair askew, makeup smudged, and one of her ridiculous heels had snapped off. Yet she struggled to maintain that mysterious I-have-a-secret demeanor. Valentine wanted to laugh, yet felt halfway sorry for the woman.

When she arrived, Madame LaChance reached out to grip Valentine's arm with one hand, Malcolm's with the other. Her signature smile melted into a haunted frown.

"*Vous avez fait sortir tous les gens, même moi*—" She cut off. Glancing at the ground, she gathered herself. "You helped get everyone out. Even me. I should have been the one, but I was scared." Her eyes glistened with tears. "You did what I could not. I think you are heroes." She pulled them into a tight embrace. "Thank you."

Valentine was almost too shocked to return the embrace. She hugged her teacher back and shared a puzzled look with her brother. When Madame LaChance let go and stepped back, the glimmer of mischief had returned.

"Tell anyone I spoke English, I will deny, and you will regret. No?" She grinned, then offered a flirty wave before leaving.

Fred stared after her. "Dude, I *gotta* take French next year."

"You're sure you're both okay?" their dad's voice blared from Valentine's phone, filling Fred's limo. School had been released early, and now they were headed to their friend's mansion.

"Yeah, nothing broken," Valentine said.

"Good. You weren't close by when that whatever-it-was happened, were you? The news made it sound kind of weird."

Valentine exchanged a look with her brother, who only offered a shrug. No help at all. "Uh, well, not close enough to get hurt, I guess."

There was a pause. The twins held their collective breath. Would he buy a response that flimsy?

"Good, good," Neil said.

Malcolm pumped his fist. Valentine stifled a chuckle.

"So, you kids coming home for dinner? Callie's here. We were hoping . . ."

Though he trailed off, she knew what he was fishing for. Another dinner, in a more relaxed setting. But could she be relaxed around this woman? What if it went badly again? Would it hurt things with her dad? What would that mean for the future? Would they be destined to grow apart?

"Fred already asked us!" she blurted.

Malcolm eyed her, looking disappointed. She stared at the floor. There was another pause over the line, followed by their dad's faint sigh.

"Okay, then. Have a good time."

The call disconnected. Valentine kept her eyes downcast as she slid the phone back into her pocket. This was the last thing she wanted to talk about right now. But, of course . . .

"Well, that was kind of rude," Malcolm said. "Even if you do think Callie's the enemy."

"Wait, what?" Fred said.

"She thinks Callie is the Frost Hammer," Malcolm said.

"Ouch, that would suck for y'all," Fred said.

"I just didn't know what to say," she muttered. "I felt awkward. And it's naive to say she couldn't possibly be the Frost Hammer, Mal. A year ago, our chemistry teacher couldn't possibly have been from the future. Right?"

"You were still rude," he insisted, then turned to their friends. "Wasn't she?"

"Ain't no way I'm getting in the middle of a twin fight," Fred said. "Y'all are crazy."

Winter had been staring blankly at the floor. She looked up now, her face twisted and bitter. "I think you're both idiots for not realizing how good you have it."

The car felt frozen again. Fred sat as still as possible, as if he were trying to be invisible. As if the very next action would decide the course of this day.

Which was right, Valentine realized. She balanced on a knife edge between two possible reactions. Whichever one she chose—whichever way she decided to feel—it would change things. So she could choose to get angry, or . . .

She switched seats and planted herself next to Winter. Sliding close, she reached out for her friend. Winter leaned away, protesting, while Valentine kept moving in. Gently relentless, she imagined herself an unstoppable comfort machine. Resistance was futile.

Then Winter crumpled. Her protective shield fell away, and she folded into Valentine's arms as tears began to fall.

"I'm sorry," she whispered.

Valentine stroked her cheek. "Don't even think about it."

The air thawed. The guys were smiling, which was a good sign—guys didn't like to draw attention to themselves when girl drama was happening. Valentine sighed in relief. *Nice try, universe, but we're not losing any more friends today.*

"Soooo," Fred began. "Y'all are staying for dinner?"

"I guess, if that's okay," Malcolm said.

"Yeah, no sweat."

"But we're going to have to eat at home sometime." Malcolm eyed Valentine.

She kicked his leg. "At least you won't spend tonight drooling over Callie."

"Whoa, hold up," Fred said. "Your dad's new lady is hot?"

"Oh, uh . . . I don't know, man." Malcolm shrugged too casually. "I mean, whatever."

Grinning, Fred shook his head. "A'ight, villain or not, I gotta see. Y'all are uninvited to my house."

Valentine frowned. "What?"

Pulling out his phone, he started tapping. "And reinvited to dinner at yours. I'm buying, but only over there. I can make the order right now. So call your dad back and tell him we're coming over."

Valentine cringed while Malcolm grinned. "Sounds like a plan."

Well, that backfired.

Then she saw something and felt instantly better. As Fred's driver stopped at his impossibly huge front porch, John was waiting for them. Her heart leapt, as it always did.

Seconds later her lips were on his, drinking in his warm, quiet passion. His hands on her waist made butterflies dance in her stomach. Something inside her relaxed as if she'd been bursting with pressure and he'd turned a release valve.

When they parted, she caressed his cheek. "Hi."

John smiled and drank in the sight of her with those deep brown eyes. "Hello, my love. I missed you, too."

"Get a room, you two," Fred called.

"You have one thousand of them to spare in this house, Fred," John returned.

Hand in hand, they followed their friends into the massive entryway. Ahead of them, a balcony overlooked a living room the size of their school's gymnasium. Multiple wings branched off from this central hub, and the far wall boasted three stories' worth of glass looking out on the massive backyard.

"I still can't get over how flawless this looks," Malcolm said, gesturing to encompass the whole house. "You'd never know anything happened."

"Yeah, dawg, it's crazy. And my dad bought the story about the storms and earthquakes tearin' everything up."

Valentine's mind flashed back to that day six months ago, when they'd been betrayed by Miss Marcus and ambushed here by Lucius and Ulrich. Mayhem and destruction had resulted. Collapsed walls, shattered glass, broken bones.

A person had died that day. A bad person, but still.

"Come on," Fred said, eyeing the twins. He led everyone down the curved staircase to the living room, and then toward the doors in the glass wall. "Someone's waitin' for you two."

Valentine cocked her head. "Waiting for us?"

Fred grinned over his shoulder. After preceding them through the doors, he stepped to the side. Then she saw.

Standing straight and regal, Tyrathorn and Asha glistened in the afternoon light. The wavy designs on their ornate armor seemed to catch and channel every golden ray of sun. Asha held a *qama* in each hand, edges glinting as if eager to be wielded.

John's hand slipped away from Valentine's. Puzzled, she looked after him and saw that he was backing away with Fred and Winter. When she faced forward again, the Corvonians were approaching.

She'd expected to hear a pronounced *clink-clank* of battle armor as they walked. But their movements were light-footed and nearly silent, as if the metal weighed little more than normal clothes.

The Corvonians stopped before the twins with proud posture. Everything felt formal somehow, though she had no clue how they were doing it. *They really are the children of royalty.*

"Malcolm and Valentine Gilbert, protectors of Emmett's Bluff," Tyrathorn said as if he were reading a kingly decree. "Are you ready to begin?"

Valentine cleared her throat. "Begin what?"

Asha grinned. "Your training."

CHAPTER 14

Steel clanged against steel. Malcolm fell back a step and swung Asha's blade in a wide arc. Sweat poured from his face after hours of exertion.

Sharp edges flashed in the sunlight filtering through the trees. Feet danced over dirt and grass, leaping rocks and fallen logs in a wooded clearing on Fred's vast estate.

"No!" Asha snapped. "Follow the pattern as I showed you, *kuputsa*. Master the basics before you improvise."

Gone was the hesitant demeanor of a young girl lost in the timeline. In her place was a warrior, powerful and unyielding. And kind of scary.

Malcolm resisted the urge to ask what that word meant—the one she kept calling him. He wasn't sure he wanted to know. Instead he reset his stance.

She came at him like a snake, darting in and out with blade and fist and foot, an attack pattern demonstrating core combat techniques. He countered with the moves she'd shown him, silently repeating the names for each. All the while, she spat commands and criticisms.

Hold your weapon this *way. Plant your feet* there. *Watch me, not my blade. Do* not *turn your back to me unless you want to die!*

Even giving it everything he had, Malcolm barely kept up. He bore the welts and shallow cuts to prove it.

She hadn't even broken a sweat. For her this was probably like kindergarten, and she wasn't even wielding Time. Her equipment lacked the red glow.

Malcolm buzzed with a tiny flow of energy. Strapped to his left wrist, the nexus whirred as it connected him to Time. According to Thorn, a Chronauri's rate of cognition increased dramatically this way. Time was literally on their side, making them better.

Except for what happened next.

"Get ready," Asha warned.

"For what?"

"Level two."

Her speed doubled. Like it was nothing.

Malcolm now faced a lethal gray blur. Vibrations rattled his arm as he parried the first attacks, then felt the sting of new cuts on his leg, his chest, his earlobe. Not enough to injure, just enough to annoy. Even so, in that moment he panicked.

Instinct took over, kicking open the door of his nexus and drinking in a torrent of power. As he blocked Asha's next swing, Time rushed through his body and down the length of the *qama*. The weapon blazed red.

The two blades collided with a bright flash and an earsplitting clang. Asha flew backward and collided with a tree, dropping her weapon as she crumpled to her hands and knees. She heaved, gasping for breath.

Oh, crap. Dropping his own weapon, Malcolm sprinted to her side and placed a hand gently at the back of her neck.

"Don't stand up," he said. "Breathe slowly and—"

Next thing he knew, he slammed against the tree with Asha

clutching his throat. Her *qama* was somehow in her hand again. She leveled the tip at his eye, glaring through labored breaths.

"I said no Chronauri attacks," she snapped. "How do you expect to survive if you meet an enemy without your nexus?"

"Accident," Malcolm gurgled, half-choking. "You startled me."

"We cannot afford accidents. When you reach full power, even one slip could be our undoing. You must learn control now." She released his throat and stepped back. "There is more at stake than you could ever know. It's my duty to train you, and I will not fail."

Malcolm held up his hands. "I really am trying. But we weren't raised as warriors and this is a lot to take in." He sat, leaning back against a fallen log. "Can we take a break?"

Asha stared him down. For a moment he thought she would ignore him and start swinging. Instead she moved to the weapon he'd dropped, slipped her toes underneath, and kicked it up into her hand. Then, to his surprise, she joined him against the log.

"Never give up your weapon voluntarily," she said, handing it to him. "Next time, I will make you *take* it back."

Malcolm chuckled, trying to picture what that would look like.

"Hey, where are Val and I supposed to get our own weapons? It's not like this town has a blacksmith."

Asha studied him, eyes narrowed as if she were trying to figure him out. He stirred, uncomfortable under the scrutiny.

"I forget sometimes how little you know. How new this is to you." She faced forward, looking toward her brother.

Malcolm guessed that was all the answer he'd get. Following her lead, he watched their siblings across the clearing. They worked through a different kind of training—the kind Malcolm truly hungered for. He could sense the *shift* as Time curved around them.

"How come you don't use Time when we're training?" he asked.

Asha frowned, but it quickly became a smirk. "Do you believe you're ready for that?"

He acquiesced. That was hard to argue with.

Valentine did not look happy. With a frustrated huff she kicked a fallen pinecone, and the nexus strapped to her wrist glowed red. The pinecone flew into the air and burst into flaming pieces. Valentine gaped.

Tyrathorn gave an encouraging smile. "You see? Already you wield Time by instinct. Now we must teach you to do more than expend it as destructive energy."

"But I could barely do the stuff you showed me!"

"You are trying to think your way to mastery, but what we do requires something deeper. Time is wielded equally by heart and mind." He placed a hand on her shoulder. "Fear not, Valentine. You will learn to trust your instinct, and what you have already done is no small accomplishment. I am very proud of you."

Asha quirked an eyebrow at Malcolm. He realized he'd been laughing to himself.

"You two have, um, different training styles." Leaning toward her, he clasped his hands. "Are you proud of me, Asha?"

Her eyes narrowed. "I will cut you."

"You two," Tyrathorn called. "Fancy a trade?"

Finally! Springing to his feet, Malcolm crossed the clearing and met Valentine in the middle.

"How'd you do?" she asked.

"Got my butt kicked repeatedly." He passed the *qama* to her. "You?"

Valentine twirled the blade in a smooth, swift figure eight. Even that was better than any move he'd managed.

"I think you saw," she said bitterly. "I can access Time and speed myself up because that's just internal. But when it comes to using Time to do things . . . I don't know, it's like I can't focus. When I let go, Time just bursts out of me, all destruction."

"It's only the first day."

She stepped closer and whispered. "Does it scare you, knowing what we can do?"

"Sometimes. But if we don't get control of it, our feelings won't matter. We've only faced minions so far, and look how that went."

Valentine sighed. "We can't stop now, can we?"

"No." Malcolm studied her. "But if we could . . . would you want to?"

He saw the gears turning behind her eyes. "I guess I do wonder what else we can do."

He grinned. "Maybe we'll be like Jedi."

Valentine laughed. "Well, let's hope so, or what's the point?"

"Break's over." Standing on the log, Asha spun her weapon with panache and pointed it at Valentine. "You're next."

Exchanging a dubious glance, the twins separated. Tyrathorn stood waiting, his demeanor much friendlier and less stabby than his sister's. He began the lesson with a jovial slap to the shoulder.

"Let us bend the universe to our will, shall we?"

Excitement and fear raced through Malcolm. "I thought you'd never ask."

"To start, I shall be honest," Tyrathorn began. "I recall basic skills, but beyond that I retain only fragments. For some reason this has limited my power, and I am terribly frustrated." He touched the bruise on his temple, a flash of anger crossing his face. "I know enough to begin your training. But if you ask a question and I have no answer, now you know why."

"Have you remembered more since you got here?"

"Pieces, though not many. Enough to know the Black Tempest should be feared. I can only pray that when we do face him, I will be whole."

"Maybe training us will shake something loose," Malcolm offered. "If not, I'm sure Asha'd be happy to knock you around."

Tyrathorn chuckled as they glanced at the young women across the clearing. Asha had started Valentine on the footwork exercises, and already she was mirroring the warrior with precision—the advantage of a lifetime of dance training.

"My sister is softer underneath than she seems," Tyrathorn said. "But put a blade in her hand, an opponent in her sights, and she becomes a weapon. She is the most natural warrior I know."

Malcolm cracked his knuckles. "Well, if I learn something now, maybe I'll surprise her next time."

"One can hope," Tyrathorn said, grinning. "Observe, Malcolm. Your training begins now."

He stepped back, the nexus in his armor's chest plate glowing red.

"You know how to absorb Time, and how to use it as pure energy. But a Chronauri's true power comes from controlling *how* Time flows. What I will teach you now is the most basic application of that principle. It is the first skill a Chronauri of Everwatch learns."

Holding out his right hand, Tyrathorn concentrated. The nexus glowed red and a stream of red energy traced down his armor.

"I could blast a tree to pieces now . . . or I could do this."

A translucent red bubble formed above his palm, the size of a baseball.

"The timeline flows everywhere in the universe. I have taken control of this tiny piece of it. The energy is red because I am willing Time to flow faster. Now, what would you say is inside this sphere?"

"Um . . . air?"

"What else?"

Malcolm pondered. "Other particles, I guess. Water, meteor dust, micro-organisms."

"What happens to anything when its atoms move faster?"

"It heats up."

Tyrathorn smiled. "And if they move fast enough? If they get hot enough?"

The bubble became a ball of fire. Malcolm gasped, falling back a step.

"In controlling this bubble, I control how Time flows for everything inside it. So I willed the atoms of *some* particles to move faster. This increased their friction against the particles moving at normal speed, until finally they reached combustion temperature."

The concept blossomed in Malcolm's mind. "So, instead of just blasting out the energy you'd absorbed, you spent it to control a little part of the universe. You told Time to move faster and it obeyed."

"Exactly so."

"If you use more energy, can you control bigger areas?"

"You can, you will, and that is only the beginning. Observe."

The flames unraveled and the red sphere disappeared. Malcolm felt a different *shift* as Tyrathorn's nexus glowed blue.

"Water and other particles also have a freezing point. Slow their atoms enough, and you will reduce their temperature." A blue bubble appeared above his left palm. "Are you familiar with the principle of sympathetic cooling?"

"Not really. Val's the science geek."

"Ah. Your scientists discovered how to do it with lasers, yet they have barely scratched the surface." With a crackle, the bubble began to solidify. "If I reduce an atom's temperature this way, its electrostatic interaction with neighboring atoms will cause them to cool as well. Just as I showed you with flames, a skilled Chronauri can choose which atoms to affect . . . to do something like this."

The bubble froze, but not as a solid chunk like Malcolm expected. No, what hovered over Tyrathorn's palm was a work of art—a delicate sphere of spiderwebs rendered in sparkling ice.

"Wow. It's beautiful. And you did it so quickly."

"Both were quite slow, actually, for demonstration," Tyrathorn explained. "But yes, my talents lean more toward slowing Time, so making ice is easier. I suspect the same will be true for you. However, if called upon . . ."

The next *shift* felt different again, and Malcolm saw why. Rays of red and blue mingled in Tyrathorn's nexus, dancing around each other as they traced the lines of his armor.

A ball of fire combusted above his right palm, contrasting with the ball of ice above his left. Both hands twitched and the fire and ice smashed together, bursting into steam.

". . . a Chronauri can employ multiple skills at once."

"Okay," Malcolm said. "That was the coolest thing I've ever seen."

"The only thing better?" Tyrathorn grinned. "Trying it yourself."

Malcolm's heart raced. Absently he tightened the straps holding the nexus to his left wrist. The leather harnesses had been another gift from Clive, so the twins wouldn't have to carry something so important in their pockets.

"Now draw a small flow of Time. Direct it to pass through your body like a wave, from your head to your toes."

Concentrating, Malcolm followed his instructions and cool refreshment passed through him. The ache of sore muscles faded, the sting of a dozen cuts dulled, and his senses sharpened as if he'd gotten a week's worth of rest. A lazy smile crossed his face.

Tyrathorn chuckled. "I do believe he likes it."

"I could definitely get used to that."

"Remember this always, Malcolm. Time is not just a weapon—it is your ally. Treat it as such, and one day you will master it." Tyrathorn gestured to the nexus. "Draw more, and mimic my ice trick."

Malcolm frowned. "How?"

"You already know how I did it." Tyrathorn tapped his own temple. "Pair that knowledge with your will. Hold that mental picture in your mind, and let Time filter through it."

Could it really be so easy? Closing his eyes, Malcolm held out his right hand. As he pressed on the nexus with his will, the connection to Time opened wider, like a quantum doorway.

Time flowed into him, bright and eager, as if it were matching his excitement. Tamping down a spike of fear, he clutched it to keep it from bursting out uncontrolled.

"Focus, Malcolm," Tyrathorn said, calm and steady. "Time helps give order to the universe. But when it breaks from the natural flow, it remembers that it is energy, wild and pure. You must show it the way."

Malcolm replayed in his mind all that Tyrathorn had shown him. For one moment, a small part of the universe had been his to command. He'd held it with confidence, as if it was his birthright. *If it's his birthright, then it's mine, too.*

Mustering his confidence, Malcolm mentally grasped the Time he'd absorbed. A thrill shot through him as it responded, steadying as if it awaited his direction. He focused his thoughts on the ice ball, on what was required to make it. Then he willed the energy to match it.

Time *shifted.*

Bending to his will, it flowed out from him. Then a chill wafted over his right hand, and Tyrathorn gave a triumphant hoot. Malcolm opened his eyes and suppressed the urge to leap and shout.

Above his palm, a grapefruit-sized ball of ice sparkled in the sunlight. It was the most beautiful thing he'd ever seen. And he'd made it using Time.

Tyrathorn clapped him on the back. "I can scarcely believe it!"

That broke Malcolm from the spell. "You didn't think I could do it?"

"Malcolm, my friend, let me explain." Palming the ice ball, Tyrathorn held it high. "In the history of the Ember Guard— the finest Chronauri warriors in all the timeline—not one of us accomplished this in the first month of training, let alone the first hour. You are truly gifted." He shook his head. "When you are ready . . . you will be a sight to behold."

A series of clangs echoed across the clearing, followed by an *oomph* and a heavy thud. They turned toward the sound and their jaws dropped.

"Another miracle," Tyrathorn muttered.

Valentine lay on her back, the point of her weapon driven into the dirt. That came as no shock. What did come as a shock was Asha, also sprawled on the grass with her *qama* fallen at her side.

"Whoa," Malcolm said. "They took each other down?"

Retrieving her weapon, Asha kicked out. Valentine twisted away and vaulted into a back handspring. The move would have been perfect if she'd managed to pull the *qama* from the ground and defend herself . . . but she missed.

Asha charged, and then Valentine was on the ground again, with her opponent straddling her legs and the tip of a blade in her face. She held up her hands to yield.

For a tense moment Asha kept her threatening stance, eyes flashing with the promise of violence. Malcolm held his breath. *If she doesn't stop, will I even be able to help?*

Then Asha visibly grabbed hold of herself and relaxed. Lowering her blade, she sat back on her heels. For a brief moment the nexus in her chest plate glowed red, and from a dozen feet away her *qama* flew into her hand.

"Well done," she said. "You learn the basic forms quickly, and your power helps you move with speed. I did not expect it—that was my mistake."

Malcolm gaped again, which was beginning to feel like his natural state. "What in . . . how did . . . ? Thorn, her sword came back to her!"

"Do not look at me. I did not remember she could do that." Thorn's surprise turned to mischief. "Would you like to see how two trained Chronauri practice? Asha! *Zeur datzeko!*"

Asha's attention snapped to her brother. Then she was on her feet and sprinting toward him. Tyrathorn stretched his arms wide and a cascade of blue energy poured from his nexus. Disks of ice appeared in his hands, and with a flick of his wrists they flew toward his sister.

The ice disks converged on her path. Without breaking stride, she swung her weapons and they burst into fragments.

Tyrathorn's wrists flicked one after the other, hurling wave upon wave of projectiles, a hailstorm of frozen death. Asha flowed like living wind, twisting and ducking and leaping, blades flashing as they sliced through air and ice like cyclones of steel. Wreathed in a growing swarm of ice, she seemed a figure out of legend, charging through a blizzard and into battle.

Asha leapt, breaking through the hailstorm and landing near her brother. With a hollow clang, her blade glanced off his chest plate. She showed an instant of surprise, then swung again. Tyrathorn retreated, arms up to block.

"Come on!" she chided. "It's not fun if you don't fight back."

She swung again and again, teasing at the edges of his defense, goading him to strike. But what he couldn't dodge, he only batted away.

"Asha, I—" Tyrathorn began, then cut off to defend himself. "I cannot—"

Her blade barely missed his nose. "What?" she taunted playfully. "Afraid of a Second-*sev* now?"

"I cannot form my weapons!"

Asha stopped in her tracks. Tyrathorn studied the ground, ashamed.

"I remember the way a Chronauri fights, Ashandara." He held out his hands, staring at them as if they'd betrayed him. "But I cannot remember *how*. My weapons are a half-remembered dream. I reach for them and they slip away." His voice thickened with emotion. "If I cannot remember what I was—if I cannot reclaim my full power—I fear the Black Tempest will tear through us like paper. What chance will our people have then?"

The twins shared an uncertain look. Their training session had suddenly taken on a desperate tone. What did Tyrathorn mean about being unable to form his weapons?

Asha grimaced. As she stared at her brother, Malcolm thought she looked lost. Like she wanted desperately to help him but had no clue how. She began to reach toward him, then stopped herself.

"Thorn, I . . ."

Tyrathorn stood hunched, staring at the dirt. Bereft and forlorn, he looked to Malcolm like a statue of some legendary warrior, long since faded and forgotten.

Should he say something to help? *And what would you say? You don't actually know anything yet.*

When Malcolm's attention returned to Asha, though, something had changed. Gone was the tender, worried expression. Something flickered behind her eyes now—a storm of fury and determination and maybe even flashes of . . . fear? When she spoke next, all traces of doubt were gone.

"Do you remember what you told me when I was a child? When our father forbid me to train with the Ember Guard, do you remember what you said?" Tyrathorn barely looked at her. "You said, 'No one can tell a warrior that they are not one. If the battle lives in your heart, no one can take it away.' You told me that a thousand times, and I believed you." Her voice raised, seething with anger. "And so help me, Thorn, if it kills us both, I will make you remember!"

Asha suddenly glowed red. Blades up, she charged. Tyrathorn retreated step after step from his sister's vicious assault. Sparks danced off his armor as he deflected a flurry of blows.

"Do not run from me!" she shouted.

Asha drove forward, a relentless blur of glowing steel. One instant she was on the ground and swiping at Tyrathorn's legs, the next she was flipping through the air and slashing at his head. Malcolm stared in awe, barely able to track her movement.

"Fight, *du kolda!*" She kicked Tyrathorn's chest plate. With a grunt, he fell back against a tree. "What's a Second-*sev* to you? Fight me! Give me my brother back!"

As he dodged under her blade, Asha's armored knee shot up and smashed him in the face. He rocked backward, clutching his nose. She danced back a step, set for another attack, and launched at him again.

She never got close.

Tyrathorn's face twisted with rage. Blazing with blue light, he threw his palm forward and a wall of ice appeared between them. Still in mid-charge, Asha bounced off the barrier and stumbled back.

With a roar, Tyrathorn burst through the wall. Ice formed over his gauntlets, and like frozen clubs they bashed against Asha's chest plate. She flew back amid a shower of glittering shards. As soon as she hit the ground, he pinned her down.

"We are beyond childhood tantrums!" he spat. "Why do you do this?"

To Malcolm's surprise, Asha's rage was gone. Instead she wore a satisfied smirk. "Look at your hand, brother."

Tyrathorn blinked at her, taken aback. Then he looked down at his right hand, and his face went slack. Malcolm nearly choked. *Whoa.*

A crude approximation of a sword rested in Tyrathorn's palm . . . made entirely of ice.

"I used to watch you practice," Asha said softly. "You created such beautiful weapons—like works of art. You'd hold out your hand and they would just appear. I always envied that."

In a daze, Tyrathorn released her and fell to his knees. While Asha scrambled to her feet, he stared down at the weapon in his hand. Then his body began to shake. Silently his shoulders bounced up and down, his gaze never leaving the blade.

Oh no, is he crying? Malcolm braced himself for an awkward moment. No one wanted to watch a dude cry—especially other dudes.

Then Tyrathorn threw back his shoulders, casting his face toward the late afternoon sky. No tears. He'd been laughing, and now that laughter broke forth in great bellows. With a whoop of joy, he sprang to his feet and grabbed Asha by the waist to swing her in a circle. She beat against his arm but quickly gave way to laughter.

Driving his sword into the ground, Tyrathorn approached the twins and clapped them on their arms. "Mark this day, my friends. We have taken our first step toward victory."

Malcolm wore a broad smile. Finally something had gone right.

"Thank you, sister. You were right—it was in my heart all along. Hopefully, soon more memories will follow."

They shared an affectionate look before he moved to retrieve his sword. It would probably melt soon, but Malcolm figured he wouldn't want to part with it until he had to.

"I dare say that is enough for today," Tyrathorn announced. "Now we celebrate."

"I'll celebrate with a shower," Valentine said.

Side by side, the warrior siblings marched toward Fred's mansion. The twins followed, Malcolm's heart aglow. Sure they had each hit walls in their training, but they had also excelled at other things. Maybe soon they'd feel like Chronauri for real.

Glancing at Valentine, he noted her tight expression. She walked stiffly, as if bracing for another fight.

"Hey, relax," he whispered. "We've got to enjoy the good times, right? For tonight, the hard part's over."

"Not for me," she muttered, then sped up to walk at Tyrathorn's side.

Malcolm stared after her, puzzled. Then it dawned on him. *Dinner at home.* Very soon, Valentine would face Callie de la Vega again. Or, as she suspected, the Frost Hammer.

CHAPTER 15

"Your fighting style is unique," Malcolm said. He drew up beside Asha as they hiked back to Fred's house. "Strong but fluid. Sort of like, um, water flowing over rocks."

Asha eyed him, brow furrowed.

"I mean, uh, not water. Something scarier, like . . . lava or hornets." He nodded. "Right. You fight like hornets on rocks. Wait . . ."

Her stoic expression crumbled. She laughed—not out of derision or sarcasm, but for real. Malcolm paused, caught off guard by the change, which made her laugh more.

She was showing him her true smile. It changed her whole face, and he felt himself smiling back.

"I'm sorry," Asha said, wiping away a tear. "It's just, even after learning what you are, you're still so . . ."

"Dashing? Charming?"

"I was going to say regular." Her ice blue eyes sparkled. "But maybe you're a little funny, too."

So here was the girl hiding under the warrior. He had caught fleeting glimpses before, but this was the first moment her shield had truly dropped. She really was beautiful. *Stop that. You know why.*

Asha noted the change in his expression. "What is it?"

"Oh, um," he raked through his thoughts to find a good answer. "I was just, uh, wondering . . . about the *sevs* you talk about. What do they mean?"

"I've been wondering that, too," Valentine said.

"Ah." Asha's smile faded a bit. "*Sev* is a ranking system for Chronauri ability. All of us are born at the lowest *sev,* and over the years we grow."

"But not all reach the same level," Tyrathorn interjected.

"Yes, each has an inborn limit. We grow until we reach that level, and then we plateau. No one knows their limit until, one day, they can go no further."

"Wow. Then we were born with this and never knew." Malcolm shook his head in wonder. "You're Second-*sev.* Is First-*sev* the highest?"

Asha gave a muted laugh. Tyrathorn also chuckled. The siblings glanced at each other with wistful smiles.

"We all start at First-*sev,*" she explained. "I reached my plateau early."

"Not that you would know it," Tyrathorn said. "She fights like the devil is inside her."

Asha gave him a grateful look. "I work hard to make up for what I lack, but the three of you can do things I never will."

"Like what?" Malcolm asked.

"Like draw your power from the Time stream."

Malcolm nearly tripped. "But, wait, all the stuff we've seen you do. The red blades and the armor and the jumping around?"

Asha nodded. "First-*sev* Chronauri cannot absorb or manipulate Time. Their powers are sensory. Some feel *shifts* in the timeline; some read your past or future—that is our father's talent; others track you by the ripples you make in Time; and there are more. They feel, they perceive, but never touch it themselves." She paused, as if steeling herself. "Second-*sev* cannot draw Time from the universe, but we can access the Time we were born with—our personal store of it. A rare type of nexus allows this."

Thunderstruck, Malcolm stared at Asha, then at Tyrathorn, then back at Asha. What she was describing—did it imply what he thought it implied? By Tyrathorn's downcast eyes, he knew that it must.

"You can't be serious," he said. "You still choose to fight, when it . . . ?"

Asha shot him a challenging glare. "To protect my people, I would make the same choice a thousand times over."

Then it dawned on Malcolm. "That's why you don't use your power when we train. You're preserving it for the real battles."

Asha hesitated, then nodded. "I'll last longer that way."

"Wait, so what does it mean if—" Valentine's eyes went wide. "Oh, no. You're sacrificing your own life span to fight with the Ember Guard?"

Malcolm shook his head. "I can't imagine—"

Asha whirled on him, poking his chest with every sentence. "And what did you do last year? Hmm? From what you said, I'm guessing you both risked your lives to save this town. Are you so different from me? Am I to be pitied by you or anyone because I make the same choice?"

With a scowl she spun back around and stalked away. "I may live half as long, but my life will mean something before it ends."

Malcolm just stood there, rocked by the discovery. As they

often did, his thoughts returned to Walter. He'd been a soldier, too, and not unlike Asha in some ways. Rough around the edges, with that fighting spirit alive behind his eyes. Yet he possessed a depth of soul that few ever saw.

Malcolm blinked as the first hint of tears stung his eyes. *Please, not now.*

"Give her an hour alone. That is all she will need," Tyrathorn said. "And fear not, my friends. You are far from the first to react this way. Truthfully, I am shocked our father relented, and eager to remember why."

He began walking again, the twins following.

"So, about the levels . . ." Valentine said.

"Ah, of course." Tyrathorn resumed by holding up three fingers. "Anyone above Second-*sev* can access the Time stream, but Third-*sev* Chronauri come with a limitation. They can only bend the flow in one direction."

"So, they can either speed up Time or slow it down," Malcolm said.

"But not both. Correct."

"Man, that's a bummer," Valentine said.

"Perhaps," Tyrathorn replied. "Consider, though—is it better to be quite good at two things, or extremely good at one? Third-*sev* will often make up for their limitation by honing their skill with relentless focus. If ever you come against one—and I suspect you will—never underestimate them."

"Good to know," Malcolm said. "How many levels are there? And which one are you?"

"Fourth and Fifth-*sev* wield Time as they please," Tyrathorn continued as if Malcolm hadn't spoken. "They are limited only by skill and the strength of their will. What separates them is how much Time they can draw. A Fourth-*sev*'s power is impressive, but a Fifth-*sev* . . . well, that is truly stunning. Even among our kind, they are rare as an eclipse."

"Wow," Valentine said. "So, Fifth-*sev* is the highest?"

Tyrathorn didn't answer that, either. Malcolm thought to ask again, but hesitated. *Is there some reason he's holding back?*

"I did not remember my *sev*," Tyrathorn said before he could ask. "At least, not until today. But I believe I know now."

For two dozen steps, the only sound was the nearly imperceptible clink of his finely crafted armor. Pursing his lips, he stroked his chin as if pondering something. Malcolm began to wonder if that was all they would get tonight.

"A memory returned this morning," he finally said. "When the Black Tempest appeared, he wielded only ice, but he did so with unparalleled precision and force. Many concluded that he was an unusually talented Third-*sev,* and so their fear waned. They could contain a Third-*sev.*"

He paused, letting out a slow breath.

"One day, a squadron of Watchers caught him alone."

"Watchers?" Malcolm said.

"Non-Chronauri soldiers. Half of them perished in seconds. The other half fled to a nearby fortress, where they believed themselves safe inside."

He gave a mirthless laugh.

"Only one scout made it back to Everwatch, and her report became quite famous. It said, 'He raised his hands to the sky, and the clouds trembled. The very wind cried out in pain. And then death rained upon us.'"

Tyrathorn stopped and faced the twins.

"The Black Tempest ripped the clouds apart and froze them into ballistae. Ice missiles as long as one of your telephone poles and as thick as five. He bombarded the fortress and reduced it to a pile of stones. When the scout told what this man had done, everyone knew he could only be Fifth-*sev* . . . which meant that only I could stop him."

THIS thing is starting to feel like a second home. The limousine's leather squeaked as Valentine squirmed. Once again she was packed in with all her friends, plus two new ones, hurtling toward doom.

Tonight, doom had taken the form of a 33-year-old journalist with perfect skin and perfect teeth. And perfect hair. And she seemed really nice. And . . . okay, so maybe their Dad's attraction to Callie de la Vega was valid. And yes, the notion of her being a villain in disguise was insanity, but didn't they deal with the insane on a daily basis? *What if I'm wrong, though? Will I ever be able to let her in?*

Her only comfort was John, pressed against her side and radiating calm as he always did. As their fingers intertwined, he leaned over to plant a gentle kiss behind her ear. A shiver went through her, and instantly the tension melted.

"Better?" he whispered.

She nodded. "Thank you."

Across from her, Tyrathorn couldn't sit still either. He tugged at the clothes borrowed from Fred as if he couldn't get comfortable. Maybe this era's fabrics didn't feel right. Or maybe it was the color.

"I am not a variety of flower," Tyrathorn had said upon seeing the bright pink button-up. Asha had openly smirked.

"Dude, it's a party shirt," Fred had replied. "And every night's a party with your boy. Relax, dawg, you look dope."

To Valentine's amazement, Tyrathorn had done his best to be gracious. Now, though, his distant expression pinched as if he were troubled by some internal thought. Did he really hate the shirt that much?

He turned to Asha. "I really turned twenty-two?"

Caught off guard, Asha stammered. "A-a few months back."

"So that would make you . . . fifteen?"

She nodded. "We were born on the same day, seven years apart."

"Oh. I should have remembered that." Tyrathorn grimaced. "I have lost so many days. With you, with our family. Time I could have spent with the Guard, defending Everwatch from that monster." He shook his head. "I have seen too many people die, Asha. I do remember their faces, and I cannot bear to add more."

"You won't," she said. "Those days you lost—we're making up for them now."

He brightened, taking her hand in his. "And one day soon I will regain my memories. I will become who I once was and be whole again."

Asha blinked, almost frowning, and leaned away from Tyrathorn. Disentangling her hand from his, she busied herself tightening her customary ponytail. An odd reaction. *She's an odd girl,* Valentine reflected. *So self-contained.*

A good girl, though. She had a short fuse, but didn't seem to hold a grudge. When they'd all showered and changed, she'd already returned to normal. Or at least it appeared that way. The girl was hard to read underneath all those layers of armor, and Valentine didn't mean the metal ones.

"Yo, the vibe in here is way too heavy right now," Fred said.

Scooting forward in his seat, he tapped the ceiling controls and turned on the stereo. Phone in hand, he navigated to his party playlist and a hip-hop beat started blasting.

"A'ight now," he called over the thumping bass. "Y'all know this song, so sing! Ain't no excuses for Time travelers either, just jump in. Go!"

And he went. No one sang but Fred, but they did laugh along with his attempts to rap. Not that he cared—this was heaven to him. Malcolm tried to belt out the chorus, but then his voice cracked and everyone laughed even louder. Halfway through the song, Winter started punching Fred's arm along with the rhythm, wearing a bigger smile than they'd seen in days.

"Ow, girl, don't cramp my style!" Fred protested.

"You're my drum now!" she taunted.

By the time the limo turned onto Pleasant Point Drive, Valentine's ears rang from the improvised concert, her chest ached, and her eyes watered from all the laughter. She reveled in that feeling, savoring it. For a few minutes, they had just been friends taking a drive together.

Even the Corvonians had not been immune. Though puzzled by the strange noises that twenty-first century teenagers enjoyed, they had celebrated right along with them.

"At the risk of breaking the mood," Tyrathorn said as their laughter subsided, "I must say how much I admire your bond. It reminds me of the Ember Guard. For a moment, Fred, I felt very much at home. Thank you."

"Ain't no thing, brother. That's how we do it."

Tyrathorn nodded, looking thoughtful. "There is a saying in your era—blood is thicker than water. It implies 'family over friends,' yes?"

"Yeah," Valentine said.

"It is taken from a very old proverb—one that means exactly the opposite. The original saying is, 'The blood of the covenant is thicker than the water of the womb.' It means that a bond forged by choice holds deeper meaning than one forged by biology. The family you are born with is not half as strong as the family you choose." He studied them all, lingering on Winter. "I believe this describes all of you. How fortunate you are to have found each other."

Malcolm leaned toward Tyrathorn, holding out his hand. "Then count yourself fortunate, too. You're becoming one of us, after all." His eyes flicked to Asha. "You both are."

Tyrathorn accepted the hand and gave a hearty shake.

"Yeah!" Fred pumped his fist. "Nothing like the threat of a horrible death to bring people together."

"So, wait," Winter said. "Does this mean we can make fun of them, too? 'Cause I've been holding back all kinds of jokes about Thorn in that shirt."

They burst into laughter again.

CHAPTER 16

With eleven people packed around the dinner table, there was barely enough room for plates, much less luxuries like personal space. Everyone sat shoulder to shoulder, jostling whenever their neighbors moved. No one cared.

To Valentine, the room practically shook with laughter. The mood in the car had followed them inside and carried through dinner, as if everyone was relieved to be having a normal evening. They'd each spent dinner telling embarrassing stories.

"Fred, my boy, this meal is wonderful," Oma Grace said.

"For sure. But please tell me there ain't more food comin'," Clive added, patting his stomach. "You know I won't be able to resist."

"Naw, this is all," Fred said.

"How many places did you order from again?" Neil began ticking off his fingers. "Let's see, there was Italian, Chinese, Mexican, um, Japanese."

"And Huey's, the burger place," Fred finished. "Pretty much everywhere that delivers."

"I've never had takeout from five places at once," Callie said, flashing that movie star smile.

Even on a Monday, she was dolled up like it was a night on the town. In high heels and a sleek charcoal pantsuit, she somehow managed to look professional and flirty all at once. By some miracle, she made that odd silver bracelet work with this outfit, too. Valentine couldn't help staring at it, on high alert just in case it hid some exotic weapon.

"The best part was when three delivery guys showed up at once," Malcolm said. "They didn't know what was going on. I opened the door and they were just standing there, staring at each other."

The table broke into laughter again. Valentine joined in, halfway enjoying this night in spite of her suspicions, and halfway distracted by the shadow hanging overhead. She'd spent the last hour maneuvering out of spots that would force her to engage Callie.

"Yo, I almost forgot!" Fred exclaimed.

Reaching into his jacket, he withdrew a stack of what looked like postcards. Made from thick and beautifully textured paper, they were covered front and back with intricate scrollwork that reminded her of Malcolm's Renaissance history books. Fanciful lettering sparkled gold in the lamplight:

Emmett's Bluff Restoration Ball

"My dad and his business friends are sponsoring this charity thing. Got people comin' from all over the state. I got all y'all tickets! This party's gonna be dope. Costs like a thousand bucks to get in." He began passing them around the table. "Unless you know the dawg, that is. Just save the date in July."

The event had been big news when it was announced—an elegant party to aid their town's recovery. The scars of what Lucius had done were still evident, but they were slowly disappearing, and this would only help. Rumors said they were planning amazing food, a live big band, and tons of surprises. *Still, a thousand dollars per ticket?!* She'd have to find a new dress.

Her attention snapped back to the group, all of whom were thanking their friend for his generosity.

"I'll have to find a new dress!" Callie said to Neil, brimming with excitement.

Of course. Perfect.

As usual, Fred waved it all away. "Wouldn't be a party without all my peeps."

Dinner began to wind down, everyone leaning back in their chairs with satisfied sighs. Neil stretched, parlaying the motion into resting his arm around Callie's shoulders. With a subtle twist, she snuggled deeper into his embrace. For an instant they shared a look that drove a burning dagger into Valentine's chest. A look she'd not seen on her father's face in two years.

"I know someone who hasn't shared a story," Neil said, too casually. "Which is ironic, since she writes them for a living."

All eyes turned to Callie, whose bright smile turned sheepish. She jabbed a finger into Neil's side, eliciting a yelp. They grinned at each other, driving the dagger deeper.

"That was by design," Callie said. "Hey, did I mention the pies should be ready soon?"

Fred sat up. "Whoa, you can bake, too? Nice!" Glancing at Malcolm, he wiggled his eyebrows in a completely unsubtle and Fred-like manner. He barked as Winter kicked his shin.

"Down, boy," she said.

"Oh, pies, of course," Neil said. "After a story. A good one."

Callie gave an exaggerated sigh. "Okay, you got me. Let me think."

Glancing at the ceiling, she bit her bottom lip. Which must be catnip to boys, because none of them could stop watching. Valentine fought the urge to roll her eyes.

"Okay," Callie said. "So I was visiting family in Santo Domingo—that's the Dominican Republic capital."

"That where you're from?" Clive asked.

"My family is. I was born in the States, but most of them are still back there." Callie gave a self-conscious smile. "They all tease me about my American accent."

"Aw, don't worry none 'bout dat, mon," Fred said with a grin.

Winter elbowed him. "That's a Jamaican accent, genius."

"And not a good one," Malcolm said.

Fred actually had enough manners to look embarrassed. "Hey, no offense or anything, girl," he muttered.

"I'm not offended, don't worry." Callie turned her smile on him and his face reddened. "Anyway, my family lives on the edge of the city. One day I was bored, so I borrowed a moped and went into town. I just needed some sun and wind and . . ." She shot Neil a knowing look. ". . . maybe a little coffee."

"Oh, there's a shock," he said, giving her a playful squeeze. "This girl can put away coffee like a machine."

"Writer," she said, pointing at herself. "It's either coffee or whiskey, so I chose to get hooked on the stimulant."

Valentine couldn't remember when her dad had last smiled this much. His face could break in half at any moment. *Stop that, and stop suspecting her! Why can't you be happy for him?*

She studied Callie as everyone laughed at the story, pleading with her brain to tell her why this was so hard. Why her thoughts insisted that Callie de la Vega was not what she seemed. Was it really about Callie, or was it about her own issues?

"You okay?" John whispered in her ear.

She nodded, wanting it to be true but knowing it wasn't.

"So, like a huge idiot, I'm now driving a moped one-handed while holding this scalding hot coffee. I wanted to find somewhere nice to sit and drink it. I'm cruising around downtown searching for a spot, when . . . it happened. The moment." Her smile disappeared. She paused for dramatic effect. "The defining moment."

Everyone was leaning toward her.

"What kind of moment?" Tyrathorn asked, enraptured.

"Have you ever had a moment when all that you are is suddenly put to the test? When it all boils down to this one time, this one place, and everything that you'll ever be hangs in the balance?" The group held its collective breath. Callie leaned forward, as if preparing to share a secret. "For me, that moment came on a moped at thirty miles an hour, one hand on the throttle, the other clutching my prized coffee . . . when a roach suddenly crawled inside my helmet."

"Eeewww!" Everyone recoiled in their chairs.

"So, did you pass the test?" Asha asked.

"I screamed and crushed the coffee cup, which burned my hand. My other hand squeezed the throttle and pulled to the right. The engine revved, which popped up the front wheel. Next thing I knew, I crashed into a curb. That's when the moped and I, um, parted ways."

"Parted ways?" Malcolm said. "Where'd you part away to?"

"Well, the moped flew through a shop window. I rolled onto the sidewalk, where not only did I scrape every visible piece of skin, but the sun dress I'd been wearing flew up and wrapped around my arms *and* my helmet. So there I was, laid out on the sidewalk, tangled in my own dress, still trying to rip off the helmet and kill the cockroach, and completely failing until a young and very cute policeman happened by and rescued me." Raising her glass, Callie looked toward the sky. "That's the first and last day I ever rode a moped."

By the time Callie had finished, everyone was doubled over and clutching their sides, gasping with laughter. Even Valentine did her best to share in the moment. Callie covered her eyes, at once laughing and mortified.

"I cannot believe you got that out of me. No one knows that story!"

"You never even told me that one," Neil said.

"Apparently, I was waiting to embarrass myself in front of all your loved ones. Mission accomplished?"

The entire table agreed that she'd thoroughly trumped everyone else's story, which made her the official winner, a dubious honor that she seemed happy to accept. And why wouldn't she? Everyone loved her. Callie de la Vega was a hit.

"Don't forget your prize," Neil said, and planted a quick kiss on her lips.

Callie's cheeks reddened. "Best prize ever."

Valentine shot to her feet, suddenly needing to be somewhere else. Anywhere else. Releasing her death grip on John's hand, she gathered the dirty dishes within arm's reach and bolted into the kitchen.

She busied herself at the sink, caught up in her own head and failing to notice that all the laughter had ceased as she left the room. Instead she focused on soap and hot water.

It was only five minutes before someone joined her. By then the group had recovered most of its happy vibe, and sounds of lively conversation filled the house again. Scrubbing furiously at a stubborn spot, Valentine didn't look up when Neil set down more dishes.

"I shouldn't have done that," he said, eyes fixed on the dishes. "We were having so much fun, it all felt so natural, and it just . . . happened. But it was inconsiderate. I'm sorry."

"I'm not angry, Dad," she forced out. "You don't have to apologize."

She meant it. Among the storm of emotions inside her, anger was not one of them. *So what am I feeling? Why is this so hard?* His eyes were on her now, and she could feel his uncertainty.

"I mean it. You're happy." *And hopefully not dating a psychopath.* "That's a good thing, right?"

"She's pretty great." Neil sighed. "But I've got more to think about than just me. So, whatever you're feeling, I should have waited until you were more comfortable." He kissed the side of her head. "Maybe, when you're ready, try to meet me halfway? You don't have to be best friends, but being friendly would be nice."

He returned to the dining area, leaving her gaping and infuriated. Try to meet him halfway? Didn't he see how hard she was trying? It was like trying to cross a windy chasm on a rickety bridge. He was her dad. Couldn't he, of all people, see she was working through something huge?

Valentine turned to grab more dishes and gasped. Malcolm stood behind her, leaning against the counter and studying her like their dad had just done. She narrowed her eyes at him.

"You here to lecture me, too?"

"I wouldn't dream of telling you how to feel, Val. That's your business," he said. "But here's how you looked during dinner." He adopted a frown, crinkling the spot between his brow like something bothered him and he couldn't figure out what it was. "Now here's you during Callie's story." The frown morphed into something between a smile and a grimace, as if he were in pain and trying to hide it. "And here's you whenever you just *look* at her." The grimace changed to a hawkish stare that made Valentine feel examined and judged.

"You're being unfair."

"I know you're trying." Malcolm stepped closer. "But you suck at hiding how you feel, Val. You always have. Sometimes that's good, but this isn't one of them. So while you're working this out, you've got to pretend things are good."

"You want me to lie? Even when I don't trust her?"

"Yeah, I do," he said without hesitation. "Because when you love someone, that's what you do sometimes. And even if you're right about her—which I don't believe you are—why hurt Dad in the process?"

At that moment the oven bell dinged. Valentine's heart raced as she realized what that meant. Her brother flashed an impish grin.

"Oops, that's my cue," he said, backing toward the door.

"Wait, Mal!" she whisper-shouted after him. "Don't leave me here with—"

Malcolm fled back toward the dining room, exchanging pleasant smiles with Callie as she passed by. Just inside the doorway, her eyes locked with Valentine and her smile froze in place. Valentine backed away from the oven, every word she knew stuck in her throat.

"I, uh, just need to get these cooling," Callie said, pulling out three pies and setting them on the stove. "One of them is custard. Your dad said that's your favorite." After a moment, she glanced at Valentine again.

Too late, Valentine realized she'd let too many awkward seconds pass before answering. "Um, yeah, it is, thanks."

Callie studied the pies, wringing her hands. Valentine noticed they were trembling but tried not to stare at the silver bracelet. Was she nervous? What did she have to be nervous about? Everyone loved her.

Callie turned toward her. Gingerly she moved closer, every step seeming a struggle, as if they carried her toward a firing squad. Valentine braced herself for another lecture. Instead Callie's voice dropped to a whisper, her smile melting into a grief-stricken frown.

"I'm so terribly sorry," she said.

Valentine blinked, taken aback.

"You barely know me, and I kissed your dad in front of you. It's not right. I just get carried away around him. I've never felt anything like—" She cut off, huffed, then visibly regathered herself. "I would love for us to be friends, but I haven't earned it. I have no clue what I'm doing and I treated you with disrespect tonight. If you're mad or hurt, it's my fault, and . . ." Callie's voice faltered. She quickly wiped away a tear. "I'll just leave you alone."

Valentine almost reached out to stop her. She almost said something. She very nearly broke into tears herself. Instead she just watched as Callie plastered on her winning smile and returned to the dining room.

Could Malcolm be right about her? Would an undercover supervillain care about Valentine's feelings?

No one on Earth had ever felt this wretched. *How about, thank you for the apology, you're nice and I'm weird? Or, I don't know, maybe thank you for making my dad happy?* A thousand words in a thousand combinations would have been better than what she had said, which was nothing.

The pies smelled amazing. Of course Callie would be a great cook, too. Valentine turned back to her dishes, wishing she could physically kick herself.

Great job, Val.

CHAPTER 17

Mercifully, someone suggested a movie while they all feasted on pie. Valentine and John moved to the living room first and grabbed a spot on the couch. Slipping an arm around her, he pulled her close and she luxuriated in his presence.

"What do you need?" he said.

She gave a relieved sigh. "Exactly this."

As the rest of the group arrived, Valentine watched the Corvonian siblings. Tyrathorn wore a neutral expression, as if he knew what to expect, but Asha's passive mask covered total bewilderment. No, not bewilderment. What was it?

"Ever seen a movie before?" Malcolm whispered to her. She shook her head. "But you've heard about them, right?" She nodded stiffly, working hard to school her face.

Is she actually excited? Valentine grinned. "Your very first movie? We have to pick something special!"

"For sure," Malcolm said. "And I know just the one."

Five minutes later, the 20th Century Fox anthem was shaking the living room as the original *Star Wars* began to play.

Valentine practically inhaled the custard pie, which was the best she'd ever had in her life. *Yep, that figures.* If a secret supervillain could also bake like this, it would shake Valentine's faith in the way the universe worked.

As the opening scenes unfolded, she took special note of Asha, who stared at the screen with the wide-eyed wonder of a child watching her first fireworks display. *She'll go back home a movie geek. Let's see what they make of that!*

It was half an hour before Valentine realized Winter was missing. She craned her neck to examine every corner of the living room. No Winter, anywhere. *Could she have left? No, where would she go?* With all the world-changing stuff going on, it was sometimes hard to remember that she was going through the worst turmoil of her life. Her world hadn't just changed—it had shattered.

Forcing a casual air, Valentine stood and went quietly up the stairs. She fought the dread in her heart with every step. It was only natural for someone in pain to need solitude, after all. Winter was probably just reading a book or having a private cry. Valentine mentally prepared herself to offer comfort.

She stepped softly to the end of the hall, where a faint glow emanated from the half-closed door to her room. On entering, she caught sight of her friend and her heart lurched.

Winter sat on her bed, curled up against the headboard and staring blankly out the window. One hand clutched a stuffed bear to her chest. The other clutched a bottle of vodka, which Valentine recognized as her dad's preferred brand. It was more than half-empty.

"Winter, no!"

Valentine leapt onto the bed and pried the bottle from the smaller girl's impressively strong grip, then set it out of reach. Winter deflated. She squeezed the bear with both hands, resisting half-heartedly as Valentine wrapped her in a firm embrace.

"Go be with your family," she said, her words slurring. "You still have one, after all."

"So do you. I can't imagine what you're going through, but you have to believe things will get better. It's the hardest thing in the world to do—trust me, I know—but you have to give it time."

Winter scoffed. She opened her mouth to speak and Valentine braced herself to accept a cutting remark.

Then, just on the verge of lashing out, Winter crumbled. Heavy sobs burst from her chest as fresh tears poured down her face.

"You don't . . . understand . . . anything . . ." she said between heaving breaths.

"You're right. I'm sorry, I—"

"I lied to you," Winter sobbed. "About everything. It's so . . . much . . . worse."

Then, trembling as she pushed through the tears, she gave the rest of the story. On arriving home that night, news of her mother's cheating had only been the first shock.

Winter's father—the man she'd called *dad* her entire life—wasn't really her father. Nor was he father to her little sister, Summer. After uncovering the infidelity, he'd secretly ordered DNA tests and learned the truth about his daughters. They'd been fathered by two other men.

All in one night, Winter discovered that her mom had deceived them, her dad wasn't her dad, and her sister was only her half-sister. Instead of being full Chinese as she'd believed her whole life, she'd been informed that she was half-Chinese and half some-sort-of-white-European.

She'd arrived on the twins' doorstep after discovering her entire life had been a lie.

"And you still haven't heard from your mother?" Valentine asked, horrified.

Winter shuddered, sucking in a hard breath. "I . . . lied about that, too."

"It's okay."

"It's not okay!" Winter pushed her away. "I . . . I cried myself to sleep. But I woke up later and she was in my room. Kept making excuses, defending herself. Never even said she was sorry. Val, I got so mad . . . I . . ."

She covered her eyes in shame.

"She said she was leaving and wanted me to come. I told her never. That I hated her. That I never wanted to see or talk to her again. Then I turned my back . . . and . . . pretended to sleep until she went away."

"You were upset. I'm sure she understood."

"No. I woke up and wanted to say I was sorry. Can you believe that? I'm such a sucker—she's the bad guy, and I felt guilty. But she was already gone. She left me there!"

Valentine blew out a breath, at a loss for what to say.

"How's your dad?" It was all she could think of. "Does he need anything?"

Winter stiffened. "I tried to sit with him. Hug him. But he hates me, Val."

"That can't be true. You're his—"

"He hates me. That's why I left. He said I'm not his daughter and never was. That I'm just the evidence of his wife's treachery." She choked back another sob. "He said I was nothing but poison."

Then the floodgates opened again.

As she held Winter, Valentine glanced down at the bear

she was clutching and noticed a name stitched over its heart. *Summer*. All over again, her heart broke for her friend.

"I'm sorry," she whispered. "I am so, so sorry, Winter. It must feel so . . ."

"Like I'm a hole with no bottom," Winter said. "I have no idea how to fill it up again." She clutched at Valentine. "Sometimes I forget. I wonder what Mom picked up for dinner or something. Then it comes back, and that hole . . . it just gets deeper."

Valentine found herself nodding. She did know that pain, or at least a piece of it.

"When my mom died, I knew my life was over. Because how could anything good happen after that?" She paused, blinking back tears. "I couldn't see the bottom either. No matter how much I cried, it all just disappeared inside it. I knew one day I would disappear, too, and I wanted that. It didn't seem right that one heart could feel so much pain."

"How did you do it?" Winter's watery eyes found hers. "How do you survive?"

Bracing herself, Valentine allowed herself to go back to those days. She opened a vault that kept those memories safe and away from the light, trembling as they resurfaced. For her friend, though, she would endure it.

"You let yourself cry. Let friends help. Tell yourself it's okay to feel broken. You don't rush to try feeling better, or it just gets worse." A deep sigh swelled from within her. "You wake up one day and decide to get out of bed. You do the same thing the next day, and then the next. You keep getting up. Then one day you smile again. Another day, you laugh. You just . . . live. Then you keep living, and it gets a little better."

"That's how I beat this?"

Valentine hesitated, then shook her head. "You never beat it, not all the way. But you learn to accept it. Keep it somewhere private, somewhere just for you. But then, one day, you realize you can be happy again. I am happy again." She squeezed her friend's shoulders. "And you will be, too."

Winter wrapped both arms around her waist and held on tight. Valentine smiled down at her as they shared tears together, glad to be the anchor for a friend lost at sea. Glad that she could do now what others had done for her.

"Looks like she's okay," Malcolm whispered after peeking into Valentine's room. "Just drank an epic amount of vodka for someone her size. She's asleep now."

When the movie ended and the two girls still hadn't returned, Malcolm had stolen upstairs to check on them with Fred and Asha following. Surrounded by Time travelers and supervillains and cosmic powers, it was too easy to forget that their friend was in anguish. He mentally kicked himself for being too distracted to notice.

"Can't believe I didn't notice, man. Girl's been hurtin' fierce." Fred shook his head. "Throwing parties, I'm good at. Being awesome, got that covered. But this is so messed up."

"Just be her friend," Malcolm said. "That's what you both did for us last year. Maybe you don't realize how much that helped, but it did."

Just then, Valentine slipped into the hall and closed the door behind her. Malcolm noticed her red-rimmed eyes and the downward slump of her shoulders. She looked exhausted.

"How is she?" Fred said.

She leaned back against the wall. "It's so much worse than we thought."

Fred snorted. "Don't see how that's possible."

Valentine hesitated, then told them everything.

All Malcolm could do was stand there, shocked, attempting to absorb the Greek tragedy that had become his friend's life. As his sister finished the story, he grasped for something to say. Everything he thought of felt pitifully inadequate.

"What can we do?" Asha asked, and Malcolm wanted to hug her. That was better than anything he'd come up with.

Valentine shook her head, at a loss. Fred made a move for the door, but she stood in the way. "She's out like a light, Fred. Hopefully until school tomorrow."

"Oh, wow, that's right," Malcolm said, running a hand through his brown hair. "Tomorrow's only Tuesday. Jeez, it feels like we've lived a month these past few days. We haven't even—"

Tyrathorn appeared at the top of the stairs. "Come quickly; you must see this!"

By the look in his eyes, Malcolm knew somehow. A sinking dread coated his stomach. "More ice pillars. Where were they found?"

"Not found. Filmed live, near the middle of town," Tyrathorn said. "They are appearing as we speak."

CHAPTER 18

On the western side of Emmett's Bluff, a small industrial park held four large warehouses and an office building. The northwest warehouse had been converted five years ago, half of it becoming a skate park and a venue for local punk bands.

Halfway through a concert, the ice pillars had appeared. Everyone had seen them on the news, so they must have been curious and wanted to get a closer look. When the dark truth had become obvious, the panic had begun.

Malcolm stared in dread at the grainy images on his TV. Valentine and John gripped each other's hands like a lifeline, as did Neil and Callie.

"I couldn't film everything. It happened too fast," said a dark-haired, tattooed woman. "I stayed in there as long as I could but . . . I was afraid they'd get me, too."

A twenty-year-old music blogger, her live stream had been picked up by local news within minutes. Judging by her footage, the town would probably hit national news again in the next hour. As she described the sights and sounds and terror, the video looped back to the beginning.

Malcolm watched helplessly while a tiny object flew across

the screen—a blur punctuated by blinking lights. The blur flew into the dancing crowd and latched onto a tall man with a mohawk, who lurched as if he'd been bitten. An ice pillar appeared where he'd been standing.

"You said there were about a hundred people," said the news anchor. "How many made it out?"

"Um, I'm not sure," the woman said, her voice trembling. "Maybe half."

On the screen, dancers and even members of the band approached the ice pillar, tapping it or taking pictures. Then a second pillar appeared. Then a third, then a fourth and fifth. A young girl began pounding on the sixth, pleading for help.

Malcolm saw realization ripple through the crowd. The pillars hadn't appeared randomly, and their victims hadn't disappeared. They were trapped deep inside the ice. A dozen more appeared, and then the stampede for the exit began.

Malcolm glanced at Tyrathorn. Eyes practically aflame, he gave Malcolm a nod. Valentine did the same. Asha next, then Fred, then John, and finally Clive. With the tiniest of signals, they indicated agreement with his unspoken question. Each of them knew.

It was time to go to work.

"Weeeellll, this old body's tired," Clive said. Standing, he gave a lazy stretch. "I'm 'bout ready to get on home. Anyone need a ride?"

"Yo, right here!" Fred leapt from his seat.

Tyrathorn stood next. "Perhaps I could stay with you again this evening."

"Me, as well," Asha said. "I shouldn't overstay my welcome here."

"Why don't we come over, too?" Valentine said. "Just to hang out."

"I don't know; it's getting late," Neil said. "You still have school."

"Oh, let them go, son," Oma Grace jumped in. "It's their last week."

At that, their dad relented.

Giving his hand a squeeze, Callie stood. "I should get home, too, Neil. My deadline's getting close, and that article won't write itself."

"More's the pity," he replied, oozing affection. "I'll see you soon?"

"Count on it."

As the group hurriedly gathered their things, the twins hugged Oma Grace goodbye. She favored them with a sly smile. *Old and retired, but still in the fight,* Malcolm thought.

"Thank you," he whispered.

"Just come back safe."

"Don't worry," Valentine said. "We'll watch each other's backs."

"I'm your grandmother, dear. It's my job to worry. Now, go show them who runs this town."

Minutes later, they climbed into Clive's restored 1985 Land Rover Defender and roared into the night. Malcolm joined Clive at the front while Valentine, John, and Fred filled the middle bench seat. In the rear cargo area, Tyrathorn and Asha struggled to don their armor in the limited space.

"So," Valentine said. "Anyone else think it's weird how Callie left when we did? Almost like she had to be somewhere, too."

Malcolm rolled his eyes. "Totally. She's going to wear armor over that pantsuit and kick some tail."

Valentine bristled. "You're blind because she's pretty."

"Yes, it couldn't possibly be that she makes Dad happy."

Malcolm locked eyes with his sister in a tense moment of silence. Eventually, she gave way.

"Let's just focus on now, I guess," she said.

With that, preparations resumed.

"I assume y'all got your magic boxes," Clive said to Malcolm. He nodded and strapped the device to his wrist.

"Never leave home without it," Valentine said.

"Indeed," Tyrathorn said. "The enemy will offer no quarter."

"Then I s'pose we better even the odds." Clive hooked his thumb over his shoulder. "See that box in the back? Open it."

Tyrathorn handed the box to Fred, who tore open the top. On catching sight of its contents, his eyes lit up.

"Whoa, sweet!"

Malcolm turned to look and burst into an excited smile. "No. Way."

He pulled out a coiled black and gray belt, made of materials both hard and soft. It unfurled to reveal small compartments of varying size and shape. A strange buckle capped each end. It almost looked mechanized.

Malcolm turned to Clive. "Have I told you how awesome you are?"

Valentine unfurled hers and laughed. "You guys are total geeks."

Fred snorted. "Says the science genius."

"I quite like it," John said, clicking open one of his belt's compartments to reveal the handheld shield device.

"Really." Valentine studied her boyfriend, who seemed to be avoiding her gaze. "John? Did you help build these?"

Clive chuckled. "It was his idea."

John couldn't hide his grin. Valentine shook her head, but smiled. "You're just encouraging them, you know."

"What is it?" Asha called from the back.

"It's a belt for all the gear!" Malcolm said. "One step closer to being Batman."

"Hmm." Valentine tapped her chin. "So, now you're at Step One, right?"

"Keep laughing and we'll make you be Robin," Malcolm threatened.

"Dude, Winter's gonna hate that she missed this," Fred said. "She'd say it was lame, but then she'd play with all the toys."

"And there are plenty," Clive said. "Everything I showed you the other night is stored on that belt, plus earpieces. Managed to keep it light, too, so you should barely know it's there."

"What are the materials?" Thorn asked. Now fully armored, he and Asha studied their belts.

"Some nylon, some carbon fiber, bit o' Kevlar," Clive said. "Better get familiar quick—we're almost there."

"We should talk about strategy," Malcolm said.

"That will be easier when we survey the scene," John offered.

"Maybe." Valentine pulled out her phone. "But we should check for updates."

In moments she had acquired a live feed from the local station. Turning her phone, she held it up for all to observe.

"And this phenomenon seems to have stopped," the news anchor was saying.

"Yeah. Once we got out of there," the blogger said.

The live stream from her phone showed open warehouse doors behind her. To Malcolm's surprise, most people were still there, crowding the door frame and peering back inside. *Why haven't they run?*

Then, as the news anchor droned through predictable questions, Malcolm really looked at them and the reason became painfully obvious. Some stared with hollow eyes. Others wept. Even the blogger teetered on the edge of breaking down. *They have friends in there, family, people they love. And no idea what's happening to them.*

"We're here," Clive announced.

Malcolm looked toward their destination and his heart sank. "You've got to be kidding me."

The warehouse complex sat on a corner lot at the crossing of two main streets. A tall chain-link fence encircled the property, opening in only two places to allow cars in and out. Those openings were now overflowing with vehicles trying to force their way in. The parking lot was packed with news vans and other unmarked cars. *Probably all those phenomena freaks,* Mal thought bitterly. It also explained why there were no police in the video—they were out front, trying to keep rubberneckers from making things worse.

"Freakin' tourists, man," Fred spat.

"Don't worry now," Clive said, as calm as ever. "For every problem, there's a solution."

Juking the wheel, he hopped the curb. The vehicle bounced onto the open lot adjacent to the warehouses, crunching scrub brush under its knobby tires. Clive hugged the fence until they'd reached the halfway point, then skidded to a halt.

"A wise strategy," Tyrathorn said. "We can simply crush this area of fence and enter more quickly."

Clive chuckled. "I had some'n a little quieter in mind."

He pulled a large tablet from his seat pocket, followed by a black and white orb the size of a volleyball. Holding the orb out the window, Clive tossed it into the air. Malcolm gazed in wonder as it unfolded into a four-rotor camera drone. Whirring, it shot into the sky and banked toward the warehouses.

"You and John have been busy," Malcolm said.

Clive grinned. "Just doin' what I can."

He switched his tablet on. The black surface became a glowing grid, thousands of tiny hexagons outlined in green light. In the top right corner, a few raised up to form a number ten. A second later, they dropped and new ones lifted to form a nine.

"Well, that looks familiar," Valentine said dryly. "You guys copied more of Lucius's tech."

"Best we could, anyway," Clive replied.

"They're only tools," John added. "In the right hands, they can save lives."

The countdown completed and the hexagons spelled out *DRONE IN POSITION*. Clive tapped a few buttons and more hexagons lifted to form a three-dimensional layout of the industrial park. He pointed to four equally sized rectangles arranged together. The alleys between them formed a T-shape, with a large open circle in the center.

"These are the warehouses," Clive narrated. "Circle in the middle's a roundabout for delivery trucks."

Leaning over the backseat, Asha pointed at the bottom corner. "What are these?"

"Office building and parking lot. Nothin' to worry about, the stuff we've gotta plan for is here." Clive pointed at the top left warehouse. "Based on the news lady's pictures, we want this one. Doors open right near the roundabout."

"Guys, look!" Valentine turned up her phone's volume. "Something's happening."

"—more activity inside now." The blogger affixed the phone to her bag strap, showing them her point of view. "It's hard to see past everyone, but there's some kind of light and I hear . . . I'm not sure what—"

Red light burst from the doorway. With a boom, a shockwave threw bystanders off their feet. The blogger cursed and stumbled back as the red light coalesced into a spinning vortex. Four figures leapt through, and the light behind them disappeared.

Malcolm's insides went cold. He recognized three of them—the minions of the Frost Hammer. They charged, wielding their impossible weapons and scattering the panicked crowd.

"Oh my god, oh my god!" the blogger shouted.

"We gotta get out there!" Fred yelled, flinging open his door.

Tyrathorn grabbed his shoulder and pulled him back in. "No! We need information."

"What's happening now?" the news anchor asked.

"What do you think is happening, you moron?! They're trying to kill us all!"

Another vortex opened and the four disappeared into it as if they'd never intended to stay. Turning, the blogger fled with others down an alley between the west-side warehouses, toward the perimeter fence.

Halfway to freedom, she screamed and skidded to a halt. At the end of the alley, another red vortex opened to block their escape, and spat out one of the same minions—a tall, dark-haired young woman with leather armor and a wicked grin.

As she flung out her hands, two electrified whips appeared and sliced through the air, arcing and buzzing. She swung hard and two people collapsed. She swung again and two more bounced off the warehouse walls before tumbling to the ground. With a whoosh, all four disappeared inside ice pillars.

Screaming, the blogger turned and fled the other way. Just as quickly, she halted again.

On the far side of the roundabout, in the alley between the eastern warehouses, more people tried running to safety. Before they reached the fence, a vortex burst open and another minion appeared in their path. The blogger turned again . . . and came face-to-face with her whip-wielding foe.

"No! Please, no—"

She dropped to the ground with a scream. Then the scream cut off. The camera lens coated over with ice, and the feed went dark.

Malcolm stared at the screen, stunned. "But . . . but that's *crazy!* Why would they trap people in ice?"

"Only to carve them out later," Valentine added. "The pillars we found were hollow."

"And now they're attacking people," John said. He gritted his teeth. "Innocent people."

"Dudes," Fred said. "This ain't a recon mission anymore."

Asha nodded. "It's a rescue."

Tamping down his fear, Malcolm reached for Clive's tablet. "We need a new plan, and we have about thirty seconds to make one."

"I have an idea," Valentine said. She hesitated, eyeing the group. "But, uh, it's a little crazy . . . and you'd really have to trust me."

CHAPTER 19

Kaylee screamed until her voice gave out.

All she'd wanted was to listen to some music and drool over Tyler as he practiced on the half-pipe. Now she huddled against the wall, terrified, as others tried to escape and failed.

They had fled down the east alley, but another red glowy thing happened and a man blocked their escape. Shirtless and as big as a mountain, muscles rippled under his obsidian-black skin.

Running was useless! He always got around them and blocked their escape. When someone got too close, one punch would toss them like a rag doll, and then they'd disappear into the ice.

She cringed away as he searched for his next victim, squeezing her eyes shut. But the next thing she knew, heavy footsteps were stopping in front of her. She peered up to see the dark behemoth towering overhead. As he reached for her, she loosed a bloodcurdling scream.

From high overhead came a crackling sound. Kaylee looked past the giant as something silvery white was spreading above the warehouses, blocking out the sky. Her attacker turned as a tiny chunk of whatever-it-was fell. Bouncing off his forehead, it clinked to the ground and broke into pieces. Kaylee stared in wonder. *Is that . . . ice?*

It grew toward the ground and blocked the end of the alley. Her heart sank—whatever it was, it had put the fence beyond their reach now.

The giant turned back to her now, refocusing. But before he could reach for her again, something insane happened.

Across the alley, a shadow came to life.

It moved so fast that Kaylee barely followed it. The shadow struck, and the giant man slammed into the ice before stumbling to his knees. A wicked cut appeared across his cheekbone.

Looming over the giant, the shadow melted away.

ASHA stood between the screaming girl and the mountain of a man.

Snarling, he leapt back to his feet. Bright red light snaked up his arms and across his chest, as if his veins were filled with lava.

"I know you," Asha said with disdain. "You're Wrathbane—a Second-*sev* like me. They say you implanted a nexus in each hand so you can burn twice as fast." Her expression darkened. "They also say you killed a Watcher scouting squad by yourself. One of them was my friend."

"Then he died screaming," Wrathbane said, his deep voice harsh and guttural. He nodded toward her *qamas*. "I know *you*. Spoiled princess, makes play with big boy toys."

Asha considered that, and as vengeance burned in her veins, it occurred to her how much more satisfying her fists would be. Channeling power into her blades, she flung them at the ground. With a reverberating clang, they buried in the concrete.

Fists up, she burst into motion.

Closing the distance, she dodged a wicked right cross and

slipped inside his defenses. Her fists became a blur as she delivered a flurry of punches into his exposed flank. Wrathbane grunted and swung again. Crouching, she spun underneath his attack and delivered two swift jabs to his solar plexus before dancing out of his reach. Or so she thought.

Wrathbane surged forward. With no time to dodge, Asha crossed her forearms, set her feet, and braced. Her armor blazed red from shoulders to fingertips.

Wrathbane struck like a thunderclap. Asha's bones rattled. The force of the blow shoved her back, pavement digging up under her feet as she ground to a halt.

Shaking her head to clear the stars, she reset for another round. Asha noticed Wrathbane favoring his right flank, and his bottom lip was bleeding. Meanwhile her arms ached, and a glance revealed knuckle dents in her armor.

She nodded in admiration. He was the enemy, but she had to admit the man could throw a punch. For the plan to work, she had to keep him fighting, keep him chasing her to the right spot. So she might as well enjoy it.

He glowered in return. "I swear you will feel pain unlike—"

Asha scoffed. "Shut up and fight."

She charged again.

Malcolm's nexus blazed blue. Waves of energy coursed over his skin. Every cell in his body rang like a tuning fork as Time rushed through him.

"This is . . ." He gasped. ". . . intense!"

"Do not stop," Tyrathorn said through gritted teeth. "If we fail, so does the plan!"

Malcolm opened the core of his being wider. Even more Time surged through the nexus. Beneath his hands and

Tyrathorn's, the ice shield kept growing from their projection of slowed Time. From their perch on the roof of the southwestern warehouse, it spread over the buildings and curved toward the ground.

Now no one else could approach. With fewer people getting in the way, hopefully their friends could get the enemy where they needed them. He lowered his arms with a relieved sigh.

"Keep going, Malcolm!" Tyrathorn cried. "The shield is not yet stable."

Malcolm slapped his hands against the ice and channeled Time just as the silvery dome began to shudder. It lasted only an instant before subsiding, but he could feel small shards of ice breaking loose.

"Sorry!" he said with a wry grin. "It's my first day building one of these."

Tyrathorn chuckled. "Just continue extending your power. I will help you direct it and build the dome's support structure."

"You remember how to do that?"

Tyrathorn hesitated. "Only glimmers. I will improvise the rest." He shot Malcolm a grin. "Then, with good fortune, there will be enemies left for us."

John counted fifteen people huddled at the end of the southern alley. They had almost made it out. But the Archer had found them first.

With tall, spiky blond hair and dark blue paint around his eyes, he looked less like a warrior from the past and more like an anime character. *Maybe he's not from the past,* John mused. A sleeveless coat completed the picture, as did the bracer on his left arm, which glowed with some sort of holographic display.

A captive woman attempted to stand, and the Archer

sneered. In a flash of light, an arrow bloomed on the wall just above her head. Seconds later, the Archer released his arrow and it disappeared in an identical flash.

John forced himself to hold back. *There will be no second chances.* Pressed against the warehouse wall, he let the shadow device do its camouflaging work while he strategized.

Every detail soaked into his mind. The dimensions of the alley, the location of every object, every person, all came to life in his head as a three-dimensional map. He spun it in his mind's eye to examine from every angle.

Running his hand along the gear belt, John recalled the gadgets it stored and overlaid them onto the map, testing their tactical advantages.

And then he had it. A way to get the Archer exactly where John needed him to be. The mental map stopped spinning, and every extraneous variable disappeared.

Just then, a rushing sound filled the air overhead. The Archer and his captives gawked at the silvery dome, and John knew his moment had arrived.

Aw, crap, Fred thought. *Probably shoulda made a plan or something.*

In the western alley, he watched the black-haired girl intimidate her captives. He hadn't expected to need a strategy. With the Accelerator ring he was way tough, and Clive's shadow thing kept him hidden. When it came to bad guys, he preferred cheating to win.

But this chick was scary. It wasn't the head-to-toe leather, or the spiked boots, or even the steel-banded whips that hummed with electricity. No, it was that look in her eyes. They lit up whenever she snapped those whips and sent someone else to the ground, writhing in pain.

A rushing sound passed overhead then. Malcolm and Tyrathorn's ice dome was spreading across the sky. Whip It—that was his name for her—looked up, eyes narrowing as the ice blocked the western escape.

Time was running out, and Whip It wasn't going to move on her own. She would need motivation. He had to do something.

"WoooOOOoooOOO!" Fred shouted. Keeping his shadow device active, he leapt to the center of the alley and flailed his arms. "I'm the Frozen Ghost, lord of . . . cold stuff and . . . uh, protector of these warehouses! This ice belongs to me! Leave these people alone or I'll show you, like, my true power!"

Fred stepped closer, but Whip It didn't run. She smirked.

"Seriously, yo! Get outta here or—!"

Her arm twitched, and then Fred was flying, searing pain across his ribs. Rebounding off the warehouse, he flopped to the ground and rolled onto his back. The shadows dissipated.

He groaned, rattling his head as Whip It appeared above him.

"Frozen Ghost, huh?" she said, snapping her whip. "Let's see if you can bleed."

VALENTINE dropped to the ground as sheets of flame spread out above her. Breathing hard, she drew in more Time and soothed the burns she'd sustained.

Despite wearing thick robes, her enemy barely sweated. The Monk's serene expression never changed even as he tried to roast her alive. His nexus glowed, and a device on each wrist glowed with it.

Valentine bent the flows of Time back on herself. Every molecule inside her accelerated, and the world around her slowed to a crawl. She launched forward.

Bursting through the wave of fire with blinding speed, she delivered a spin kick to her enemy's face. He stumbled to the ground but instantly rolled back to his feet.

The world returned to normal. Overhead, the ice dome completed its trek across the sky. Valentine would need to act quickly for her plan to come together.

The Monk bowed. "I honor your skill. But please, let us cease fighting."

"Why? So you can keep attacking my town?"

"So that I do not have to kill you." The Monk's tone betrayed no ego, only certainty. "You have great power, but do not understand it."

Remembering her goal, Valentine stepped to the right, moving in a semicircle. The Monk mirrored her to keep the distance between them. She projected as much confidence as she could muster.

"If you know my power, then you know I'm holding back."

"Because you are afraid. Why must we fight when you are not ready?"

"Tell me what you're doing here and I'll think about it."

Valentine stopped and he mirrored her again. Behind him, she could see the roundabout where each alley met. *Right where I need you.*

"Why are you doing all this?"

The Monk looked thoughtful. Then, instead of answering, he flicked his wrist.

Before Valentine could react, a blunt projectile smashed her between the eyes. She rocked back, dazed, and his foot collided with her stomach. Aching nausea swept through her.

Bent over and clutching her middle, Valentine looked up to see a wall of flame envelope her.

Asha flew back and hit the ground on all fours. Her fingers raked furrows into the pavement as she crunched to a halt. She crouched at the mouth of the alley while Wrathbane barreled toward her. *That's right, come to me!*

As he came within range, Wrathbane drew back a giant foot and aimed for her head. Spinning, Asha kicked his other foot and swept it into the air. He crashed onto his back with a thud.

Leaping on top of her enemy, she sat on his chest.

"All your strength . . ."

A blur of motion, she punched his eye, then his jaw, then his other eye.

". . . all your power . . ."

She dodged his fist and slammed her forehead into his nose.

". . . and you're still losing!"

Asha leapt to her feet and backed onto the grassy area at the center of the roundabout. She savored the sight of this bully clutching his face.

"Really?" she said with a pitying smile. "Is that all you have?"

Eyes blazing, he clambered to his feet with a heavy grunt. Of course there was fight left in him. Wrathbane was a tank—she had been counting on it. And now she needed him to be right where she was standing.

Quirking her eyebrow, she beckoned him forward.

THE Archer shouted for his captives to be silent, aiming a nocked arrow at a terrified boy's face.

NOW.

Clutching Clive's Skipper device, John dashed up behind the Archer and carefully aimed one single kick. As he did, light flashed and an arrow hit the warehouse wall high above them.

The Archer's head whipped up. "What the—?"

John kicked the bottom of the bow. Shocked, the Archer lost the arrow and it flew high, disappearing in another flash and emerging several seconds in the past.

Next, John separated the Skipper's two rings and threw one as hard as he could back toward the alley entrance.

The Archer spun. John barely dodged as an arrow burst from a flash of light, raking a deep furrow in his shoulder. *That'll need stitches.*

Accepting the pain, he jammed the second ring against the Archer's chest and gave it a slap. In a blink, the Archer folded and sucked through the ring's three-inch opening. He reemerged through the second ring, which was still flying down the alley. His cry of shock echoed along the walls as he plummeted toward the ground.

John chuckled as he ran toward his enemy, trading the shadow device for his shield generator. His body sang with the massive boost from the Accelerator ring. In the distance, the Archer crashed to the ground and rolled to his feet. Instantly, his eyes locked onto John and he reached for his quiver.

Four arrows appeared in midair. The Archer's arm flicked four times in quick succession. Inches away from John, the arrows bounced off his shield. At least half of the shield's charge was spent now—he had to get this done or risk being skewered. He poured on every ounce of speed his body could manage.

The Archer drew again and took aim . . . too late.

Like a human arrow, John plowed into the Archer and sent them both to the ground, tumbling in a mass of arms and legs. They came to a stop on the roundabout's grassy center, leapt to their feet, and faced off.

The side of the Archer's face bore a deep scrape from the pavement, and his bow had slid a dozen yards away. Reaching behind his back, he drew out two wicked-looking knives. John mentally searched his inventory of gadgets, but nothing on his belt had been designed for a knife fight. Except, maybe . . .

Clicking the buckle, he unwrapped the belt from his waist. With a flick, he twirled it like a *nunchaku* and set his feet, preparing to dance.

WHIP It gazed down at Fred with that evil grin. Apparently she wanted to enjoy defeating him. Well, if she could play that game, so could he.

"Yo, you're pretty cute when you throw down," he said. "Wanna get a coffee or something?"

She snorted. "You're a child."

"Yeah, but I'm taller than you, so . . ."

Whip It glanced toward the roundabout and the cruelly flirtatious expression slid off her face, replaced by burning hatred. "Ashandara!"

She wouldn't be distracted for long. Pulling his knees to his chest, Fred kicked up. Both feet impacted her gut with enough force to lift her off the ground. She toppled onto her back hard enough that one of her ice devices went skittering across the pavement.

Clutching at her midsection, she spat a string of curses between dry heaves. Smirking, Fred stood over her.

"Wow, now that had to hurt," he said. "You want some ice?"

Growling, Whip It lashed out from the ground and wrapped her whip around Fred's arm. Wide-eyed, he tried to pull away until the other whip wrapped around his waist. Her weapons crackled.

The next thing Fred knew, he was falling against the warehouse wall, leaning on it for support. The cold heat of electricity seared his nerves. Teeth chattering, he struggled to stay on his feet.

"You will die tonight," she said, regaining her feet. With a flick of her whip, she released his arm and looped it around his throat instead.

Fred couldn't cry out or breathe in. He bathed in white hot agony as blackness crept across his vision. There had to be some way to survive. Some way to . . .

Then it came to him—his last and best option. And yet, he hesitated. *Your friends will need you.* He closed his eyes and worked to picture their faces. *You have to live.*

She was killing him. He could feel himself draining away. Only the Accelerator ring was keeping him conscious. If he was going to cross that line, he would have to do it soon.

"Open your eyes, pet," Whip It purred, stepping closer until Fred could feel her breath on his face. "I want to—"

Fred's eyes snapped open. Reaching out, he clamped his fingers around her throat. She screamed as electricity raced from his body to hers.

With his free hand, he tapped a spot on his gear belt. A small compartment popped open and a round object dropped into his hand. As Whip It cried out in agony, Fred jammed the object into her open mouth. She gasped in shock.

Clive's Time grenade required three squeezes to activate. Fred clamped his hand over Whip It's mouth and punched her in the jaw once, then twice, then a third time. Dazed, she fell back a step and let go of her whips.

As they parted, he threw an uppercut and her teeth crunched through the grenade's delicate glass. She could only stare at him in shock.

Fred threw himself out of the way as a fire-red vortex enveloped her. For five eternal seconds he watched it swirl around her like a storm, pulsing and arcing with energy. Then it dispersed and nothing remained of her but dust.

Sucking in a sweet breath of air, Fred kissed the Accelerator ring and collapsed. He trembled as that last moment played over again in his head. He wouldn't doubt or second-guess—that was for fools. But still, it . . . changed things.

Val and Mal are gonna be peeved. Funny how that concerned him more than anything. The twins were so good, so determined to win the right way.

Then again, did they have to know?

Fred glanced toward the mouth of the alley. None of his friends were close enough to see what happened.

Through everything, his mission had always been to protect the people he loved. Winter, Valentine, Malcolm—they were family. The world was better with their goodness in it.

But goodness didn't win battles. This was something the twins couldn't see, and even if they could, they would never live that way. So if his friends were going to survive, what kind of friend would they need at their backs?

He'd have to get up soon, get back out there and rejoin the fight. But he could spare a few minutes. So for now Fred lay there and thought. About the enemy that threatened his town. About the danger his friends faced. And about the kind of friend they would need him to be.

Whether they knew it or not.

VALENTINE felt a stab of mortal terror as the wall of flames enveloped her. Unless she found a way out, in seconds she would be dead.

Her reflexes caught up, and Time poured into her again. Mimicking her brother, she bent the energy back toward herself and began to heal. But it wouldn't be enough. She could feel it— the Monk's assault had been stronger than her ability to recover.

Trying to heal would kill her. Trying to leap away would take too long and kill her. With her life hanging in the balance, Valentine did the one thing Tyrathorn had warned her would be necessary. The one thing she had never managed to do. She let go of all thought and reason, surrendering completely to instinct.

Her deepest being blossomed open. Something inside her *shifted* a different way.

Blue energy cascaded across her skin, a soothing wave of coolness. Valentine realized now that she was *slowing* the flow of Time!

Cold and invigorating, it formed a protective shell around her. In wonder, she nudged it with her will, and the temporal shell became a layer of ice, like frozen armor. Just like that, the fire could no longer touch her.

As her fear subsided, the outline of the Monk stood out in her senses. Energy rushed from deep inside him, into his nexus, and then to the fire devices on his wrists.

Recalling Tyrathorn's training, she seized the flow of Time in a thirty-foot bubble around them. Guided by inborn Chronauri instinct, she chose an array of particles and commanded them to *slow*.

Including the particles in the monk's weapons. They fought against her, struggling to create combustion, working harder as Valentine clamped her will down on them. Sputtering, they gave a mechanical whine and a loud pop, then melted.

The Monk fell back a step as Valentine came through the dissipating flames, sheathed in ice. A flash of fear crossed his face. Quelling it, he drew a sword from the folds of his robe, shouted a battle cry, and charged.

Valentine faced the warrior without fear. On embracing her true self, she had seen possibilities beyond simple fire and ice. Working through the principles Tyrathorn had taught, she froze particles of moisture and dust into ice and snow. She willed air particles to move faster. In seconds, she became the center of an ice storm, frozen particles carried by racing wind.

As much as she could, Valentine matched the conditions of a high-altitude thunderstorm.

Her senses stretched down to the subatomic. Through the currents in Time, she could feel electrons gathering. Frozen particles collided in rapid succession, building up a massive negative charge. The attacking Monk was now the closest object to her storm, and she sensed the responding positive charge building up around him.

The Monk came within reach and swung.

Valentine released her electric charge. A lightning bolt arced across the space between them and struck the Monk full force in the chest. A crack of thunder shook the walls.

Asha saw Fred arrive alone, without his enemy. *Curious. Did he fail?*

Wrathbane's gigantic fist whooshed too close to her face. Instinct took over as she arched backward to avoid it. Forcing herself to refocus on her enemy, she leapt into a backhand spring and tagged his chin with her heel.

"Whatever your plan, it has failed," Wrathbane said. He glanced up at the dome. "And now you are trapped with us."

"Fool." Asha grinned back. "That was always the plan."

A burst of light flashed from the north, along with a deafening crack. A man in flaming robes flew from the northern alley like a human rocket.

Her jaw dropped as another figure emerged.

Swathed in ice, Valentine glittered with every move. Catching up with her enemy, she grabbed him and skidded to a halt next to the grassy circle.

All fighting ceased as everyone's attention pulled toward her. Setting the robed man on the ground, she waved her hand and his flames disappeared under a layer of frost. Then she looked toward Asha and nodded.

Asha shook off her astonishment and tapped the comm in her ear. "Thorn, Mal, we have them."

In response, a different kind of rumble filled the air. Sweeping across the ice dome in waves, the rumble traveled down into the alleys where the hostages waited. Only now, their captors were too far away to threaten them.

At the end of each alley, the ice parted like a curtain, revealing four escape routes.

With shouts of relief, the hostages barreled toward the openings and escaped into the night. It took only seconds, and then the ice folded shut again.

"NO!" Wrathbane bellowed.

Now things would get interesting. Flexing her hands, Asha

sent a mental call through her nexus. Her *qamas* spun back into her waiting hands. As Wrathbane turned to bellow his rage at her, she pressed the tip of a blade under his chin.

"Since we're alone now," she said, "we can discuss what you were doing here."

"You don't know what you've done!" he shouted, breathing hard. "Now she will come."

Asha blinked, taken aback. Now she saw beyond her enemy's mask of rage, to what lay beneath. It was fear.

He shook his head. "Now we all will fall."

Alarmed, Asha looked to Valentine. "Do you sense anything?"

Valentine shook her head. "No, only . . . wait—"

A red vortex burst open, cutting a hole through the fabric of the universe. Gusts of hot wind rushed from the opening as *she* emerged, clad in nightmarish black armor.

The Frost Hammer had arrived.

CHAPTER 20

A deep *thrum* vibrated through the air.

Time ripped away from Valentine's grasp. Her ice armor shattered. Shocked, she reached for the power again but found herself blocked by some unseen force. She collapsed to the ground, shoved down by rippling distortion waves.

The Frost Hammer approached, distortion waves lifting her minions off the ground. As she spoke, Valentine could feel the amplified voice prying at her mind, but once again the intended effect seemed to bounce off her.

"Our master does not tolerate incompetence."

Red energy coursed down her gauntlets. A glowing orb formed in each palm, then flew out to strike the Monk and the Archer. Explosions threw them back and they flopped to the ground, unmoving.

As if dead minions meant nothing, the Frost Hammer turned to Valentine and her friends. "And you were warned."

The *thrum* intensified, grinding them harder against the dirt. Valentine could hear her friends struggling in pain. Over and over she reached for Time through her nexus, to no avail. *Is she blocking me? How can she do that?*

"You think this a victory? Tonight was only a test."

The distortions hoisted Valentine into the air beside John, Fred, and Asha. The Frost Hammer faced them, the strength of her presence practically filling up the space under the dome. She raised her hand, aiming an open palm at Asha.

"No!" Valentine cried out. "Take me—I'm the threat to you. I'm a Fourth-*sev* Chro-*wait, NO!*"

Distortion waves sent Asha rocketing backward. As she flew, the pavement beneath her cracked and the warehouse wall behind her buckled.

Asha crashed through the wall of the southwest warehouse. Then the Frost Hammer's hand dropped and the *thrum* abated. She turned to Wrathbane, lowering him to the ground.

"Finish it."

Valentine twisted against her bonds. "If you're all so strong, why not fight *me,* you coward?"

The giant man just nodded to his master and he sprinted for Asha.

"Hey!" Valentine shouted. "Come back and—"

The force holding her, John, and Fred disappeared, dropping them back to their feet. Valentine tapped into her nexus and felt the bridge to her power unblocked. Like a parched woman in a desert, she drank in everything she could, savoring the rush.

"Brave little Chronauri," the Frost Hammer mocked.

From behind her back, she drew an object about two feet long, made of black and silver metal. Its design mimicked her armor—all sharp curves and jagged edges. At the press of a button, gleaming blades unfolded from each end. She tossed it to stick in the ground at John's feet.

"And her brave little men."

Dread filled Valentine. She glanced at the boys. "Run."

John shook his head. "No."

"Not a chance," Fred echoed.

"Please—"

"I won't leave you." Reaching down, John pulled the weapon free. "Not ever."

Fred put up his fists. "Let's do this."

The Frost Hammer beckoned them forward. "Tonight, you will know pain."

METAL screeched as Asha ripped through the warehouse wall like a bullet. She hit the floor and rolled, smashing through row upon row of storage shelves. Her weapons skittered away.

She rolled onto a pile of construction materials and stole a moment to catch her breath. The warehouse was mostly dark, but still she examined it for any possible advantage.

No heavy machinery. Bricks over there. On a nearby shelf, she spotted white metal canisters emblazoned with warning pictures of an explosion. *My last resort.*

Metal screeched in the distance. Asha saw a hulking form darken the hole she'd made in the wall. Wrathbane had come to finish her.

He would leave disappointed.

Asha sprang from the shadows and dove at her enemy, her hands clamping around his throat. In a tangle they crashed through another set of shelves.

Wrathbane spun hard to shake Asha loose, flinging her halfway across the warehouse. She skipped across the floor like a stone and tumbled to a stop on bags of concrete mix. The dust made her sneeze.

Asha flipped over to see her enemy sail toward her, clutching a jagged length of metal like a spear. She coiled, ready to move. Just let him get a little closer . . . just a little—

The warehouse ceiling ripped open. Freezing gale-force winds raced through the hole and flung Wrathbane against the wall. A figure dropped through the ceiling, riding a wave of ice down to the floor. Asha's heart leapt—style like that could only be Tyrathorn's.

Then the figure stepped through the vapor cloud, and her jaw dropped.

"Jeez, that guy's huge," Malcolm said. "You okay?"

Standing, Asha called to her *qamas*. "I didn't need rescuing."

Malcolm shrugged. "We're a team. Just thought you could use a hand."

Her cheeks colored in embarrassment. "I'm sorry, I—"

In the distance, Wrathbane rose, a white object clutched between his massive hands. Asha stalked toward her prey with Malcolm trailing behind, intending to finish this fight for good. Her blades flew back into her hands.

As she approached, a danger sense prickled at the back of her neck. She stopped in her tracks. Wrathbane's eyes—they were wrong. All along, those eyes had glared at her with murder. Now they regarded her coldly, with death.

Wrathbane spun the object in his hands, letting her see the warning picture of an explosion. Only then did she realize that dozens of identical canisters littered the floor around them. Wrathbane had lured them into a giant bomb.

Asha yanked Malcolm's arm. "Run!"

Wrathbane's veins flared as if the sun were bursting through his skin. With a roar, he crumpled the canister and smashed it down.

They made it five steps before the world exploded behind them.

Asha ran for her life from the shockwave. *Too slow . . . not enough* . . . Flames licked at the edge of her vision, adrenaline making them appear to move in slow motion. Even she couldn't run from an explosion.

Then a second *boom* shattered the air—this one different somehow. The concrete beneath her feet cracked, and a strong arm clamped around her waist.

Malcolm pulled her close, running with her body tucked against his. His face pinched in concentration, nexus emanating dazzling rays of blue. As he reached out with his free hand, pointing toward the warehouse wall, bright rays of red joined the blue.

Molten hot fire shot from his palm like a laser beam. The metal warped and peeled back.

He's using fast and *slow Time!*

The pressure built in Asha's ears as Wrathbane's blast wave reached for them like a predator. Shrapnel screamed by, trailing smoke and flames.

With a strained cry, Malcolm leapt through the hole in the wall. As they hit the ground and tumbled away, his concentration burst and Time rushed back to normal. With an ear-splitting *crack,* the rest of the wall ripped open and gouts of flame jetted into the night.

"You okay?" he panted.

She nodded. The blast wave had come so close. A screech and a crash from inside told her the roof was collapsing, too.

As her danger sense faded, Asha became aware of another sensation. She and Malcolm lay tangled together, his arm around her waist, their faces only inches apart. Her skin prickled where it touched his, as if the nerves were overstimulated.

"How did you do that?" she said, wanting it to come out as a demand. Instead it came out as a whisper.

"I . . . I just had to do something. So I pushed harder than ever, even when I felt myself breaking inside. Burning." Malcolm shook his head. "Then, suddenly, I could do *more*. So I pushed Time to speed up and it did."

She gazed at him in disbelief. "You thought your power was burning out, and you still kept going?"

"I couldn't let him . . ."

He trailed off, and as he gazed at her, Asha could see the struggle behind his eyes. His mouth worked as if it were trying to find the words—or maybe he had found the words and held them in. *Good. You are a warrior, and that is all you need. Anything else is a distraction.* Yet her senses buzzed at the nearness of him.

"And now you're Fourth-*sev*." In that moment, it was all she could think to say.

Malcolm nodded, not seeming to believe it himself. "I . . . guess so."

His gaze slipped past her. Suddenly tense, he leapt to his feet. Asha stood with him, doing her best to shake off the moment between them.

Valentine, John, and Fred danced furiously around the Frost Hammer. The woman barely moved, yet she deflected them all with ease. Even Valentine's elemental storm got within inches of her and disappeared.

"Let's see how she handles two more," Malcolm said.

Asha hefted her blades. "Right beside you."

Malcolm's eyes seemed to catch fire—an intensity Asha had never seen before. The small-town boy disappeared, and a Chronauri took his place.

Just as they charged, their enemy made a move.

Swinging her palms toward the ground, the Frost Hammer brought down a massive distortion wave that knocked Valentine,

John, and Fred to the ground with an audible *clap*. The distortions above Valentine swirled like a tornado. She screamed while her red-and-blue corona faded, as if her power were being stolen.

Halfway there now. The air sizzled around Asha as her *qamas* and armor blazed. Malcolm glowed like a furnace.

Then the distortions rushed toward them. Asha smacked onto her back, the wind knocked out of her as distortions dragged her toward the enemy. Beside her, Malcolm's corona faded. They slid to a stop next to the others.

"You think yourselves strong?" she said. "I will show you true power."

The Frost Hammer snapped her fingers.

Valentine felt a *shift*. Another red vortex opened behind their enemy. Then another. Then another. Valentine sensed them opening faster and faster, encircling the roundabout—over three dozen.

As each vortex opened, a figure came through and took a position around the Frost Hammer. Men and women, large and small, some dressed as warriors from old kingdoms, others from lands and civilizations that didn't exist yet.

The Black Tempest's own private army. Valentine's heart sank. *We are so screwed.*

After discovering how to perceive the Monk's flow of Time, she could feel that same power all around her now. Only now it was far stronger. Except for the Frost Hammer, that is—somehow Valentine couldn't sense anything about her.

"You begin to see it now?" With a flourish, the Frost Hammer produced a cell phone and tapped the screen. "No? Not yet?"

Valentine heard mechanical beeps from every corner, each followed by a distinct *shift*. The devices that had trapped people in ice—they were all lighting up.

The pillars twisted and shivered, chunks of ice crumbling away as something inside struggled to break free. With a series of thunderous cracks, massive shapes emerged to stand on their own. Valentine's mind reeled. *It can't be . . .*

"You gotta be kidding me!" Fred shouted. "Now we got ice monsters?"

There was no other way to describe them. Ten feet tall, each a different monstrous configuration. Some were spindly with razor-sharp claws, others thick and blocky with hammer-like hands. All moved with surprising speed. Their joints crackled as they marched, arraying behind the Frost Hammer, a company of nightmares at her command.

"Oh, god," John said. "Do you see what's inside them?"

Valentine did see, and it filled her with dread. Deep inside each creature was a dark and blurry form—the trapped hostages.

"I warned you. I spoke of consequences."

With another tap on her phone, a spindle-limbed ice monster approached, impossibly long claws crackling as they flexed. The Frost Hammer's attention fell on John.

"Kill this one first."

Valentine went cold. As friends shouted protests and threats, she pounded against the invisible bonds with all her will, desperate for Time. It felt like pounding against steel. The creature stood over her boyfriend, frozen claws poised to strike. John reached out and gripped her hand. Tears welled in her eyes and she heard herself scream.

Something flashed overhead. A quick flutter of movement, a dark spot against the dome. Then a roiling mass of shadows slammed to the ground beside John, blocking the ice monster's attack. Twin blades of flame lashed out to slice both arms and legs clean off. Now just chunks of ice, they fell to the ground and shattered.

As the limbless torso toppled to the ground, the shadows dissipated. Tyrathorn stood there, fire blades held high. Valentine's heart soared as the Frost Hammer stumbled back with a gasp.

"Challenge *me,* mortals!" Tyrathorn roared.

Gouts of rock and fire exploded from the ground, spewing like volcanic eruptions. The rogue Chronauri broke ranks, scattering to avoid the unexpected onslaught.

Valentine's bonds disappeared. She leapt to her feet, whips of flame bursting from her hands. Her companions readied themselves in a blink and stood back-to-back, bracing for a fight.

All around, Valentine felt a dizzying array of *shifts* as each rogue Chronauri opened a nexus. Through all the chaos, Tyrathorn and the Frost Hammer stared each other down.

It was their enemy that flinched. Backing away, she raised a fist and shouted.

"Volle tirada!"

A blue vortex opened behind her. Following her lead, the rogue Chronauri turned toward their own unfolding portals. Even the ice monsters followed, dragging the de-limbed monster behind them.

"Yes, run!" Tyrathorn taunted. "Flee with your minions and your *Skrim!*"

As quickly as they had arrived, they disappeared. The last to leave was the Frost Hammer, who stood at the edge of her portal, staring at Tyrathorn. With a nod, she stepped back and melted into the light before it winked out of existence.

Everyone had their way of recovering. In the moments following the fight, they all retreated into their own worlds. Asha sheathed her swords and stood with eyes closed, as if willing herself to relax. Malcolm stared blankly into space. Tyrathorn sat cross-legged, lost in some kind of meditation. Fred just sprawled on the grass like they were on a picnic.

Trembling, Valentine locked eyes with John. Now he stood before her, shaken but alive.

She grabbed him and kissed him more deeply than she ever had. Momentarily surprised, he then clutched her waist and pulled her close. She felt a sigh bubble up from deep inside, the need for him driving her, as if she could never be close enough to him.

Her lips sought his over and over, soft yet frantic. *I almost lost him . . .* Her mind melted into a storm of fear and love and relief and radiance. They had survived together. Nothing else in the world mattered.

"I'm sorry," she whispered. "I'm sorry I couldn't protect you."

"We survived," John said. She could still feel him trembling. "We always make it through somehow."

"Not everyone made it last time, John," she said. "Why should this be any different than fighting Lucius?"

Grief flickered in his eyes. Walter's loss had been tough on Valentine, and she had barely known him. How must it have been for John, one of his oldest friends?

He wiped a tear from her cheek. She hadn't realized she was crying. Instead of words, he simply placed little kisses on her nose and eyelids until she couldn't help but smile.

"Why would they retreat?" Tyrathorn said. "We were clearly outmatched."

Asha flinched. "Not in their eyes," she said quickly. "They know your power, Thorn, and they fear it. Always have."

"Before you got here, she blocked my power," Valentine said, haunted by the memory of that helpless feeling. "I couldn't touch Time at all. You never said another Chronauri could do that."

"She did what?" Tyrathorn said.

"Happened to me, too," Malcolm said. "When she started using those waves, I couldn't do anything."

Puzzled, Tyrathorn turned to his sister. She shrugged.

"I didn't feel it. But . . . my power is different than theirs."

Tyrathorn's gaze went internal, as if he were searching his broken memory. He shook his head, frustrated. "If there is a way for one Chronauri to block another's access to Time, I do not know it."

"It matches her reputation," Asha said. "Others have said she wields Time in strange ways."

"Maybe it worked because we're so new at this," Valentine said. "She ran when you showed up, Thorn. Maybe she knows it wouldn't have worked on you."

"Perhaps," he replied. "We shall have to think on this, and train harder."

Valentine hoped that would work, though she didn't intend to count on it. If there was some other way to get around the Frost Hammer's trick, they would need to figure it out quickly. As if that weren't enough, another question struck her.

"Why would she disguise her voice?" Valentine said. "Lucius did it so no one would recognize him, right? Even people who knew him."

"Lucius changed his voice with a mind control device," Malcolm said. "The disguise part was secondary."

"And this woman's voice was freaky," Fred said. "Maybe it's to cause fear or something?"

"I know what you're getting at," Malcolm said to Valentine.

"Tell me it's not possible," she said.

"Of course it's *possible* that she's Callie. I just don't think it's likely."

They just weren't going to see eye-to-eye about this, apparently. It reminded Valentine of their early days in Emmett's Bluff, when Malcolm insisted there was something strange about the house across the street—the one with no doors. Back then, Valentine was the skeptic and Malcolm had eventually been proven right. Were their roles reversed now?

"So," Fred said, "can we talk about why on God's green earth someone would turn people into those . . . things?" He pointed at Tyrathorn. "What'd you call 'em?"

"Skrim," Tyrathorn replied. "In our tongue, it means abomination."

"Yeah, the Skrim, that works," Fred said.

"She said tonight was a test," Valentine said. "What could that mean?"

"Was she testing us somehow?" Asha said.

John shook his head. "Unlikely. They didn't seem to expect us."

"Escalation," Malcolm said. "At first, the ice pillars appeared one at a time, right? Then a few more, and now look what they did tonight. Big group, lots of people."

"Yes!" Valentine said. "Just like any science experiment. You go small-scale to test a theory, work out the kinks, then build up to full-scale."

"Which means they're making progress, but we've barely figured out anything." Malcolm shook his head. "We can't hesitate anymore. We have to go on the offensive."

"How?" John asked. "At least with Lucius we knew where to look, but this town doesn't have more houses with no doors."

"Ha!" Fred perked up. "Hold on a sec, y'all. I got it."

He turned and jogged toward the alley where he'd fought the girl with the whips. Now that things had calmed down, Valentine realized she hadn't seen that girl at the end.

Fred returned with a triumphant grin.

"What happened to the whip girl?" Valentine asked.

"Huh? Oh, right." He shrugged, dismissive. "Knocked her out, didn't feel like draggin' her here. Frost Hammer must've taken her when she left. Anyway, check this out."

One of the Frost Hammer's devices rested in his palm.

"I knocked this outta Whip It's hand before she could use it on me." He passed it to John. "Maybe you can figure out what it does."

"And how to counteract it," Malcolm said. "Whatever the Skrim are meant for, those are innocent people inside."

"We still need to find them," Asha said. "You all live here. Where could they hide?"

The twins gasped. Their eyes met and Valentine knew they'd realized the same thing.

"All those portals they jumped through," Malcolm said. "Could they . . . ?"

"It's a long shot, but it makes sense." She grinned. "Let's find out!"

With renewed vigor, they dashed toward the western edge of the ice dome. Clive and his truck waited on the other side. A thrill raced through Valentine as they ran. For the first time, they might be one step ahead.

CHAPTER 21

Clive's Land Rover clawed at the rough terrain, tearing through thick underbrush to climb over the rocky hills. Glued to the front passenger seat, Malcolm clutched the handle above his door.

"What did you do to this thing?"

Clive grinned. "Oh, just a few modifications to the suspension, custom tires, titanium reinforcement. And a supercharger as big as your head." He paused. "I mighta added sonic and thermal imaging, and maybe it feeds into a HUD on my side o' the windshield."

Malcolm craned his neck to look through the windshield from Clive's point of view. Sure enough, it painted bluish outlines around every element of the terrain, offering readouts for velocity and elevation and other figures he couldn't decipher. Occasionally a flash of red-orange would pass across the display—probably the heat of some forest animal.

"Why am I surprised anymore?" He chuckled, hefting the Skrim device. "Something tells me you and John won't have a problem with this thing."

"If there's a clue in there, we'll suss it out." Clive shook his head. "Gotta admit, what y'all saw got me shaken. It ain't right."

The vehicle leapt over a deep, muddy ditch and began climbing a tree-covered hill. Near the top, Clive's HUD chimed and flashed red.

He jammed on the brakes. Malcolm heard groans of protest as everyone was thrown forward in their seats. The Land Rover slid to a halt near the crest of the hill.

"Okay, stay low," Malcolm said. "We want to look without being seen."

He clambered out of the vehicle, dashed farther up the hill, then dropped and crawled to the crest. The others followed his lead.

"This is where our foe hides?" Tyrathorn said.

"I'd bet money on it," Malcolm said.

"Even one vortex takes massive power to generate," Valentine said. "We saw that with Lucius. This is the only place where they could steal what they need."

Half a mile away, in the center of the valley below, sat Rayner Nuclear Power Plant. It fed Emmett's Bluff and surrounding towns the vast majority of their power. In the deep night, only utility lights lit up its massive structure. The river flowed along beside it, tranquil and smooth and lit by the half moon.

Their enemy had to be here. But there was a problem.

"Yo, that place looks sorta normal, right?" Fred said. "I mean, I've been down there before with my dad. It always looks like that."

Malcolm had noticed it, too. *What'd you expect, a castle with a sign reading Evil Lair?* Yet literally nothing seemed out of place.

Sighing, Malcolm pinched the bridge of his nose. "We have to know for sure, and since we can't know from here . . ."

Valentine eyed him, incredulous. "Mal. You've got to be kidding."

"This is crazy, this is crazy, this is crazy!" Valentine whispered through Malcolm's comm.

He stifled laughter. "Val—"

"This is crazy!"

He couldn't help it, barking out a sharp laugh before clamping his hands over his mouth. He could hear the others fighting their own laughter.

"Hey, Val," Fred said. "How d'ya feel about what we're doing?"

The living shadow that was Valentine stopped short, facing the three other shadows. "Fred, when I figure out which one you are . . ."

"Stay on target," Malcolm reminded them. As much as he wanted to keep the joke going, they had to be serious now.

"Remember, we may be in enemy territory." Asha punctuated the statement with the slow rasp of her blades leaving their sheaths. "Be ready."

Tyrathorn had elected to stay and guard Clive, John, and the truck while serving as long-range recon. The others had activated their shadow devices and scaled the perimeter fence. They tried their best to blend into the natural darkness.

"Take the lead, Fred," Valentine said.

"Uh, what? Me?"

"You're the only one who's been here before," Malcolm said.

Fred moved to the front of the group. On tiptoes, staying close to walls and dark corners, they explored anything not closed off behind security doors.

For twenty minutes they made a stealthy circle around the

power plant. Halfway through, a sinking feeling began to settle in Malcolm's stomach, but he was determined not to voice it until they finished. When they reached their starting point again, Asha beat him to it.

"I see no signs of an enemy."

"True that," Fred said. "This place is dead, y'all."

"Yeah. But where else could they be?" Valentine said.

"I don't know," Malcolm said. "But we must have miscalculated. Nothing looks out of place or—"

He paused, struck by a new thought. Every part of the power plant looked and sounded normal. But did it *feel* that way? Until now, he'd been exploring like a normal person with normal senses. But that description didn't apply to the twins anymore.

"Val." Crouching down, he leaned his back against a gray block wall and stared at the ground. "Let's try a different way."

Reaching through his nexus, he absorbed a small flow of Time, just enough for a cool glow to fill him. With his will he flicked at the energy, gently pushing it outward in a radiating pulse.

Too weak to have any real effect, it simply moved in an expanding sphere, sliding along the flows and eddies of the Time stream, bouncing everything in the valley. With his awareness tuned, Malcolm painted a picture of their surroundings that his Chronauri senses could interpret.

"Oh," Tyrathorn's voice came faintly through the comm. "How did you do that?"

"Wow," Valentine breathed in awe. "It's like you built a sonar out of Time. I can sense everything now."

"I'm kinda surprised it worked." Malcolm's next comment died on his lips. As the pulse reached the edges of the valley and dissipated, he tilted his head in curiosity. "Did anyone feel that? Or see it, or whatever?"

There was a brief pause, and then Valentine joined him on the wall. "Huh. Yeah, I think I see what you mean. Weird."

"What is it?" Tyrathorn said. "Perhaps I am too far away."

"Here, look again," Valentine said.

A similar pulse radiated from her, though with a different energy signature. Expanding again, it traced along the same lines that Malcolm's had, refreshing the image he'd painted.

Malcolm bumped her in appreciation. "Nice."

"Thank you." She turned toward the distant hill. "Thorn, watch how my pulse changes. It flows through the plant like normal, but as it expands into the valley—"

"I see it," Tyrathorn said. "Curious."

"Yo, what *is* it?" Fred interrupted. "Y'all are killing me!"

"Time warps slightly around the plant," Malcolm explained. "It's *really* faint, but definitely there."

"Imagine a river," Valentine said. "When there's a rock sticking out of the water, think of how the current flows around it. It doesn't affect anything in the grand scheme, but the flow changes right there. That's kind of what's happening here."

"This place generates massive amounts of power," John said. "What if the warping is a result?"

Malcolm prepared to protest, then stopped. "Maybe you're right. It's so slight, it could be something natural." He bumped Valentine again. "What do you think?"

"My gut says this means something more, but . . . maybe I just want it to." She sighed. "Either way, I don't think the Black Tempest is here."

Reluctantly Malcolm stood. "I guess they found another way."

"We survived the enemy, and managed to save innocent people," John said. "I count tonight as a victory."

Valentine smiled. "You're right."

He was. Malcolm tried to take comfort in that, and maybe even a little pride. "I guess we've earned some rest. And I can't believe I'm saying this, but we still have school tomorrow."

"Ugh, dude," Fred said. "Major buzzkill."

"You all did fine work tonight," Clive said. "Let's head home."

VALENTINE waved a silent good night to Malcolm. Before closing the bedroom door, she flashed her best everything-will-be-okay smile. He mirrored it before his own door closed. She hoped they were both right.

A snore came from the bed. Spinning, she held up her fists. Then the covers moved and hair spilled out, half black and half purple. *Winter.* They'd left her to sleep off an epic battle with vodka. Though it had only been a few hours, it felt like weeks.

Moonlight painted the world outside and lit up her room. With an exhausted sigh, Valentine sank into her desk chair and stared out the window. In this first moment of solitude, as the night's events tumbled down on her, she began to tremble.

They'd all stared death in the face tonight. And John . . . *oh, John . . .*

Cupping her hands over her mouth, Valentine squeezed tight to muffle the sobs. Her chest and shoulders heaved, silent tears sliding between her fingers. *Oh god oh god oh god.* She'd been seconds from losing him.

Fear for her own safety had been a glimmer next to the raging fire that was fear for his. How could the world survive without John Carter, her deep and quiet Time traveler, with his gentle touch and bottomless brown eyes?

She and Malcolm had held firm to their no-killing conviction. But in her moment of desperation, Valentine knew the truth deep in her bones—to save John, she would have killed that woman in a heartbeat.

She trembled harder, terrified by that truth. A truth she would never admit to anyone. Tomorrow, when they were all together, she would have to be her strong and good self again. She would smile, train hard, and look to the future with optimism no matter what they faced.

But for now, alone in the moonlight, Valentine would let the tears flow. She would falter, doubt herself, give in to the fear of what would happen if they failed. She would imagine the cruel things she could do to the woman who dared threaten the ones she loved.

Then she would take control, wrapping up this dark corner of herself and putting it out of sight. She would sleep, and when the sun rose she would be a simple high schooler in her last week of freshman year. She would wear the guise of a normal teenage girl with normal problems. That's what she was.

At least, as far as anyone knew.

As soon as his door clicked shut, Malcolm sagged, deflating like a balloon with a slow leak.

Turning, he leaned against the door and stared into space, still stunned by how much stronger his enemy was. He'd felt outmatched against Lucius and Ulrich, but this was something else entirely.

There had been moments of triumph, too. The intoxicating

rush of cosmic power as he broke through to Fourth-*sev,* the deep pride when Valentine did the same. *The feeling of Asha in my arms.* He shoved that thought away.

Yet tonight had been his biggest failure. In the end, Tyrathorn had been the one to save them. Malcolm owed him a debt.

All these things we can do, all this power . . . and tonight I was helpless.

How could they defeat an enemy whose power somehow blocked the twins from theirs? More than ever, he felt Walter's absence. His friend would have pointed him the right way, or at least told him to man up and get this done, whatever it took.

Malcolm crossed to his side window—the one that looked out on a small brick house next door. A house that had sat dark since that day six months ago, when Walter had sacrificed himself for his friends. He leaned against the window frame.

"What would you do?"

If they were going to have a fighting chance, he'd have to find the answer soon.

BLACKNESS *all around.*

Dizzy. Lost. Where am I?

Tyrathorn's boots scrape across the stone floor. He peers down at them. The floor is smooth, its pattern familiar. But no walls, no ceiling—only the dark.

His movements are slow, weak. It would take days to reach the edge of the darkness. The pattern on the floor is so familiar. Where do I know this—?

Laughter in the distance. A young girl's. He knows her voice. The laughter chokes, becomes a scream. He knows her scream. And he knows now where he is.

Everwatch. Throne room of the Eon Palace. He is home. Home with his family.

And something is wrong.

A wave of dread sweeps over him. From his left, a tap and then a rumble. A tap and then a rumble. A tap and then a rumble. Then the floor changes.

A silvery sheen spreads over the polished stone, swallows the intricate mosaics. Like a living thing, a crystalline entity, it advances growing growing growing. Tyrathorn tries to back away. Cold. So cold. Cold so strong and so bitter that it echoes. How can cold echo?

A tap and then a rumble. A tap and then a rumble. To the left, a foot comes into view, then a leg, then a whole body, backing out of the darkness. A man, tall and strong, clad in Ember Guard armor. Steps back, his armored foot makes a tap on the icy floor. A rumble answers from the darkness.

The Ember Guard turns, a quick glance behind to check his path. Tyrathorn's heart races.

Garris. Garris is here.

Garris steps back. Tap. Rumble. Steps back again. Tap. Rumble. The Black Tempest emerges from the darkness, clad in shining black.

Garris plants his feet, yells. Tyrathorn cannot hear the words, but he sees Garris's face. Not angry. Pleading. Imploring. Holds up his hands as if to halt the Black Tempest.

The enemy advances on Garris, a monstrosity in jagged black ice. Tyrathorn tries to run to his brother's side. His limbs respond as if half asleep. Numb, lumbering, too weak to help. He shouts in frustration.

Garris's pleading becomes sorrow. Resignation. His armor

radiates an intense red glow. A broadsword of flame blazes to life in his hands. He speaks again. The Black Tempest hesitates.

Then strikes.

Flame. Cold. Steam. Fire on ice on ice on fire. Captain of the Ember Guard, Third-sev master of all things fast and flame, battling against the embodiment of a frozen storm. Black, soul-numbing dread brought to life. Unstoppable Fifth-sev lord of ice.

Garris fights and yells. Falls back. Fights and pleads, takes a wound, falls back. Pleads. Rallies, advances, launches a flurry of attacks with tears in his eyes. Scores a hit. Then another. Two frozen plates fly away in pieces. The Black Tempest falls back, armor constantly growing and changing. He bleeds, flesh and blood underneath.

Black fists tighten with rage. A massive shift. Tyrathorn yells at Garris to run. His words die on the wind.

Garris feels it. He stands firm, proud, body wreathed in flame. He will not yield.

Black ice slices through the air. Garris unleashes a storm of fire. Waves of ice melt. Waves of ice shatter. Then waves of ice penetrate. Too many. Too powerful.

Tyrathorn screams.

Quiet now. Fire and storm fade. The Black Tempest stands over his prey, armor half melted. And Garris . . .

On his back. Shards of ice protrude from his chest plate, thick as Tyrathorn's arm. Still he struggles up to his knees. Bursts of flame pop around him.

The Black Tempest raises a hand. A fourth shard of ice blooms in Garris's chest. He splutters, collapses to hands and knees. Tyrathorn begs him to fall, to surrender. Garris cannot hear.

Again he rises. Face twisted with agony, set with determination. Almost to his feet. A fifth shard pierces his armor. On his back again, Garris strains. Strains so hard. Waves of heat rise from his body.

Flames jet from his palm, envelop his foe. Not enough. Not nearly enough. He is spent.

The Black Tempest stands over him. Raises his own hand. Open palm toward Garris's heart.

But then he stops. Hand falls back to his side. Steps around his fallen enemy. Walks away with a rumble, disappears into the darkness.

Tyrathorn gasps, blinks, and is at Garris's side. Still alive. Barely. He is spent. His tears still fall.

More tears, now in Tyrathorn's eyes. "Garris. Oh, Garris, please no."

Garris sees him now. Smiles.

"Remember your heart, boy." Taps Tyrathorn's chest. "Always remember."

His expression goes slack. Hand drops away. Open eyes see nothing now.

Tyrathorn crumples to the floor, wracked by sobs. Garris is gone at the Black Tempest's hand. And the world is—

He awoke crying.

Safe in Fred's manor once again. Yet agony kept bubbling up from a deep chasm, a black pit of grief and despair and rage. Tears poured from a bottomless well.

The dreams came every night, relentless and cruel. They tormented him until sleep itself grew bitter and he forced himself awake.

But this one had been different. So much worse. It had felt personal in ways the others had not. Why?

He knew why. It hit him like a thunderclap—a truth that

had been hiding just beyond his injured mind's ability to grasp. A mind that was slowly healing.

It wasn't just this dream that had been different—many of them had. Because the truth was, some of them weren't dreams at all.

They were memories.

ASHA snapped awake.

A presence filled the room. As her mind awoke, her trained body vaulted to its feet and drew her *qamas*. The weapons blazed, a rush of energy bringing her fully alert.

The red light illuminated her brother. He stared at her in accusation, tears painting his face.

"Thorn? What is it?"

"I saw the Black Tempest."

Asha twisted, scanning the room. "Where?"

"In my dreams."

". . . Oh." She relaxed, her weapons going dark.

"I saw his power. Watched him kill. I remember now." He stepped closer. "Why did you not tell me?"

She stiffened. "Tell you what?"

"That the Black Tempest killed our brother."

CHAPTER 22

Friday. The last day of freshman year. But no one was talking about summer vacation.

Since Tuesday, the videos from Monday night had gone viral across the world. Plenty thought it was all a hoax, but Valentine had been surprised just how many true believers were out there. More tourists flooded the town, scrambling for pictures of the mysterious ice dome before it melted two days later.

For the people of Emmett's Bluff, though, this wasn't just some crazy story or strange adventure. They were living it. Walking the halls of Emmett Brown High School, Valentine saw enough tears to prove that. Some had friends and family that hadn't come home that night.

The hostages that did escape told their stories, too, a thousand times over. As the world pieced their accounts together, one thing became clear. Their survival had not been an accident. Someone had intervened, and because of them many had escaped with their lives. Which meant someone out there knew what was really going on.

Strolling across the gym floor, Valentine shook her head. *If they only knew.*

"What?" Malcolm said.

"Just wonder how fascinating everyone would find that dome if they knew what was really happening."

He hiked his bag onto his shoulder. "Totally. Call me crazy, but if we get through this it'd be nice to, oh, I don't know, just go to school. Maybe get a job. Hang out with friends."

"Like normal teenagers? That does sound crazy."

They approached the exit. Coach Boomer lounged against the wall, relaxed in his shiny track suit. One hand held a clipboard while the other absently spun a basketball.

"Gilbert twins," he called, diverting their attention. "Good first year?"

And there it was—the perfect question to sum up the absurdity of their lives.

Valentine stifled a laugh. "It's been, um . . . electric."

"Yeah," Malcolm said. "Time is really flying by."

She did laugh then, and quickly disguised it as a cough. Malcolm covered his mouth to hide a grin. The coach looked sidelong at them, puzzled. Valentine knew how crazy they must look. *Maybe we've gone a little nuts, too.*

"Well, uh, anyway," he continued, "have a good summer, and see you next fall. Might want to zip up those jackets—still pretty chilly out there."

Stifling more insanity giggles, they thanked the coach and bid him a good summer. He was right about the weather, at least. Almost June, yet the cold held on as if winter was determined to show summer who's boss. Lucius's antics had done quite a number on the climate.

Valentine zipped up her jacket, tucking wavy red hair inside the collar. They crossed the school grounds, aiming toward the next class. Just a couple more hours and they would be free for the next three months. She was a thousand percent ready.

"Next year, we start a new chapter," Malcolm said.

"I'm so ready. New classes, new teachers."

"No Chemistry or U.S. History."

"That especially, yeah."

Last year, Lucius Carmichael began as their awesome chemistry teacher—and Valentine's mentor—and ended as the nemesis who nearly vaporized Emmett's Bluff. Miranda Marcus, strange though she was, had grown to be more than just their history teacher. She had become a friend. Until she betrayed them and sided with Lucius.

Every day they walked into those classrooms, the replacement teachers only reminded them of what they'd been through. The friends they'd lost. It would feel good not to have a constant reminder.

"And, hey, we'll get to geek out over new stuff," she said, brightening. "How about Physics next year?"

Malcolm made a face. "That means we'll have to take Calculus. How about Biology?"

"Maybe. Just don't make me take U.S. History 2 or anything like that."

"Don't worry." Malcolm's eyes gleamed. "Next year, I'm thinking European History."

She didn't bother to stifle a groan.

MALCOLM could hardly believe his ears.

Pacing at the head of the class in a pleated gray skirt, Madame LaChance grew increasingly animated as she read to them. They'd finished the textbook last week, so she was using her own book of French history.

A beautiful French woman who loves history? What could

be better? To top it all off, on the last day of the year she had broken her sacred "no English" rule.

It was almost enough to distract him from the scent of smoke, the black marks on the wall, and the covered window. Valentine had certainly done a number on this room. Hopefully it would be fixed over the summer, because whenever she saw it she looked guilt-stricken.

For days now they been discussing key moments in French history that the textbook hadn't covered. Joan of Arc leading troops at the battle of Orleans and ending a British siege. The expansion of power under Louis XIV's rule. The construction of Versailles.

The storming of the Bastille, an action that sparked the French Revolution. This was Madame LaChance's favorite period by far, and she'd educated herself thoroughly on the actions and motivations of both sides. On their final day, this was the history she had chosen to teach them.

Though she clearly sympathized with the rebels, Madame LaChance didn't shy away from talking about heroes on both sides. The Revolution had been a dark and violent thing, but not everyone wanted blood for blood's sake. Those were the people she talked about.

Mirabeau had many personal vices, but was described as an "adventurer of genius in a dissolving society." Though belonging to nobility, he disagreed with much of their greed for power. A fierce debater and charismatic presence, he received a miles-long funeral procession after his death.

Jacques Cathelineau was a well-known peddler, but became much more after the French First Republic was born. Extremist revolutionaries committed violence and injustice against the common people during the Reign of Terror. In defense, Cathelineau organized the peasantry into an army and struck back.

Charlotte Corday, the Assassin of Marat, killed an oppressive leader in an attempt to halt his violence. Before her execution, she said, "I killed one man to save one hundred thousand." There was even a famous painting about it, *The Death of Marat*. Madame LaChance had a small copy, and it hung in her classroom between other French paintings.

She spoke with such passion, it was hard not to get swept up in it all. Malcolm found himself wondering what it must have been like. What he would have done in their position.

"There is still evil in this world, my lovelies," the teacher said in French. "If you have the strength, I hope you will do as they did. I hope you will not shy from the burden. That you will be brave and choose to fight, no matter the cost. God knows the world needs more people that will."

The bell rang and the students gathered their belongings with an excited buzz, in anticipation of freedom. Though Malcolm shared their excitement, he couldn't help sparing some attention for their young teacher. She regarded her students with a bittersweet smile, as if she would genuinely miss them.

"*Mangez bien, riez souvent, aimez beaucoup,*" she said.

It meant *eat well, laugh often, love abundantly*. A popular French saying. Malcolm grinned. The French were so dramatic, and he loved it. As she tossed thick chestnut locks over her shoulder, his heart raced and he pondered signing up for French 2 next year.

She looked right at him. Malcolm froze, wondering if she'd caught him staring. What kind of look was on his face? Then she looked at Valentine as well, and beckoned them to her desk. As they approached, she sat on the desk and her voice dropped to a whisper.

"Your final scores," she said.

Malcolm's eyes widened. They'd done well in the class, but their final grades had been bumped up to a perfect 100!

"You deserve it, *mes amours*," she said with a smile. Glancing at the floor, she bit her lip. "I hope you will consider taking my class next year. It would not be the same without you."

Yes, of course, you're a fine teacher and that would be wonderful, Malcolm tried to say. What came out was more like a giggle. He cleared his throat and tried again, but for some reason his voice wouldn't work.

"That might be nice," Valentine said, rescuing him. "We don't know what our class load will be, but we'll try."

He nodded. "Yes! Um, thank you."

"I hope so. Please do have the very best summer."

As they left, Malcolm walked as if wrapped in a cloud, a silly grin plastered on his face. Valentine rolled her eyes.

"Boys. You fall for that stuff way too easily."

"Yeah, but we know it and we don't mind. Then the girls keep doing it and everyone's happy. So, who's really pulling the strings here?"

She shrugged. "The world may never know."

"You'RE talking about next year?" Winter said. "You know school just ended ten minutes ago, right?"

"Y'all are raising the bar for geeks everywhere," Fred said.

In the back of Fred's limo, the twins sat on the seat across from their friends. Only minutes ago they'd piled into the sleek black vehicle, and the chauffeur was now waiting for their turn to pull out of the parking lot.

Valentine feigned surprise. "You mean, you haven't planned all four years?"

Fred started to respond. Then his jaw went slack as a cluster of cheerleaders strolled by in uniform.

"Well, maybe," he said. "If I can take Intro to Blonde Studies."

Without looking, Winter slugged his arm.

"Ow! Don't be hatin'. Players gotta play."

"Oooh," Winter said. "So, where did you meet these players?"

Fred shook his head. "That's cold, girl."

The twins burst into laughter, and Winter shot them her signature evil grin. More than anything, it warmed Valentine's heart to see her friend regain some of herself. She would still have hard days—a lot of them—but deep down Winter was still Winter.

Finally, the car slipped into afternoon traffic. Fred tapped the intercom button.

"We still going to Clive's?"

Valentine nodded. "He analyzed the device you gave us."

"Cool. Yo, Jeeves, we're hitting up Clive's shop. Cool? Cool."

"Still can't believe I missed the whole fight," Winter said. "No one tried to wake me up?"

"We would have," Malcolm said. "But you'd already had your fight."

"Yeah," Fred said. "And vodka won."

Winter punched his arm again.

"Ow!"

Ten minutes later, the limo stopped outside Clive's red

brick shop. Valentine wondered what kind of exotic cars he was working on today.

"You guys can stay in the limo if you want," she offered to Winter and Fred. "This may not be that exciting."

Winter snorted. "No way am I missing anything else."

"For sure," Fred said. "I may not get all the sciencey stuff, but we're in this, too."

They exited the limo and invaded Clive's pristine shop. As soon as they crossed the threshold between his office and the shop floor, they spotted the tall black man nearby, his salt-and-pepper hair bobbing in and out of an engine bay.

"A 1963 Aston Martin DB4," Malcolm said reverently. "Awesome."

Valentine's heart leapt. John stood beside Clive. Seeing them together—a fifteen-year-old boy and a man well over a century old—it was hard to fathom how long they'd been friends. Yet, watching them now, it was easy to see the familiar atmosphere of friends who'd shared a bond for many years. One was old, the other had an old soul.

John noticed Valentine and his smile deepened. She smiled back as if the sun had just begun to shine on her. *How does he still do that to me?*

Holding her gaze, John nodded toward the back door and tapped Clive's shoulder. The two groups met there, where John greeted Valentine with a soft kiss and wrapped her hand in his. She beamed at him.

"Hey, you."

"Hello, Valentine." John put his lips to her ear and whispered. "You look lovely. That blouse is one of my favorites."

She blushed fiercely as John drank in the sight of her. He

had commented on this top before—shimmering green and just tight enough to show off some curve—and she'd worn it specifically for him.

"Shall we?" Clive said.

At the back of the yard, the wide bay door of Clive's private clubhouse whirred upward. As the group stepped inside, Clive bent toward the hidden retinal scanner. Blue beams played across his face.

"Place is starting to feel like home," Malcolm said, grinning. Then he glanced at the rows of lab tables and stopped short. "Whoa."

Most of the tables had been pushed together in a U-shape. They held an exotic array of tools, electrical and mechanical components, and the half-removed guts of at least two industrial 3-D printers. Nearly every piece was new, even since the last time they'd come here.

At the center of the U sat a machine that dwarfed everything else. An open cube six feet across, it was a mass of steel framing and whirring clockwork. Gears spun while electric arcs and bursts of acetylene-fueled fire lit up the inside. Mechanical arms moved to and fro, piecing components together as the cube fabricated them—everything from tiny circuit boards to curved metallic pieces that seemed to be forming a shell of some kind. Affixed to the front of the cube, two tablets displayed wire frame models that constantly morphed from one shape to another.

"Whoa is right," Winter said.

"We weren't here that long ago," Valentine said, agape. "How were you able to do all this?"

"Workin' night and day, pushin' twice as fast," Clive said with a sly grin. "I tell you, lately it's like I got four hands."

"Dude," Fred said. "I got no clue what that is, but it looks totally sweet. What's it do?"

"Aw, just testin' out a theory. If it pans out, might be some'n we can use." Clive swept his hands across the tablets to clear the displays. Donning his spectacles, he motioned toward the round table in the corner. "Okay, gather 'round."

Everyone took a chair except for Clive and John. They approached the bank of sealed containers, focusing on one that looked like a rare antique. The size of a bread box, its weathered copper surface still gleamed in the low light. Its small door was literally covered with an intricate puzzle of clockwork gears. Malcolm's eyebrows climbed. Clive took his security measures seriously, but it seemed they really didn't want anyone to get inside that box. As they worked together to turn the gears, Clive and John conferred in low voices.

"Good thing we got tech nerds on our side," Fred said as they settled around the table.

Clive and John approached with their hands full. Clive set the piece they'd recovered from the warehouses in the center of the table, while John set down something Valentine hadn't seen before. Silver and black and about the size of a book, its surface had a series of grooves on one half and four lenses on the other.

John set the spectacles into the grooves and clicked them into place, facing the foreign piece of tech, then pressed a button. With a soft hum, the lenses flared to life. Lines of bluish light traced through the air above the table, a holographic projection of the information captured by the spectacles.

"Nice!" Fred said. "Where do y'all come up with stuff?"

"The spectacles themselves help," John said.

His manner had grown more serious, like Clive's. Instead of smiling at Fred's compliment, his expression tightened. It was a subtle change, but it made Valentine sit up in her chair. John may have been quiet, but he rarely looked grim. He gestured at the images rotating above the table.

"Here is what we could decipher about the para-nexus."

The hologram separated into individual components. Lines of data scrolled beside each piece, outlining materials and function and power requirements.

"Para-nexus?" Valentine asked. "You mean it's like a nexus, but not the same?"

"I mean para," Clive said. "As in parasite."

Everyone at the table stiffened.

"Parasite, how?" Malcolm asked.

"Wasn't sure 'til we got a look at this." Clive tapped the projector and a second image appeared. The two images shared a surprising number of similarities. "That's our friend Asha's nexus. Hers is unique from yours. Instead of tapping into the universe, it taps into her personal store of Time. In a way, she *is* the battery for her own powers. The para-nexus works on a similar concept."

"With key differences," John added. "Only a Chronauri can use Asha's nexus. This other device will work on anyone, and they are not required to operate it themselves. In fact, they may not be able to."

He paused to let the implication sink in. Valentine stared at the projections, thunderstruck. Horrified.

"You're saying—" She swallowed, her throat suddenly dry. "These things force people to be batteries for the Skrim?"

John sighed. "I believe so."

"And the Frost Hammer controls them," Malcolm said. "We saw her do it."

"How long could someone survive that?" Valentine asked.

"Takin' a guess?" Clive said. "Long as they got Time left in 'em. From how you described the Skrim, it may not take long to drain a person dry."

Winter's voice came out strained. "What would they do with this?"

"With just a few of these, maybe nothing," John said. "But with more . . ."

"With more, they could build an army," Malcolm said. "The Black Tempest could have legions of Skrim, and he could use anyone he wanted as hosts."

Fred rubbed his temples. "Man, this is so messed up."

"There's more," John said.

Everyone groaned.

John gave a thin smile. "This may be the good news, actually. Observe."

He tapped more buttons. The images shrank and moved to the side, except one, which grew larger. This component was identical in both devices.

"Not sure what its real name is," Clive said. "We took to callin' it the Beacon."

"From what we can tell, it's a temporal emergency exit," John said. "Activate it, and the nexus pulls you through a portal and sends you to a preprogrammed day and location. They can do this once, and then the Beacon burns out and must be replaced. We can't tell where or when these Beacons are programmed for, but we did learn how they work."

Clive gestured at the twins. "You two like nonlethal solutions. Well, this could be it."

Malcolm's brow furrowed. "I'm not sure I follow."

"If all the Black Tempest's people have these," Valentine said, "could we find a way to trigger them?"

"Oh," Malcolm said. "Use the Beacon to send them away. Kind of like what we did with Lucius."

Clive grinned. "Maybe. We're workin' on some ideas."

"Except these guys might just come right back," Fred said.

"One problem at a time," John said.

"What about the Skrim?" Malcolm asked. "How do we shut down a para-nexus without hurting the person inside?"

"And what if the Frost Hammer blocks our powers again? How do we get past that?"

John began to answer, then paused, uncertain. And sad. Valentine's heart ached for him. She knew John to his core, and right now it was killing him that solutions were elusive. He wanted so badly to help those people.

"I . . . know so little about the nature of your abilities," John finally said. "All I have are guesses. I can at least start tinkering with ideas, but they may not help."

She squeezed his hand. "It's okay. We'll figure it out together."

He squeezed back, giving her a grateful smile.

Winter leaned forward, an eager glint in her eye. "How can we help?"

"I'm in, too," Fred, said. "We got all night, and I can send Jeeves to get Asha and Thorn. Just tell us what to do."

Valentine exchanged a knowing look with Malcolm. She pursed her lips, and he looked as displeased as she felt. It would have been so much better to spend an evening here, working on something to give them an edge in this fight. But it could not be this evening.

She sighed. "You'll have to keep going without us. For tonight, anyway."

"We have obligations," Malcolm added.

John leaned closer. "Obligations for what?"

CHAPTER 23

"Family comes first, my dear," Oma Grace had said this morning before school. "Even when a supervillain is in town."

The last day of freshman year was a special occasion, according to their dad. Every completed year of school was a milestone to be celebrated.

"You've got to enjoy the good days, kids," he'd said when they expressed reluctance. "Never know when they'll come around."

Valentine supposed there was wisdom in those words, but tonight she didn't want to acknowledge it. They were going to a semi-fancy dinner, wearing semi-fancy clothes, and generally acting semi-proper with their dad and Oma Grace. And Callie de la Vega.

She suppressed a sigh and resumed brushing her hair. Tonight had been mostly Callie's doing, actually. Neil had had the initial idea, but Callie had picked it up and run with it. Somehow she'd pulled strings to get them into an exclusive dining club in Abilene, an adjacent town.

She was trying so hard, being so nice. The possibility of being a stepmom to two very weird teenagers must have been daunting, yet Callie hadn't shown it. At least, not yet.

Valentine stopped brushing and shivered. *Stepmom.* The word hadn't crossed her mind until now. But if her suspicions about Callie were right, would it ever get that far? Were her suspicions even valid, or was she just desperate to keep any new woman out of their lives? *And how did I become such a tangled mess?*

Many of her classmates had a step-something and they seemed okay. Valentine had seen the way Callie looked at her dad. Affection that genuine couldn't be faked, could it?

If Valentine was being fair, then so far, Callie seemed like nothing more than a good person. So why did Valentine lock up around her? Why did she insist on suspecting her? And what if—?

A knock on her door broke her train of thought. "Come in," she said, pinning up one side of her hair with an iridescent butterfly clip.

The door swung open to reveal Malcolm in dark jeans and a blazer with a button-up shirt. His unruly brown hair had been corralled into some semblance of style. He chuckled, wearing an easy smile.

"Might want to pick another expression before she gets here. You look like you're dressing up for a firing squad."

She mock-glared at him. "And you look like a stationery salesman."

"No wonder they're taking us out tonight. We are so fancy."

"Malcolm, Valentine, are you ready?"

"Coming, Dad," Malcolm called. He faced Valentine again. "You'll be fine. She doesn't bite. At least, not yet."

"Yet," Valentine said with a grin. The grin faltered. "I know she's being nice. I'm trying. It's just . . ."

"You suspect she's secretly a Time-traveling supervillain?"

Valentine deflated. "Sometimes. Other times, I'm not so sure."

To her surprise, Malcolm gave her shoulder a sympathetic squeeze.

"I see you're trying. That's good, but you need to try harder. We've fought plenty for this town. Just once, I'd like to fight for Dad. Can you do that?"

"I'll try." Valentine stood tall, squared her shoulders, and saluted. "Sergeant."

He saluted back. "Sergeant."

Before she could freak out and change her mind, she marched through her bedroom door.

"So, freshmen no more. How does it feel?" Neil said. He spoke from across a table covered in white linens, silver, fine china, and crystal.

"I, um, still feel kinda like the new kid, actually," Valentine admitted.

"But if it makes you feel better, we'll start giving wedgies next year," Malcolm said.

"One year closer to real freedom," Callie said. She leaned in, lowering her voice conspiratorially. "Most adults won't tell you this, but growing up is the best. You can do everything you used to do, plus new grown-up stuff, and no one tells you when to come home or go to bed."

"I knew it!" Malcolm said. "Most adults lie and say it's harder."

"Oh, it's harder," Callie said. "But it's worth it."

"Careful, dear," Oma Grace said to Callie with a smile. "These two are difficult enough to parent. They're like little adults."

"The smart ones always are, from what I've seen." Callie winked at the twins.

Yeah, she was really trying hard. Callie worked overtime to build a rapport with the family, while Valentine watched for any inconsistencies. Any hint of deception. Which was extra hard while trying to appear receptive to the woman's friendship.

The fancy restaurant in Abilene turned out to be The Fox, a converted historic inn situated next to a rushing stream. As their little group ate and drank the evening away, the moonlit water flowed by outside their window. Despite her growing suspicions about Callie, Valentine found herself more enchanted by this place.

Callie kept trying to gently engage her. With each attempt, Valentine had struggled to bury her suspicions, and she'd experienced varying degrees of failure. Which meant their interactions were still painfully awkward.

At least Malcolm was there. He'd managed to distract the others from her more embarrassing failures, jumping in just before the moments became unbearable. She owed him big time.

"How did you make such a lovely meal possible, dear girl?" Oma Grace asked Callie.

"Oh," Callie said. She glanced down with a half-smile, as if embarrassed. "I wrote an article on this place last year. How the owners restored it, turned it into this. They loved it and offered something special to say thanks. I, um, held onto the invitation until now."

"And we're grateful, sweetie." Neil leaned in to kiss her cheek and take her hand. "This is amazing. Thank you."

Valentine echoed her thanks with everyone else, which Callie waved away with a smile that bloomed full and warm. "I can't imagine being here with anyone else."

Valentine wracked her brain for something to say. Everyone else had introduced a subject or asked Callie something about herself. Everyone else was contributing, while she sat there radiating weirdness.

She had to try something. Ask Callie something unexpected, maybe. Not only would it appease her family, but it would be an extra chance to learn about this woman. So, why was her mind such a blank slate?

Then Callie brought up her left arm and swept silky dark hair behind her shoulder. Her wrist sparkled with the same intricate silver bracelet with the red gems. It didn't belong with her jade green cocktail dress at all.

"Um, Callie," she said. All eyes turned with varying degrees of surprise. "Your bracelet. Do you, uh, always wear it?"

For an instant, Callie's eyes were a tornado of emotions. Valentine barely registered them flickering from one to another before it was over. Then Callie smiled.

"It doesn't really match this dress, does it?" she said. "I admit, it does have . . . sentimental value. I'm so used to it, it's hard to take off."

She held out her arm and Valentine leaned in, studying the bracelet for anything out of the ordinary. Anything to suggest it could be more. To her disappointment, it was a beautiful and finely crafted piece of jewelry.

Why are you disappointed? Because you really don't trust Callie, or because you don't want to trust her? She hardly knew anymore.

Suppressing a frustrated sigh, Valentine leaned back in her chair. Then her eye caught something else and she came forward again. Head tilted in curiosity, she peered beyond the bracelet to the skin underneath . . . and the small tattoo.

"Rectify?"

A little too quickly, Callie pulled her arm back. She flashed an adorably sheepish smile.

"Oh . . . right. Um, personal mantra, I guess? *Rectify.* You know, set wrong things right, save the world. That kind of thing."

A tattoo about changing the world? *Interesting.*

With effort, Valentine buried all her suspicions and forced a smile. The next three words took as much effort as moving a mountain. "I like it."

Callie beamed. "Thank you, Valentine," she said. "So, what do you have planned for the summer?"

It was a simple question. Yet Valentine's mind reeled as if it had been shoved over a cliff. She'd expended everything she had on that one tiny engagement.

Unbidden, her thoughts raced out of control. *Why is she asking? Is she just curious, or is she trying to make plans with me? Is she trying to find a weakness? Am I supposed to hang out with her all summer now? What would we talk about? Why is she trying so hard can't she just relax I mean come on this is crazy it's just a question Val don't freak no YOU don't freak out! Everyone is staring . . .*

Valentine stared back at the group wide-eyed, wondering how long she'd been oblivious while her own thoughts fought with themselves. *Oh, god, please tell me I didn't say anything out loud.* She didn't think she had. But Callie eyed her now with uncertainty.

Valentine stared down at her hands, clutched together in her lap. "Um, not sure yet," she mumbled. "Hanging out with friends, I guess?"

Callie pursed her lips, then nodded. "Oh. Well, that sounds nice."

After another awkward pause, Malcolm took pity on her and asked Callie something that got real conversation rolling again. Not that Valentine was listening. She spent the rest of dinner—and the ride home, and the goodbyes at the end—straining to be present and failing.

Later, when Callie had gone home and the adults had turned in, Valentine sat alone in front of her mirror. Glad to be out of her dress and heels, glad to be finished failing and able to rest, she absently brushed her hair before going to bed.

Someone at her door cleared their throat. She glanced over to see Malcolm leaning against the doorjamb and suppressed a sigh. These after-Callie conversations were becoming a routine.

"Don't say it," she said.

"Okay, I'll just sarcastically imply it."

Despite her mood, Valentine laughed. "Fine, go ahead."

Malcolm grinned. "Well, that was interesting."

"I still don't trust her, Mal. Something is screaming at me that she's not what she seems. But, for Dad, tonight I really did try."

"I know. I saw."

"Do you think they did?"

"Hard to say. They're smart, but they don't have mystical twin powers."

"Too bad."

"Yeah."

She fiddled with the hairbrush before giving up and setting it down with a huff.

"Can we talk about something else now? Like that crazy

machine Clive built but didn't want to talk about. Or your drama. I'm sick of mine."

"You know Clive—he doesn't like to reveal his gadgets until they're perfect." Malcolm shot her a quizzical smile. "And what do you mean, my drama? I'm all sunshine."

"I mean your will-they-won't-they thing with Asha."

"I don't know—" He cut off as she gave him her don't-give-me-that-story look. His smile faded and he looked away.

"For what it's worth, I see her struggling, too."

His eyes snapped back to her. "You've seen that?"

"You have chemistry, but for some reason, you both run from it. She's got that whole soldier-for-life thing, and probably doesn't want anyone messing with it. You, though? You've played dumb with every girl at school who came after you."

Malcolm shrugged. "I wasn't into them."

"Fair enough, but you didn't even act tempted. I mean, Shelley Stafford? She's one of the hottest girls in school—even I can see that. She was sweet and she totally gave you an opening. Which you shut down."

"I just . . ." he began, but didn't finish.

Valentine softened her voice. This wasn't an interrogation, and she didn't want him to feel attacked. Just to know that she cared.

"Asha's different, though, right? All it would take is for one of you to try, and you might have something." She tried to catch his eye but he wouldn't look at her. "You've been like this for a while now. At first, I thought it was because we lost Mom. But the more I think about it, that's not the reason. You changed after what happened with Lucius. Why?"

Malcolm finally met her eye. He furrowed his brow in thought, as if debating with himself, and moved to speak. Then he hesitated. The intensity drained from his expression as he adopted a casual air again.

"It's not a big deal, Val," he finally said. "I have my reasons, but they don't have to be reasons forever. So don't worry about me, I'll be fine."

He gave a reassuring smile and bid her good night. As he closed her door, Valentine stayed on the edge of her bed. For long moments she pondered over her brother. Over what he was thinking, why he had really taken this path.

And why he had just lied to her.

TYRATHORN snapped awake.

Breathing hard, dripping with sweat, he rolled to his feet and paced the edges of the guest room—one of many in Fred's modest estate.

He no longer found rest in sleep. Battles and rage, fear and pain, killing and being killed—they dominated his dreams. Realizing the truth about them had done nothing to stop them. It was impossible to tell which were dreams and which were memories.

Some felt so vivid, so familiar. Others swept over him like surreal flashes of color and emotion. He was a soldier dying at the Black Tempest's hand. He was Garris, standing against a terrible foe. He was devoid of physical body, forced to watch as evil covered the world in black ice. And tonight, he had watched more friends die.

After a dozen walks around the room, Tyrathorn decided he needed something else to clear his head. A few splashes of cold water might help. He slipped into the hallway and padded around the house until, finally, he stumbled onto a bathroom.

The bright overhead light would not do, so he opted for a

small lamp by the sink. He reached for the switch, then stopped halfway, the hairs on his neck raising.

Someone else was there.

Adrenaline pumped through his veins. He reached out to draw Time and realized his nexus was still sitting beside his bed. So it would happen the old-fashioned way, then. Preparing to strike, Tyrathorn switched on the lamp.

A shape in the bathtub recoiled. Tyrathorn prepared to launch at whatever threat had been foolish enough to face him. Until the shape turned toward him.

He relaxed. "Winter. Apologies, I did not realize you were here."

Small already, she seemed even smaller when curled up in the massive bathtub. Hugging her knees to her chest, she clutched a stuffed bear. She sniffled and scrubbed a hand across her tear-stained face.

"Decided to give Val a break from me," she said. "I'm not much fun right now."

Tyrathorn turned to leave her in peace, but stopped. *I may be almost a stranger,* he thought, *but this one has been left alone enough, I think.*

Turning again, he climbed into the bathtub and tucked himself into the end opposite Winter. She stared as if he might be unhinged, but did not object.

But what could he possibly say that would give her comfort? He had not the faintest clue. So he just began speaking.

"I met a man once, in my travels," he said. "He is one of the few things I remember clearly. A noble warrior, one of the finest. At least, he had been before war swept across his homeland. Before the enemy killed his wife and daughter. I remember thinking I had never seen a man so lost. My heart ached for him. So, as we do on occasion, I invited him to come back with me. To live in Everwatch and be one of us."

Winter tilted her head. "You do that?"

He nodded. "My kingdom is full of more than just Chronauri and fighters. We are more than two hundred thousand people from every corner of history, past, present, and future. Some are born there. Others, we invite. Yet in all my travels, I had never invited anyone . . . until him."

He had her full attention now.

"Why him?"

Tyrathorn considered. "Because I had seen what he was before, and so I knew what he could be again. Not just a warrior, but a man of passion. A man who knew love and beauty, and cherished them so deeply that losing them had broken him. A man who, despite what he himself believed, wanted to find the light again. He only needed to be guided back to it." As he spoke, the memory brought a smile to his lips, and tears welled in his own eyes. "He builds toys for our children now. Amazing toys full of wonder! On Regeneration Day, he comes to Meridian Square and gives them to anyone who desires one."

Winter held the stuffed bear to her heart. Her gaze fixed on Tyrathorn. "Is he happy?"

He nodded, then smiled again as hope filled her eyes.

"Do you think . . ." she began, then hesitated, her voice almost a whisper. "Do you think that . . . someone like me would fit in there?"

He studied her, reminded so much of the man he had invited. Brash, tough, yet with the soft core of a lover. A true nature carefully hidden.

"The Japanese have a word—*kintsukuroi*. It means 'to repair with gold.' " Winter gave him a puzzled look, but he continued.

"They say that a bowl made of clay, formed by hand, has honor and beauty. When broken, it loses those things. But when repaired with precious metals such as gold or silver, it becomes even more beautiful than before. So when you would think its life is over, in truth, its real life began the moment it was dropped. It becomes more beautiful for having been broken."

Tyrathorn looked deeply into Winter's eyes, wanting her to know how truly he meant his next words.

"This, I believe, will be your story. These days are dark, but they are not your end—they are your beginning. Wherever you find yourself in this life, Winter Tao, and whomever you find yourself with, I believe you will heal. I believe you will know joy again. You will find the light, and then bring your own light into this world. And the world will shine all the brighter for it."

As Winter gazed at him, fresh tears fell from her eyes. But these tears were not made entirely of pain. Tyrathorn thought he saw a seed of hope. He reached toward her with an open hand.

"Until then," he concluded, "know that you have true friends who love you. Who will never leave you. And two new friends who think the world of you. We will stand by your side as you have stood by ours."

Winter studied his outstretched hand. Then she leaned forward and grasped it.

CHAPTER 24

Sunlight dappled the ground in their training spot on Fred's property. Yet, the golden rays paled next to the twins. They stood side by side, Malcolm's corona glowing blue and Valentine's red. Tyrathorn beckoned them forward.

With a surge of will, Malcolm exerted his power, and blades of ice appeared in his hands. Whips of fire appeared in his sister's.

Malcolm dove in, carving cold lines in the air and stepping in a circle to keep his opponent at the right distance. Valentine danced in the opposite direction, a mesmerizing blend of aggression and beauty, fighting techniques combined with her training in dance and gymnastics. All the while, her whips spun and cracked around her body, each staccato snap igniting a burst of flame.

Tyrathorn flowed between them like a snake, quicker than a blink, dodging while launching strikes of his own. Longswords appeared in his hands, one of ice and one of fire.

Malcolm saw what Tyrathorn was doing. Now that they'd reached Fourth-*sev,* he was making sure they didn't rely on the powers they were most comfortable with. Valentine tended to accelerate Time, Malcolm tended to decelerate it, but they could each do both. So they needed to learn them equally.

Somewhere behind him, there was a shout and a thud. Malcolm glanced over his shoulder for an instant, then dodged backward as Tyrathorn's foot whooshed by his face. *Focus!*

At the other end of the clearing, Asha stood surrounded by John, Fred, and Winter. Blades set aside, she taught them using only her skill, while the three used every gadget on their belts to try and bring her down. Asha was a blur between them, accepting the good attacks and doling out her own, calling out instruction and criticism.

She knocked them down, taught them how to roll with a strike and counter with their own, how to fight someone faster and stronger and survive. That was the life of a Second-*sev,* and she had mastered it better than anyone.

Refocusing, Malcolm threw one of his swords like a javelin, hoping to push his opponent off balance. Following his cue, Valentine cartwheeled behind Tyrathorn and attacked with her whips.

As Tyrathorn twisted between their strikes, Malcolm formed a Time bubble around him and mentally squeezed, slowing it down. Now the warrior moved at a snail's pace.

Then he made a countermove. Recognizing what Malcolm had done, Tyrathorn encased himself in a giant block of ice, thick enough to repel most elemental attacks. Malcolm grinned. *Gotcha.*

Falling back, he dropped the bubble around Tyrathorn and formed one around himself. As a temporal storm enveloped Malcolm, he re-created what Valentine had discovered fighting the Monk. The air around him crackled like a thunderstorm, and a bolt of lightning lanced from his hands.

The lightning hit home, shattering Tyrathorn's ice. He flew backward, right into Valentine's waiting arms. She conjured a dagger of flame and held it to his throat.

Tyrathorn burst forth with a full-bellied laugh. "My friends, in mere days you have mastered what should have taken years. I suspect soon you may join me in the Fifth-*sev*."

Malcolm beamed at the praise. When Valentine released him, he clapped them both on the shoulder.

"Well done. Your instincts are taking shape, and I can feel your power growing." He tapped his chin in thought. "Your coordination is also admirable—I suspect in part because of your twin bond. You fight together much like the Ember Guard. One day, perhaps, you shall see for yourself."

A thrill raced through Malcolm at the thought of seeing Everwatch. He exchanged an excited grin with Valentine.

"Just say when!"

"I shall. For now, however," Tyrathorn faced the other group. "Ashandara! Let us trade."

The others paused mid-battle and faced Tyrathorn. When they did, Asha dropped and spun to sweep Winter's and John's feet out from under them. As they hit the ground, she flipped up and caught Fred in the chest with an armored heel. He reeled backward and tripped over a bush to end up on his back.

Asha stood over them. "Never drop your guard when the enemy is near. Say it!"

"Never drop your guard," the three groaned.

"Now I'm ready, brother." Asha's eyes found the twins and narrowed, looking hungry.

"Switch!"

Tyrathorn dashed to the other group while Asha retrieved her blades and rushed at the twins.

"Let us start with dodging," Tyrathorn said, wrapping his fists in ice and his feet in flames. "Do not let me touch you."

He launched a series of attacks, though not as quick or strong as what he had thrown at the twins, all the while sharing tips and encouragement. It seemed as if he wanted them to feel confident against their enemies, despite lacking Chronauri power. Underneath his muscle, Tyrathorn possessed a soft heart.

Asha did not share her brother's sentimentality. As she approached, her blades pointed at the twins. "This will hurt."

She attacked as if they were enemies. But this time Malcolm had sensed Asha's nexus activating. He had felt stirrings of Valentine's power like vibrations through the air, and he knew that she felt his as well. So as Asha came at them in a hail of steel, he was ready.

Frozen sword and shield appeared in his hands, and flaming whips appeared in Valentine's. They swarmed in a deadly dance of fire and ice and metal, flowing like storm winds and clashing like thunder.

What Asha lacked in power, she made up for with ferocity. Malcolm froze her hands up to the elbows and she punched him hard enough to break the ice. Valentine enclosed her in a cage of fire and she burst through the flames, accepting scorch marks as the price of freedom.

"You're holding back," she accused.

"You're outnumbered," Malcolm said.

"And, technically, overpowered," Valentine added.

"That would not stop the enemy, *kuputsa*. They will press every advantage. Now, attack!"

She redoubled her assault, coming at them again and again. On both sides of the clearing, all battled and trained until they were red-faced and dripping with sweat. Then they kept going, pushing beyond what each believed was their limit. For Malcolm, all thought and existence blended together in a blur of motion.

Then Asha nicked his earlobe, drawing a line of blood. This would have been nothing, but in the instant it took him to retreat, Asha turned the flat side of her blade and slapped him playfully on the cheek. A devilish grin flashed across her face.

From out of nowhere, Malcolm's anger blazed.

His nexus slammed open, and power flooded into him. He heard Valentine gasp. His corona poured off his skin in glowing waves. The energy crested, ready to surge forward at his command.

A split second before lashing out, Malcolm caught himself. *Holy crap, what am I doing?* Reining in the energy, he willed it to disperse. Like a breeze, it flowed out of him, reabsorbing into the Time stream.

Only the space of a breath had passed. Which meant Asha was still within arm's reach. Though he'd shed his anger, her little stunt couldn't go unanswered.

Malcolm willed the Time around his arms to move faster. With impossible speed, his hands clamped onto Asha's wrists. Holding her right arm down, he bent her left arm back toward her body and gently smacked her cheek with her own blade.

"Hey, stop hitting yourself," he said. Copying Asha's evil grin, he slid out of reach.

Asha stared at him, wide-eyed and bewildered. Nearby, Valentine fell to her knees, laughing until she gasped and wheezed. Even their companions practically fell over each other with laughter. Fred rolled on the ground, howling and clutching his stomach. Malcolm let himself chuckle, though he kept a wary eye on Asha.

Then her intensity cracked to reveal a smile. Approaching,

she offered her hand, and when Malcolm accepted it, her expression grew warmer.

"Nicely done . . . apprentice."

Tyrathorn approached, barely maintaining his composure. "It may be good to stop for today. Shall we take a rest before returning to the house?"

Happy but exhausted, they reclined right there, sprawling on soft grass or leaning against trees. The late afternoon light was turning a deeper gold, and a colder breeze began to rustle the leaves.

"So, when are you gonna teach these guys how to make a vortex?" Fred asked. "That'd be a cool trick."

Tyrathorn gave a wry chuckle. "I have yet to meet a Chronauri who can. I suspect it is not possible. We all must rely on something mechanical to access our power, and the same applies when traveling through Time."

Malcolm sat up. "Why is that, exactly? There seem to be rules for what we can do with Time, so where did they come from?"

"And why are they changing?" Valentine added. "I get the feeling that what Lucius did—what the Black Tempest is doing—wasn't always possible."

Tyrathorn shrugged. "You would have to ask the Chrona."

Malcolm faltered. "The who?"

"The Chrona," Tyrathorn said as if it should be obvious. "The authority over Time? You know, the—"

He turned to Asha, eyes wide.

"Of course they don't know," she said. "Who would have told them?"

"Really lost here," Winter said.

Tyrathorn tapped his chin. "Where shall I even start?"

"The Shift," Asha said.

"Yes! Of course, the Axial Shift."

He stared up at the sky, collecting his thoughts.

"No one knows when this happened—or how, or why—but at some point in the timeline, there was an awakening. We call it the Axial Shift. It was then that three siblings—two sisters and one brother—first touched Time. After absorbing this energy, they discovered how to bend it to their will. Not only were they the first of us, but they are the only recorded Sixth-*sev* Chronauri to ever exist."

"Whoa, wait," Valentine said. "Sixth? You only told us about five."

"Because only five are relevant," Asha replied.

"Correct," Tyrathorn said. "The rest of us can only access Time because of what they did, and we must rely on machines to aid us. They did not possess this limitation."

"So, they caused all of this?" Malcolm said.

"In a sense, yes. When the Axial Shift occurred, that same awakening swept through the timeline in all directions, past and present. People began to manifest a lower form of their power. When enough gained the ability, the three Prime Chronauri felt the ripples through Time and realized what had happened."

"Musta freaked 'em out," Fred said.

"Perhaps," Asha said. "But they were still figuring out how to use the power, and what to use it for. The only truth they knew from the beginning was that the timeline must be protected."

"At first, anyway," Tyrathorn continued. "Eventually the brother and one sister became intoxicated with their power. For a Sixth-*sev*, it could eventually grow to limitless heights. They came to think of themselves as gods, and determined to bend the course of history to their will, shaping mankind how they deemed best. Only one sister remained true. Fortunately, she was the strongest. She alone opposed them, until eventually the conflict came to a head."

He stood and paced, growing more animated.

"Their battle was so vast, so powerful, that it created cracks and distortions in the very fabric of the universe. This disrupted the natural flow of Time, and those disruptions spread from one end of history to the other."

"Please tell me they're not still fighting," Winter said.

"Eventually, the sister prevailed," Asha replied. "The other two were killed. But she realized that more would follow in their footsteps. For every Chronauri who wanted to help, there would be others who wanted to destroy. So she had to do something about it. She became the entity we know as the Chrona."

Tyrathorn took over. "From then on, she worked to protect the timeline from others who would threaten it. As her knowledge and power grew, she learned how to separate herself from the timeline and view it from a higher vantage point. This allowed her to observe all points in history at once, and to create laws that govern how Time can be used."

A shadow fell over Tyrathorn's face.

"However, something has been happening. The laws have been weakening. Some have become lopsided and uneven. Loopholes have opened. It is why Everwatch was founded. Our parents led a fellowship of Chronauri that saw what was happening. When they reached out to the Chrona for help, they no longer received a response. So they created a kingdom hidden in Time, and dedicated it to protecting history as much as they could."

"The irony," Asha added, "Is that those same loopholes allow us to do what we do. Yet, even with our help, the timeline is slowly breaking. We fear what may happen if it breaks beyond repair."

"And that is why we are here," Tyrathorn concluded. "To protect the people and shield the timeline from further damage."

Malcolm had been staring wide-eyed at the ground, and now he shared a glance with Valentine. She looked as overwhelmed as he felt. It was as if something heavy sat on his chest.

"Wow," he said, swallowing hard. "That's, uh, a lot to take in."

"I am sorry," Tyrathorn said. "In Everwatch, these are truths we grow up knowing."

"At least you know now," Asha said. "You know what's at stake, and what will happen if we lose."

Silence fell as they processed knowledge that so few people possessed. Ultimately, Malcolm knew Asha was right. They had to learn this eventually, and it made what they were doing seem even more important.

Fred seemed to arrive at the same conclusion. Leaping to his feet, he clapped once.

"Don't know about y'all, but I'm ready to throw a few more punches. Anyone wanna keep going?"

Grinning, Malcolm stood. "Yeah, I could do that."

One by one, they stood and got back to work. Time was running out, and if they were right, the Black Tempest's plans were nearing completion.

He could strike at any moment.

CHAPTER 25

Six Weeks Later

"They are escaping into the wild!" Tyrathorn's voice burst through the comm. "Squad Three, press their right flank!"

Malcolm and Asha dashed to the border of the industrial park. Dodging and leaping between stacks of shipping containers, they came to a twelve-foot-high chain-link fence topped with razor wire. On the other side, the southeast edge of town faded into fields of tall grass and then dense forest. By the time Malcolm caught sight of their two targets, they were almost halfway across the field.

"Jeez, they're fast!"

Skidding to a halt, he laced his fingers to form a stirrup. Without breaking stride, Asha planted her foot in his grip. Malcolm heaved upward and she sailed over the fence. Somersaulting, she touched down and kept running.

Malcolm's nexus blazed red. He threw a blast of searing heat, then dove through the hole where chain links had melted.

They still lagged behind. He could create a bubble of fast Time, but that would affect his ability to coordinate with the team. Even so, Malcolm knew he would have to do something. Gritting his teeth, he grabbed Asha's hand. *Hope this works!*

Absorbing a rush of Time, he split it into two flows. One energized his own body, the other he shunted through Asha's nexus. She gasped as the power boost fed into her armor.

Their speed doubled. Asha's armor blazed so hot that the grass around her flashed to cinders. The field passed in a blur and the tree line drew closer. Yet the enemy still outpaced them.

"They're too fast, Thorn!" Malcolm called. "We need—"

Far to the left, Squad Two appeared. Valentine and Tyrathorn lifted their arms, and storms of lightning and fire fell across their adversaries' path.

The fleeing Chronauri accelerated too quickly for even Malcolm to track. Dodging between the storms, they plunged into the forest. Malcolm and Asha followed with Squad Two close behind.

"Squad One, prepare to close the net," Tyrathorn commanded.

"Set and ready," John whispered over the comm.

Then Malcolm felt two *shifts* and his heart sank.

Two vortices bloomed open in front of their targets, glowing blue. *Oh, come on!* The Chronauri vaulted into the light, and the portals winked out of existence.

"Whoa! What just happened?" Winter shouted.

Malcolm stopped in the small clearing where the rogue Chronauri had used their last resort. He gave a frustrated huff.

"They used their Beacons," Asha said.

Malcolm heard rustling as the other squads moved to their positions. He looked to Asha, intending to ask her thoughts on their next move, then noticed her staring down at their hands.

They were still locked together.

Malcolm's heart raced, a jolt passing through him like an electric shock. Simultaneously, they pulled away and turned in opposite directions.

John, Winter, and Fred appeared. They had been waiting in the trees, the third point of the triangle designed to close around their enemy. Valentine and Tyrathorn arrived last. Frustration poured off of everyone—except Tyrathorn, who fumed with barely contained rage.

"Yo, that was crazy," Fred said. "How'd they move so fast?"

"Third-*sev* Dashers," Asha explained. "Some Thirds choose to specialize in one skill. Dashers focus on increasing their own speed. Not great fighters, but hard to catch."

"Weeks of work," Tyrathorn spat. "Weeks of tracking and planning, of struggling to remember something—anything. Our one good lead, and what happens? We lose them in the *daotan* trees!"

As he swung to punch the nearest tree, a massive scythe of fire appeared in his hand and cleaved through the trunk. The trunk of the towering oak burst into fiery shrapnel, and a shockwave split the tree in half all the way to the top. The pieces toppled to the ground with a crash.

Malcolm stared wide-eyed. *Whoa.*

Tyrathorn recoiled from the remnants of the tree. He faced the group with shock, his anger smothered by embarrassment.

"I . . . I am sorry. I never intended . . ."

Turning, he fled into the forest.

Stunned silence fell over the group. Malcolm's gaze drifted to Asha, who stared after her brother with a potent concoction of emotions contorting her face. Chief among them, he thought, was worry.

"Well, that was new," he said to her. "Will he be all right?"

"He's . . . just frustrated."

"Oh, really?" Fred said. "I couldn't tell."

Asha shot him a warning glare. "The memory of our brother weighs heavily on him."

"I can imagine." Malcolm's heart went out to his friend. How terrible would it be to carry the memory of your brother's murder?

Asha moved in Tyrathorn's direction. "Hold here. I'll calm him down."

Her eyes lingered on Malcolm for an instant longer. Then she disappeared into the trees without a sound. A wave of heat swept over Malcolm. He buried the feeling quickly, hoping he hadn't blushed.

"Gotta say, Thorn's not alone," Fred said. "All these weeks, and whatta we got to show?"

"Clues, guesses, and two escaped Chronauri," Valentine lamented. She gestured to John. "And we didn't get to test your Lance."

They'd been certain the Black Tempest's endgame would start any day. So they'd trained relentlessly. They'd investigated, running down even the thinnest clues. They'd remained on high alert, wanting to be ready at a moment's notice.

Separately, John and Clive had worked night and day on a solution for the twins. Something to keep the Frost Hammer from shutting down their power. They hypothesized that she had found a way to concentrate Time so much that it took on physical form—the distortion waves.

If she hit the twins with all that condensed energy, she could possibly create a temporal wall that would disrupt their ability to draw the energy themselves. So John had Clive build each of the twins a Lance—a device meant to store Time like a battery and release it all in one focused burst, hopefully punching through the Frost Hammer's wall. Now the only thing to do was test it against their enemy.

Six weeks later, though, nothing. As if their enemy had fallen off the Earth. Where was the Black Tempest? What was he waiting for?

Finally they had pieced a few tidbits together. For months, a percentage of shipping trucks had been disappearing along the highway routes near Emmett's Bluff. Deeper digging revealed the theft of an intriguing cross-section of items—everything from computers to copper and palladium.

So they'd set a trap, hoping to capture and interrogate the Black Tempest's minions. And now, even that had failed. They needed a win, and soon, or all this waiting would take a toll.

"I can't stay still," Valentine said. "Anyone want to walk?"

"I will," John said, taking her hand.

"Me, too." Winter hesitated. "Uh, unless 'take a walk' is code for make out."

Valentine laughed. "We'll try to control ourselves."

The three left Malcolm and Fred alone with the wind and rustling leaves. Fred sat on the ground. With an exhausted sigh, Malcolm sagged against a tree.

"What are we doing wrong?"

Fred shrugged. "Least we're gettin' to train a lot."

"The Black Tempest is a sphinx—he's not giving anything away. Lucius was an open book compared to this." He stared at the ground, plagued by doubt. "Sometimes I wonder if we're just too outclassed."

Picking up a broad leaf, Fred pulled it slowly to pieces. He focused on the repetitive task, chewing the inside of his cheek.

When half the leaf was gone, he looked up again. Malcolm waited for a silly comment, something undeniably Fred.

"I ever tell you how Winter and I got to be friends?"

Malcolm raised his eyebrows, taken aback. "No. I just assumed you grew up together."

"Mm," Fred acknowledged. "Back in sixth grade, that girl was already stirring up trouble. Football team never won a game, so she writes this snarky article and sneaks it into the school paper. Totally called out the team, got in some good jokes. Still the funniest thing I ever read."

He went back to tearing at the leaf.

"Next day, I'm in the hall and I see this tiny Chinese girl trapped in a corner. Giant linebacker hadn't cared for her article and wanted to knock her out. Girl wasn't backin' down, though. This guy was a tank, and she got right up in his face. Said most of her jokes were about him specifically, and she was just surprised he could read. Dude was about to take a swing, and he woulda demolished her." Fred shook his head. "Don't know what I was thinking."

"What happened?"

"I jumped in front of her, dawg."

Malcolm gaped. "Seriously?"

"Yep. Got all in his face, said he should fight someone his own size, which was stupid 'cause he was twice my size. But I acted all whacked-out to scare him away."

"Did it work?"

Fred gave a wry grin. "Nope. Busted my lip wide open. I got some blood on his shirt, though, so I still count it as a win. Winter helped me up, then called me a moron. Been friends ever since."

Malcolm laughed. "I should've known it'd be something like that."

Fred laughed with him. Then his smile faded. "I was in his face, thinking, 'If he starts swinging, I'm dead.' Didn't really matter, though. It was about the principle. Ain't no bully gonna push someone around in my town."

He stared into the middle distance, reliving the old memory. After a moment, his eyes came back to the present.

"Compared to me, y'all are giants. The things you can do . . ." He blew out a rush of air. "I figure the Black Tempest will be the same. In the end, though, it still don't matter."

He looked up, locking eyes with Malcolm.

"I may not be able to warp Time or make fire, Mal . . . but I'll be there when you need me. Always."

Malcolm regarded his friend, forced once again to reevaluate him. Every time he thought he'd figured Fred Marshall out, the guy went and surprised him again. Reaching down, he grasped Fred's hand and nodded his thanks.

"I wouldn't want anyone else at our backs."

Footsteps and laughter echoed nearby. Valentine, John, and Winter reemerged in better spirits than when they'd left. They gathered around Fred and Malcolm, and for a few precious minutes it all felt so normal. Just friends and adventures and not a care in the world.

Soon after, Asha arrived with Tyrathorn in tow, contrite and embarrassed.

"Apologies," he said. "I owe you all a debt."

Winter slapped his arm. "I'd have blown up a tree, too, if I could."

"Yo, sounds like we just gotta unwind," Fred said. "You know? Take a couple days off."

"I would prefer a week," John said.

"Where do I sign up for that?" Valentine said.

"No, seriously." Fred leapt to his feet, picking up steam. "It's Tuesday now, and Saturday is my dad's charity ball, so it's perfect! Let's just take Friday and Saturday off and have fun."

The group eyed each other awkwardly, no one wanting to speak up first. They'd been working so hard for so long, to Malcolm it almost felt like giving up to take a break.

"Come on, y'all," Fred pushed on. "Two days off the clock ain't gonna hurt anything. If we don't relax, we'll explode."

Like steam, Malcolm realized. If a steam-powered machine never released any steam, eventually the pressure blew it to pieces. Could they afford to take that chance?

"He's right," Malcolm said finally. "We can't do this every minute. We've got to decompress." He grinned. "Let's do it."

After that, it didn't take long for everyone to agree.

Look out, world, Malcolm thought. *We're about to try acting like normal teenagers!*

CHAPTER 26

Just knowing that a break was coming made all the difference. For the next few days, they trained harder than ever. They ran down every possible clue. As Thursday night fell, they even squeezed in an extra training session. Then, eager to begin their vacation early, everyone stayed at Fred's house for a night of pizza and blasting aliens on his giant theater screen.

For the first day in many weeks, they laid their weapons down. They took a break from looking over their shoulders. For just a little while, they let themselves be teenagers. When the rainy Friday morning dawned, an aura of peace had settled on Fred's house.

At least, at first.

"Woooooooooooooo!"

Valentine snapped awake as the bedroom door burst open. In a flash of panic, she reached for her nexus and prepared to defend her friends. Across the room, Winter and Asha leapt from their beds.

Then Valentine saw their "attacker" and fell back to her pillow with a relieved sigh. Fred stood in the doorway, wearing a ridiculous red and sparkly cowboy hat. In each hand, miniature foghorns blasted earsplitting tones.

"Vacatiooooooooon!" Fred bellowed. Dropping the fog-horns, he pulled out a handful of party poppers and pulled their strings. The doorway filled with tiny explosive pops and sprays of confetti. "Come on, ladies, daylight's wasting!"

"Fred, I will straight-up *murder* you," Winter said. "Go bother the boys!"

Grinning, Fred bounced down the hall. Then Valentine heard another door burst open so Fred could do his routine again. Scrubbing hands over sleepy eyes, she laughed as the boys yelled the same protests.

"What is he celebrating?" Asha asked.

Winter smirked. "He takes being lazy very seriously."

No one changed out of their pajamas. One by one, they emerged from their rooms and shuffled toward the kitchen. John greeted Valentine with a kiss that sent her heart soaring, and together they made breakfast for everyone.

Of course, they got teased, so they took revenge by giving each other dumb pet names. She called John Schmoopie-Face and he called her Perfect-Honey-Bear. As they cooked, their friends gathered around the marble island to share donuts that Fred had called out to have delivered.

He'd actually gotten a donut shop to deliver. The Marshall name carried enough prestige that he could get away with stuff like that. Fred just shrugged it off. The money and glamour only mattered to him as far as its ability to do silly stuff like that.

Stuffed full of breakfast, they piled onto the huge couches in Fred's theater room. After their trouble last year, his dad had used the house repairs as an opportunity to remodel. One result had been this room, with its wall-sized projector screen, impossibly comfortable couches, and a pile of giant cushions and bean bag chairs in the middle.

Valentine picked a corner of a plush L-shaped couch and curled up with soft pillows and John, who whispered sweet things in her ear and stole kisses when no one was looking. Fred and Winter busied themselves by tossing pillows at each other's faces.

In honor of their new friends, they decided to watch *The Empire Strikes Back*. On hearing that it was the first sequel to *Star Wars*, Asha burst into a thousand-watt smile. She picked a spot close to the screen, sprawled across the floor cushions.

She soaked up the epic tale, only turning from the screen to whisper questions to Malcolm. Overjoyed, he obliged by providing all the facts that anyone could ever want about the Force and the Jedi Order. She drank it all in, cheered for the Rebellion, fell in love with Yoda, and even critiqued the Jedi fighting style. When Darth Vader revealed his true identity, she gasped and grabbed Malcolm's arm, eyes wide in shock.

Tyrathorn sat in a recliner, hands laced behind his head, the very picture of contentment. From across the darkened room, he watched his sister with a faint smile, as if he saw what Valentine was seeing. What Malcolm and Asha refused to acknowledge, yet kept happening anyway.

As the credits rolled, Asha practically begged to watch the third movie, but of course Malcolm refused. *Star Wars* couldn't just be watched, he said, it had to be experienced. That required a period to appreciate each movie. They followed up next with a comedy.

Wrapped in the warm comfort of John's arms, watching her friends laugh their heads off, Valentine reflected on what her expectations had been for this day. She'd thought everyone would run around like crazy, trying to cram excitement into every minute.

Watching them now, though, she realized excitement had been the last thing anyone wanted. With what they would soon face, what they needed now was stillness.

These weren't needs that anyone spoke, and no one laid out a plan. But they were needs that everyone shared, so minute by minute, the day was giving it to them.

FRED had planned a party for later in the evening—just a small one, he'd said, since it was rainy and cold and he wouldn't be able to use the pool. Of course, to Fred, a small party probably meant a hundred people. Until then, they had the rest of the day to themselves, and an urgent piece of information had just been revealed.

The Corvonians had never seen a mall.

So, after hours of lounging and eating way too much snack food, they leapt into Fred's limo and Jeeves drove two towns over to Winnick. It wasn't as pretty, but it had the Arrowhead Galleria, the best mall for hours in any direction. Fred's dad owned part of it, of course.

Valentine's favorite part was watching their visitors gawk at the "towering monument to commerce." That was how Tyrathorn described it. Asha examined every storefront with the quick, eager eye of someone excited but not wanting to show it. As they passed by a store with fancy cocktail dresses, she had even stopped walking for a split second before catching herself. Valentine filed that away for later.

They bought a few silly things, then hit the food court for a late lunch. The meal was spent making fun of the ridiculous hat

Fred had insisted on buying, and teasing Asha for how much she loved her little toy lightsaber. Malcolm had bought that for her.

Eventually, discussions turned toward the *Emmett's Bluff Restoration Ball*. It would be a fancy affair, everyone in high society sporting their best suits and dresses.

That was when it dawned on them—the Corvonians possessed only battle armor and borrowed jeans.

AN hour after they invaded Nordstrom, Asha found herself wandering alone among vast racks of gowns. Valentine and Winter had doted on her, but finding a dress had proven more difficult than expected. Asha had taken pity and released them to find what they needed for themselves.

Which also granted her solitude. Wandering among the finery, she traced her fingers along the soft fabrics in a rainbow of colors. These days, she would prefer to wear something made of metal as opposed to—

She stopped in her tracks. *The* dress filled her vision, calling to her with the deepest, truest red she could imagine. Somehow it pulled her closer until it was resting in her hands. The silky, sparkly material brought back old memories of attending royal celebrations as a little girl. Those occasions had never been her favorite, but sometimes—once in a while—the dresses were nice.

"You find the one?" a male voice said behind her.

Flinching, Asha released it and whipped around as if she'd been caught. Fred stood there with a bag full of new clothes. Craning his neck, he looked past her with raised eyebrows.

"Oh, yeah, slammin' dress. That's definitely it." He glanced around. "The girls leave you alone?"

"They're finding shoes," Asha replied, unable to meet his eyes. She hesitated. "How . . . do you know this dress is right?"

Fred grinned. "Let's just say I've bought dresses for too many girls. But you're a princess, right? Shouldn't finding a dress be easy?"

"If my parents had their way, yes. But I prefer armor."

Fred nodded. Stepping past her, he plucked the red dress from the rack and held it up to her figure.

"Well, that's the great thing about bein' tough," he said as he examined the dress. "It don't mean you can't still be a girl. 'Feminine' and 'tough' go together just fine. Know what I mean?"

Without waiting for a response, he called over a saleswoman.

"This works, right?" he said, gesturing at Asha and the dress.

She nodded emphatically. "It totally works. You're going to be gorgeous."

"Sweet. If it fits, she'll take it."

"Wait!" Asha said. This was all happening so fast. "I-I can't actually wear this. And the price—is that expensive?"

Fred smirked. "First—it's a formal ball, so you totally can wear it. Second—remember who you're talking to? I ain't royalty, but I do all right." He looked to the saleswoman. "Where's your dressing room?"

The saleswoman barely hid a smile as she led them across the store. Asha vacillated between excitement and the desire to tackle her. On seeing Fred's satisfied expression, she buried the latter impulse.

"Thank you, Fred," she forced out. "I'm in your debt."

He waved it away. "Don't worry 'bout it, girl. You'll rock that dress." Under his breath, he added, "Mal's eyes are gonna pop outta his head."

She heard him. He didn't notice when her steps faltered.

MALCOLM closed the giant glass door behind him. Stepping onto Fred's patio, and then onto the grass beyond it, he left behind the bustle of party preparations.

Cloudy gray skies scuttled by overhead. Occasional breaks in the clouds allowed brilliant rays of light to bathe the earth. Malcolm shed his jacket, enjoying the cold droplets as they speckled his shirt and *tink*'d against the nexus strapped to his wrist. He'd been wanting to try this for days.

He drew in a deep breath and savored the damp, green-scented air. Lifting his hands, he closed his eyes and reached through the nexus. Time responded, and a gentle stream washed through him.

The nexus glowed blue as Malcolm created a large temporal bubble with himself in the center. Though he kept his own Time flowing normally, anything else entering the bubble would *shift,* its Time flowing more slowly. *That should do it.*

He opened his eyes and smiled. As raindrops passed through his bubble, their descent toward the earth slowed to a crawl. Like liquid gemstones, each drop sparkled in the sunlight. Malcolm swiped his fingertip through a droplet as it fell inch by inch. *So beautiful.*

"I've never seen that before," a voice behind him said.

Malcolm gasped and nearly lost his grip on the bubble. He turned to see that Asha had stepped inside it, and come close enough to him that her Time flowed normally. Either she moved like a ghost or he'd been far too preoccupied.

"Clever," she said, eyeing the droplets as they tumbled languidly. "And pretty. But why do you do it?"

Malcolm gave a sheepish grin. "It must look strange to you—using cosmic power to play in the rain. But this kind of stuff matters to me."

"Yes. It teaches fine control, helps you learn the nuances of your power."

She was right, and yet completely wrong.

"Yes, but that's a side benefit. The real reason is . . . well, less tangible."

Asha's brow furrowed. "I don't follow."

"A real warrior wouldn't," he said with a wry smile. "No practical application. But that's why I love it." He flexed his fingers as if reaching for better words. "I want to be stronger, and of course I'm learning how to fight with my power. But I can't just be a fighter, Asha. All of this—it has to mean more than that. It has to add something to the world, be more than just another weapon." He gestured at his bubble. "So I made something, and its only purpose is to be beautiful."

He braced himself for criticism. Using Time to make pretty raindrops must seem ridiculous to Asha. She gazed at him and his bubble before responding. But then . . .

"You fight like an artist," she said. A week ago it would have been an insult, but today her tone was softer. "A Second-*sev* focuses on ferocity. We must because our enemies are stronger. But you—you fight with the universe at your back. I see its poetry in you." She looked away. "I . . . envy that. Not just how you fight, but how you see the world. I would like to find more beauty in it."

Malcolm stared at her in wonder. More than ever, he saw the different sides warring within her—the fighter, the princess, and the girl. However much she pretended, Asha Corvonian was far more than a weapon.

She fidgeted under his gaze. "What?"

Malcolm's hand twitched. *Don't.* His hand lifted an inch. *Don't do it. Do NOT do what you're about to . . .*

He held out his hand. "Let me show you."

With the barest hesitation, Asha took his hand. Gently he pulled and she stepped forward until only inches separated them. She gazed up at him with equal parts fear and anticipation.

He closed his eyes and focused. The power was already inside the bubble. Now he just needed to concentrate it the right way.

When each new raindrop passed into the bubble, he wrapped it in deeper layers of slowed Time, using atoms to cool other atoms, the way Tyrathorn had shown him. As molecular activity inside each raindrop decreased, so did its temperature. *Good. Now to spin each micro-bubble, just enough to bend its path to the ground . . .*

He heard Asha gasp and opened his eyes, knowing already that it had worked. Now as each raindrop fell through the bubble, it froze into a pure white snowflake, and the gentle spin caused each snowflake to swirl around them before touching the ground.

Malcolm had turned his bubble into a life-sized snow globe, with himself and Asha at the center. She stared in awe, laughed in amazement, drinking in the sight for a long moment. Then her eyes rested on Malcolm.

"How did you do this?" she whispered.

Her ice blue eyes and full lips beckoned to him. Malcolm felt himself leaning closer.

"I had the right motivation."

Asha leaned in, too, as if a magnet were pulling them together. She was so close now. The scent of her hair filled his nostrils. The touch of her hand buzzed through his body.

Electricity. Lightning. Malcolm blinked, memories invading his thoughts. Pain, loss, dark days, and after all of that, realization.

A lightning bolt of true understanding. About himself, about his path. About why something like this couldn't happen.

For the barest instant, he hesitated. As if looking in a mirror, he saw Asha hesitate, too. Then he saw her see *him* hesitate. In the blink of an eye, the spell unraveled.

"Um . . ." he said, uncertain.

Neither moved forward but neither pulled away. Locked together, they teetered on the edge of a cliff, unsure which way they would fall.

Fred's appearance answered for them. "Yo, Mal! People are gettin' here, bro."

They released each other, stepping away as Fred approached the edge of the patio and caught sight of them.

"Aw, man, awesome trick with the snow! Anyway, party's starting." He pointed at Asha. "You ready to dance, girl?"

Asha fixed him with a no-nonsense stare. "Warriors do not dance."

"Pssh, we'll see. Come on, let's get our swerve on!"

Malcolm shared a glance with Asha—equal parts embarrassment and relief at not having been caught—and followed Fred inside. Mentally, he crossed his fingers in the hope that a little partying would help him forget what had almost happened.

Deep down, he knew it wouldn't.

Valentine's blissful sleep shattered as someone pounded on the bedroom door. With a groan, she threw back the covers and stumbled groggily toward the unwelcome noise. Halfway to the door, she noticed the other girls stirring.

"Yo, you gotta get up!" Fred called through the door.

Valentine's bleary eyes narrowed. *He is not doing this two days in a row!*

"Hey, Asha," Winter said. "Can I borrow your swords? I need to murder Fred."

"Only if I can help."

Valentine laughed, then resumed her angry face and whipped open the door. "You're not our alarm clock, Fred."

But he wasn't celebrating. "We all crazy overslept."

"Your 'little' party didn't end until 3 a.m., genius," Winter said from her bed.

"Yeah, and now it's 3 p.m. Saturday! You know what that means, right?"

A wave of horror washed over Valentine. She turned to the other girls. While Asha appeared unconcerned, Winter's expression mirrored her own.

"Oh. Crap." Winter sprang out of bed. "Code red, we've gotta go."

"What have I missed?" Asha asked.

"We have to leave for the charity ball in three hours." Winter threw back Asha's covers. "Come on, move!"

"Oh, no," Valentine said, despairing. "Everything except my shoes is at home."

"My stuff is there, too," Winter said. "What do we—?"

"Relax," Fred interrupted. "I already got Jeeves ready to drive you. Get fixed up there. We'll come get you."

Valentine laid a grateful hand on his arm. "Thank you, Fred. You're a lifesaver."

Fred beamed. "Hey, it's cool. Do your thing."

As the door closed, they exploded into action.

Malcolm lounged in Fred's theater, playing a game on his phone. John sprawled on the floor reading a book. Tyrathorn lay atop the pile of cushions, eyes closed and blissfully lazy.

A few minutes ago, Fred had checked his watch and bounded out of the room with a yelp. Now he returned and flopped down on one of the couches. Humming absently, he picked up a tablet and thumbed through his movie library.

"Were they still asleep?" John asked, still reading his book.

"Yep," Fred said.

"Did they panic?" Malcolm asked, still playing his game.

"Yep."

"How long do we have?" Tyrathorn asked, eyes still closed.

"About three hours."

"Mm," Malcolm replied. "You guys wanna watch a movie?"

John closed his book. "Sure, we have time."

"Already on it." Fred mirrored his tablet display on the projector screen. "What looks good?"

CHAPTER 27

Valentine's favorite playlist thumped in the background as the girls completed their ensembles. They were going to a party, so they might as well set the mood now.

She took one last look in the mirror on her door, making sure everything was in its place. *Not bad.* With a nervous smile, she pressed a hand against her stomach to quiet the butterflies. When she'd shown pictures to John, this was the dress he'd reacted to—lavender, floor-length, sleeveless with a scoop neck.

"All these months and you still get nervous?" Winter teased. "You know he thinks you're gorgeous."

"It's still fun to remind him."

Winter grinned, slipping on her shoes. "That'll do it."

"What about you?" Valentine said. "You look like a movie star."

Despite her teasing, Winter had spent forever picking out a short cocktail dress of black lace. It fit as if it had been made for her. Still, she scoffed like Non-Fancy Winter.

"No guy wants a part of my drama right now. I'll stick to dancing like crazy, thank you very much."

Winter stepped up behind Asha, and Valentine followed.

Their new friend sat at her vanity, hair and makeup nearly finished. The red dress would come next. Right now, Valentine found it difficult to recall the fighter they trained with every day. All she saw was a princess.

Asha plucked uneasily at her new curls. "I'm not sure about this."

"Trust me, you look super hot," Winter said.

Asha shook her head. "It's so long since I've done this."

"I'm sure it's like riding a bike," Valentine said. "Or, whatever your equivalent of a bike is."

"You'll feel better in that dress," Winter said.

"It's so beautiful," Valentine said. "And Mal loves red."

Asha looked at her sharply in the mirror. "Why would that matter?"

"Oh, um . . ." Valentine stammered. *Nice going, Val.* "Just, uh, thinking out loud. He likes red, and really *any* guy would love that dress on you. I mean, I don't know if Mal is a typical guy, but—"

"He's not," Winter said.

"Okay, he's not. Then, um—"

"He's better."

Valentine and Asha both eyed Winter. She held up her hands in defense.

"Don't get me wrong, he's just my friend. But Mal Gilbert is better in one day than most guys are all year. That boy's special."

". . . Oh," Asha said.

"Plus, I think his tie is red, so you might sort of accidentally match," Valentine finished.

Asha gave a noncommittal nod before returning to preparations. Though she tried to hide it, her stoic mask was becoming less convincing as they got to know her. Which was how Valentine knew she was excited. *Maybe she's not made of steel like she pretends.*

Someone knocked on the door. "Valentine?"

"Come in, Dad."

Cracking the door open, Neil Gilbert poked his head into the room. "Hi, sweetie. Got a minute?"

"Um . . . ." She took a quick inventory—she only had to don her shoes to be ready. "Sure."

"We can finish somewhere else," Winter said.

"Don't worry about that, girls," Neil said. "We can talk in my room."

Valentine followed him to his room at the other end of the hall, next to the stairs. They stepped inside and he closed the door behind him. For a moment, he kept his hand the doorknob. Then, squaring his shoulders, he turned to face her.

Everyone is nervous tonight, she thought. Though he put on a smile, he couldn't hide it from her. To put him at ease, she reached out and touched the lapel of his suit.

"I like this. Is it new?"

"Oh. Yeah. Um, Callie helped me with . . ." He trailed off, his smile fading. Suddenly, he pulled her into an embrace. "You look beautiful. I hope John knows how lucky he is."

Pulling back to arm's length, she smiled at him expectantly. "Thank you, Dad. But . . . ?"

"Right." He let go of her and stood straighter. "I want you to know first. Before Malcolm or Oma, or even Callie. It concerns everyone, but . . . I wanted a moment with you."

Her brow furrowed. "Are you okay?"

"Ha!" He burst out, then reined himself back in. "Yeah, I'm fine. In fact, I'm great. Best I've been in a long time. That's why we're talking." He paused to take a long, slow breath. "Valentine, I'm in love with Callie. I haven't made any final decisions, but we make each other happy. If that continues . . . I'm going to ask her to marry me."

Valentine stared, feeling at once numb and kicked in the gut. Did he want her to say something? If she tried, nothing would come out.

"I know you've struggled, but I've seen you trying, and I want you to know how good that makes me feel." He stepped closer. "You're a wonderful girl, and Callie is wonderful, too. When you're feeling better about this, it would be great if you could be friends."

She had been struck by lightning. Now she was floating in the haze of someone else's weird dream. She managed to put on a brave smile, kiss her father on the cheek, and promise she would try.

On autopilot, she floated out of his room and down the stairs. *Water. I need water.* Turning, she floated into the kitchen and stopped dead. The haze around her evaporated.

Callie stood at the counter.

Her back to Valentine, she tapped on her phone screen with one hand while sipping a glass of red wine with the other. In a coral-colored evening gown, with sparkling gems at her ears and throat, she looked ready to walk a red carpet. Turning at the sound of footsteps, she caught sight of Valentine.

"Hi, Valentine," she said with a broad smile. "You look gorgeous."

"Oh, um . . . uh, thanks, I . . ."

No matter how hard she tried, words wouldn't connect into sentences. She stood there dumbfounded, caught in a loop of failure. Slowly, Callie's smile died.

She held up her hand. "It's okay. You don't have to do this. If you want to just go back to your friends . . . it's okay. I'm okay."

But she wasn't. Looking into her eyes, Valentine believed it this time—she was hurt. As Callie turned and picked up her wine glass, she seemed weary.

Valentine's heart sank. *Is this my life now?*

She wanted to go. Turn and run as fast and as far as possible. Because her father had fallen in love with a supervillain.

Or had he? Looking back on her experience with Callie de la Vega, Valentine couldn't point to even one real piece of evidence against her. So, was she really trusting some deep instinct about this woman, or was it a convenient reason to dismiss her?

There were other reasons to reject Callie. They'd lived in the back of Valentine's thoughts from the beginning. Real reasons. Human reasons. Reasons strong enough that they may have subtly fueled her suspicions.

Her dad was trying to be happy, and at least for now, Callie was his way to get there. *If there's even a one percent chance you're wrong about her, shouldn't you try? For him.*

When it came to family, maybe that was the only truth that mattered. So, with monumental effort, Valentine grabbed all her nebulous suspicions and shoved them to the back of her mind. If she focused on fixing the real stuff, maybe there was a chance this could work.

Staring at this exotic woman draped in glamour, Valentine felt it *click*. Before she knew it, she was speaking.

"You're so different from her."

Callie stiffened.

"Emily Gilbert was my mother, and my dad loved her so much. Even as a kid, I saw it. I knew that when I grew up, all I'd ever want is what they had." She paused, her chest tightening with emotion, then pressed ahead. "I really thought I'd gotten over it, and if he'd brought home someone just like her, I would have understood. But you . . . you're ball gowns where she was sundresses. Refined where she was simple. You're—"

She cut off. Those were enough, but she was stalling. She had to say the rest.

"I looked at you and thought, maybe he wasn't so happy with Mom after all. Maybe this is what he wanted all along. If it wasn't, then how could someone so different make him so happy?" She shook her head ruefully. "I blamed you for that. But now . . . I think maybe love doesn't work that way. Maybe just because you're what he wants now, it doesn't mean he wanted her any less. Maybe as your heart heals, it changes, and other things change with it."

Callie turned toward her, eyes glistening. Valentine clamped down on her own emotions. *Don't cry. Not now.* But she had to keep going.

"So, if you're who my dad needs now—if you make him happy—then shouldn't I try to love you, too?" She looked down. "I'm so sorry for how I've been. I hope I haven't ruined things. Please . . ." Her voice cracked and stuttered. ". . . please tell me I haven't—"

Then Callie was there, pulling her into an embrace. Valentine shuddered, sighing, overwhelmed with relief. With soft sobs and a teardrop on her shoulder, she realized Callie was crying for real now. Something inside her broke open in response. Burying her face in the crook of Callie's neck, she let loose a rush of tears.

"Thank you, Valentine," Callie said. "You're an incredible girl."

Valentine squeezed tighter. "Can we just start over?"

"I would love that."

They stood there for long moments, resting against each other in relief. There would still be difficult days ahead. Valentine still had her suspicions. But for the first time, in her heart she truly hoped she was wrong. If she was, then maybe one day they could be a family.

She blinked hard. "We're going to have to redo our makeup in the car."

They burst into laughter.

Pulling back to examine her, Callie brushed her thumbs under Valentine's eyes. "Worth it. Right?"

Valentine nodded. "Totally worth it."

"I feel like sitting for a minute before everyone's ready." Taking Valentine's arm, Callie led her toward the living room. "Maybe we could talk a little?"

"Yes," Valentine said, beaming.

Then they rounded the stairs and entered the living room, and her smile faded. Everyone sat there waiting. Everyone. Her family, her friends, everyone except Asha, who was probably still getting ready.

She felt her cheeks turn vermillion. "Oh."

CHAPTER 28

Malcolm bit the inside of his cheek so he wouldn't laugh. Seconds ago, Valentine and Callie had each been a blubbering mess when they came into the room. Apparently they hadn't realized everyone was just one room over.

Valentine shot him an alarmed, inquisitive glance. He nodded to indicate that, yes, everyone had just heard her embarrassing moment. Her shoulders fell.

"Hi, everyone," Callie said, eyes wide. "Uh, doesn't Valentine's dress look amazing?"

For a moment everyone was quiet. Even Neil seemed lost about the right thing to do here. Then Fred stood up.

"Yeah! Way to get your cry on, Val." Approaching, he held up both hands until they gave him high fives. "Nothin' brings ladies together like a few tears. Am I right?"

With everyone laughing now, the awkwardness broke. Neil hugged them both, after which Malcolm sidled up beside Valentine with a smile. She gave him a smile of her own—one unburdened from the weight she'd been carrying.

"We wouldn't be us without something dramatic happening today," he teased.

"The night's still young. Maybe it's your turn next," Valentine shot back with a devious grin.

Malcolm cocked his head. "Huh?"

Then he heard footsteps on the stairs. The last of them was about to arrive. Unconsciously, Malcolm straightened his red tie and readjusted his suit jacket. As the footsteps touched the floor, he turned to welcome Asha the warrior.

And saw Ashandara, Princess of Everwatch.

He exhaled sharply, words dying on his lips. She was clad in a floor-length gown of the deepest, richest red. A single strap clung to her right shoulder, shining with silvery accents. The line of silver continued down her right side, following her curves all the way to the floor. As she turned into the living room, tiny sparkles in the dress caught the light.

Her dark hair, normally pulled into a ponytail or a tight bun, now tumbled over her shoulders in gentle curls. He hadn't realized how long it was until now. From behind subtly smoky makeup, her ice blue eyes shined like crystals. She was always beautiful to Malcolm, but this . . .

It was more than just a veneer of finery. A buried part of Asha had reemerged. As the others caught sight of her and the compliments began to pour out, her smile lit up the room as if bathed in spotlights.

She was so breathtaking, Malcolm thought there should be sparkles floating in the air around her while a romantic song played in the background. He attempted to give a compliment, but found his mouth inexplicably dry. All he could do was stare.

As everyone headed for the door, he stood rooted. Only his eyes could move, and they could only follow her. Asha moved to join the group, then stopped and turned a sharp look on him. She narrowed her eyes, and a glimpse of the girl he knew reappeared.

He was caught and they both knew it. Cheeks heating, he turned away, but couldn't resist and glanced at her again. Her glare softened into a smile.

"Thank you," she whispered so only he could hear, then swept by him and out the door.

Malcolm noted then that she was carrying Valentine's duffle bag. Tyrathorn had brought something similar. Only the faint clink of metal hinted that they were bringing their armor. *Always ready.*

With every step toward the door, he repeated the promises he had made to himself. Yet, with visions of Asha swimming in his head, that voice was losing ground. *This is a test,* he told himself. Now, more than ever, he must cling to his convictions. He just had to get through tonight.

Just one night.

Malcolm had never seen anything so grandiose. The massive ballroom looked as if it had been pulled from the pages of *The Great Gatsby*, all art deco and plush furnishings and deep amber lighting. The glass ceiling revealed a thousand bright stars. Musicians sat at the far corner, playing everything from Glenn Miller classics to swing dance numbers to orchestral covers of pop songs. Dining tables surrounded the wooden dance floor in the center of the room.

A lavish buffet filled the corner adjacent to the band. Champagne flowed like water for more than five hundred guests—the elite high society of Emmett's Bluff and a dozen surrounding towns. Fred had reserved a special table beside the dance floor. After setting down their belongings, everyone scattered to the buffet.

Malcolm made himself choose lighter food. Fred would

probably drag everyone onto the dance floor, and he didn't want to feel sluggish. While the others lingered over the plethora of choices—Clive's eyes had bulged at the Dungeness crab, his favorite—Malcolm chose quickly and returned to their table.

As he prepared to take his first bite, the chair directly across from him slid back. With a sparkle and a swirl of red, Asha sat down, her plate only half full. Even her eating habits reflected a lifetime of discipline.

Malcolm paused with the fork halfway to his lips, and she paused halfway into her seat. With a quick scan of the table, she realized they were the only two occupying it. A guarded smile brushed her lips as she sat the rest of the way down. He forced himself to eat the grilled shrimp on his fork, taking far too long to chew while he figured out what to do next. *You'll have to talk at some point.*

"So, uh," he gestured at her plate. "Ever tried *uni?*"

"I have no idea what that is."

"Sea urchin. A lot of fancy restaurants serve it."

She spooned some into her mouth, looking up as she processed the unfamiliar flavor. Her expression bounced between approval and rejection.

"It tastes like the ocean."

"Ah. That's okay, I guess," Malcolm said, dying a little at the painful small talk. "If you like the ocean."

Asha took another bite, then turned her ice blue gaze on Malcolm. "May I ask you something?"

"Uh, sure."

"Weeks ago, when I tapped your cheek with my blade? It made you angry, but you didn't respond that way. Why?"

"Oh. Um," he fumbled, caught off guard. "Haven't really thought about it. I guess it felt condescending, sort of like an insult. But then I realized you were just teasing. My first reaction was wrong, so I let it go."

"Mm." Asha moved to ask another question, but then her thoughts seemed to turn inward.

Malcolm leaned forward. "Did I just fail some sort of test?"

She considered before answering. "There are some high-ranking Ember Guards—not all, but a few—who would say it's disrespectful to their power and position. They would want me reprimanded."

"Oh." Malcolm shrugged. "Well, I'm not ranked high in anything. I'm just me, you know? I can handle being teased."

Nodding, Asha focused on her plate. Was she hiding a smile?

Tyrathorn sat down next to her. In his sharkskin gray suit, the handsome young man was no doubt drawing many admiring eyes. Much like his sister, the royal blood had emerged as he donned something finer than jeans. A cross between confident swagger and regal poise.

The next hour passed by in a blur of good food and laughter. Occasionally some of them joined the crowd on the dance floor, returning with smiles and stories of bumping elbows with local celebrities.

Malcolm found contentment in his spot at the table, soaking up the festive atmosphere. Occasionally his gaze and Asha's would brush each other, sending a spark through his chest. He focused on ignoring that.

Then, in a quiet moment when dinner was finished and the plates had been cleared, when an air of relaxation had settled over the table like a soft, warm blanket, he felt Asha's attention on him fully. He turned to see her examining him, and gave her a questioning smile.

Her expression froze. "I . . . like your suit. It, um, fits you well."

Malcolm leaned back, caught off guard. "Th-thank you."

Peripherally, he noted that the music in the background had changed. The orchestra had taken a break, leaving only a young woman and her acoustic guitar. With a few strums, she began a light yet soulful ballad.

Callie shot from her chair, phone in hand. Staring at the screen, she bit her lip in consternation and rapidly tapped the screen.

"You okay?" Neil asked.

She looked at him as if just remembering he was there. "Work emergency. Sorry, everyone, I need to step out and make a phone call."

After squeezing Neil's shoulder, she melted into the crowd. Malcolm idly watched her go, wondering what type of work emergency a writer could experience. Then his eyes fell back on Asha and all other thoughts vanished.

She bit her lip, fidgeting with her spoon. Her eyes darted everywhere except to Malcolm. Then, without warning, she stood.

"Malcolm," she said, holding out her hand, "would you like to dance?"

The entire table fell silent. Malcolm sat thunderstruck, as if the whole room had darkened and a spotlight had lit up his chair. He realized he hadn't answered. *Move!* He shot to his feet.

"Yes. I would like that."

Accepting her hand, he followed her onto the dance floor as if floating into a dream. They came together, her off hand resting on his shoulder while Malcolm held her waist. His whole world shrank to impossibly blue eyes, a red dress, and her body so close to his.

Together they swayed to the music. The motion of her hips filled him with a buzzing sensation, as if every nerve in his body had come to life. *It's just a dance*, he told himself. *That's all*. But as they drew closer, as their eyes met without looking away, he found his resistance evaporating.

His lips quirked up in a smile.

Asha squinted. "What?"

"I thought warriors didn't dance."

She gave a coy shrug. "Maybe I don't feel like a warrior tonight." She looked ready to say more, but then her mouth snapped shut.

He studied her. "What is it?"

She almost looked away. Unconsciously he leaned closer, his voice falling to a whisper.

"Tell me."

She shook her head, pursing her lips tighter.

Malcolm gave her a knowing look, affectionate yet chiding. "You know, there's a weak spot in the whole 'bulletproof soldier' thing. If it's a shield, then it works both ways. It keeps people at a distance. It may be the safe way to live, but . . . I'm not sure it's the happy one."

"Just me?" Asha mirrored his expression. "I see your shield, too, Malcolm Gilbert. It goes up when . . . whenever you look at me." Her hand slid up from his shoulder, resting on the back of his neck. "I wonder, is it to keep others out? Or to keep yourself in?"

Now it was Malcolm's gaze that turned inward, focusing on his conviction. On the truth behind it—something he had never spoken aloud, not even to Valentine. Yet somehow Asha had seen it. Before he could stop himself, he was speaking.

"After what happened last year—after I saw what I could

do—there was this moment. Something happened. Not a big thing, but the way I felt, I knew the truth right then. I knew I couldn't live the same life most people did. And I knew everything that meant. So I *couldn't* let someone in." He shook his head. "Then you fell out of the sky, and before I knew it, I . . ."

Asha leaned in, focusing all of her crystal blue attention on him. Those eyes held him captive, peeling away his armor. "You what?"

Pulling gently at the back of his neck, she drew him so close that their noses almost touched.

"Tell me," she whispered, almost desperate.

Flashes appeared in the night sky above them. They looked up in alarm as fireworks painted the glass ceiling and the dance floor below, drawing *oohs* and *aahs* from the crowd.

While the bursts of light continued, they focused back on each other. To Malcolm's delight—and dismay—the distraction had done nothing to break the spell. They fell toward each other inch by inch, and he found himself wanting nothing more in his world than to feel her lips on his. *Maybe just once,* his intoxicated mind said. *Just once, that's all I—*

He felt a *shift*.

Pulling back in alarm, Malcolm scanned the room. Asha noted the change and her hand tightened around his.

"What is it?"

Another *shift* occurred, this one close by. As he swung left, a *shift* occurred to his right. He spun himself and Asha to find the source, and yet another *shift* occurred behind him. Then a torrent of *shifts* assaulted his Chronauri senses. His insides went cold.

Asha gave him a shake. "Malcolm, what—?"

"Get your bag," he said. "Now."

The glass ceiling exploded.

Shocked screams filled the air as the crowd turned from celebratory to panicked. Ducking away from the glass, Malcolm and Asha rushed back to their table. She dove underneath to retrieve the duffel bag.

"Everyone okay?" Clive called.

"What is going on?" Neil shouted.

Malcolm thought he knew. Then, as the first para-nexus dropped through the broken ceiling, he knew for certain. A sinking dread gripped him.

The Black Tempest had arrived.

CHAPTER 29

The ballroom's main doors had been barricaded. The guests were fish in a barrel, trapped with para-nexus swarms.

"Your armor!" Malcolm called.

"No time!" Asha twisted her nexus free of the armor and slapped it against her chest. The device sprouted tiny metallic appendages that latched onto her dress and the skin underneath. She winced, then drew her *qamas*.

Beside her, Tyrathorn whipped off his jacket and tie and mirrored her with his own nexus. "We need a plan of attack."

"A plan of *defense* for now," Malcolm said. "Have to destroy those things before—"

He cut off as light flashed across the room and the first ice pillar appeared. Another appeared near the bar, then two more on the dance floor. As the crowd saw the glittering spires form, their panic became more desperate. They had all seen the news reports.

The Corvonians took in the sight with grim determination. Tyrathorn looked to Malcolm.

"A dual strategy, then."

Asha pointed to John, Fred, and Winter. "You three, destroy every para-nexus you can. Let nothing past you."

"You got it," Fred said.

Opening Tyrathorn's bag, Fred drew out three gear belts. He and John tossed away their jackets and strapped on the belts.

Winter fastened hers over her cocktail dress, then reached down to remove her stiletto shoes. After a quick glance at the shards of glass littering the floor, though, she snapped the heels off instead.

"Use your Accelerator rings." John slipped a black metal band over his finger. "Knock those things from the sky."

After ripping the thick legs from a nearby table, they waded into the fray, swinging the legs like baseball bats. Clangs and sparks filled the air wherever they walked. Already they were fighting a rising tide—dozens of ice pillars dotted the ballroom.

Meanwhile, Malcolm shed his jacket to reveal the nexus strapped to his forearm, with John and Clive's Lance right beside it. Valentine came to his side, fastening hers as well.

"Callie leaves, and five minutes later we get attacked?" she said.

"I thought you were getting past that."

She gave him a level look. "I was. But tell me you don't find that convenient."

Malcolm had to admit it was at least curious. Still, they needed to focus.

"Well, if we see the Frost Hammer, maybe you can ask for her name."

"Maybe I will." Valentine peered up at the shattered ceiling. "They're close. I felt those *shifts*. So, what are they waiting for?"

"If we destroy enough of these, I bet we'll draw them out."

"Valentine? Malcolm?"

The twins turned at their father's quivering voice. Kneeling behind the table, Neil Gilbert regarded them with confusion.

"What's happening?" their dad asked.

Malcolm stopped short, at a loss for words. What must his dad be feeling at seeing his children—his perfectly normal children—preparing to fight? There would have to be hard conversations later.

Oma Grace clutched Neil's shoulder. "Ask questions later, son."

"We'll look after 'em, don't worry," Clive told the twins. He pulled two Accelerator rings from his pocket and gave one to Oma Grace. "Do what you gotta do."

Relieved, Malcolm nodded his thanks.

"We'll explain everything later," Valentine said as they moved to join the Corvonians.

"Be careful among the civilians," Tyrathorn admonished. "Wipe out these machines and the enemy may present themselves. Attack!"

They split into family groups and headed in opposite directions. Malcolm opened his nexus and Time rushed in at his beckoning.

"Arrows," Valentine said.

With a flick of her wrist, she sent a dozen fire arrows into the air. Each found its mark, and a dozen devices burst to flaming bits. Malcolm followed with his own, made of ice.

Despite the danger, Valentine grinned. "Awesome."

They stood back-to-back, an eye of power inside the storm. Wave after wave of para-nexuses fell before them.

Peripherally, Malcolm noticed John, Winter, and Fred shielding groups of party guests, working feverishly to smash every para-nexus that came near.

In a far corner, entire waves had targeted Asha. *Probably exactly what she wanted.* All he saw were streaks of red, flashes of gray, and para-nexus pieces falling around her like rain.

Tyrathorn stalked around the room, hunting swarms like prey. After trapping them in hollow shells of ice, he ignited fireballs inside to melt each device while protecting bystanders.

Malcolm shook his head. They were helping, but not enough. If the room were empty, they could cut loose and this battle would last five minutes. But they had people to think about, and they had to be precise. Which meant they couldn't stop everything, and ice pillars were still appearing.

"We have to attack the source," he said. "And why haven't they—?"

The main doors flew off their hinges and a dozen rogue Chronauri rushed in. A dozen more dropped through the ceiling, surrounding the twins on the dance floor.

"You had to ask," Valentine said.

Malcolm braced for attack. But instead they turned away from the twins and dove into the crowd, roughly catching guests one by one and slapping a para-nexus to their chest.

In that moment, Malcolm saw the truth. *This isn't a test anymore. It's an invasion.*

Which meant they couldn't hold back anymore. Valentine had apparently reached the same conclusion—her corona flared red as she drank in a burst of energy. Malcolm's flared blue as he did the same.

"Be careful," Valentine said.

"No promises," he replied. With a grim smile, he set a rogue Chronauri in his sights and prepared to unleash frozen fury.

Then everything went wrong.

A deep *thrum* passed through everything. The floor, the

walls, Malcolm's teeth, everything vibrated to something deeper than mere sound.

Time ripped from his grasp. He loosed a frustrated cry as distortion waves slammed them to the floor. His heart sank—they still weren't strong enough to resist.

Tables and chairs and people were cast aside as their friends were dragged to the dance floor, chained by the same force. They struggled fiercely and futilely, spitting curses.

"Val," Malcolm whispered. "The Lance!"

To his relief, the device still pulsed quietly in his senses, its stored Time waiting to be unleashed. Waiting to punch through the temporal blockade around them. All he had to do was will it to open like a nexus.

The Frost Hammer floated through the ceiling on a cushion of distortion waves. Two minions floated down beside her, carrying a black and copper machine as tall as a man and twice as wide.

With the enemy in sight, the twins shared a quick look. Valentine's whole body tensed as she gave Malcolm a single nod. They were as ready as they were ever going to be.

He braced himself. "Now!"

Malcolm threw open the Lance. Time burst out of it like a missile, focused energy aimed right at the distortions holding them hostage. His hopes swelled as the two opposing forces collided.

Then those hopes died as his attack unraveled like loose thread, dissipating to nothing. Half a second later, Valentine's did the same and she released a cry of despair.

A complete failure. How could they have gotten it so wrong? How was the Frost Hammer really doing this?

The Frost Hammer didn't even appear to notice. Touching down, she turned away from them and regarded her minions. "Your task is not finished. Continue."

They resumed capturing the screaming party guests. With each crackle of a new ice pillar, Malcolm felt a punch to the gut. Each was another innocent they had failed to protect. Yet, through the anguish of failure, he still couldn't help wondering . . .

Where is the Black Tempest? If their endgame has started, why is he still in the shadows?

The Frost Hammer pointed at a table nearby. Her minions flung it aside to reveal Malcolm's father. His grandmother. Clive. *Where's Callie?* The minions dragged them toward the enemy and stood them up.

The punch to the gut became an arrow in Malcolm's heart. He tried to reach out, tried to find words to beg for his family's safety. For them, he would beg. He didn't care.

The Frost Hammer tapped a series of commands on her machine. With a beep, the top irised open and a para-nexus flew out, then another, then two more. They buzzed forward and latched onto his family's chests, and in a blink they were frozen in pillars of ice.

Malcolm's friends cried out challenges to their enemy. He fought down the panic and the rage that threatened to overwhelm him. If they were going to survive, he needed a clear head.

Soon the rogue Chronauri finished their work. All five hundred party guests were now ice-bound. Malcolm clenched his jaw, silently promising his family that it would not end here.

Though he couldn't see her face, the Frost Hammer radiated smug satisfaction. "No room left for mercy. Tonight it begins, and soon every soul in this town will power our army."

"That's your plan?" someone asked. Malcolm thought it was John.

The Frost Hammer nodded.

"Then you," John said, "are a moron."

Valentine closed her eyes, likely praying that her boyfriend wasn't about to die.

"We examined your devices," John continued. "They'll suck their hosts dry in months at most. Very soon, you will lose your army."

The Frost Hammer scoffed. "And when these cattle are spent, we will find another inconsequential town in a meaningless corner of history. There we will create the next wave. This will continue until Everwatch is conquered."

Now Malcolm grasped the full weight of their trouble. If they failed here, not only would Emmett's Bluff fall—other towns would follow. Countless masses sacrificed for a slave army. And if Everwatch fell, the entire timeline was at risk. Once again, he fought a rising tide of panic and despair.

We'll find a way to beat them. We have to.

But the Frost Hammer was not finished.

"Now that our moment has arrived, the need for secrecy has ended."

Reaching up to her helmet, she pressed a small button on the jawline. Malcolm tensed—they were about to see the Frost Hammer's face. He gave a silent prayer that Valentine would be wrong, but had the sinking suspicion that she would be right. Whatever happened, they would deal with it. He just hoped their father wouldn't be hurt too much in the process.

The helmet separated into pieces, then folded and slid into a compartment behind her neck. As it retracted, luxurious chestnut brown hair spilled over her shoulders.

Malcolm nearly choked.

"What the . . ." Valentine said. "Madame LaChance?"

Malcolm shook his head in denial. But this was no illusion. Their French teacher stood there in jagged black armor, smirking as she prepared to destroy them and everyone they loved.

"Actually, I prefer my real name," she said. "You may call me Charlotte Corday."

Malcolm could only whisper. "The Assassin of Marat?"

She nodded, looking pleased.

"You're not Callie," Valentine said in shock, more to herself than anyone.

She scoffed. "Your father's woman? She has been captured."

"Dude!" Fred shouted. "Is *anyone* at our school actually just a teacher?"

Malcolm flipped through every shred of knowledge he'd learned about the French Revolution. Charlotte Corday had assassinated a radical political figure to save her country. On being sentenced to death, she had expressed no regret, declaring that she would have killed many more to help her people. And yet . . .

"Someone got you out! Did another woman die in your place?"

"Those history books are lies!" she spat. "About why I killed Marat, and how. What I did, I did to remove his evil from the world, and it warped Time so strongly that it drew the Black Tempest's attention. He found me, and I joined his cause. A greater cause."

She stalked back and forth, like a panther deciding which prey to devour first. As her little speech ended, she stopped above Tyrathorn, who stared up at her with unbridled hatred.

"And now, we lack only one thing before beginning. The key to everything."

Curling her fingers, Corday lifted Tyrathorn onto his feet. She stepped closer and Malcolm tensed, expecting a killing blow. The Black Tempest would want someone so powerful out of the way. He bit his lip to keep from crying out.

Corday opened her hand, and the distortion waves around Tyrathorn disappeared. Malcolm felt a *shift* as Tyrathorn reached tentatively through his nexus. Gazing up at him, Corday's expression changed from aggression . . . to devotion.

Bowing her head, she dropped to one knee. "All is ready, my Lord Tempest. We await your command."

CHAPTER 30

Shock hit Malcolm like a mountain. *No. It can't be.* Yet, how much did they really know about Tyrathorn Corvonian? Could they have been so thoroughly fooled?

Tyrathorn looked like a breeze could blow him off his feet. Swaying as if in a daze, he shook his head vehemently.

"You are lying. I am a prince of Everwatch, a High Protector of the Ember Guard!"

Corday rose, brow furrowed. "The need for pretense is over, my lord. We must move forward. Your covert mission has failed, and I am sorry. But we both knew it would be difficult to turn the Gilbert twins to our side."

What?!

Glaring at Tyrathorn, Valentine gave voice to Malcolm's thoughts. "We were your mission? You knew about us? How?"

Corday regarded Valentine with mock pity. With a flick of her wrist, she lifted everyone onto their feet. Their bonds disappeared, and she gestured for each to be flanked by two minions.

"Did you believe we chose this town at random? Why take just any place when there was a chance to turn two powerful Chronauri in the process?"

"That's the reason," Malcolm said, the truth exploding in his mind. "When we first met in the alley, you didn't kill us. When you had us beaten at the warehouses, you retreated. It was—"

"—because you planned it that way," Valentine said, astonished. "It wasn't about mercy in the alley, and you weren't scared of Thorn. You were following a plan with him."

"A plan that must now be abandoned," Corday replied, her eyes locked on Tyrathorn. "It has failed, and now they must be dealt with."

"But, I remember . . . I . . . I can't . . . can I . . . ?" Tyrathorn swallowed hard, his eyes darting feverishly as if searching for something he couldn't find. "My memories, my dreams . . ."

Corday's face suddenly went slack. Rushing to Tyrathorn's side, she examined his temple. There was still a bruise where his skull had been cracked. She prodded at his flank, where he'd been cleaved open when they found him. Finally, she stared deep into his eyes as if searching for something.

With a stunned gasp, she fell back a step.

"You don't remember," she breathed. "All our work. The creation of the Black Tempest. You . . ." Her faced twisted with rage. Whirling on Asha, she pointed an accusing finger. "You!"

Asha glared back in defiance.

Corday continued, "That night, when you attacked us at the Empyrean Bridge. *You* did this to him! Have you been filling his head with lies ever since?"

Malcolm's jaw dropped. Had Asha known all along?

"No," Tyrathorn kept repeating. "No. No, I'm not. I can't be."

"Asha," Valentine said. "Tell me it's not true."

"Is it?" Tyrathorn pleaded, his voice trembling. "Asha. My injuries at the bridge. Did you . . . ?"

He stared at his sister in desperation, as if barely holding on to his own sanity. She wouldn't meet his eyes, and her silence dragged out for too long, until they all knew the truth.

Tyrathorn's gaze hardened. "Why would you attack your own brother?"

Asha's brave front melted. A sob burst from her chest. Tears began to fall, and she spoke as if every word broke her heart.

"Because you are the Black Tempest, Thorn. Because when I discovered where you were going, I went there to kill you. Because it was the only way to keep Everwatch safe!" Her voice cracked as she finally looked at her brother. "But after we fell through the portal . . . you said my name and responded to yours. You spoke like before. I looked into your eyes and saw my brother again—not the monster you had become. So I tried to destroy the Black Tempest *and* save my brother. Please, Thorn, I never wanted to lie!"

Tyrathorn trembled. Breathing hard, his gaze turned inward. "I am the Black Tempest?"

With those words, a violent spasm shook his body. He gasped and groaned, jerking as if an invisible foe was assaulting him. Gritting his teeth, he clutched his temples. Malcolm felt a series of *shifts* as power sputtered and raced through Tyrathorn.

"The Guard, the Watchers . . . all those soldiers . . . dead from ice, from *my* ice. Travels through Time . . . I-I see it, I see the . . ." His eyes widened in horror. "Oh, Garris, my brother! Garris, I . . ."

Finally, Malcolm understood. With the revelation of Tyrathorn's true self, the floodgates of memory had opened. All at once he was remembering what he was—the villain that he himself despised. The villain that his injured mind had re-membered as a phantom, a specter of destruction. A monster.

Tears streamed down Tyrathorn's face. Lifting his hands,

he regarded them now as if they were foreign things. Then Malcolm felt another *shift*, and his friend's corona turned blue.

Intense cold radiated from Tyrathorn's hands, washing over his body in waves. The cold began to solidify into ice, layers on layers of it sculpting over his body. As they hardened, their edges turned jagged and sharp. Beautiful plates of ice melded together in one harmonious form, turning as black as midnight. Tyrathorn stared down at himself in horror.

"I am the Black Tempest."

This time it wasn't a question.

Then his body lurched in revulsion. His armor shattered and rained to the ground in pieces. Chest heaving, he fell to his knees and looked up to the sky.

"What have I done?"

CHAPTER 31

Everwatch, Three Years Ago

The throne room doors burst open with a *boom.* Tyrathorn stumbled through, scorched and bleeding, his face contorted with rage.

"FATHER!" he shouted.

King Jerrik stood by his throne on the dais, conversing with Queen Meliora and their oldest son, Garris. As Tyrathorn entered, their heads whipped toward the door in alarm. Even though he was limping, he stalked toward his family as fast as he could.

Before he could reach the steps up to the dais, an Ember Guard appeared at his side. Placing a gentle hand on Tyrathorn's shoulder, he presented a friendly smile.

"Prince Tyrathorn, allow me to help you, please. At least until—"

Tyrathorn grabbed his hand and twisted. The Ember Guard cried out in pain. A wave of deepest cold enveloped him, and Tyrathorn punched him full force in the chest. Armor shattered with a deafening crack. His feet flew out from under him, and he dropped onto his back with a bone-shaking thud.

"Son, calm yourself!" his mother commanded.

His family came to the edge of the dais. In their eyes he saw fear and confusion, as if a wild animal had charged into the Eon Palace.

"Attacking a High Protector?" his father, King Jerrik, said. "If you were anyone else, you would be in chains. Explain your—"

"Wieluń, Poland, September 1939. They bombed it to nothing. Hundreds are dead!"

"You tried to save them?" Meliora asked.

"You were commanded not to interfere," Jerrik said.

Tyrathorn pointed accusingly. "And you let them die, knowing we could have prevented it!"

"Thorn, please," Garris said, his tone conciliatory. "What would you have us do? Save every innocent life throughout history? It is not possible, and if we tried—if we bent history to our own will—we would be as guilty as the rogues we fight against."

"Yes. Above all, we protect the timeline," Jerrik said. "And we have saved lives along the way. You know this."

"And how many more could you save without your precious rules to hide behind?"

Meliora pursed her lips. "And how might the timeline be corrupted, were we to act so rashly? Even we could not predict it."

"I know you made friends in that town," his father said. "And I am sorry. But we cannot decide who lives and who dies, Tyrathorn. We are not gods."

"Gods?" Tyrathorn said, fuming. "You are not even a man."

The king's jaw tightened and his fists clenched. Then, on the verge of lashing out, he seemed to seize control of himself. With great effort his expression calmed, and the worry that was hidden underneath rose to the surface.

"I see your path through Time twisting, my son. You were

not always so angry. But where once I saw joy in your future, I now glimpse a deep shadow. You walk a dangerous road—one I do not know how to bring you back from."

"Please listen, *atali*," his mother said, wringing her hands.

Atali—she'd called him that as a child, always with affection.

Slowly, Garris stepped toward him. "I know your heart, Thorn. How it aches for all those we cannot save. Mine does as well. But we mustn't let that pain blind us."

"No, Garris," Tyrathorn said. "It has allowed me to *see*. What we do for the timeline is a paltry bandage. The people of history need so much more."

Images of Wieluń rose up in his mind. Memories of fire, of that earsplitting roar . . . and then after, the screams.

Shaking his head, Tyrathorn opened his nexus and drank in power. Coils of slowed Time radiated from him. The stones at his feet frosted over with a crackle, spreading up the steps to the dais. An intricately beautiful broadsword formed in his grip. Only now, as it froze to polished completion, the ice turned black.

"If you will not help them . . ."

Raising the weapon, he approached the first step and plunged the blade through the polished stones. They split with a heavy *crack*. A spiderweb of fractures radiated from the sword as he drove it in halfway to the hilt. In cold fury he glared up at his family.

". . . I will find a way to do it myself."

Protests and questions and pleadings peppered him from all sides. But he couldn't let their cowardice matter anymore. Ignoring them, he spun and stormed from the throne room.

Through the grand entry hall he stalked, and then out the main doors to the grounds of the Eon Palace. It was a beautiful sunny day with just a hint of chill in the air, yet Tyrathorn registered nothing except the storm raging inside.

Until a small young girl appeared at his side.

"Are you all right?" she said. "I could hear the yelling from here."

Short black hair tossed over her shoulder as she gazed up at him. As always, she twirled daggers between her fingers like they were children's toys. Practicing dexterity, just as he'd taught her. Despite his rage, Tyrathorn felt a spark of pride.

He worked to keep the anger from his voice. "Nothing you need worry about."

With a casual flick, she tossed both daggers in the air and caught them with the opposite hands. "Want to spar? I'll let you use my favorite blade."

"Not now, thank you. I must go, and you must stay here."

"Where are you going?"

His steps faltered. ". . . I do not know."

"Oh. For how long?"

He shook his head.

"When will you be—?"

"I do not know, Ashandara!"

His sister studied the ground, trying to hide her hurt. When she spoke, her voice was subdued.

"I . . . I'll miss you."

Tyrathorn stopped, pierced to the core. Gazing down at her, he suddenly felt as lost as he did furious. With a sigh, he sank to his knees and looked her in the eye.

"And I will miss you. But there are people who need saving—so many people—and I must find a way to help them."

Asha brightened, flourishing her blades. "We can help!"

He smiled sadly. "Our parents do not approve, so I must go

on my own. You are young, but one day you may choose your own path as well."

She gave a puzzled frown. "Then who's going to help you?"

In recent months he had wondered the same thing. Though he had never been sure why, that question had driven him to study historical records of multiple eras like never before. But, instead of studying kingdoms, he had studied people.

Only now, at the verge of embarking on this insane quest, did he realize what he had been searching for. Kindred spirits. Those who might join this grand rescue he envisioned. Those who weren't afraid of the tide even when it flowed against them.

Just recently, he may have found a place to start. A young woman who made a name for herself during the French Revolution.

Yes. She might prove to be a powerful ally.

CHAPTER 32

Present Day

The sound of Tyrathorn's sobs filled the vast room.

Malcolm watched him with warring feelings of pity and revulsion. Here was the villain they had feared, and in this moment he was so small. He was surprised to find he believed Tyrathorn's struggle with his identity. Maybe there was hope in that.

"What have I done?" he said again, as if pleading with the universe.

The Frost Hammer studied Tyrathorn, her expression unreadable. Malcolm prepared himself for her fury. Based on what history said about Charlotte Corday, she didn't seem the type to give up easily.

She shocked him by kneeling, too, putting her face on a level with Tyrathorn's. Her hard eyes softened, and she reached out to cradle his face.

"What you have done," she said, "is what few ever have the courage to do. As we worked together to save humanity, we realized together that they are unable to guide themselves.

So you must do it for them. You must be the compass they so desperately need."

There it was—the true reason Charlotte Corday was so dangerous. Studying the two of them together, Malcolm could see it now. It wasn't her seemingly invincible command over gravity. It was the manipulations—deft and subtle and performed so masterfully that the object of them would never see it. Never realize. Until suddenly they woke up years down the road to find they'd been swallowed by shadow.

Tyrathorn shook his head. "No! That is exactly what the Chrona's adversaries intended."

"Yes, and they were right! Now the Chrona's influence is slipping—you have seen it, as I have. Someone must save humanity from itself, Thorn. Who else is there?" She poked the nexus on his chest. "Everwatch? They hide in their great city, content to place bandages on a dying timeline."

"So, you would have me start by sacrificing these people? These three years, Charlotte, you have been the closest I had to family. Tell me, from your heart, how such evil can lead to good."

Pursing her lips, she looked away. For a moment, she appeared almost as lost as Tyrathorn. But when she turned back, her eyes had hardened.

"Power is not free, my lord," she stated. "Not even the power to do good. If we would save history, then we must have the full power of Everwatch behind us. That is what drove you to this revolution. No others would do what is necessary, so the burden falls to us. To you."

Tyrathorn's whole body heaved, as if it were a struggle just to pull in the air. *I know how he feels.* Malcolm had nearly gone numb, unable to process everything at once.

Still the battle raged inside Tyrathorn. Malcolm could see it in the twitch of his muscles. There were two Tyrathorns now—the idealistic prince and the unstoppable villain. He spoke under his breath, shaking his head as if different voices inside him were wrestling for control.

Malcolm wracked his brain for a plan for if they were forced to face the Black Tempest. Tyrathorn's psyche teetered on the edge of a knife blade, threatening to fall in either direction. Anything, even the slightest word, could push him in one direction.

That's when it struck Malcolm. *We've just been standing here watching! Corday's been drilling her voice into his head. He needs to hear from friends before it's too late.*

"Thorn."

He stopped short as Tyrathorn turned to look at him, realizing he had no clue what to say. What could he say that would make a difference?

"What you've done with us—I know it wasn't an act. In your heart, you know what's right. And this," he nodded at the ice pillars, "is not it. When you think about good and bad, it doesn't really matter what you remember, does it?"

"Or who you were before this moment," Valentine added.

"You will be silent," Corday commanded.

"The Tyrathorn I know—he's my friend," Malcolm pushed on. "It doesn't matter if he's an old version of you if he's the *right* version."

Corday stood, taking a step toward the twins. "I have warned—"

Malcolm raised his voice. "Don't you see how that injury was a gift? It didn't make you forget who you are—it let you remember. You're not a monster." He paused to stress each word. "You're. A. Good. Man."

Snarling, Corday pointed at Malcolm. A red orb of energy appeared in her palm. "You will not keep him from his destiny!"

Tyrathorn knocked her arm skyward, sending the orb up through the shattered ceiling. Malcolm blew out a relieved breath.

"I cannot see the way ahead, Charlotte," he said, grimacing. "I no longer trust myself. But here among these people, I have seen kindness. Goodness. Bravery. Faith in people."

He squeezed her arm now, in an almost pleading way. Turning, he gestured to the twins.

"In them, I see all that I once aspired to be," he continued, his voice finding its old strength. "And I wish to be that again. I see it now—we were wrong. We must find another way."

Releasing her arm, he stepped back and addressed the army of rogue Chronauri. His army.

"But first we must dismantle this plan, release these people, and I will submit myself to the authority of Everwatch. I have committed wrongs—so many wrongs—and I must begin by paying for them." He paused, shaking his head. "I am sorry to have led you all astray. Please, I beg you . . . join me once more. Follow me into the light."

Corday stared at him, her face a mask of shock. Of betrayal. For a long moment, not a single person stirred.

Then one of them did.

A rogue Chronauri stepped forward, gaining confidence as he approached Tyrathorn. Though young and small, he moved with the confidence of someone possessing power. He stopped in front of Tyrathorn, looked him up and down, then nodded.

"I will join you, Lord Tempest."

Tyrathorn broke into a warm smile. "That is no longer who I am, my friend. The Black Tempest is dead." He offered his hand. "From now on, I hope you will know me as a better man."

The minion held out his own hand, ready to accept Tyrathorn's friendship.

But before their hands could touch, Malcolm felt a strange warping in the flow of Time. Not a *shift,* but a sudden distortion. Then Corday raised her hands.

"No!" she screamed.

Concentrated distortion waves shot from her hands and pierced the minion through. He dropped to the floor and didn't move again. Tyrathorn whirled on her.

"Charlotte, why?!"

"All that we have worked for, all that we have done—I will not let your weakness destroy it!" Pointing at him, she charged two red energy bombs. "I will not leave history in the hands of evil men!"

Tyrathorn rose to his full height, causing a massive *shift* as a flood of Time poured through his nexus.

"Will you attack your commander now?" A blazing ring of fire burst to life around him. "I am a Fifth-*sev* Chronauri, a High Protector of the Ember Guard, and a prince of Everwatch. Before, I asked for your allegiance. Now I am not asking. Stand down."

For a tense moment, they faced off, power versus power, the air trembling between them. Then, looking down, Corday released her energy and lowered her hands in surrender.

"Swear allegiance," Tyrathorn commanded. "Stay by my side and see this through."

Face downcast, Corday's shoulders began to shake. Softly at first, the shaking quickly grew until they were bouncing up and down. Malcolm began to let himself relax. *He did it.*

But she wasn't crying.

Her laughter grew louder, dripping with bitterness. Intense waves of distortion poured from her body. Malcolm tried to reach through his nexus, but met a brick wall once again.

Corday's distortions seized Tyrathorn. With a surprised grunt, his body jerked as flame and ice disappeared. He stared wide-eyed as Corday forced him to his knees. Malcolm gaped at the spectacle. *How could she be stronger than Thorn?!*

"Impossible!" Tyrathorn cried. "You are not Fifth-*sev!*"

"Oh, My Lord Tempest," she mocked, gesturing to Asha. "I am no more a Chronauri than this puny girl."

What could that mean? Malcolm was not alone in his confusion. Tyrathorn stared up at her with the question in his eyes.

"Did you really think that Time is the only force at work in the universe?" she continued. "You Chronauri are so impressed with your own power, you never stopped to look for more."

"Gravity!" Valentine blurted. All eyes turned in her direction. "Gravity can distort the flow of Time. That's how you block our powers! That's how you appear Chronauri. Because when you manipulate gravity, it warps Time, too. I'm betting your armor even converts gravity into those energy bombs."

Corday regarded Valentine with a glimmer of respect. "There may have been hope for you, had you joined us."

Malcolm's mind reeled. The idea of Chronauri had been strange enough. Now there were gravity manipulators out there, too? At least it explained why her power felt so different. Why she dominated them so easily.

"You knew you were stronger from the start," Malcolm said, shaking his head. "All along, you've been waiting for your moment."

"No. I was content to follow," Corday said. "Until there was a reason not to."

Tyrathorn squared his shoulders. "Will your dark purpose start with me, then?"

She circled him, tracing her fingers along his jawline. "Of course not, my love. I have something else in mind for any Chronauri who stands against me." She circled behind Tyrathorn now, dragging her fingers through his hair, and bent to speak in his ear.

As she leaned down, Malcolm caught a flicker of movement over her shoulder. Behind Corday's back, Asha's disposition had changed. The tears had stopped, and in their place Malcolm saw white-hot rage. Malcolm tried to catch her eye. What could she be thinking of—?

Asha shouted in defiance, and her nexus blazed to life.

What? Malcolm gaped.

Throwing back her elbow, she shattered her first guard's nose. The woman fell to her knees with a cry, clutching her face.

Of course! Malcolm realized. Corday was blocking everyone from accessing Time through their nexus. But Asha was her own power source. Short of destroying her nexus, there was no way to block that.

The second guard slashed at her with his serrated knife. Asha dodged and then flung herself onto him. As he fell backward, there was an audible crack and he dropped to the floor in a heap. She somersaulted back to her feet.

Asha had struck like a coiled snake, almost too quickly to follow. Which meant Corday hadn't had time to react. Charging,

Asha leapt toward her enemy and slammed both feet into her chest.

Corday flew, smashing through the door to a smaller banquet room. Racing after her, Asha leapt through the hole and disappeared inside.

The gravity distortions unraveled and Malcolm felt the shackles over his nexus disappear. Time rushed into him. As his corona glowed, he turned and locked eyes with one of his guards.

"Oh." The guard stepped back. "Crap."

The room exploded into chaos.

Asha barreled through the doorway, kicking Corday hard in the chin before she could recover. As the woman tumbled across the small room, Asha held up her hands. Her *qamas* spun through the doorway and into her waiting grip.

Corday stood and cracked her neck, studying Asha like a predator deciding how to devour her. With a wicked grin, she made a slight gesture. Suddenly, up was no longer up, and down was no longer down.

The room spun and Asha crashed to the floor. Leaping up again, she prepared to strike . . . then stopped, realizing too late that she wasn't standing on the floor. She was standing on the wall.

Corday gestured again. Gravity reverted to normal and Asha fell off the wall. The instant she hit the floor, Corday reversed gravity's orientation and Asha smashed into the ceiling.

Gravity reverted again, and again Asha hit the floor. Before she could stand, Corday's distortion waves grabbed her by the arms and legs. She found herself hoisted into the air and held immobile.

"I could tear you to quarters, little one," Corday said. "I

spent so long pretending to be one of you. Hiding what I can do. Now you see my true self."

As if to punctuate her threat, the distortions tightened around Asha's limbs and pulled in opposite directions. She gritted her teeth, refusing to cry out from the pain even as gravity overwhelmed her body.

Just as her joints began to pop, the pressure disappeared and she dropped. The Frost Hammer drew a length of black and silver metal.

"But killing you this way will be so much more satisfying."

With a flick of her wrist, gleaming blades extended from each end. Grinning, she beckoned Asha forward.

Asha met her with a hailstorm of attacks, spinning and leaping, striking from every direction. Corday's movements were impossibly strong but slower. She relied on her power, and even though Asha landed strike after strike, her foe's armor held strong.

I won't stop, and she won't budge. Asha dodged, barely spinning away as Corday sliced a table in half. *So I'll have to play dirty.*

Asha threw a wild swing that brought her too close, then widened her eyes as if realizing the mistake. Corday took the bait and struck at her face.

And overextended herself just enough. Dropping to a crouch, Asha leapt into a backflip and kicked the weapon from Corday's hands. It flew away and clattered to the floor.

Asha's blade glowed as she sliced from Corday's chin to her eyebrow. The woman fell back with a cry, clutching her face. The cut had come within a half-inch of her eye.

Corday's arrogance crumbled into fury. The floor beneath her trembled, and she stalked forward with death in her eyes.

Asha became a tornado of sizzling steel. Corday fought with fists now, trusting fully in her armor to protect her.

To Asha's dismay, it worked. She drove her nexus to the ragged edge, surging more power into the *qamas,* and still she could not pierce the armor. Mid-strike, she changed directions and struck at her enemy's eyes.

Corday slapped the *qamas* aside. Hands wrapped in distortion waves, she punched Asha hard in the flank once, then twice. Gravitational force slammed through Asha and she stifled a groan as her ribs cracked.

She struck with her right blade. Corday grabbed her wrist like a vise and delivered a vicious overhead chop. Asha cried out as her forearm snapped. The weapon dropped from her grip.

She fell, knees turning to water. Her bones burned like fire, a mass of hairline fractures. Her movements grew sluggish. *No, I will not fall to—*

As she forced herself to stand, Corday slapped both palms against her chest. Asha blasted through the wall and rolled to a stop in another banquet room, half-buried in debris.

Get up get up get up get up!

The room whirled around her. She wheezed as fiery pain stabbed into her sides. Corday appeared above her, oozing satisfaction.

"You could never win," she said. "None of you can. One by one, I will send you all to hell."

Reaching down, she grabbed Asha by the throat and hoisted her to her feet. Asha struggled, desperate to breathe . . . and holding out for one last attack.

"But you, little one? Your death will be my favorite. I will savor it."

Asha's vision clouded. Struggling to speak, she managed only a soft gurgle. With a smirk, Corday loosened her grip.

"What was that?"

Sucking in a deep breath, Asha snarled. "Savor this."

She brought her left hand from behind her back—the hand that still clutched her remaining *qama*. Swinging hard, she aimed the razor-sharp point at her enemy's throat. Her heart sang in triumph as the blade flew. She'd done it! Everything would be—

Corday caught her hand, ripped the weapon from her grip, and spun with a flash of steel.

Asha felt a *thunk* against her flank. She stood there stunned, numbness washing over her. As her knees grew rubbery, she wondered where she was. Her head dipped, suddenly too heavy for her neck. And then she saw it.

Her own blade was buried between her ribs. Stunned, Asha made a choked noise as she grabbed for it. Her fingers clutched at it feebly, clumsily, then dropped back to her sides.

Blackness closed in from the edges of her vision. Asha felt herself falling. She didn't feel herself hit the floor.

CHAPTER 33

Malcolm flung out his arms, and sheets of flame burst from the floor. He sent them tearing across the room like fiery waves, scattering enemies and turning tables and chairs to cinders. His enemies converged in their wake and came at him from all directions.

A red *shift* behind. Spinning, he blocked the fireball with an ice shield. A blue *shift* to his left. He wreathed himself in fire until the ice attack turned to steam.

Their little band was holding on, but barely. For every enemy they put down, another one recovered. Even restored to full power, Tyrathorn could not keep going forever.

A trio of *shifts* nearby caught his attention, their red signatures as intense as Valentine's. *Dashers!* Moving like the wind, they advanced on his sister from behind. They'd waited for another opponent to distract her, and now they charged with weapons drawn.

"Val, move!"

Clamping down on Time, Malcolm created a thick wall of ice between them and his sister. As Valentine whipped around, the Dashers hit his wall full force, shattering the ice and their own bones on impact. In a blink, they were on the floor, moaning.

With a weary smile, Valentine gave Malcolm a salute. Then her eyes flicked behind him.

"Mal!"

Malcolm spun. *Too late.* A focused blast of fire hit his left flank with surprising force. He spun and then dropped like a stone as Valentine vanquished his attacker.

Pushing up his knees, he turned to thank her, only to see that he was too late to stop what happened next. One of the Dashers, a swarthy, dark-eyed woman, had fallen nearby. Palming a para-nexus, she managed one good throw.

The twins lashed out with ice and fire. They were both too slow.

The para-nexus slapped against John's chest.

Between heartbeats, everything stopped but this. John saw the device latch on, shared a last look with Valentine, and then there was a flash. A pillar of ice enveloped him.

An inhuman scream exploded from Valentine. Lifting the rogue Chronauri off the ground, she drew back her fist and wrapped it in a sheet of flames. She struck the dark woman's face. Drawing back again, she encased her fist in ice and struck with a loud *crack*. The woman collapsed in a heap.

Stunned, Malcolm stared at the ice holding his friend prisoner. Then a commotion drew his attention toward the bar, and he saw Fred go down between six attackers. Seconds later an ice pillar stood where he had fallen.

Tyrathorn desperately fought off a horde. Winter hovered behind his back, leaping out to sucker-punch anyone who dropped their guard. Then the horde closed in around them.

Something exploded and Tyrathorn sailed backward, covered in fire. He dropped to the floor, crashing through debris and rolling to a stop near the twins.

Left alone, Winter shouted curses and went down swinging. Her last taunt was lost as an ice pillar took her. Malcolm felt agony stab him deep. *One by one, they're falling. We have to save them. But how?*

The twins helped Tyrathorn to his feet, burnt remains of his shirt falling away as he stood. Only they remained, and now more than two dozen Chronauri surrounded them.

Breathing hard, Tyrathorn glanced at Malcolm. "Can you buy us a moment?"

Malcolm opened his nexus and a bubble sprang up around them. Teeth gritted, he suppressed the Time flowing outside the bubble, covering the entire ballroom—the largest area he had ever attempted to control. His corona flared blue, and the approaching force slowed to a snail's pace.

"I can't stop Time," he said in despair, shaking with exertion.

"None of us can," Tyrathorn said. "We can only slow it. So we must plan quickly."

"How do we even the odds?" Valentine asked. "Please tell me Chronauri have some kind of kryptonite."

Tyrathorn studied the enemy, the shattered ballroom, even the stars overhead. When his eyes returned to the twins, they were lost.

"They used to fear me," he said. "I raised a finger, they jumped to obey. It seems every choice I make, I only create more enemies."

Valentine gripped his shoulder. "Some enemies you should be proud to have."

"Don't take this the wrong way," Malcolm cut in, straining, "but save the regret for later. They're getting closer."

"Right." Standing between the twins, Tyrathorn locked

arms with them. "I do have one theory. Valentine, can you feel the Time flowing through my nexus and Malcolm's?"

"Yes."

"I can feel yours as well. Connected as we are now, I believe each of us may be able to draw power from all three."

"Is that safe?" Valentine asked.

"No. It may kill us, or even burn out our Chronauri abilities."

"Our ability can burn out?"

Tyrathorn shook his head. "I have so much more to teach you."

They paused, studying each other's faces for fear or doubt. Which, of course, they found. But one way or another they had to make a last stand.

Malcolm shrugged. "Worth a try. Let's do it."

They drew closer together, standing tall to face the enemy.

"On my count," Tyrathorn said. "Three . . ."

Malcolm prepared to drop the bubble.

". . . two . . ."

The bubble burst as gravity crashed down on them. Malcolm's connection to Time cut off like a slamming door. It could only mean one thing. *Oh, no.*

His heart thumped as the crowd parted. Charlotte Corday stalked toward them with murder in her eyes, breathing hard and limping. Blood streamed from a wicked cut across her face. Malcolm felt a flash of pride. *Asha hurt her.*

Then he realized why she was moving awkwardly. She wasn't limping from an injury—she was dragging something heavy. Malcolm caught a glimpse of red silk and his heart plummeted. *Oh, no.* Corday gave a disdainful toss, and the object flopped to the floor in front of them.

Tyrathorn screamed. It burst from deep in his soul—the

sound of a man having his heart torn out. He beheld his sister with hollow, tearful eyes.

Malcolm struggled to keep it together. Asha lay before him, a mass of cuts and black bruises and swollen lumps where bones had surely broken. Worst of all, her own blade stuck halfway into her side. Eyes closed, she didn't stir at the sound of her brother. The nexus on her chest remained dark and cold.

Malcolm's heart broke. He heard Valentine choke back a sob. *Don't be dead please Asha don't be dead.*

Tyrathorn fell to his knees and crawled toward her. Before he could cradle her, Corday pointed in his direction. Gravity waves launched him high, then slammed him down with a *thwack.* Then again, and again.

Malcolm shuffled to Valentine's side. Trembling, she took his hand as they stared down at their broken friend.

"Get up," she whispered. "Please get up."

Corday stood over Thorn now, chin raised in superiority. "You will suffer more than she did."

Tyrathorn glared up at her, fists clenched. "The last person I kill will be you."

She laughed. Walking a circle around the Corvonians, she began to list all the ways she would make him miserable before his end. Malcolm only heard her threats distantly. *What can we do now?*

The enemy was winning. His eyes couldn't leave Asha, as if turning away would doom her to die. Mentally he urged her to fight for life, to stay with them. With him. All his focus trained on her, drinking in everything that was Asha Corvonian.

Then, from deep inside her, Malcolm felt the tiniest *shift.*

He sucked in a breath, hand tightening on Valentine's. Though he couldn't access Time, he could still *feel* it. So he trained every scrap of that feeling at Asha, praying to feel her stirring again.

And there it was again—an infinitesimal spark.

Valentine shot him a questioning glance. He squashed the elation before it showed on his face—the Frost Hammer obviously thought Asha was already dead. So he stood stone-faced, all his powers of perception wrapped around the warrior girl, searching for a way to help her.

The spark flickered. Malcolm's senses dove inside Asha, the real world around him growing dimmer and more distant. He plunged farther and farther into her being until he reached an unfamiliar place. A place inside her that pulsed with energy.

His vision in this place was made of pure Chronauri senses. There was darkness, then a burst of golden light, and then a pulse wave. A heartbeat later, golden light burst again. Another wave of energy swept over him.

And then he knew. *Her Time battery!* The source of the energy that powered Asha—the unknowable place that held all of her Time—Malcolm had found it deep inside her.

Asha was still strong. Deep down, she had so much life left. He could feel her fighting, feel her wanting to live.

But right now her injuries were winning. Even as he watched, the golden light was waning. She needed help, and it would have to come soon. Inside, Malcolm wailed in despair. All this power and he still had no clue how to save her.

Someone was watching him now, Malcolm felt it. Reluctantly letting go, he backed away from Asha and returned his thoughts to immediate problems. As he focused on the ballroom again, he caught Tyrathorn staring.

Only a few seconds must have passed. Corday was still completing her walk around Tyrathorn, taunting him with every step. Now that he had Malcolm's attention, his eyes flicked twice toward Asha. Telling him something.

He must have felt it, too. *Wait, no.* This wasn't a look of concern. It was one of direction. *I'm missing something.* Tyrathorn's eyes flicked to Asha again, more urgently.

Malcolm examined her, searching for whatever his friend had tried to . . .

There it was.

Very clever, Thorn. It would give them one chance at survival. But Tyrathorn himself was too far away—it would only work on the twins and Asha. Was he really willing to do that?

One look in Tyrathorn's eyes told Malcolm all he needed to know. Of course he was willing. He was a warrior and a good man. Malcolm nodded to him in respect.

He squeezed Valentine's hand. "Hold on tight and be ready," he whispered.

Corday reached a crescendo. Grabbing Tyrathorn, she ripped the nexus from his chest and threw him against an ice pillar with a heavy crack.

Gravity waves emanated from her, pinning him to the ice with crushing intensity. Corday held out her hand. A para-nexus flew into her palm, and she shoved it onto Tyrathorn's chest with a snarl. In this last moment, he didn't look afraid. He looked proud.

Light flashed, and the ice took him.

Corday faced the twins now, seething. She pointed at them, and Malcolm felt Time warp as she summoned her power again.

He dove to the floor, Valentine in tow. With desperate speed he tapped the side of Asha's nexus. The device bloomed open, and with relief he saw what Tyrathorn had wanted him to find.

With Corday shouting in protest, he activated Asha's

Beacon. Gravity waves emanated from Corday, reaching out for them like a predator. Malcolm braced himself.

A blue portal opened and stretched around them. Dizziness washed over Malcolm as the universe warped.

Then the portal disappeared, leaving them in another place.

Another Time.

CHAPTER 34

Snow fell gently on them. They lay on a gray stone platform, bathed in blue light. Malcolm turned to see a massive blue vortex behind them—the biggest he'd ever seen. As the sound of rushing energy receded, the vortex folded in on itself and disappeared.

A ring spun in its place, made of polished metal and stone. Rumbling to a stop, the ring tilted to lie horizontally with two others. The machine powered down, leaving them in a wooded clearing on a dark night, snow falling gently around them.

Malcolm eyed Valentine. Though shaken, she nodded to indicate she was okay. Then something in the distance caught her attention. She came up to her knees, staring.

"Whoa."

Malcolm followed her eye and his jaw dropped. They weren't in a forest at all—this clearing sat inside a grove of trees at the end of well-kept grounds, enclosed by a wall.

At the far end of the grounds, a castle unlike anything he'd seen towered over everything—at least fifty stories tall. In fact, it looked less like a castle and more like a space ship that had landed vertically, nose pointed at the sky. Instead of blocks, its surface incorporated sleek metal, stone polished to a sheen, even broad sweeps of glass. They blended together seamlessly, grays and dark purples and silvers mingling and flowing along the curves and outcroppings of the structure. Each level was lit with bright lights that slowly morphed between complementary colors.

Never in all his studies had Malcolm seen a castle like that—which told him exactly where they must be. Asha and Tyrathorn's descriptions of their home had been passionate and detailed.

"Whoa," he echoed. "We're in Everwatch."

Malcolm shook his head and refocused on Asha. They could think about where they were later. Opening his nexus, he sighed in relief as Time responded to his call. He aimed refreshed senses at Asha and delved into her being again. *Stay with us. Please.*

He squeezed her limp hand. "She wants to live, Val, I can feel it. But her body is so broken, her Time isn't strong enough to break free. I—" He choked on his next words. "I think she's fading."

Valentine clutched her other hand. "Hold on, Asha. You're strong."

"Strongest person I know," Malcolm said, a tear falling down his cheek. He realized he was trembling. "Val . . . I don't know how to heal her. I only figured out how to heal myself, not someone else."

"We'll figure something out," Valentine said. "It'll be—"

"It *won't* be okay! Not if she . . ." His anguish turned to despair, crushing him like a boulder. He gasped for breath between every word. "What good is this power, if all it can do is destroy?"

He could feel her flickering like a candle in storm winds. If she died, the world would never be right again.

If only she had more Time. If only I could give her . . .

His thoughts screeched to a halt.

Why couldn't I?

With that one question, a plan began to form. Even as the ideas came desperately together, Malcolm knew it was insane. But the thought of losing Asha had opened a door to madness.

Without hesitation, he walked through it.

"Move back, Val." Rising to his knees, Malcolm clutched the blade in Asha's side.

"Mal, are you sure—?"

"Please. She doesn't have long."

Pursing her lips, Valentine shuffled out of reach.

Malcolm willed a small flow of Time into Asha's weapon. The blade began to glow red. It would be more powerful now, better able to cut.

With a smooth tug, it came free. He tossed it aside. Gazing down at Asha, he drank in the lines of her face. Even hurt so badly, she was still . . .

"Beautiful." He leaned closer to her. "I will not lose someone to an enemy, Asha. Not again. You're not going anywhere."

Malcolm threw his nexus wide open and an avalanche of Time crashed through his body. He gasped, gritting his teeth at the euphoric agony. *More. More!* With a groan, he forced something inside himself to expand farther, drinking in more and more pure Time.

He held his palms toward each other, focused every thought on the vision in his mind, and silvery white beams of pure Time burst from his palms. Writhing like living things, they collided. But instead of exploding or resisting each other, the beams melded together.

With his body open like a conduit, he channeled more Time than he ever thought possible. Could what he wanted even be done? He didn't know.

But he did know. Because it had to be done.

The mass of energy grew between his hands, building on itself as he fed it a constant flow of cosmic power. Though holding together, it was still shapeless, raw, incomplete. That was about to change.

Clutching it with his will, Malcolm began to carve it, mold it, give it form to match his mental picture. Energy overflowed from his body now, arcing around him in bright flashes.

Halfway to his goal, the entity began to push back. The shaping resisted him like a magnet encountering its opposite. Sweat broke out on his forehead as he exerted every fiber of his being.

He looked to Valentine, who stared as if he had gone mad. "I need your nexus."

She shook her head. "You'll kill yourself!"

"Please! Please trust me," he pleaded, tears falling. "Val . . . I need her."

Valentine hesitated. Squeezing her eyes shut, she nodded as if knowing she would regret this moment. Then she unbuckled the nexus from her forearm, approached Malcolm, and strapped it around his.

He gazed up at her, brimming with gratitude. "Thank you."

She gave a resigned nod and stepped back again.

Malcolm took a deep breath, preparing himself for what he was about to do. Counting down from three, he threw Valentine's nexus open.

Someone screamed. Distantly, he thought it might have been him. Mind and body disappeared inside the power surging through him.

Through it all, he forced his creation to weave together, to build the complex machine. *So close . . . just a little more . . .*

Valentine gasped. "Oh, my god. Mal . . . you're building her another Time battery!"

All Malcolm knew was Asha's own battery wasn't strong enough to overcome her injuries. So he had to give her another one. *One last push . . .*

The strands of cosmic power collapsed into place with a flash. Folding in on themselves, they formed a pulsing machine molded from flows of Time. In its final form, it was no bigger than his thumbnail.

Coils of energy floated freely along its edges. At his direction they plunged deep into Asha. Latching onto her insides, they pulled, and Malcolm's creation descended toward her . . . closer . . . closer . . . until it finally sank into her chest.

The coils wrapped around her natural Time battery, joining old and new together side by side. Malcolm waited an eternal moment, praying that it would work. That he wasn't insane.

Then the batteries pulsed together. A white-gold glow cascaded over Asha's body.

Cuts and bruises disappeared. Swelling decreased as shattered bones began to mend. Finally, the stab wound in her side glowed.

Malcolm felt the fibers in her chest knitting back together. He saw Asha's life force swell up from inside, bursting through the veil. Her eyelids fluttered, then opened.

Closing each nexus, he released his iron grip on Time. Numb, overwhelmed by fatigue, he toppled onto the cold stones. In his last waking moment, he felt Asha sit up. He heard Valentine grab Asha in a tight hug.

"Oh, thank god," Valentine said.

"... What happened?" Asha said.

"Malcolm," Valentine said in wonder. "He saved your life."

Darkness draped over him. He smiled, welcoming it with open arms.

CHAPTER 35

To Valentine's relief, her brother breathed normally, and her Chronauri senses showed his life pulsing as strong as ever. She sighed, returning her own nexus to her forearm.

"Is he all right?" Wincing, Asha reached out to touch Malcolm's hand. "What did he do?"

"He gave you a second Time battery," Valentine said, marveling.

"What?" Asha gaped. "That can't . . . but something *is* different. I feel it." She studied the twins as if they were a new species. "How?"

"He pulled in so much power. If something had gone wrong . . ." It was her turn to study Asha now. "But for you, he didn't hesitate."

Asha shocked her by doing something she never expected—she blushed. Looking down, she gave a bashful smile.

Clearing her throat, Valentine gestured at the immense machine. "So, we're in Everwatch?"

Asha looked up as if just noticing it was there. Valentine expected her to relax now, in the safety of home.

Instead, Asha looked from the machine to the towering

castle, then leapt to her feet in alarm. Gasping, she clutched her side.

"Ow." She paused to take a labored breath, then turned toward the ramp. "Get Malcolm. We have to move."

Valentine sprang to her feet. "Move? What do you—?"

"I assume you used my Beacon?"

"Yes."

"When someone goes through the Empyrean Bridge, their Beacon resets itself. If you activate it, you're brought back to exactly five minutes after you left. Which means, only a few minutes ago, the Black Tempest and the Frost Hammer killed these Watchers to get to the Bridge."

Asha pointed at shadowy mounds that surrounded the platform. Valentine saw now that they were armed soldiers, lying dead.

"Only a few minutes ago, I attacked them and fell through the portal."

"But why are we running?"

"By now, the Ember Guard knows there was an unauthorized jump, and that someone reappeared exactly five minutes later. Now they'll come."

"Isn't that good? We need their help."

"You don't understand!"

Valentine's senses went crazy, detecting a score of incoming *shifts*. She had barely opened her nexus when walls of fire and ice surrounded her, linking together to form a prison cell. Absorbing Time, she threw it against the makeshift prison and it burst into steam.

A dozen men and women appeared through the haze, all clad in the grayish silver armor of the Ember Guard, all glowing bright. Valentine readied her power but kept it bridled.

"We're not your enemy!" she called. "We need help to—"

A broad-shouldered, black-skinned Guard threw a crystalline orb to the ground at her feet. As it shattered, a shimmering wall of *something* appeared too quickly for Valentine to respond.

Constricting around her, it hardened into some kind of shell. Suddenly she was half-*shifting* between thousands of moments and thousands of places. They raced by in such a dizzy blur that she never regained her balance.

What other tricks would the Ember Guard have up their sleeves? Valentine found herself both embarrassed and impressed that they had captured her so easily. *Maybe they can surprise Corday, too.*

Minutes or decades later, the shell around her disintegrated. Valentine lay on a polished floor next to Malcolm. Coming up to her knees, she studied their surroundings.

A throne room. We must be in the castle. The cavernous space seemed patterned after ancient castles, with its wide columns and windows of sculpted glass. The design, though, was something else entirely. It mirrored the outside of the building—a display of sleek futuristic artistry rooted in old-world traditions. The chamber was bathed in the soft glow of those same morphing lights.

Two Ember Guards stood directly behind her and Malcolm. Farther behind, ten more formed a semicircle. They wore varying designs of the armor that was so familiar to Valentine now—fine, smoke-gray chain mail overlaid with silver plates. While every set of armor bore the same wavelike grooves, no two were exactly alike.

In front of the twins, wide steps led to a platform topped by two ornate thrones of black wood. The first step, oddly enough, had a broadsword sticking out of it. Squinting, Valentine thought she saw a faint cloud of vapor rising from the blade. *Is that . . . black ice?*

The Ember Guard who'd captured them climbed those steps now, with Asha squirming in his muscular arms. She spat a long string of her own language. Though Valentine didn't know the words, their meaning was plain—Asha was not happy with being carried like a child. He ignored her with the skill of a man accustomed to dealing with petulant royalty.

As soon as he set her down, she shoved away from him with a glare. Then her attention turned to the occupants of the thrones, and her manner altered instantly. Staring at the floor, she clasped her hands. Submissive.

Blinking awake, Malcolm gasped, his gaze resting on Asha with the purest joy. He looked to his sister for confirmation.

She smiled. "It worked."

That look in his eyes warmed Valentine's heart. His hands twitched like he wanted to reach out to Asha. He moved to stand.

A hand rested on his shoulder, pressing down just enough to stop him. The tall blond woman above Malcolm shook her head. Her expression wasn't of anger or hatred, but it was all business and the meaning was clear—stay down. Reluctantly, he obeyed.

Valentine returned her attention to the dais. The Guard had stepped to the side, leaving Asha with what must be the leaders of Everwatch—her parents. *Eternal King Jerrik and Meliora, Queen of the Infinite. Wow, she really is a princess.* They gathered their daughter in a tight embrace, the relief evident on their faces.

"Thank you, Captain Armel," the queen said.

Observing them now, there was no mistaking them as family.

Each bore the same dark hair, though theirs was shot through with gray. Each projected the same regal confidence. And while Meliora's eyes were dark as night, Jerrik's shone with the same ice blue as Asha's.

Neither appeared as composed as Valentine would have expected. Still in dressing robes, hair askew, dark circles under their eyes—hardly the picture of royalty, though it *was* pre-dawn, and they'd probably been woken to deal with this. And right now they didn't seem happy about it.

With their relief expressed, the real conversation began, and it radiated tension. The king and queen fired what sounded like accusations at Asha, and she regained enough of her composure to fire back. The king poked her wounded side and she hissed, shrinking away. He shook his head, disappointed. She began to protest, but he stopped her with a raised finger.

The king faced the twins and took one step down, placing himself between them and Asha. He studied them as if trying to see beneath their skin. The queen came all the way down to the floor, eyeing them with vitriol.

"Two uninvited strangers in the Eon Palace," she said, her English bearing the same melodic accent as Asha's. "What have you done to our daughter?"

Valentine exchanged an incredulous glance with Malcolm. "If you asked her, then you know my brother saved her life."

"And what business do you have with her?"

"She showed up in our town," Malcolm retorted. "That made her our business."

"Mother, I—" Asha began.

"Be silent, child."

"We helped her, she helped us," Valentine said. They didn't

have time for this—everyone at home was counting on them. "But something terrible has happened, and it's too big for us to fight alone. Please, our people need your help."

"Explain why I cannot sense your path through Time," the king commanded. "What trickery have you brought inside our walls?"

"I literally have no clue what you're talking about," Malcolm said.

Jerrik's eyes narrowed. "In all my years, I have not encountered a single soul who could hide themselves from me. Yet searching you is like staring into a void. Explain that, if you are so trustworthy."

Valentine scoffed, though she felt taken aback. Asha had described her father's First-*sev* talent—to glimpse a person's path through Time, observing pieces of their past and future. She hadn't mentioned the idea of anyone being immune. *So, why us?*

"We just found out we were Chronauri," she said. "How are we supposed to know everything?"

"Smooth words," Meliora said. "But the use of the Empyrean Bridge cannot be denied. We detected it, followed by an emergency return. Soldiers arrived to find our people dead and our daughter injured. If you are not responsible, then explain who is."

Valentine's teeth clenched, and she saw Malcolm's hands balling into fists. After everything they'd been through, she was not about to sit here and be falsely accused.

"Your son is," she said. "Or do you just call him the Black Tempest now?"

The queen and king paled. Whispers passed among the Guards behind them, but fell silent with a stern look from Captain Armel.

The queen swallowed hard. "How . . . how do you know that name?"

"Because for weeks we've been doing your job," Valentine snapped. "And while you slept in your palace, the Frost Hammer rained death and terror on our people."

"Explain," the king said, his voice softer now. Weaker. "Tell us everything."

"We will," Malcolm said. He tapped the armored hand on his shoulder. "But not on our knees. We aren't your servants."

The king nodded and the Guards backed away. The twins climbed to their feet, with the Guard watching them like hawks. Valentine resisted the urge to open her nexus just to feel less vulnerable. That, however, would probably not have been taken as a friendly gesture.

They launched into their story. Starting with the short version of their battle with Lucius Carmichael, they moved on to the night when the sky had torn open and two armored warriors had fallen through.

For the next twenty minutes, the twins traded back and forth. They talked of clashing with the Frost Hammer; of fearing the day they would meet her master, the Black Tempest; of training with and fighting alongside their new friends Asha and Tyrathorn; of learning what it was to be Chronauri.

Finally they talked of learning their friend's true identity, and how the only person more shocked than them had been *him*. They shared stories of the Tyrathorn they'd come to know, how forgetting had actually helped him remember his true self.

They told of the Frost Hammer's betrayal, and her plans for using Emmett's Bluff to invade Everwatch. Then they described her strange powers and the danger they posed to Chronauri who opposed her.

When they had finished, the king and queen had sunk into their thrones, stunned and gripping each other's hands. They sat silent for a long moment. Then the king turned to Asha with raised eyebrows.

"It's true," she said. "All of it."

"But we have not heard everything," Queen Meliora said. "Why were you at the Empyrean Bridge? How did you know your br—the Black Tempest would be there?"

Once again Asha examined the floor.

"You will tell us now," the king said. "You defied our direct orders. Why did you do this?"

Fire roared to life behind Asha's eyes. "Why didn't *you*?"

King Jerrik prepared to rebuke her. She didn't pause to hear it.

"I hear the whispers in the kingdom. People wonder why their king and queen don't crush the Black Tempest before he hurts more of us. If they knew his true identity, they would have the answer, wouldn't they? Because Jerrik and Meliora aren't strong enough to bring justice to their own child."

"We had him contained—" the queen began.

"Until he created his master plan." Asha jabbed an accusatory finger at them. "I know that you captured one of his servants, that he revealed everything to you, and that you refused to believe it. Someone had to do something. *Someone* had to be strong."

She pointed toward the Empyrean Bridge.

"So I set a trap. I had a spy tell Thorn that the king knew he needed the Bridge, so it would be destroyed on Regeneration Day. I forced him into action so I would know where he was. And I went there to kill him myself."

"And you caused the death of a squad of Watchers," Queen Meliora said, her own eyes catching fire. "You were foolish and careless."

"The Empyrean Bridge is never guarded on Regeneration Day. I couldn't know that you changed—"

"There is much you do not know. There is . . ." King Jerrik trailed off, staring at the ceiling to compose himself. "You have the luxury of judging us now, child. But one day you will understand the burdens of protecting a kingdom."

Asha shook her head. Awkward silence fell as both sides stewed in their own resentment. Valentine questioned the wisdom of speaking in this moment, but someone had to. There were bigger things to worry about than family drama.

"Whatever happened before, we have to act now."

"And quickly," Malcolm added. "So we ask you, please send the Ember Guard back with us. Surely the Frost Hammer can't stop all of them."

Two heavy pairs of eyes fell on the twins. Valentine refused to squirm under their weight.

"I will not make a rash decision," King Jerrik said.

"Nor will I," said Queen Meliora. "We must consider carefully, when Regeneration Day has passed. Tomorrow we will reconvene and decide our course."

"*Tomorrow?*" Malcolm burst. "Our people are dying right now and you want to celebrate some festival?"

"Be careful," Queen Meliora said. "You are a guest here."

"Do you forget what the Empyrean Bridge does?" King Jerrik said with an ironic grin. "We could take a year to decide and still send you back only a day after you left. You have seen us vulnerable here, but do not mistake us for fools."

Despite sharing Malcolm's feelings, Valentine stayed quiet. She rested a calming hand on his arm. "Of course. Thank you for hearing us."

Malcolm took a slow, calming breath. "I'm sorry. We only want to save our people. I know Asha feels the same."

The king glanced at Asha. "Whatever we decide, rest assured that our daughter will not be returning with you."

Valentine's brow furrowed. Malcolm's jaw dropped.

"Her near death proves that only Ember Guard should lead these missions. They are too dangerous for anyone else."

"But she *is* an . . ." Malcolm began, then trailed off. As he looked to Asha, she avoided his eyes. "But you're *not* one of them, are you?"

Asha shook her head, looking truly defeated in a way Valentine hadn't thought possible. She braced herself for Malcolm's anger at having been lied to again. But he only shrugged.

"Could've fooled me," he said. "You should see your daughter fight. It's breathtaking. We wouldn't have survived this long without her."

"It is not up for discussion." Queen Meliora stood with the king. "You may explore the Eon Palace freely. Should you venture into Everwatch, we require you to have an escort." She gestured and a uniformed man emerged from the shadows. "Bring our guests to their rooms. I'm certain they will want to refresh themselves."

The king bade them farewell until tomorrow, and the Corvonians left the throne room with Asha in tow. Before disappearing, she turned to gaze at Malcolm with sad eyes. Valentine felt for her. She seemed so much smaller.

Malcolm performed a silly, overdone bow. Stifling laughter,

Asha gave a little wave and turned to follow her parents. When they were gone, the uniformed man invited them to accompany him.

Before he could finish, a tall, young Ember Guard stepped between them.

"Surrender your nexus," he said. "Both of you."

Valentine scoffed. "I don't think so."

"Liam," the blond Guardswoman called, giving a subtle shake of her head.

"Those are the rules," Liam insisted, glaring at the twins. "You will follow them, or be made to."

Malcolm chuckled. Then his face grew deadly serious. "Try it. See what happens."

Liam's fists clenched. Valentine felt the beginnings of a *shift* and prepared to open her nexus. A split second before, the captain appeared over Liam's shoulder.

"Resume your place in line," he said. Liam began to protest. "Now, soldier."

Liam shot the twins a withering look before returning to his place.

"I apologize," the captain said. Asha noted that his accent was different from the Corvonians. More West African-meets-French.

He produced two copper-link bracelets encrusted with small purple gems. Valentine noticed layers of circuitry embedded in the gems.

"Please wear these. They allow us to monitor your movements, but nothing more. I will keep escorts ready in case you wish to leave the grounds."

The twins glanced at each other, then accepted with a shrug. As the captain fastened them to their wrists, Valentine caught an unexpected softness in his expression. Glancing discreetly at the other Guards, she saw them regarding the twins in the same way. Except for Liam, of course.

"Why are you being so nice to us?" Valentine asked.

The captain hesitated, then lowered his voice. "Asha is one of us, whether the King sees it or not," he said. "And you saved her life. We owe you a debt."

Valentine smiled, elated to meet warriors who lived with honor.

"If you want to pay us back," Malcolm whispered, "please help us save our people."

"The king and queen command us—the decision is theirs. But when they ask for my counsel, I will advocate for you."

Valentine nearly started crying. At least they had allies somewhere.

The captain bade farewell until tomorrow, and their guide beckoned them to follow him deeper into the massive palace. She resisted the urge to gape at everything she saw. There was high technology here, but it was under the surface, embedded in everything.

She caught glimpses of it in small things—lamps that used some sort of mineral instead of fire or filaments or LEDs; walls that appeared to be stone or metal, yet lit up with directional arrows as they neared; purple gems in the ceiling at junction points, which caused their bracelets to beep as they passed under them.

Their guide turned down a short hallway that ended in a solid wall. On either side were three curved doors with no discernible handles. He placed his hand on a small glass panel and one of the doors whooshed open. Exchanging astonished stares, the twins followed him into the lift.

"*Bisari* level," he said as the door slid closed.

Something chimed and the lift soared upward. Valentine heard no gears, no cables, no creaks or mechanical whines. *What's powering this thing?*

Malcolm cleared his throat. "So, uh, what does *bisari* mean?"

"Guest."

So he was allowed to answer questions. That was good. Valentine could ask something that had been burning in her mind.

"What is Regeneration Day?"

"It occurs once every 610 days," he replied with a mix of wonder and pride. "It is a . . . rebirth of sorts. When dawn arrives tomorrow, the celebration will begin."

Well . . . okay. It wasn't a complete answer, but he didn't seem inclined to elaborate. Maybe she would ask Captain Armel.

"How many are in the Ember Guard?" Malcolm said out of the blue. Valentine shot him a puzzled look. "What? I'm curious."

"The average, I believe, is about two hundred and fifty. However, the elite guard—the High Protectors—always number thirteen."

Valentine raised her eyebrows, surprised at the numbers and that he had openly shared them. The guide gave a little smile.

"If the captain trusts you, so do I. Also, it is not only the Ember Guard that owes you a debt. Princess Ashandara is special to us all. Thank you for saving her."

Malcolm's cheeks reddened. "She is special."

"And we wouldn't have made it here without her," Valentine agreed. Then another thought resurfaced. "Why is there a sword stuck in the throne room floor?"

"I noticed that, too," Malcolm said.

The guide's smile faltered. "We . . . do not speak of that." Recovering quickly, he brightened again. "However, we have prepared the suite with the finest view of Everwatch. Before you leave, I hope you will find rest here."

Exiting the elevator, he led them to a large, two-bedroom apartment. Though it boasted the same sleek ancient-yet-modern architecture, the furnishings offered lavish comfort. Malcolm chose the bedroom to the right of the common area, leaving an identical room on the left for Valentine. After pointing out a call button that would allow them to request anything they needed, their guide bade farewell.

Valentine closed her door and sat on the edge of the bed, relishing the moment of solitude. Her weary eyes wandered to the en suite bathroom. Already a fresh set of clothes hung there for her. Everwatch certainly knew how to treat its guests. It occurred to Valentine then how unkempt they must look. Sweaty, battle-worn, clothes torn and dirty. They probably didn't smell like roses either.

Yawning, she leaned back on her elbows. Even the bed was impossibly soft while supporting her perfectly. She ran her hands over the plush cover. Maybe after a shower, her exhausted body would actually be able to relax. Sleep was too much to ask for, but she would settle for not jumping at every noise. She yawned again.

A hot shower . . . definitely. And then we'll . . . we'll need to figure out our next . . . what's the word? Move? . . . Yeah, we should . . .

She fell dead asleep.

CHAPTER 36

Valentine didn't wake so much as ascend gently out of sleep. When she stretched, her aches and pains had smoothed over. The light outside told her she had slept for hours. Giving the mattress a grateful pat, she slipped out of the covers and indulged in a long, steaming shower.

The clothes fit perfectly. Deep purple robes hinted at old Japanese styles, almost like a kimono. Soft yet strong, warm but not stifling, they wrapped her in silky comfort. A pair of the softest leather boots completed the outfit.

Leaving her room, she spotted Malcolm on the balcony. His new clothes resembled those of a medieval European nobleman, except made from materials that could have come right out of *Star Trek*. Another meeting of old and new.

Valentine joined him. He held a steaming mug of something, and a second mug waited for her on a small table. To the west, the sun was sinking toward the horizon.

"Hey," she said.

"I see you fell asleep, too."

"I was powerless against that bed."

She leaned on the balustrade and took a sip from the mug. As she blinked away the last vestiges of sleep, her thoughts turned internal. The moments of their catastrophic loss began to play over again in her mind. The helplessness as ice overtook their family one by one. The despair as their gambit with the Lance fell apart.

"We guessed wrong and everyone else paid the price," she said. "She controls gravity. How could we have seen that coming?"

"And how do we get around it?" Malcolm said. "The only one she couldn't block was Asha."

"Think they keep an army of Second-*sevs* here?"

"Based on how Asha's parents treat her, I doubt it. Still, there's got to be a way we can use that knowledge."

"We'll figure it out," Valentine said, working to infuse her voice with confidence. Then another memory came back to her—a happier one. She reached over to squeeze her brother's arm. "That was amazing, what you did for her."

Malcolm shrugged, seeming embarrassed. "Just did what I had to do."

"Do . . . do you love her?"

Valentine watched as her brother's face morphed from denial to uncertainty and then back to denial, to fear, then resignation, and finally, after a long pause, something like cautious happiness. He gave a tentative smile.

". . . I think maybe I do."

There it was—a glimmer of something good in otherwise horrific times. Unable to contain her joy, Valentine grabbed her brother and pulled him into a hug. He gave a surprised yelp and hugged her back.

"She may not feel the same, you know," he said, laughing. "Don't celebrate yet."

"I've seen the way she looks at you, Mal. Trust me, you—"

Peering over his shoulder, Valentine truly looked out from their balcony. Since stepping outside, she had been too caught up in the turmoil of her own thoughts, but now the panoramic view finally registered. She untangled from Malcolm to get a better look and her jaw dropped.

"Whoa."

"Yeah," Malcolm said, following her gaze. "Tell me about it."

Snow fell in a gentle flurry. Sunlight broke through scattered clouds, golden rays bathing the massive valley between towering mountains. It was impossible to tell just how big it was, but every square mile overwhelmed Valentine with its beauty.

She gazed in one direction and saw gardens bursting with color, manicured and shaped into living portraits of mythical creatures, spiral galaxies, even a re-creation of Vincent van Gogh's *Starry Night*. The gardens flowed around a large structure of polished stone sculpted in the likeness of a seashell among crashing waves.

Looking elsewhere, she saw a series of glass and steel cubes big enough to serve as apartments. Arranged in a fractal design, they glimmered in the sunlight like a monument to mathematical and artistic perfection. A stream wound between them, passing underneath some cubes, then rising into the air to flow around others.

Set high up on the Eon Palace, the twins' balcony showed them everything. A thousand works of art. A thousand architectural styles. A thousand things breathtaking and wondrous in form. No matter where Valentine gazed, something new amazed.

If that weren't enough, lights of every color were beginning to flicker on across the valley. The streets teemed with people, while sounds of music and merriment traveled up to beckon them closer.

Valentine exchanged a look of disbelief with her brother. "Where are we? *When* are we?"

Malcolm shrugged. "I would guess the ancient past—some undiscovered valley—but that's all I can tell. One weird thing, though. It's snowing and we're up in the mountains, right?"

"Yeah."

"So, are you cold?"

She stopped to think, then realized she had to think about it. "Are you saying they climate controlled an entire valley?"

"Maybe. I mean, look at this place. Do you believe they couldn't?"

And as she peered across the valley, Valentine noticed something else she couldn't explain. At the northern border, a small tower stood away from other structures. It resembled a lighthouse built in the style of the Eon Palace, at once ancient and futuristic.

But instead of a light bulb or a flame, an iridescent dodeca-hedron spun at the top. As it rotated, each face shimmered in a rainbow of dazzling colors. And the mystery didn't stop there.

"Mal, look." She pointed.

"I saw that. There's a bunch of them circling the whole valley."

He was right. A dozen towers encircled the city, creating a border of sorts. She found the tower closest to them and pointed at the dodecahedron.

"Look at the top," she said. "See what's it's doing?"

"Yeah, the spinning thing. Maybe it's some kind of art piece."

"No, look at the edges."

She kept quiet as Malcolm examined it, not wanting to bias him in case her eyes were playing tricks. For a moment his expression remained blank, but then his eyebrows climbed.

"There's an energy field."

"Yes!"

Each dodecahedron was surrounded by a faint bubble of rippling energy. Reaching out, Valentine brushed the bubble with her Chronauri perceptions. An odd fluctuation washed back over her, accompanied by a sort of . . . circular feeling. As if the flow of Time somehow curved around the tower. Now that she'd identified the feeling, she sensed it across the entire valley. It was subtle, but now she couldn't miss it.

"Whoa." Malcolm clutched the balustrade. "What'd you just do?"

"You felt that?"

"It's everywhere." His head cocked to the side. "Does it feel familiar? I can't place it, but I could swear we've felt something like it before."

"Maybe." She wracked her brain for something to match up in her memories. Nothing fit just right. "I don't know. Maybe it's a shield to keep out unwanted visitors."

"Could be," Malcolm said, seeming unconvinced. Abruptly, he faced her. "How are you feeling?"

"Uh, fine?"

"No, I mean in here." He tapped his chest. "The Chronauri part. Does it feel, I don't know, bigger somehow?"

So, he'd felt it, too. She nodded. "When we fought in the ballroom, I did things I'd never even thought of before."

"Yeah. I can feel us growing. It's like every time we fight for real, we find a higher gear."

"You mean . . ." She hesitated. "You think we may hit Fifth-*sev* someday?"

"Maybe. And it's happening much faster than it's supposed to be."

"Thorn and Asha try to hide it," Valentine said. "But sometimes I get the feeling they don't know what to do with us."

"What we've done—it should have taken years, Val. I have no clue what that means or why we're different, and I don't think they do either." He blew out a breath. "Is this how it feels to be afraid of yourself?"

"It is scary. But we'll learn how to use it the right way." Valentine grinned. "And come on, it feels pretty awesome, too. Right?"

Malcolm couldn't hide a smile. "It must come with some extra confidence. You do realize we stood up to a king, a queen, and their elite guard? That was really us."

"Oh, I know. I was there. Asha couldn't keep her eyes off you." She gave him a playful nudge. "I think you've got a fan."

His cheeks flushed.

Valentine grew more serious. "She lied for good reasons, you know. Trying to save her brother and her people. If I had to lie to do that, I would. Don't be angry at her."

"I'm not. I'd have done it, too." He shook his head. "She must have felt so alone."

Alone. The word provoked an image of Emmett's Bluff if the Frost Hammer won. Empty. Desolate. A town of people who'd endured the strangest catastrophes and carried on. All those lives, wasted.

And what of the twins' family? Their friends? They were trapped in ice at this very moment, forced to power Corday's war machine. Well, technically they weren't, since this was a completely different period of history. But it felt like they were. Valentine sagged, her heart suddenly heavy.

"I know," Malcolm said before she even spoke. "I'm worried about them, too."

She sighed. "I feel guilty being here. Being comfortable while they're in danger."

Malcolm chewed his lip, lost in thought. Then, nodding to himself, he stood straighter.

"You're right, it's not fair. But Val, we're in a city so hidden there aren't even myths about it. When are we going to get this chance again?"

"What are you saying?"

"I'm saying we're stuck here until tomorrow anyway. Shouldn't we enjoy it just a little? After all, we're trying to save this place, too."

Something inside Valentine resisted, but it was quickly overruled by a different feeling—she really wanted to see what else was out there.

She smiled. "Race you."

VALENTINE had never seen a more festive place. It was like Everwatch had thrown a party and the entire valley had shown up. From the Eon Palace's front entrance, the twins had walked down a short lane until it emptied into the massive Meridian Square. It must have been a quarter-mile long and twice as wide.

It practically exploded with colors as merrymakers paraded by in every style of dress imaginable. They strolled, danced, and played music with everything from old stringed lutes to weird-looking synthesizers that synched happy electronic music with swirling light projections.

The crowds enjoyed exotic delicacies from one of a thousand rolling food carts. On smelling the rich and spicy scents, Valentine felt her stomach grumble. *When did we eat last?*

As if on cue, a cart brimming with skewered meats trundled close by and stopped. Valentine thought she smelled vaguely

Middle Eastern spices. Her mouth watered. Then the cart operator beckoned them closer.

Grabbing Malcolm's arm, she pulled him toward the cart. The owner, a tall, swarthy man in a turban, welcomed them with a jovial smile and held out two skewers. As the food danced in Valentine's vision, the man said something in another language.

"Oh, sorry," Malcolm said, patting his pockets. "I don't think we have local money."

Valentine's heart sank. But the man held the skewers out to them again.

"Please, you take. Enjoy!" he said. "Regeneration!"

"We don't use money here," a woman's voice said behind them.

Valentine looked over her shoulder. Vash—the tall, blond Ember Guardswoman—stood behind them. True to the queen's word, Vash had been waiting at the palace gates to escort them as they explored. Like a polite shadow, she had kept a discreet distance until now.

"None at all?" Valentine said.

"We barter, mostly, or just give. But on Regeneration Day, no one barters."

Valentine didn't need more convincing. Accepting the skewer, she responded with her brightest smile. "Thank you, sir." She took a bite and her eyes rolled into the back of her head. "Ohmagod that is amazing!"

Malcolm emitted a satisfied growl as he devoured everything on the skewer. With a deep belly laugh, the man clapped them on the shoulders, handed them two more skewers, and rolled on to his next spot.

"Thanks," Malcolm said to Vash. She nodded.

They continued through the crowd. Valentine did her best

to open all her senses and soak up everything. Sight, sound, smell and taste, even touch, since the comfortably cool air was punctuated by gently falling snow. Her body was incapable of absorbing everything happening around it. Yet the crowd was so immersed in glee, the mood couldn't help but be infectious.

Food wasn't the only thing being given. Dozens more danced by, handing out everything from little stone carvings of the Eon Palace—complete with miniature lights twinkling across the surface—to a tiny blue box that could hold tenfold more than it should have been able to.

Malcolm received a shiny red button that turned out to be a prank generator. He pressed the button and something invisible smacked the back of his head. He pressed it again and received a mild electrical jolt like a toy buzzer. It seemed the people here had a sense of humor, too.

"Hey, look." Malcolm pointed to the left.

A swarm of children had clustered around one man. Tall and broad, with a jagged scar across his face and the watchful eyes of a soldier, he nevertheless welcomed the children with a bright smile and open arms. They called his name, gave him hugs, and waited eagerly for what would come out of the bag slung over his shoulder.

With a showman's flair, he reached into the bag and drew out an object of bright blues and golds—a delicate butterfly made from colored glass and gold wire. As it rested in the soldier's palm, the children hushed in anticipation.

"*Magia!*"

He threw the butterfly at the ground. When the glass hit the stones, it burst into a dozen multicolored butterflies made of light. The dazzling holograms danced between the children, landing on hands and shoulders and even foreheads. Valentine laughed, caught up in the delight as the children giggled and chased the lights. Half a minute later, the holographic butterflies swirled over the toymaker's palm, then collapsed together to become glass and gold again.

The children jumped and cheered as the toymaker reached into his bag and produced a butterfly for everyone. Gazing over their heads, he noticed Valentine and tossed one to her.

Looking into his eyes, she was struck by what she saw. The soldier-like vigilance was gone, replaced by peace. Without knowing why, she curtsied in thanks. He bowed in return, a twinkle in his eye, then moved on to find more children.

Valentine studied the butterfly, admiring its beauty while trying to deduce how it worked. When they got back home, she'd have to examine it with Clive's spectacles. For now, she slipped it into her pocket.

"I officially love this place," she said.

Malcolm grinned. "We're a couple of kids from Nowhereville. Look where we are now."

"Yeah." She turned a full circle to drink in the atmosphere, feeling lighter than she had in ages. "I could get used to this."

Vash appeared again. "It is nearly time."

"For what?" Valentine asked.

"For regeneration." She pointed toward the western horizon, where the sun was almost touching the mountains.

As she spoke, the lights on the Eon Palace pulsed brighter. A cheer went up from the crowd, as if this had been the signal they were waiting for. Near the top, a wide balcony extended over the valley and its roof blossomed open, revealing dozens of men and women in robes of glittering silver.

A hush fell over the valley. Valentine marveled, never having heard such deep quiet fill such a big space. Her ears caught the faintest whine, like a stereo switching on. Then music emanated from the entire surface of the palace. Softly at first—a slow, soulful piece brimming with strings and horns and other melodic tones she couldn't identify.

As the music rose, voices joined in the song. Valentine realized then that the robed people were a choir. The music swelled, their voices lifted to meet it, and her skin broke out in chills. The song felt ancient, somehow, filling her up as if it carried the depth and weight of legend.

The sun touched the horizon. Movement caught Valentine's eye, and she turned to see each dodecahedron lift higher on beams of light from the towers beneath. They spun faster, radiating energy. The crowd came to life again, leaping and cheering in anticipation.

As the song reached its crescendo, electrical arcs burst from the dodecahedrons and connected with each other, forming a glowing net over the valley. Brighter swells of energy traveled from tower to tower, tracing a circular path around the city.

A feeling washed over Valentine, as if she stood in the center of a cosmic whirlpool. Then she felt a *shift* so massive that she gasped and clutched her chest. Malcolm did the same.

On the western horizon, the sky rippled and then changed. The evening sun disappeared, replaced by a sliver of pale blue sky and gray clouds. The ripple grew, forming a wavy line that stretched over the valley.

Then the ripple moved across the sky, consuming the snowy evening and leaving a different sky in its wake—a gently drizzling *morning* sky.

As it passed overhead, the snow disappeared, leaving cool and gentle rain in its place. The air changed from gentle chill to gentle warmth. On the mountains, trees that had been bare were now lush and exploding with greens and reds and oranges.

Finally, the ripple reached the eastern horizon. The last patch of snowy sky disappeared, replaced by the morning sun. The overwhelming *shift* faded, and the crowd's celebration reached a deafening roar. Even Vash cheered at the top of her lungs.

At the center of all that merriment, the twins gaped at each other. Valentine knew in that moment what Regeneration Day was.

"Regeneration Day," she said. "More like Reset Day."

Malcolm nodded. "They just rewound the clock 610 days."

It explained perfectly why no legends existed about Everwatch. Because to the outside world, it only existed in this place for 610 days. Somehow, they had created a repeating loop in this corner of history. When it hit the 610-day mark, the entire kingdom circled back on the loop to Day One. But this civilization appeared many decades old, if not centuries. Which meant that Time must flow normally inside the loop. They had discovered the perfect way to hide their kingdom from the world.

Even more importantly, Valentine remembered where she had felt that weird feeling before, and the memory burst in her mind like a bomb. The sensation of Time flowing around something, as if a rock were sitting in a stream.

"Mal," she said, grabbing his arm. "The power plant."

"It felt the same! Smaller, but I remember it."

"Instead of 610 days, the Frost Hammer might have used just one. That could be why it felt smaller!"

"Then we do know where she is. If we find *when,* we can bust right through her front door."

Valentine grinned. "No way she could know we would figure that out. We finally have an advantage."

"And we'll get one chance to take them by surprise."

"The king and queen need to hear this."

Malcolm agreed. "Let's go back and get to work."

CHAPTER 37

Back inside the palace, the twins parted ways with their escort. Ten minutes later, they were lost. Somehow they'd taken the lift to the top level, and, after rounding a few corners, they could find neither stairs nor the lift doors.

"This place is impossibly huge," Malcolm said. Stopping at a wall as smooth as smoked glass, he poked along its surface. *Come on, show me what you've got.*

"What are you doing?" Valentine said.

"You saw how these walls light up. One of them's bound to have a map or something."

Nothing appeared. Malcolm didn't know if he was doing it wrong or if this just happened to be a really shiny wall. Eventually he gave up and aimed toward the end of the hall, where double doors led . . . somewhere.

They swung open to reveal a lush atrium. Rain pattered against the circular stone courtyard in the center, soaking into the manicured trees and gardens around the perimeter. Petrichor greeted the twins, that after-rain smell, earthy and clean.

"Hey, look." Valentine pointed. The doors had opened onto a far corner of the atrium. In the opposite corner was a lift door. "Nice! Let's go."

Malcolm barely heard her, his eyes pulled through the trees to the courtyard. Valentine tugged on his arm, but as she followed his gaze, her grip fell away.

Asha stood at the center of the courtyard, arms spread and face tilted up to welcome the rain. After a moment, she removed an outer robe and tossed it aside. Underneath, she wore loose-flowing white pants tucked into soft leather boots, and a form-fitting black tank top. Two *qamas* were strapped to her waist, shiny and new. Drawing them with a metallic rasp, she struck a fighting stance.

Eyes closed, she lifted the blades and began to move—slowly at first, picking up speed as she progressed. Flowing like the water that drenched her, Asha spun and flipped, flicking her blades at unseen enemies, twirling them around her body to deflect unseen attacks, never stopping, each move melting into the next in a delicate battle dance. Glowing faintly red, they carved hissing lines of steam in the rain.

Malcolm could only stare, enraptured. Their weeks together awoke in his mind, every moment that had brought them to this one. The dangerous first encounter. The tense truce. The discovery of a shared purpose, and the start of their training. The beginnings of friendship and mutual respect.

Then the subtle change in her eyes when she looked at him. The first glimmers in his heart. A shared moment of beauty inside a snow globe, Asha standing so close that he could smell her scent.

Then the terror, the despair, the burning rage at seeing her broken body tossed to the floor. The need for her to survive, and the desperate measures to save her.

Watching her now, all those feelings from all those moments came rushing back on Malcolm like a tidal wave. Now he knew that what he'd been running from—what he'd denied himself, believing his path in life would not allow it—had found him anyway. The only question was, what would he do about it?

But he already knew.

"Why don't I give you a few minutes?" Valentine said before he could speak. Hiding a smile, she retreated through the doors.

Before he could back away, before he could find a reason to stop, Malcolm stepped through the trees and walked onto the edge of the stones.

Immersed in her movements, Asha didn't notice. He drank her in, following every curve of her lithe form as it spun through the raindrops. *How can I get her attention without breaking her stride? Or getting cut?* Then an idea struck, and he smiled.

Concentrating on the space around Asha, he opened his nexus. The device glowed blue as energy streamed into him, full of life and vibrancy and cosmic power. He willed it to form a bubble around Asha—exactly like he'd created for her before.

Inside the bubble, raindrops became snowflakes, swirling and dancing around Asha in response to her movements. There she was, the dark-haired warrior princess who'd somehow stolen his heart, the center of a snow globe powered by Time itself. *She's so beautiful.*

Feeling the change, Asha spun to a halt and opened her eyes. She stared up, laughing in delight at the sight of what Malcolm had done. Then she turned and found him through the snow, and when she gazed on him her smile didn't fade. It warmed.

Still, she guarded herself. He could see it. In her eyes he saw a question, and a shadow of fear. She had lied to everyone. Would he be able to forgive her? Would things change between them?

With a purposeful gait, Malcolm approached her. With

every step, her blades lifted higher—the unconscious defense mechanism of a vulnerable warrior.

As he drew near, the Time bubbles disappeared, and the rain poured on them both again. Never breaking stride, Malcolm marched up to Asha, cupped her face in his hands, and kissed her with all the passion he possessed.

With a faint gasp, Asha stiffened. Malcolm could feel her standing rigid, blades still ready. He pressed on, letting his lips caress the soft contours of hers. She almost pulled away.

But instead her body relaxed into his embrace. Malcolm heard a metallic clatter as her blades dropped to the ground. Then her hands were on him, clutching at his arms and shoulders and neck. Pressing into his body, she sighed and kissed him back hungrily, as if the touch of his hands and his lips could never be enough.

For long moments they surrendered to what they had been burying, letting it rush back and forth between them like fire and starlight and bursting colors. For those moments, they were the center of all Time, the glimmering heart of the universe.

When their lips finally parted, Asha clung tightly to Malcolm, keeping him close. Breathing heavily, they leaned against each other for support. Malcolm cradled her face, resting his forehead on hers, while she stroked the back of his neck.

He opened his eyes again. Asha's ice blue eyes were already gazing softly at him.

"You devil," she said with a dreamy smile.

He laughed. Asha giggled like a girl who'd forgotten, just for a moment, the burdens of a soldier.

"Me? You fell through a crack in Time and changed my whole world."

They laughed, holding on to this moment for as long as

possible. Asha leaned her head against his shoulder and traced a fingertip along his jawline.

"I never wanted to lie to you."

"I know."

"I didn't think I had a choice, and—"

"I understand."

"—was trying to save my brother and my people, and—"

He stopped her with another kiss.

"I get it, Asha. I'm not mad."

"Not even a little?"

He shook his head. With a relieved sigh, she closed her eyes and clutched him tighter. Her voice fell to a whisper.

"Thank you for saving me."

Malcolm pulled her close. "I didn't have a choice. I don't want to know what the world is like without you in it." He stroked rain-soaked strands of her hair. "And it'll probably get me a date. So, bonus."

Asha smacked his shoulder. Then she looked up suddenly and glanced all around, as if searching.

"What is it?"

After a moment, she relaxed. "Nothing. I thought someone called my name."

They stood there in silence, reveling in each other, barely even noticing the rain.

It was in that moment of true peace that Malcolm found the solution. Or at least he thought it might be.

The vision of Asha fighting Corday when no one else could, the knowledge that her power was different from theirs, the conversation with Valentine on the balcony—they collided in his mind and burst into a single burning question. One that he kicked himself for never asking before.

"Asha," he said. "Second-*sev* Chronauri use a unique kind of nexus, right? One made just for them?"

She nodded. "It pulls our power from within, rather than from the timeline."

"So, has someone who's not Second-*sev* ever tried to use one?"

CHAPTER 38

It was technically still Regeneration Day. They had gone from late afternoon to around 7 a.m., except 610 days earlier. But the twins could never have waited until tomorrow—not after everything they had discovered.

They hadn't bothered to change. Instead they made a nuisance of themselves until the king and queen had agreed to meet them. So here they stood, in the throne room once again. Waiting for a chance to save their family.

"Do you really think it could work?" Valentine whispered. "I mean, it makes a crazy kind of sense, but . . ."

"Asha thinks it might, though she can't remember anyone trying it," Malcolm said. "When she gets here, we'll find out for sure."

He faced the dais, trying to look serious and focused, but every few seconds it would slip and his joy would shine through. *Come on, get a grip. They'll be here any minute.*

Valentine eyed him with a grin.

". . . What?"

"Oh, nothing," she said, facing forward as well. After a moment of silence she added, "Asha must be a good kisser."

She bit her lip, stifling laughter. Malcolm narrowed his eyes at her, but couldn't hide his joy.

Footsteps entered the room behind them—without looking, Malcolm knew it was High Protectors of the Ember Guard. Suddenly, it was much easier to be serious. He stood straighter.

Six of the Guard stood several paces behind them. Three moved to flank the left side of the dais, three on the right. The thirteenth, Captain Armel, ascended the steps to stand by the thrones.

Thirteen of the most elite warriors in all of history surrounded them. Despite his growing power, Malcolm couldn't help feeling small. How many years had these soldiers trained to wield Time? He gave a respectful nod to the captain, and received one in return.

Behind the thrones, an intricate metal sculpture covered the wall, and now its shining segments began to unfold. Layers of copper and gold curled outward, and the wall irised open to reveal a hidden door. King Jerrik and Queen Meliora stepped through, looking far more regal than they had before.

Asha followed, wrapped in a dark purple robe and a gold belt, dark hair hanging loose and wavy after drying from the rain.

Though she kept her expression neutral, her eyes sparkled as they met Malcolm's. She nodded, signaling that she'd acquired what they needed.

The king and queen did not look happy. Clearly, they didn't appreciate being summoned in their own home, in the middle of the kingdom they ruled. Malcolm just hoped they would listen.

"Thank you for coming," Valentine began as they sat. "We meant no disrespect, but what we've discovered sheds new light on our enemy."

"Actually, it was your command to wait that made this possible," Malcolm added. "Regeneration Day gave us the key."

"Explain," said Queen Meliora.

"We could never locate the Frost Hammer. We tracked every lead, but still couldn't figure out where she was attacking from. Time flowed oddly near our town's power plant, but for all we knew, that was natural."

"Until today, when Everwatch reverted," Valentine took over. "On a bigger scale, it was the exact same feeling. The Frost Hammer must have created a short loop around the power plant, and has been operating from inside it."

"Which explains why we could never find her," Malcolm said. "We looked in the right place, but not the right day."

"How certain are you?" King Jerrik asked.

"Very," Valentine said. "The more she's able to repeat that loop, the longer she has to prepare. We can't let her have more time."

"We also think there's a way to get around her block on our powers," Malcolm said.

He gestured to Asha. Reaching into her robe, she pulled a nexus from each pocket and held them up for all to see.

"The Frost Hammer can block a nexus from drawing power from the timeline," Malcolm continued. "So, what if we took the power from ourselves instead? Use a Second-*sev* nexus to leverage our own Time? The effects wouldn't be permanent, after all. As soon as we could access the timeline again, we would replenish."

"In light of all this, we've come here to ask you again," Valentine said. "Please help us. We can't do it alone."

The king and queen examined them for a long moment, then

turned to each other and whispered. They beckoned Captain Armel over, but glared at Asha when she tried to join.

Two minutes later, it was clear that they had made a decision, and that Captain Armel was not pleased. As he returned to his place, he shot the twins a look of apology.

"Thank you for alerting us to this danger, and for suggesting a strategy," the king said. "It must be dealt with immediately. A strike force will be sent this afternoon."

Malcolm sighed in relief. "Thank you so much."

"You will be informed of the outcome when the Ember Guard returns," the queen added.

"WHAT?!" the twins shouted in unison.

"A threat of this magnitude must be met only by trusted, capable agents of Everwatch," King Jerrik said. "Two untrained youths may introduce more danger. You will be perfectly comfortable here in the meantime."

Malcolm clenched his fists. "Last year, a man from the future tried to vaporize our town, and we beat him with no help. Where were you then?"

"She has our family," Valentine said. "We will not be held captive here!"

"Mother, Father," Asha broke in. "Please don't—"

"We cannot base tactics on your emotions," Queen Meliora said to the twins. "This threat came from Everwatch, and it will come back upon Everwatch if we do not quell it properly."

Fury boiled Malcolm's blood. "I've heard enough. We're going back home to protect our family now."

Valentine stared daggers at the royals. "Just try and stop us. Let's go, Mal."

Turning, they marched toward the main doors of the throne

room. *We'll get to the Empyrean Bridge,* Malcolm thought, *and then figure out how to get home.*

Six High Protectors stood in their path. Five eyed the twins and the royals in turn, uncertain what to do. The sixth, of course, was brash Liam. Conjuring a massive broadsword of fire, he faced them with a grin that said he was eager for a fight.

"Move or be moved," Malcolm warned.

In response, Liam created a flaming tower shield in his off hand, bellowed, and charged.

"Stand down, Liam!" Captain Armel shouted.

But the young Guard was beyond reason. Drawing close, Liam raised his weapon to strike.

He got no further.

Malcolm opened his nexus just as Valentine opened hers. Their coronas burst with dazzling light.

Wrapping the broadsword in slowed Time, Malcolm flexed his will and matched fire with ice. The weapon flashed into steam. He focused those same flows on Liam's feet and froze him to the ground.

Sheathed in fast Time, Valentine danced a complete circle around Liam before he could blink, her fire whips snapping in rapid succession. When she returned to Malcolm's side, Liam's silver plating fell away and clanged to the ground.

They could have let it end there. They *should* have. But Malcolm was angry, and he could feel the same heat from his sister.

With an extra nudge, he encased Liam's body in a solid block of ice. Valentine unleashed a lightning bolt and hit the block dead center. The ice shattered and Liam flew backward. Tumbling onto the dark stones, he slid to a stop and did not get up.

Their counterattack had taken less than three seconds.

Malcolm felt a series of *shifts* as the High Protectors each opened their nexus. He heard shouts of outrage and the clatter of weapons. The twins spun, preparing for an epic fight.

They turned to see Asha running at them. Her robe flapped in the wind, revealing shiny new Ember Guard armor to complement her new *qamas*. As she reached the twins, she whirled around and skidded to a halt with weapons drawn, placing them at her back.

"They only want to defend their home! Wouldn't you?"

Looking over her shoulder, Asha caught Malcolm's eye and glanced down at her own weapons. He furrowed his brow in confusion. She repeated the pattern with her eyes, growing more insistent.

Then he understood. There was only one play that would get them out of the throne room without a battle. And every second they delayed brought the Frost Hammer closer to victory.

"Follow my lead," he whispered to Valentine.

Before he could talk himself out of it, Malcolm threw his arms around Asha, tore the *qamas* from her hands . . . and then held them at her throat. As he channeled Time into the weapons, they blazed red, and the air around them sizzled and popped.

The queen leapt from her chair, shouting a command that halted the High Protectors in their tracks. She stared murder at the twins, but he saw terror in her eyes and felt a stab of guilt.

The king wore a different expression. Sunken back against his throne, he beheld the twins with awe, terror, shock, and something like realization. The curious array of emotions puzzled Malcolm, but he had no chance to dwell on it.

Valentine caught on quickly. "Don't follow us, or else!"

She threw up her hands and her corona became a swirl of

blues and reds. A dome of fire encased them, punctuated by long spikes of ice jabbing out in all directions. Malcolm could hear electrical arcs as lightning jumped from spike to spike.

"Back away, toward the doors," Valentine said.

They followed her, the protective dome rolling along the floor with them.

"Nicely done," Asha whispered, then leaned back to give Malcolm a peck on his lips.

Despite the situation, his cheeks warmed. He noticed now how snugly her body was pressed against his. *Focus, man!*

"We're at the doors now," Valentine said. "When I tell you, drop to your knees and give me an ice dome."

Malcolm nodded. Just a few more steps and they emerged into the gigantic entry hall. Valentine counted to three.

"Now!"

Malcolm fell to his knees, arms wrapped around Asha. Concentrating, he tossed up a second dome made entirely of thick ice, shielding them from the dome his sister had created. Valentine knelt with them.

Her dome exploded like a bomb. The throne room doors ripped to pieces and the frames came tumbling down, blocking the opening with piles of debris.

"Run!" she yelled.

Malcolm's dome shattered, Asha sheathed her blades, and they sprinted across the entry hall while angry shouts echoed from the throne room. As they burst through to the grounds outside, what seemed like hundreds of Everwatch citizens stared in alarm.

Asha ignored them. "This way."

She sprinted, leading the twins across the vast grounds until they reached a familiar path through a familiar grouping of trees.

Veering away from the path, Asha cut into the little forest, and they crashed through the undergrowth after her. With each step, hope grew in Malcolm's chest.

They burst through the tree line and stopped in their tracks. Two dozen soldiers formed a double line between the twins and the Empyrean Bridge.

Out in front, a short and stocky soldier put a finger to his ear as if listening to something, then nodded and drew a gleaming rapier.

Malcolm sighed. They didn't have time for this.

"Watchers!" the soldier said. "Protect the—"

Pointing forward, Malcolm created two walls of ice down the center of the Watchers' formation, ten feet tall and thicker than a man. Following his gestures, one wall slid left and the other slid right. Like giant brooms, they swept the soldiers aside and cleared a path to the platform. Valentine and Asha sprinted through the opening.

On reaching the platform, Asha knelt and placed her fingertips on a particular stone. It glowed in response and a control panel rose up.

Before the Watchers could counterassault, Malcolm curved the walls and froze their ends together, making two perfect circles with them trapped inside. Shouting challenges, they hacked at the ice, but normal weapons would never break through. If they had more powerful weapons, Malcolm guessed they wouldn't use them so close to their comrades.

With a wave of Asha's hand, two virtual keyboards projected from the control panel and a three-dimensional holographic display glowed to life above them. She called instructions to Valentine as her fingers flew across her own keyboard. The Empyrean Bridge's three massive rings began to move.

"Found it!" Asha called.

Malcolm joined them. The holographic display showed what looked like a sphere inside a rushing stream. Inside the sphere, he could just discern the outline of a valley and an industrial facility.

"That's Corday's regeneration bubble?"

"Yes," Asha said. "It appears to span a full day."

"Mal," Valentine said, her eyes haunted, "look at the date."

Malcolm saw the day Corday had chosen to hide in. He felt sick in the pit of his stomach. "Oh, man. That's the day after we fought Lucius."

She nodded. "I remember the plant being out of commission because no one had any power. We thought it was because of what Lucius did . . . but maybe it wasn't."

"The Frost Hammer used the chaos to her advantage." For some reason, this made Malcolm even angrier. *As if those days weren't painful enough, now we have to go back there and fight again.*

"Plan quickly," Asha urged. "The Ember Guard should arrive any second."

"Jump to that day, then find a way inside the bubble?" Valentine suggested.

"We've never done that before, and I don't know how," Malcolm said. "Could we go back a few days before she did this? Stop her before she creates it?"

Asha's fingers flew over her keyboard. She smacked her fist on the console. "*Daotan!* The Frost Hammer is clever. She managed to anchor her loop, so going back before will not prevent its creation."

"What does that mean?" Valentine asked.

"The loop here in Everwatch is anchored, meaning it's a

fixed point in the timeline. Causality will only bend around it. Going back before won't prevent its creation. It's one way we protect the kingdom." She grimaced. "Corday figured out how to copy it."

"Then there's only one option," Malcolm said, the thought filling him with dread. "We jump directly inside the bubble."

Asha stared at him. "You're insane. We have no strategy, no plan once we're inside."

"You still have a Second-*sev* nexus for each of us, right?"

She nodded, reached into her robe, and handed one to each of them.

"Corday doesn't know we have these. She'll expect to shut us down like before. So we go straight for her, try to take her down while she's surprised."

"He's right," Valentine said heavily. "This may be the one shot we get."

A dozen powerful *shifts* hit Malcolm's senses. Whipping around, he saw the High Protectors charging through the trees. "They're here."

Raising his hands, Malcolm channeled a rush of energy and a dome appeared over the platform—not made of ice or fire, but of Time itself. A layer of slowed Time sandwiched between two layers of fast Time. Hopefully it would confuse their pursuers long enough.

Just as Asha entered the jump command, the first attack burst against the shield. Malcolm flinched, smiling grimly as it held firm. Then a flurry of attacks bombarded it all at once.

"The portal needs two minutes!" Asha called. She glanced up as an explosion rocked the dome. "Which we don't have."

Malcolm turned back to her just as the spinning ring became a red vortex. "Yeah, not two minutes—now!"

"The portal won't be stable—" Asha protested.

"Things aren't stable *here*," Valentine said. "Let's go!"

Hand in hand, Malcolm and Asha dashed behind Valentine to the waiting vortex. With each step, the red light filled more of his vision. As they approached the edge, Malcolm's dome shattered under the full assault of the High Protectors. Valentine faltered, looking behind them.

"Don't look, just go!" Malcolm called.

Together they leapt.

CHAPTER 39

L ight burst and streamed in the vortex as they tunneled through Time and space. Like a trio of bullets, they flew as if fired down the barrel of a cosmic rifle. Valentine worked to stay calm, but a heavy cocktail of exhilaration and terror turned her blood to fire.

The jump back to Everwatch had been little more than a flash. This was something else entirely. Centuries flashed by in a thousand sights and sounds and radiant colors from no known spectrum. This was the energy that powered the universe—that powered her and Malcolm. She savored the rush, knowing that in any second they would face mortal danger.

The tunnel shrank, constricting around them. In the distance, a narrow rift of blackness opened across their path. Before they could blink, the rift was upon them. The tunnel of light disappeared, and Valentine flew into cold blackness, knowing somehow that she was back in the real world. A heartbeat later, she smacked into a concrete floor and tumbled.

The blackness melted away, revealing the inside of an industrial building the size of an airplane hangar. As they skidded to a halt, Valentine somersaulted to her feet with Malcolm and Asha at her side, all three glowing with power.

To their right, massive bay doors stood open, revealing the two gigantic stacks of Rayner Nuclear Power Plant. It was dark outside, but a hint of gray showed on the eastern horizon. What was inside this building, though, stole all of Valentine's attention. Staring at the wall in front of them, she gaped in disbelief.

It appeared to be a makeshift command center. The wall itself was barely visible, covered by a network of metal beams and hundreds of thick power and data cables.

A strange machine dominated the left side. The size of a pickup truck, it rumbled from deep inside, working at something Valentine couldn't begin to guess. The right side overflowed with computer equipment and giant display screens, which were currently dark.

A ring sat in the center, ten feet across, like a crude facsimile of the Empyrean Bridge. A blue vortex spun brightly inside it, as if eager to be used.

Perched above everything, Valentine spotted a dodeca-hedron. Though primitive compared with what she'd seen in Everwatch, and lacking the iridescent quality, it still spun inside a rippling energy field. *That's how Corday created her temporal loop.* To Valentine's surprise, the command center sat quiet and dark, seemingly without personnel or protection.

Until she took a step toward it.

The instant she moved, she gasped as her senses were slammed with an overwhelming rush. *Shift* upon *shift* upon *shift.* Massive amounts of Time were suddenly being channeled. One by one, she felt dozens of nexuses wake up, and one by one their bearers appeared.

Rogue Chronauri. At least thirty of them. From the far corners and deep shadows of the cavernous room, they appeared to form a loose circle around the twins and Asha.

They were waiting for us, Valentine thought, wanting to kick herself.

It must have been the other reason the Frost Hammer hadn't launched the final stage of her plan. It wasn't only because she needed time to prepare. She'd been waiting for her enemies to figure out what she'd done and come knocking. *Which we did, and fell right into her trap.* With them out of the way, there would be few left to oppose her final assault on Emmett's Bluff.

Valentine couldn't imagine a world where they defeated this many hardened fighters. Yet here they were, about to try anyway . . . and they would make it hurt.

Asha raised her blades. "*My heart, my sword will ever blaze . . .*"

Valentine opened her nexus wider. *Be strong, Val.* Cosmic energy bathed her cells in its radiance. All that was Valentine Gilbert heightened and expanded, bursting with power. She felt Time *shift* as Malcolm did the same.

"*. . . for all of Time, for all my days.*"

Malcolm's corona blazed. "All right. Who wants some?"

Valentine beckoned to the horde. "Come and get it."

From roof to foundation, the building trembled with the fury of their battle. Steel bent and burned and ripped. Ice and fire and lightning burst through in waves of devastation, carrying shouts of rage and pain. For miles around the valley, the timeline quivered and warped. Any Chronauri living within ten years of the battle felt its vibrations through Time.

Ten minutes later, the three of them leaned against each other for support, battered and drained beyond measure. Half of the attacking horde lay unconscious, scattered like rag dolls. The half that remained upright were exhausted and panting.

Valentine was the embodiment of agony, her Everwatch

robes in tatters. A quick glance at her companions showed them in much the same condition. The two forces eyed each other, dreading another clash, yet knowing the fight was not over.

"What, that's all?" Asha taunted, her face twisted in pain.

Malcolm forced himself to chuckle. "Tired already? We're just getting started."

And if they were going to win, this fight had to end quickly. Somewhere the Frost Hammer was furthering her plan while they battled her minions here. Somewhere their family and friends waited to be rescued.

Valentine mustered her courage. "Come on, then. Which one of you is first?"

The enemy radiated reluctance. Valentine saw something in their eyes that hadn't been there before—respect. *Well, that's something, I guess.*

A stocky brunette woman stepped forward, short spears in each hand. With a twist of her wrists, the spearheads lit on fire. Goaded into action now, her comrades drew into a tighter circle around the three.

Malcolm visibly collected himself. His corona began to glow. Asha's blades shimmered red again. Which meant it was Valentine's turn. With a deep breath, she opened her nexus and Time rushed in. This time the feeling was bitter as much as it was sweet.

"We didn't have to be enemies," she said.

"Even the righteous path may lead through darkness," Spear Woman said. "Though it is necessary, I mourn for your people. Defend them with honor and may the best of us survive."

Valentine shook her head. "We don't kill."

Spear Woman gave her a pitying look. "Then you will die."

Valentine nodded, understanding that it was all they would

say. In her head she counted down from five—at zero, no matter what, she would attack.

Five . . .

Four . . .

Thr—

With a *whoosh,* the vortex flared brighter and a shadowed figure stepped through. A familiar *thrum* hit her deep inside. Valentine felt a stab of panic as her connection to Time disintegrated.

Then she remembered they weren't helpless anymore. Hiding a grin, she exchanged a knowing look with Malcolm. They had a plan, and no one would see it coming.

The circle of Chronauri parted as the shadow approached from the vortex, coalescing into the jagged black armor of the Frost Hammer. Madame LaChance—*no*—Charlotte Corday removed her helmet and stood two paces from them.

It was close enough. Leaping at their enemy with a cry, Valentine tapped into her *other* nexus and Time flowed from deep within. Hands raised overhead, she conjured white-hot flames in the shape of a massive scythe.

Corday retreated, wide-eyed. Tripping on one of her fallen minions, she toppled over backward just as Valentine swung her weapon. Which was exactly what Valentine wanted.

Corday slammed onto her back. Valentine felt a *shift* and Malcolm buried her under as much ice as he could create. Then, as the rogue Chronauri recovered from their shock, he and Asha turned and unleashed a storm of attacks. Hopefully enough to keep them busy.

Leaping atop the ice mound, Valentine pushed the nexus to its absolute limit. A Second-*sev* wasn't as strong, but she prayed it would be enough for one bolt of lightning. She went to work, the air crackling around her as she built up the necessary charge. *Come on, only a few more sec—*

A bone-shaking rumble was her only warning. Then the ice shattered and a burst of gravity flung Valentine to the floor. The air around her rippled with distortions. Soon Malcolm and Asha slammed down next to her.

The Frost Hammer loomed over them, panting. To Valentine's chagrin, she looked less terrified and more annoyed.

Corday gestured at them. Gravity waves ripped Valentine's borrowed nexus from her wrist, then her real nexus. Both of Malcolm's came next, and then Asha's tore through her armor. As one they floated up to hover around Corday's outstretched hand.

"Please, no," Valentine heard herself say. "Without those—"

The Frost Hammer closed her fist. With a sickening crunch, the devices crushed to the size of marbles, then ripped to shreds. Valentine gasped, feeling as if she'd been kicked in the gut. Malcolm made a choked sound.

That's it, then. It's all over. Without a nexus, the twins might as well be normal people. An aching emptiness filled her.

"You Chronauri and your tricks," Corday said, shaking her head.

Malcolm seethed. "This won't end well for you. Your last mistake was taking our family."

"Still you speak this way, *mon cheri.*" Leaning over, she traced a fingertip tenderly across his lips. "As if you do not realize the truth—that you are already defeated."

Turning to Spear Woman, Corday made a gesture. With a nod, she marched to the computer array and flipped a single switch.

Behind Valentine, something huge made a series of *clanks.*

Twirling her hand, Corday spun the three companions to face the wall opposite her command center. With each metallic sound, the corrugated steel shook until the clanks became a mechanical whirring.

Then the wall began to move, and Valentine saw the simple deception unfold. What she had thought was a main wall of the building turned out to be a partition separating the building's second half. Now the partition folded like a curtain.

When she saw what was on the other side, her insides froze. *They've been here all along. Oh, no.*

Her dad. Oma Grace. John. Callie. Clive. Fred. Winter. Tyrathorn.

The Frost Hammer had kept them here, waiting for this moment. She had hollowed out the Skrim that held them captive, leaving their heads and chests exposed but the rest still trapped. A para-nexus blinked on each of their chests, slowly siphoning their Time—yet they were all still conscious. Which meant they could see and hear everything.

Terror and rage washed over Valentine in equal measures. *We'll figure something out. We have to.* But the Frost Hammer wasn't finished.

Corday strolled toward their family, strands of gravity pulling the twins and Asha along the floor behind her. As they drew closer, Valentine heard voices challenge their enemy to a fight, while others taunted or insulted her. There would be no pleas for mercy from them.

Valentine couldn't help swelling with pride. They would be strong to the last moment. The only face that gave her pause was her father's. Neil Gilbert beheld his children with tear-stained eyes, his face a mask of fear and confusion. She looked away to keep from falling apart.

"Afraid to fight with honor?" Asha called. "Will that satisfy you—a victory you didn't earn?"

Corday scoffed. "Any victory that is achieved, is earned."

Bands of gravity tightened around the three, and then they were flying. Lifting them onto their feet, the Frost Hammer faced them toward their family. Though they worked hard to appear strong, Valentine saw fear in their eyes.

"Oh, hey, y'all," Fred said with a casual air. "When'd you get here?"

"Come on, you know they just had to make a grand entrance," Winter said.

Valentine almost laughed. Leave it to them to cut through certain death with a joke.

"We're fine, my dears," Oma Grace said. Valentine could see her working to project calm. "Don't you worry about us. We're fine . . . no matter what."

Of course she would try to take care of them. Next to her, Clive gave them an encouraging nod despite the bloody cut across his forehead. Callie appeared less afraid and more annoyed that this was happening to them. Tyrathorn just stared at the floor, shame pouring off him in waves.

Finally, her gaze fell on John. He must have been so afraid, yet his eyes gave her only love. It filled her, lending her strength. She gave him a grateful smile, regretting only that she couldn't kiss him.

"John," she began, "I love—"

The Frost Hammer spun them to face her command center again. This time she anchored their restraints to the floor with strands of gravity. Valentine couldn't move an inch, and now she was forced to look at her enemies instead of her family. Somewhere beneath the despair, a spark of anger ignited.

Had she ever felt so helpless? Time glowed in her perception, begging her to reach out and take it. Yet when she tried, she bounced off what felt like bulletproof glass. The wall that her nexus had allowed her to pierce.

"Do not look so sad," Corday said. "With a strong guiding hand, this world will become a much a better place."

"Well," Asha said, "I hope that makes up for your face."

Corday frowned, unconsciously touching the nasty cut from eyebrow to chin. The cut that Asha had inflicted.

Asha tilted her head now, feigning curiosity. "What happened to it, again?"

Corday lashed out and Asha's head rocked back. Smiling through a split lip, she spit, and a fleck of blood landed on her enemy's cheek. Corday put her face only inches from Asha's, trembling with rage.

"What happens now, it is because of you. Remember that, *petite.*"

Flinging out her hand, she curled her fingers. With a scraping sound, Tyrathorn's icy prison dragged across the floor until it stopped next to her. He kept his face downcast.

Clutching his long black hair, Corday yanked back and slapped him across the face. Then she drew back and slapped him again. Finally his attention focused on her. Valentine could see his jaw clench.

"There you are, my old friend," Corday said. "You can thank your sister for this."

She pressed an open palm against his chest. The air thickened as dense gravity distortions rose from the ground to gather around her. Corday tensed, as if straining to wield as much as she could. The waves coursed up her body and then down her arm, concentrating at her palm. Valentine swayed, dizzy as gravity twisted the flow of Time into unnatural patterns.

"I will not take your life," the Frost Hammer said through clenched teeth. "I will take what is most precious to you."

As Valentine looked on in revulsion, the flows of Time inside Tyrathorn shredded, giving way to claws of gravitational force. He winced, twisting away from the invasion. Corday only tightened her grip.

Gravity dug deeper, ripping through Tyrathorn's presence in Time and space, until finally they reached the deepest center of his being. Valentine saw then what the Frost Hammer was aiming for, and she cried out in horror.

"No!" Malcolm shouted. "No, you can't—"

The Frost Hammer twisted her palm, and the claws inside Tyrathorn struck. He screamed, an inhuman cry that pierced the air like a knife. Something inside him cracked and then burst.

A shockwave exploded from his body, carrying light and temporal distortions and a thousand sensations of agony and loss. The blast broke his icy prison and threw Tyrathorn to the ground along with Corday.

Valentine trained her senses on their friend, searching for the inner spark she'd felt before. But where it had been, now there was only a dark void.

"Tell me she didn't . . ." She swallowed hard, unable to finish.

Malcolm gave a hollow nod. "She just broke his Chronauri ability."

Asha strained against her bonds, desperate to reach her enemy. Tears streamed down her face. "I swear on all Eternity, I will cut you to pieces!"

Tears burned Valentine's eyes. Back at the charity ball, the Frost Hammer had promised Tyrathorn that he would beg for death. For someone so strong to suddenly lose it all—what would that do to him? Even now, Valentine saw the emptiness in his eyes. Though his restraints were gone, he lay unmoving.

"I'm sorry, Thorn," Asha whispered. "I'm sorry, I'm so sorry . . ."

Standing, the Frost Hammer nudged him with her armored boot. He didn't respond.

"We could have ruled all of Time together," she said. "But you were not strong enough."

"Let me free and I'll show you strong enough, *kaga!*" Asha spat.

Corday ignored her, instead turning to her minions. Those that had fallen were conscious again, and stood now with their brethren.

"You all know your tasks," she announced. "Let's save the world."

The minions gave a shout of triumph and leapt into action. Valentine could only watch, her heart sinking through the floor. *This is a bad dream. It has to be.*

They split into teams. The first took control of the computer array, switching on two giant display screens. The left screen showed a hundred different gauges and columns of cascading numbers.

The right screen showed a dusty brick room, its roof mostly gone. *That must be in town, somewhere that hasn't been rebuilt yet.* The para-nexus launcher filled the center of the room, sur-rounded by a series of metal containers. Valentine strained against her bonds. *We have to get to that!*

More than anything, that launcher must be destroyed first. Without it, the Frost Hammer would be forced to capture Emmett's Bluff person by person, which would give them a chance to mount a defense. But where exactly was it hidden? And when?

As for where, the room itself offered few clues. But when? Valentine thought she knew. *Probably six months from now, in our present.* When all of Corday's ice pillars had appeared.

But knowing didn't get her any closer to destroying it. Overcome with frustration, she slammed her will against that bulletproof wall again. The glow of cosmic power flowed behind it, an unreachable salvation.

The strange machine in the room with them grew louder. Minions swarmed over it like ants, making constant adjustments. Once more, Valentine puzzled over what the monstrous thing might do . . . and then it showed her.

A mechanical arm extended from beneath the machine, capped by an open ring about a foot wide. A second arm positioned above it, this one holding a series of tubes that opened directly above the ring.

Valentine felt a *shift* and the ring glowed with a tiny red vortex. A para-nexus fell from the tubes and disappeared through the portal. Then a small flash drew her attention to the screen displaying the brick room, where she watched the para-nexus drop through an identical vortex. It landed in one of the containers surrounding the launcher.

The process repeated over and over again, growing faster. *They're creating the final para-nexus waves, and keeping their machines separate so we can't destroy it all.* Oh, the Frost Hammer was clever.

Against the wall, the larger ring *shifted* from blue to red, and the last team of rogue Chronauri dove through. Valentine watched the screen now, where a red portal appeared on the brick wall. All ten minions spilled out and surrounded the launcher, double-checking every inch. Soon one of them approached the camera, his face growing large on the display.

"All is ready," he said. "We await your command."

Slowly, deliberately, Charlotte Corday turned to look her enemies in the eye—first Asha, then Malcolm, then Valentine. As their eyes locked, her lips quirked up in a satisfied grin.

"Begin."

CHAPTER 40

With a heavy *thump,* the machine fired a para-nexus through the open roof. The device blinked to life in midair and curved away, flying under its own power. A quarter-second later, another para-nexus launched. Reliable as a clock, the launcher began to spit a steady stream.

If we don't do something, this town won't know what hit it until it's too late! Valentine wracked her brain for some strategy to buy more time.

Time. That was ironic. The one thing they should have an inexhaustible supply of, and now it flowed just beyond reach. Again she lunged and bounced off the cosmic barrier.

With her back to them, the Frost Hammer surveyed all the moving pieces of her grand plan. "Display progress."

Two numbers appeared on the screen displaying the launcher. One ticked up when a para-nexus deployed, but the other stayed at zero. Activity slowed as her minions watched, waiting with baited breath for . . . something. Every moment it remained at zero, their tension seemed to grow.

Did something go wrong? Valentine clung to the hope that—

The zero changed to one, then two, then five, then shot up like a rocket. The minions shouted in triumph, the Frost

Hammer held up a victorious fist, and Valentine's despair deepened. She knew what it was now.

Every number meant another person captured. Another doomed to power Corday's army. And if they did nothing, eventually the numbers would stop ticking. Because no one would be left.

"Good," Clive said under his breath, though Valentine heard him. "Now he'll find it. Now you'll learn."

Craning her neck, Valentine shot him a quizzical look. Clive just flashed a grim smile and winked as if they'd shared a secret.

Malcolm grew restless, straining against his bonds. "It can't go down like this," he whispered. "There's got to be something we missed."

Valentine's gaze flickered to Tyrathorn, crumpled on the floor. She might have thought he was dead, if not for the rise and fall of his chest. The Frost Hammer had known exactly what she was doing, breaking the strongest of them.

Valentine focused back on Malcolm, struggling to project hope. He read her expression anyway, and his shoulders slumped.

"Some Chronauri we turned out to be."

"Come on, man," Clive muttered. "Get there. Get it done."

But the minutes ticked by and the machine kept working. Valentine silently apologized to everyone as the numbers increased. Before she knew it, twenty minutes had passed. Nearly five thousand of those evil things had launched, and more than four thousand had found victims.

What sort of panic must be racing through Emmett's Bluff right now? With another surge of frustration, of rage, Valentine punched her will against Time's barrier. *Why won't you just help us?*

Another para-nexus launched. Valentine's heart chased it through the air, praying for a miracle, begging the universe for something to turn the tide. Then, before the device had a chance to curve out of sight, it blew to pieces.

Valentine gaped. "Mal, look!"

Another para-nexus launched and exploded into fiery bits.

"What's happening?" The Frost Hammer snapped. Her minions scrambled.

"We detect no defects," one replied.

"The problem must be external," another said.

"What do you mean, external?" Corday demanded.

Behind Valentine, Clive chuckled.

With a flutter on the screen, a dark shape dropped through the open roof and landed in the center of the brick room. A man, Valentine saw now—wearing a long black coat and armored gloves, a deep hood that shadowed his face, and some kind of high-tech goggles.

Reaching under his coat, he produced two metal orbs the size of tennis balls—one black and one silver. Connected by a thick braid of cables, they reminded Valentine of the old *bolas* throwing weapon that Malcolm used to have.

Before the minions could move, he flung his device toward the ring and its red vortex.

Midflight the black orb halted, hovering at the edge of the vortex without plunging through. It split open, its insides emanating green light, and with a beep the vortex suddenly *shifted* from red to blue.

The silver orb kept flying. As the vortex changed, it disappeared through the blue light . . . only to burst through the portal in the Frost Hammer's command center. It split open, too, radiating the same green light.

"Destroy it, you fools!" Corday shouted, sprinting for the portal.

She only made it five steps.

Tethered to each other across the temporal vortex, both orbs emitted a high-pitched whine. They exploded in unison, and with a *whoosh* the vortex collapsed on itself. Valentine shut her eyes as a wave of hot air whipped across her face.

When she opened them again, the ring was a twisted pile of wreckage.

"Whoa!" Malcolm said.

"That's it," Clive whispered, sounding pleased. "Now she can't help them."

He was right, Valentine realized. Corday's para-nexus launcher existed months in the future, relative to the date they currently occupied. With her portal destroyed, she was effectively cut off from the machine until she found another way to jump through the timeline.

Valentine ached to ask Clive more questions, but everything moved too fast. Shaking with rage, Corday pointed up at the screen, where her minions on the other side were picking themselves up.

"Kill him!"

Two rogue Chronauri lunged for the hooded man. He shimmered and disappeared, leaving them to dive through the empty space and topple to the floor. They cast around the room, searching.

Behind two other minions, the air shimmered, and the hooded man reappeared. With a flick of his wrist, something burst at their feet and the floor turned to dust. They plummeted through the hole with a shocked cry. The hooded man faded away as fire filled the air where he had stood.

Seething, the Frost Hammer seized her nearest minion. She drew him close and shouted into his face. "Get me to my launcher! *Someone* find me a way!"

On the screen, the hooded man reappeared beside the launcher. Facing it, he clapped his hands together and a thunderous shockwave burst from his palms. The machine rocked with a metallic groan.

Valentine smiled. *He's trying to destroy it!*

But the launcher had taken little real damage. He moved to try again, then ducked away as a gout of flame jetted over his head. Rolling across the floor, he regained his feet and clapped. Another shockwave tossed his attacker across the room.

"Yes! Go!" Asha called.

Valentine saw Tyrathorn twitch, roused by his sister's voice. He gazed up at her, then followed her eyes to the screen. As he watched *someone* still fighting, his eyes regained a hint of their old fire.

Stuck in her prison, Valentine could only watch as their strange ally appeared and disappeared. He attacked Chronauri and launcher alike, catching his enemies by surprise, leaping through holes in their defense. He fought dirty, and one by one they fell.

All the while, the Frost Hammer screamed at her people while Valentine cheered with her family. Even Tyrathorn raised a fist in salute. By now only three minions remained, and each had taken a beating.

But then the hooded man made a mistake. Perhaps too eager to win, he reappeared right next to the launcher. His next shockwave dented the casing . . . but he had taken too long. Before he could disappear, four ice arrows sliced through the air and pierced his torso.

"No!" Valentine cried.

The hooded man flew back and smacked against the wall. Dazed, hood askew, he sank to the floor. As his goggles broke and fell away, Valentine finally saw his face. *What?!* She stared in disbelief. Even the attacking minions stopped in confusion.

Clive leaned against the wall, breathing hard. Valentine spotted the same cut across his forehead, but the wound had nearly healed. Agape, she turned, and all eyes followed her to the Clive in the room with them.

He grinned, shrugging. "I may've kept a few things secret lately. Sometimes, only thing that can help a man is himself. Ain't that right, Old Man?"

On the screen, *Clive* saluted the camera. "Right you are, Young Man."

"How are you doing this?" Corday demanded.

Clive winced, gasping. Looking down at the arrows in his chest, he shook his head wistfully. "You understand what's happenin' here?"

Clive nodded. "Yessir, I do."

"Know what you gotta do, then . . . when your time comes?"

Clive's grin faded into determination. A look like chiseled stone. "I do. I'll get it done."

"Good man. So will I. In fact, I'm gonna do it right now."

Valentine found her voice. "Clive, what's happening? I don't understand."

Eyes glistening, he gave her a reassuring smile. "Just watch the screen, my girl. And don't worry—everything's gonna be all right. Promise."

She shook her head, still lost, but listened to her friend and turned back to the screen. Just as she did, *Clive* somehow regained his feet. He took a heavy step toward the nearest rogue Chronauri.

"Stay down!" the minion said.

Two more frozen arrows struck home and *Clive* rocked back in agony. He forced himself upright again. Reaching under his coat, he flipped a switch, and Valentine spotted the distortion of a personal shield.

"You got one chance to stop me, son," *Clive* said. "Think you got it in you?"

To Valentine's surprise, the giant man hesitated. Then *Clive* flared his coat wide open, and her surprise turned to horror.

The entire inner layer of his coat was lined with Time grenades—at least a hundred of them. He must have done something, because they were all glowing. It dawned on her then what he had planned. What he must have known would happen. Because that *Clive*—the *Clive* on the screen—had already seen all of this happen before.

Oh god, Clive, please no.

"I'm comin' now, son," *Clive* said. "Better make it count."

Gathering his last shred of strength, he ran toward the launcher.

"KILL HIM!" Corday bellowed.

With every pounding step *Clive* took, the rogue Chronauri covered him with elemental attacks. Some burst against his shield, some glanced away, others broke through to pierce his body. *Clive* took every fatal hit and drove forward, relentless as the tide. Nearing the launcher, he coiled like a spring and leapt.

With his coat flared open, *Clive* flew through the storm and collided full force with the launcher. All at once, every Time grenade shattered.

Red light swarmed the machine like a tornado. Brighter and

brighter it glowed, faster and faster it spun, each bomb building off the last until the room itself began to disintegrate. Finally, the blast enveloped the building.

The camera flew to pieces, and the screen turned black.

CHAPTER 41

S tunned silence blanketed the room. Valentine worked to process what she'd just seen. Some future version of Clive had just paid the highest price, giving them their one and only advantage. Caught between grief and gratitude, she couldn't look away from the numbers on the screen.

4,629

Each one a para-nexus that had claimed a victim. Before this ended, they would have to find a way to free every single host. And if *Clive* hadn't done what he did, they would have faced many more.

Valentine heard a choked sob.

"Clive, no," Oma Grace pleaded. "There must be another way."

Clive gazed at her with tenderness, his eyes conveying a friendship that had lasted over a century.

"We've lived long past our time, anyway, Grace," he said. "If I gotta walk in shadow to save my friends, well, that's all right with me. I just wish I had longer to say goodbye."

"Clive," John said, choking back his own tears, "I . . ."

Clive understood. Though he smiled, a tear fell down his

cheek. "When this is over, go to my shop and open the safe. I left some'n there for—"

"YOU!"

The Frost Hammer glared at Clive, quivering with hate. As she stalked toward him, waves of gravity burst through her feet and cracked the concrete around her. Her palms glowed as red energy filled them, fed by her suit of armor. Clive watched her calmly.

Again Valentine lunged for Time and found an empty space where her nexus used to be. She hammered at the invisible wall to no avail. *You're only Fourth-sev—what did you expect?*

Shut up, I know! she answered herself. *But I have to try. Even if it's not enough.*

Corday raised her hands at Clive. "You will not live to—"

A blur slammed into her, knocking them both hard to the floor. The red orbs flew up to blow holes in the ceiling. Corday rolled onto her back with her attacker on top.

Straddling his former ally, Tyrathorn rained down punches. Corday covered her face, as if forgetting for a moment that she was stronger.

"S'pose that's my cue," Clive said. "My turn to go back now, look after Young Clive."

How could he possibly escape now?

Yet he radiated certainty. Quickly as he could, Clive met each of their eyes, a split-second to say goodbye. Valentine searched for something to say but came up short. It was Malcolm who summed it up perfectly.

"Thank you, Clive," he said, his voice choked.

He nodded, flashing that easy grin. "Thank you for being my friends."

He flexed, and something rippled in his chest just beneath the skin. With a subtle *snap*, blue light radiated from him. The soft glow traced across his body, growing into a dazzling display as it spread. Then the light twisted around Clive as if he stood at the center of his own personal vortex.

Valentine felt a *shift,* and then Clive was gone. She stared, barely believing that it would be the last time she ever saw him. A choked sob burst from her chest.

A shout pulled her attention back to Tyrathorn. Remembering herself, the Frost Hammer struck, and a deep *thrum* rattled Valentine's teeth. Tyrathorn rocketed sideways and bounced off the wall with a bone-shaking *clang*. He fell to the floor, clutching his side and glaring at her in defiance.

Corday turned back toward Clive, only to find his empty prison. She stopped short and her eyes went wide.

Valentine's insides leapt with triumph. She knew what his escape meant. In failing to kill Clive, the Frost Hammer had ultimately failed to prevent her machine's destruction. The Charlotte Corday of the past would not be prepared for him, and she would end up right back here again with her plan in tatters. A loop in Time, now inescapable because she had failed.

The enemy realized it, too. With molten rage and frenzied eyes, she turned back to Tyrathorn. He struggled to his feet and faced her proudly.

"You privileged *fils de pute*," she spat. Her chest heaved, breaths coming ragged. "None of you are even worthy to power my army! None of you!"

The air around her twisted, distorted by gravity. Valentine felt a sinking dread. The Frost Hammer had murder in her eyes. In her desperation, all Valentine could do was pound against the unbreakable barrier between herself and Time.

Gravity compressed around Corday's hand until it was smooth as glass. Like a blacksmith, she forged it into the shape of a lance, razor-sharp tip pointed at Tyrathorn's chest.

Her friend had only seconds to live. Valentine threw herself at the Time barrier, screaming at it in her mind. She heard someone else screaming, too, and thought it might be Asha.

Corday drew back, aiming for the heart. Tyrathorn squared his shoulders and adopted a regal posture. Once again Valentine saw the prince inside him. *Chronauri or not, the world needs you, Thorn. You can't die. I won't let you.*

With a deep, centering breath, Valentine gathered all of herself, every part of her being—every moment she'd lived, every memory, every thought and hope and dream, every shred of Chronauri power and instinct. All that was Valentine Gilbert focused in one shining point. Summoning all of her will, she shaped that point into a spike . . . and hurled herself.

The barrier shattered like glass.

Floating in a void, Valentine looked upon what she'd done in utter disbelief. With her eyes she saw the Frost Hammer, still moving, but at a snail's pace; with her mind she beheld the sea of Time itself, its radiance stretching to eternity, driving the universe with infinite power.

In a flash she understood the purpose of the barrier. Why the Chrona restricted them to only what a machine—a nexus—could draw. Because in the wrong hands, unlimited Time could break not just the world, but the universe and all of reality with it. After the original three Chronauri, none had possessed the strength or ability to transcend that barrier. None had reached Sixth-*sev*.

Until now.

Valentine gazed out on the endless ocean as it flowed by.

In her mind's eye she reached out with a tentative hand, wary of unbridled Time's reaction to a new presence. Her fingertips brushed its radiance, and warm relief flooded her. This power wasn't a stranger—it was a friend. She'd spent months getting to know it, letting it get to know *her*. And now, as it flowed around her, it greeted her as if it had missed her.

Okay, she thought, trembling. *I'm ready. Come to me.*

As if a dam had broken, energy rushed into Valentine. Her body felt like a paper cup trying to catch Niagara Falls. But then her cup grew large and turned to steel and caught every drop of those raging waters. Her mind slammed back into her head, into the present moment, and the flow of Time resumed.

Power burst from her body, overflowing with physical force. Her gravity chains fell to pieces. The building trembled around her. Her corona radiated like a star—instead of plain blue or red, it shone a silvery white. The outer corona burst around it in every color of the spectrum and beyond.

With just a finger of power, Valentine reached out and flicked the Frost Hammer. The woman flew backward and flopped onto her back, her gravity weapon disintegrating.

And with that one touch, Valentine knew that the fight was not over. Although she had taken her enemy by surprise, gravity still held greater sway over Time.

Yet, in her moment of communion with the universe, an insane idea had come to her—a way she might turn the tide. But even now she couldn't do it alone.

She turned toward Malcolm. Surely, if she had found her way to this power, her twin could—

Malcolm erupted in silvery white light and his gravity chains flew to pieces. By the look in his eyes, she knew he'd seen what she had. Turning to her, he grinned.

"Well, look at that," he said, his voice vibrating with power. "Did we just . . . ?"

"I think so. We leapfrogged Fifth-*sev* . . ."

". . . and hit Sixth-*sev* instead."

Valentine nodded. "And I have an idea."

"I knew it!" Tyrathorn shouted. They turned to see him clinging to the wall. Bathed in their light, he gazed up at them with tears in his eyes. "I knew it. You *are* a sight to behold!"

Valentine smiled, overjoyed to see her friend alive.

"Attack!" Back on her feet, Corday turned on her minions as they shrank away. "I am your master, you cowards! Attack them *now!*"

With their Time machine destroyed, cutting off escape, they must have seen no other option. So, trembling, they formed a battle line and charged. Valentine moved to face them but felt a staying hand on her shoulder.

"Relax, Val," Malcolm said. "I've got this."

As the horde approached, he raised an open palm in their direction. He extended his will, and every enemy's nexus burst. They stumbled and lurched to a halt, overloaded and bleeding energy they could not replenish.

Malcolm gestured again. A coruscating capsule closed around each rogue Chronauri. Valentine felt them sink into a *shifting* stasis, much like the Ember Guard had done at the Empyrean Bridge, trapping their enemies in suspended animation. She nodded approval.

Then Valentine felt the familiar *thrum* of an impending strike. Appearing in front of them with fists raised, Corday loosed a scream and powered up for a devastating assault.

Malcolm grabbed Asha by the shoulders. Her gravity chains

fell apart, and he shoved her out of harm's way. She flew backward, tumbling to a stop near Winter.

Fists clenched, Malcolm enclosed the twins in a temporal bubble. Time flowed at normal speed inside the bubble, while outside it the Frost Hammer's attack slowed. Malcolm groaned with great effort and Valentine could see his body shaking.

"Holy crap," he said. "I can't stop Time, Val. It feels like trying to stop the Amazon River—the *whole* thing."

Tyrathorn had been right, Valentine realized. It seemed that completely stopping Time was impossible even for a Sixth-*sev*.

"Just keep it slow, then," she said.

"Can't hold this for long. We'd better think of something fast."

"I have a plan. Well, just a theory, but . . ." She paused to collect her thoughts. "Okay, gravity warps the flow of Time, right? That's how she could suppress our powers."

"Right."

"So, what if the opposite were possible? What if you could use Time to influence gravity?"

Malcolm's brow furrowed. "I don't remember you saying that was possible."

"Maybe no one *knows* it's possible. Maybe you'd have to control such an enormous amount of Time that no one's been able to do it."

"Then why is gravity so much stronger?"

"No idea. Maybe I'm wrong. Or maybe the Chrona's control of Time is tilting the balance. Either way, we have to try something, and this is my only idea."

Malcolm stared at the Frost Hammer, at their friends and family, at Asha, and finally back at Valentine. She could see his wheels turning, calculating what would happen if they failed.

Setting his jaw, he gave a single nod. "So, we try to suppress her gravity and capture her?"

"Actually, I had another idea," Valentine said. "Remember when Clive said he almost built a gravity grenade, but didn't want to risk creating a black hole?"

"Yeah."

"What do you know about how black holes are made?"

Then Valentine shared her plan and Malcolm agreed without hesitation. It was their best shot, they both knew it immediately. Having decided, the twins spent an extra moment of quiet, steeling themselves for what was about to happen.

"We still may not be strong enough," Malcolm said. "We could drop this bubble and she could squash us like bugs."

"So . . . pretty much a normal day, right?"

They grinned at each other. As always, Valentine drew comfort from her brother's presence. Whatever happened, they would face it together.

"Ready?" he said.

Valentine absorbed all the Time she could, preparing to match her newfound might against the Frost Hammer's. With a last deep breath . . .

"Do it."

Malcolm let the bubble burst. Corday's scream resumed and her gravity hit like the fist of a god.

Hands raised, the twins met her power and shoved back against it. The walls around them bowed outward with a horrible screech, and the concrete beneath them crumbled to dust.

The force of Corday's attack drove them to their knees, but they were alive! Her gravity hovered above them, held in place by their opposing force.

"Impossible!" the Frost Hammer shouted. "You can't!"

With effort, the twins climbed to their feet, holding their enemy's power at bay. As Corday watched them move, the first hint of trepidation crossed her face.

"We can't?" Malcolm said.

Valentine grinned. "Just watch us."

They stepped forward once, then again, then again, closing the distance to their enemy. Corday's gravity battered against their Time, but still they approached. Separating, the twins spread out until they stood on either side of Corday, with her in the center.

As she looked back and forth between them, her uncertainty twisted into hatred. Valentine knew the woman's arrogance—she had counted on it. Being surrounded by inferior Chronauri would only push her harder.

For an instant, the distortion waves disappeared as Corday regathered her power. Then, spreading her arms wide, she pointed at Malcolm and Valentine and unleashed twin blasts of pure gravitational force.

Valentine slid backward, churning up rubble under her feet. Still she held on, crying out with exertion but containing Corday's power with the help of her brother. Over Corday's shoulder she could see Malcolm's corona blazing.

Now came the hardest part. The twins had successfully placed Corday in the center of her own gravity field. All that remained was to hold on.

We need to outlast her, Valentine had told Malcolm. *If we can do that, physics will beat her for us.*

But even that would test them to the limit. Gravity micro-storms burst around them. Valentine groaned as her arm snapped from the force. Half a second later, Time swept through the break and left it perfectly healed.

Another burst cracked five of her ribs, and once again Time protected her. Malcolm grunted and she knew he must be experiencing the same. Valentine pushed on, trusting that cosmic radiance to keep her alive.

A constant roar shook the valley. They were stalemated, each side pushing their power to new limits but neither side gaining ground. Which was what the twins wanted.

Valentine lost track of how long she fought. How long she stretched her power, held it just at the edge of breaking. The passage of Time lost all significance, her world shrinking to this one single point and this one single purpose.

Corday shrieked—not in anger this time, but in agony. With one last titanic push, she threw enough gravity at the twins to shatter a mountain.

Then her power faltered. Her attack sputtered and died.

For an eternal instant the world seemed to hang motionless, weightless, Timeless. Everything hovered in that dreamlike moment between flying up and falling down. Between victory and defeat, life and oblivion.

Instead of just deflecting Corday's gravity, the twins had *contained* it, letting it build up around her. This was why they had surrounded her—to ensure that when her strength failed, she would be at the center of the gravity field she herself had created.

And now, as her energy ran out, there was nothing inside her to counterbalance all the gravity she had expended. Which meant there was only one place for it to go.

In one instantaneous rush, the gravity field collapsed back on Corday with a clap like thunder. Deep inside, the source of her power imploded until it formed a microscopic black hole.

The gravity storms disappeared. Corday dropped to the floor.

CHAPTER 42

With a cry like her insides had been ripped out, the Frost Hammer writhed on the floor. Clutching at her chest, she wailed with rage and grief and loss. Her body lurched as if she were trying to force the power inside her to work again.

But it never would.

Finally she passed out. The twins fell to their knees, leaning against each other for support. Malcolm swayed from a rush of dizziness.

"We just . . ." he panted.

"I know," Valentine breathed.

Behind them, something scraped across the floor. Leaping to their feet, they whipped around to face it. Malcolm tried to reach through his nexus, then remembered it was gone. Time responded anyway, bathing him in its radiance.

Then his whole body sagged in relief. Valentine laughed as they rushed into the arms of their waiting family. They formed a giant group hug in the center of the decimated building.

The shockwaves had destroyed everyone's Skrim prison. Now, as they held each other, the twins helped each of them remove their para-nexus and crush it to bits.

No one had escaped unscathed. There were cuts and bruises and broken bones. Everyone hurt. No one cared. They were alive and together and that was all that mattered.

Tyrathorn's damage had been the deepest, but he worked to put on a brave face. Malcolm couldn't fathom what the warrior might be feeling at this moment. So instead of words, he simply offered his hand and then pulled his friend into an embrace. Tyrathorn accepted it gratefully.

"Yo, that was freakin' sweet," Fred said.

Winter jabbed his side. "Eloquent, as always." Then she shrugged, unable to contain a smile. "He's not wrong, though."

"She was so strong," Oma Grace said. "How did you do it?"

"Physics," Malcolm said, sharing a look with his sister.

Valentine nodded. "Basically, we re-created the conditions to form a black hole and let her power destroy itself."

"If Val's right, she has a tiny one inside her now. With all that gravity pulling inward, it cancels out her power. She'll never be able to wield it again."

Oma Grace hugged them both, choking back tears and telling them how proud she was. More embraces followed until, somewhere in the mass of bodies, Malcolm and Asha found each together. She fixed him with a fierce stare, then wrapped her hands around his neck.

"Silly *kuputsa*," she whispered into his ear. "I'm never letting you go."

Then she kissed him, and every ache and pain faded, slipping away with the rest of the world around them.

"So, I'm guessing I've missed a few things," Neil said.

Malcolm's lips parted from Asha's. He turned to see his father watching, and a sudden fear surged in him. What could he be thinking after all this?

Neil beckoned the twins closer. Gingerly, Malcolm untangled from Asha and approached. Valentine left John leaning against Winter and did the same.

With his good arm, Neil swept them both into a hug. "I want to know everything," he said. "But right now, I'm just glad you're okay. You are, aren't you?"

The twins glanced at each other, a thousand thoughts exchanging in that instant.

"Yeah, we're good," Malcolm said.

"And we'll tell you everything. No more secrets."

"Sir, I have never beheld *anyone* like your children," Tyrathorn told Neil. He turned to the twins. "I believe I understand now. How you built a nexus with no instruction. Accomplished in months what should have taken years. Performed tricks with Time that even I have never seen. And, today, how you leapt completely past Fifth-*sev*."

"So . . . we *are* Sixth-*sev* after all," Valentine said, looking relieved and overwhelmed all at once. Malcolm knew the feeling.

"I believe so. Which means you will have a bond with Time unlike any others." Tyrathorn grinned. "Very soon, I hope to see our people learn from *you*."

"I'd just be happy to visit Everwatch again," Malcolm said. He forced himself to stand straighter. "But right now, we aren't finished."

The group shot him an exasperated look. He understood that, but this wasn't like their battle with Lucius. It didn't end with defeating the villain.

"Back in our present, there are still almost five thousand people trapped, waiting to become Skrim. We have to free them."

"And destroy that thing," Valentine said, gesturing at the

dodecahedron. "It's what they used to repeat this day over and over. Once we do, we should slide back to our present."

"I can help." Producing another nexus, Asha clicked it into her chest armor. A flash of red washed over her. "From my old armor. I thought a spare might—"

Glancing over Malcolm's shoulder, she tensed.

The twins turned to see Corday stand. Chest heaving, she glared at them with bitter hatred. Her right hand moved, and with alarm Malcolm realized what she was holding.

Corday tapped the device and a series of beeps answered from her command center. Incredibly, some of the computers still worked. Though hanging askew, one of the screens blinked, and Malcolm saw a familiar number again: 4,629 of her devices had found a host. Beneath it, one word appeared in bold red letters: ACTIVATED

"You think it ends here?" she spat. "I still have an army, and now I've set it loose on your people. How many will die before you can save them? That is . . ." She held up her hands. ". . . if you can save yourselves!"

Her armor powered on again, creating red energy bombs in her palms. Malcolm's eyes went wide, a memory emerging in his mind. Back in the ballroom, Valentine had theorized that the armor powered *itself* with gravity. Now he knew she was right—the Frost Hammer had saved one trick for the very last.

As the twins moved to defend, a screaming red blur hit Corday with thunderous force. Asha tumbled across the floor with her, clanging to a stop against the wall. Corday shoved her away and they leapt to their feet.

This time, Asha was faster. With a snap-kick to the chest, she launched Corday through the wall and into the woods beyond. Turning to the twins, she pointed at the screen.

"You handle that. She's mine!" With that, she dove through the wall.

Malcolm resisted the urge to run after her. But Asha could take care of herself, and she was right—the twins had their own work to finish.

FLYING through the hole in the wall, Asha somersaulted and came to her feet, blades drawn. As she reached through her nexus, power unlike anything she'd ever felt rushed through her. Her weapons and armor blazed like a wildfire.

Corday stood and drew her dual-bladed weapon. Summoning every ounce of rage, Asha stalked toward her enemy. One way or another, it would end here.

Corday flashed a feral grin. "I will enjoy killing you twice. Come—"

"Shut up and fight."

They clashed like tornadoes, staccato clangs echoing like machine gun fire as they circled each other, raining steel. Within seconds it became clear—this time something was different.

Corday swung her blade. Asha dodged and landed a spin kick to her face. Corday fell back clutching her crushed nose.

Sliding closer, Asha swung her left *qama* and knocked Corday's weapon from her grip. She swung her right *qama* and cleaved it in two. The dual blades flew away to stick in the ground.

Corday opened her fist and fired an energy bomb pointblank. Dancing past it, Asha stabbed clear through her arm. Corday tried to kick her. Asha dodged and stabbed through her leg, too. Hissing in agony, Corday backed away to put distance between them.

Asha flashed a satisfied grin. Corday glared back, but

beneath the anger Asha saw something more. She saw frustration, and doubt.

They'd only been fighting a few seconds, but each was experienced enough to see what was happening. Without gravity powers for Corday to hide behind, it became clear who was the better fighter.

So Corday didn't fight. Instead, she summoned every scrap of her armor's stored energy and pumped it all into one massive bomb.

Asha's insides went cold as she realized why Corday had retreated. With distance on her side, she could take aim and lock onto Asha, reducing her ability to dodge. Even if the bomb missed, the blast might kill her all the same.

Corday was gambling everything on one unstoppable kill-shot. As Asha watched the weapon burn bright in her enemy's hands, she knew she would have to take the same gamble.

With a focusing breath, she reached down into her deepest places and summoned all the power she could. Then she broke into a sprint—not away from Corday, but toward her.

The bomb leapt from Corday's hands and flew at Asha, screaming through the air like a missile. They hurtled toward each other, drawing closer and closer until she could feel the crackling energy on her skin.

A fraction of a second before the bomb hit, Asha crossed her blades in front of her. Blades forged for a Chronauri warrior, with the sole purpose of channeling *energy*. Catching the bomb between her *qamas,* Asha spun in a circle to redirect its momentum.

Then she leapt.

My heart, my sword will ever blaze . . .

Asha sailed toward the woman who threatened her people.

The woman who hurt her brother. The woman who tried to kill Malcolm. Blades forward, she flew like winged death.

. . . for all of Time, for all my days.

Before Corday could react, Asha buried the blades in her chest armor with a resounding *clang*.

Corday stumbled back in shock. For half an instant they locked eyes. The emotion Asha saw most clearly, the one she would savor the rest of her days, was terror.

Spitting in her enemy's face, Asha yanked her *qamas* free and ran as fast as her feet could carry her. Corday screamed, and Asha turned to see the bomb erupt.

A burst of light, an ear-splitting *boom*. Corday's armor peeled away like an onion, the skin underneath turning black. Her scream cut off as a shockwave blasted her exposed body backward through the woods. Asha never even heard her hit the ground.

Sinking to her knees, she let the *qamas* fall from her grip. With hands clutched to her chest, she laughed in relief as tears streamed down her face.

For you, Thorn.

WINTER smacked the computer and swore. She and Fred typed furiously at the consoles that hadn't been pulverized, searching for something—anything—that could disrupt the Skrim.

"The commands are locked down!" Winter said. "Even *she* couldn't reverse it now."

"Some kinda fail-safe." Fred looked from his screen to the twins. "Sorry. We can't stop 'em from here."

Malcolm huffed. Then another idea struck. "If you can't stop the attack command, can you change their target?"

The keyboard clattered under Winter's fingertips. "I think so, yeah."

"Good. Send them here."

"Yo, are you serious?"

Malcolm exchanged a glance with Valentine. He saw his own fear mirrored in her eyes, but with it, understanding.

"We can't let them attack people in town," she answered. "And if you send them here, it'll give us a chance to figure this out."

"What about the nuclear plant workers?" John said. "The Skrim won't attack us here in the past, they'll attack our present."

At that moment, Asha climbed back through the hole in the wall. Though she wasn't smiling, she somehow seemed . . . unburdened. Sighing with relief, Malcolm met her with a tight embrace.

"Are you okay?"

"Yes. And she will never threaten us again."

Although they weren't finished saving Emmett's Bluff, Malcolm let himself appreciate the significance of that victory. The Frost Hammer had been vanquished. Now they needed to do the same to her army.

"You said she made this Time loop a fixed point," he said. "Could you *un*-fix it?"

"I could try. Why?"

"Before we break the loop, we need to move it to our present. That's when the Skrim will attack."

Asha considered, then gestured at the dodecahedron. "That's the source of the loop. If I can recalibrate it, then yes, it should be possible."

Valentine beckoned to John. "Can you help her? We need to work fast."

"Of course," he said, nodding to Asha. "Just tell me what you need."

While Asha and John replaced Fred and Winter at the computer stations, Malcolm and Valentine turned their attention to planning their tasks. If the loop moved successfully, everything would have to happen quickly.

"Which one do you want?" Valentine said.

"Want to take down the loop? Then I'll handle the workers."

"Okay. After that—"

The room pitched to the side. Or it seemed to, as Malcolm's equilibrium suddenly failed. He grabbed at his sister for support, only to find her doing the same.

"Whoa, what's happening?" she said.

"You feel that?" John called. "Sorry. Didn't know it would affect you."

Malcolm's vision swam while his stomach did backflips. It took all his concentration to focus on Asha, who gave him a tight smile.

"It's working," she said. "The loop has to slide up the timeline until we reach your present. Just hold on."

"And try not to puke," Fred said.

"Shut it, Fred." Winter smacked the back of his head.

Despite the intense nausea, Malcolm found himself chuckling. He closed his eyes in the hope that it would stop the room from spinning. Or at least slow it down.

"How long?" he asked.

"About thirty seconds," John said.

"Will you count us down?" Valentine said.

John obliged, calling out every five-second interval as the present drew closer. Twenty-five, then twenty, then fifteen.

Malcolm absorbed a small flow of Time, taking a moment

to marvel at no longer needing a nexus. It felt like the universe recognized him now and shared its power willingly. Instead of a guest standing outside and knocking on the door, he was family.

He prepared himself, holding ready to act as soon as Valentine did her part. Then the room stopped spinning, nausea fading as they arrived.

"Five . . . four . . . three . . . two . . . one . . . *now*."

The instant John stopped counting, Malcolm felt a temporal *shift* as Valentine went to work. Her bubble of super-slowed Time enveloped the dodecahedron. Freezing at a molecular level, the device cracked and then shattered. Its energy field faded and the Time loop fell apart, depositing them in the present.

"Your turn," she said.

Malcolm flicked at his Time and sent it rippling across the valley—a temporal sonar like the one he had created before. His Chronauri senses found every plant worker by their signature in Time. Barely a breath after Valentine destroyed the loop, he wrapped each person in a capsule of temporal stasis, as he had with the rogue Chronauri.

"Got them!"

He opened his eyes, sharing a triumphant smile with Valentine. One more challenge down.

"We have the workers in stasis," he said to their family. "Can you bring them here? We'll need to protect them, too."

Agreeing, they left to start the search. Then, after only a few seconds to breathe, it was time to consider what came next.

Malcolm turned to Winter. "You sent that command to the Skrim?"

She nodded, looking grim. "They're on their way."

"How long do we have?" Valentine said.

"If they're fast . . ." Fred shrugged. "Dunno. Maybe an hour?"

Malcolm gave an ironic smile. "One hour to come up with another miracle."

"Can't y'all just . . . I don't know, blast 'em?" Fred said.

Malcolm shook his head. "It's not that simple. They have real people inside."

"And we have no idea how much we can do," Valentine said. "Five thousand Skrim would be a lot, even for us."

Malcolm wondered about that. How far did their power stretch now? How far could it? The desire to find out burned in him, but that would have to wait. Right now, they had people to save and no clue—

He felt a *shift*.

Instantly alert, he scanned the room. Valentine went stiff beside him. Another *shift* and his heartbeat raced. Then he felt more—a lot more.

"Mal?"

"I don't know, but they're coming fast."

Pressure built in Malcolm's senses as something hurtled toward them through the timeline. The twins held ready to act.

At the center of the room, a red vortex opened and three tall figures leapt through, clad in gray and silver armor. When they were clear, the portal winked out of existence and another opened a half-second later.

Three more figures appeared through the next portal. This continued on until twenty-five Ember Guard stood before them, Captain Armel at their head. Last, a mass of non-Chronauri Watchers rushed through the final vortex to take up position behind them. Captain Armel bowed at the twins.

"This really isn't the time to finish our disagreement, Captain," Malcolm said.

Valentine pointed at the soldiers. "If you're not here to help, go back—"

"We are. King Jerrik knows you face an impossible force. Which happens to be our specialty." With a smile, he offered his hand. "And we would be proud to fight alongside you."

CHAPTER 43

A flurry of activity surrounded the twins. Malcolm had pointed out the hillcrest to the south, where the Skrim would be invading from the direction of town, and the soldiers had busied themselves with battle plans. The twins' family slipped quietly along the edges of the room, carrying the last of the plant workers.

Right now, neither twin had attention to spare for any of it.

Valentine clung to John. Eyes closed, foreheads touching, they soaked in each other's presence. Soon Valentine would have to leave him with the civilians and go to battle.

Asha had returned, sore but beaming. The Frost Hammer had been vanquished, and Malcolm's admiration for his . . . girlfriend? . . . grew to new heights. Her arms encircled him, her face nestled against his neck.

Malcolm held her close and breathed in deeply. "Cinnamon."

She stirred. "What?"

"I figured it out," he whispered. "You smell like cinnamon."

"Do you . . . like cinnamon?"

"It's my favorite."

She gave a lazy smile and nestled closer. "*You're* my favorite."

Malcolm laughed. "We'll have to find arch-nemeses for you to defeat more often."

Movement caught his attention. He straightened as Captain Armel approached.

"Princess Ashandara," he said. "I am pleased you're well."

With a warm smile, she grasped his hand. "I'm grateful, Captain. Your training kept me alive today."

Armel mirrored her affection. "How long have I watched over you?"

"As long as I can remember."

"Every day has been my honor."

Malcolm cleared his throat. "I don't want to sound ungrateful, but why come now? Why not earlier, when things were so bad?"

"I'm curious about that myself," Valentine said.

"When you showed your power in the throne room, King Jerrik was finally able to glimpse your paths through Time. He will not reveal what he saw to anyone—not even the queen."

Asha made a noise. "She must *love* that."

The captain gave a coy shrug. "Whatever he saw, it changed his mind. We were told to chase you to the Bridge, but not to catch you, then to arrive at this specific moment." He hesitated. "If you would like my opinion . . ."

Malcolm gestured for him to continue.

"I suspect the king saw that, were we to come sooner, you would not have unlocked your true power."

Valentine pursed her lips. "I feel like I should be upset. Funny, though, I'm not."

Malcolm felt the same. Maybe someday they would discuss it with the king. For now, they had business to attend to. He nodded toward the Ember Guard.

"Are they ready?"

"Very nearly." Captain Armel studied Asha. "Can you fight, Princess?"

Despite her fatigue, flames lit behind Asha's eyes. "I wouldn't miss this, Captain."

He smiled as if he'd expected nothing else. "We will make what repairs we can to your armor. As for the others?"

"Our family," Malcolm said. "They'll guard the Time capsules."

"I will leave Watchers with them, in case the enemy gets past us."

"I appreciate that."

Armel gestured toward the southern hills. "When we deploy . . ."

He trailed off, the air of calm around him shattering. His face, always so controlled, contorted into a mask of rage. Malcolm followed his eye and his stomach plummeted. *Oh, man, I didn't even think about that.* Their family and friends had entered the building with the rest of the plant workers in tow.

The last to enter had been Tyrathorn.

A wave of tension burst from Captain Armel and swept across the room. One by one, soldiers turned to see the prince who had become their most hated enemy. They stopped in their tracks, glaring.

Tyrathorn was the last to notice. When he did, his expression flowed from puzzlement to realization, then to shame.

As his eyes met Armel's, the captain moved like a snake. In a flash he drew his weapon, a massive iron warhammer. It glowed red as Armel stepped forward, sizzling like Asha's *qamas*.

Malcolm clamped a staying hand on his shoulder. "Captain,

the Black Tempest is dead. Since coming here, Thorn has been with us. He saved our lives."

"And the Frost Hammer broke his power," Valentine added. "He's just a normal man."

The captain gritted his teeth. "Only half the punishment he deserves."

As if walking to the gallows, Tyrathorn crossed through the army that wanted his head. Three paces from Captain Armel, he sank to his knees and bowed low, exposing his neck.

"Words cannot convey my remorse for what I have done, Captain. Though I am no longer the Black Tempest, I know that I deserve no mercy." He paused, steadying himself. "If you wish my life, I beg of you, please . . . take it now. You deserve justice."

The hammer raised higher.

Malcolm tightened his grip. "Captain, please."

The Captain's arm quivered as he warred within himself, wanting desperately to let the hammer fall. Then, in a blink, his face calmed, and the hammer returned to its place. Stepping closer to Tyrathorn, he loomed overhead.

"When this is over, you will return with us. In chains."

Tyrathorn bowed and moved far from the soldiers. Armel made a small gesture and the army returned to work. Malcolm released a breath he didn't realize he'd been holding.

THE battle line stretched across the hillcrest, the air thick with anticipation. In minutes, the Skrim would arrive.

Malcolm stood hand in hand with Asha. With her skin on his, it was hard to concentrate on the approaching battle. Though exhausted, she kept alert and ready.

"Thank you for heeding my counsel," Captain Armel said.

"We'll do our best."

"Yeah," Valentine replied. "We'll find a way."

Earlier, he had approached them in the warehouse. "I want to propose a strategy for you," he had said. "I hope you will be open to it. But you're not going to like it."

Correct on both counts. The twins had hated the strategy, but it was the right one. This fight couldn't be won with brute force alone. So, despite their desires, they had agreed. Malcolm just hoped they could deliver.

"I will carry you into battle with me," Asha whispered, resting her hand over her heart.

He beamed at her. "Have I told you how hot you are when you fight?"

Asha's cheeks reddened.

"It wasn't just training that kept me alive. Whatever you did . . . I have so much more energy. More life." She tugged on his hand, pulling him closer. "I used to shut people out because I knew my life wouldn't be normal. I was going to spend it fighting, protecting my people, and then die young. That's the price of a Second-*sev*."

A tentative smile brushed her lips

"But I'm different now. I feel it, deep down. I don't know for sure, but after what you did . . . I think maybe I'll have a normal life span."

Malcolm stared in amazement, his heart soaring.

"So thank you, Malcolm. Thank you for my life."

Asha pulled him into a kiss. He felt her affection pulse through his body, and kissed her back with all the joy inside him.

Then he felt the barest ripple in the timeline, and something crashed deep in the woods. As they parted, Malcolm gave Asha's hand one last squeeze.

"They're coming, Captain," Valentine said.

"Watchers! Ember Guard!" Armel shouted. "Prepare for battle!"

A symphony of weapons echoed through the trees, the song of rasping steel as the Watchers produced swords and axes, staffs and hammers, every variety Malcolm could name and some he couldn't.

The Ember Guard followed with their weapons of ice and fire and steel, some glowing like Asha's. One and all, the soldiers stood ready.

The first line of Skrim came crashing through the trees— hundreds of them, and fast. Malcolm tamped down his fear. If he had anything to say, they would never reach the valley behind him.

"Form up!" the captain shouted.

The battle line drew together like one organism. Bunching in the center, they created a wedge-shaped formation with Ember Guard at the edges and Watchers behind.

Only seventy-five yards away now.

"Hold!" Armel commanded.

The Skrim advanced like thunder, heavy footfalls vibrating through the earth. Even sixty yards away now, they looked like giants.

"Hold!"

Asha gave Malcolm one last, lingering gaze.

The Skrim reached fifty yards.

"Charge!"

With a fierce cry, they rose to meet the oncoming horde. As Asha joined them, Malcolm's heart flew from his chest to go with her. He prayed she would be safe.

"Ready?" Valentine said.

He nodded and refocused on his task. On the captain's words.

"You are Sixth-*sev* Chronauri—quite possibly the first since the Three," Captain Armel had said. "Your connection to Time is now beyond the understanding of Everwatch. Only a foolish commander would use you as soldiers. Instead, find a way to stop this army at its source. We will hold them for you as long as we can."

How could they have argued? So now, as their allies flung themselves into battle, the twins would stand on this hill and search Time for a way to shut the Skrim down.

Thirty yards ahead, the battle line erupted. Explosions, flashes of red and blue light, clanging steel, cries of pain and aggression, all spread like wildfire through the forest. Malcolm flinched as a tree splintered from the swing of a Skrim's club-like arm, toppling to the ground with a hollow *boom*.

Malcolm closed his eyes and let the battle fade into the background. Bit by bit, he shut out the physical world and stretched his Chronauri senses over the forest. It felt like stretching a new muscle.

As physical forms—every tree and soldier and all things in between—faded from his perception, all that was left was Time. Time came from everything that lived, flowed through everything that didn't.

Perceiving only Time, Malcolm saw the world laid bare. He saw the trees as tall plumes of Time streaming upward, reaching for the sky. He saw the warriors of Everwatch, Time pulsing in radiant waves from deep inside them. Their weapons and armor were slowly eroding, breaking down imperceptibly as Time flowed through them. Shining bright, Asha's signature blazed like a star.

Malcolm floated among them in his mind, passing through the flows and bursts of Time like rivers of glowing mist. He moved through them until he beheld the Skrim. Before, he had felt their wrongness, and now he could see it as well.

Stifling his revulsion, he singled out one Skrim and focused on the para-nexus at its heart, searching how it worked for a way to shut it down. The host hovered there, his Time pulsing from deep inside. Malcolm watched it cascade through the man's body, sustaining his life like the beat of a temporal heart. Then he watched in horror as the para-nexus sucked that pulse away, absorbing and using it as fuel. With each passing second, the para-nexus drained his life away.

Focusing closer, Malcolm traced every piece of the intricate machine. He observed how they worked together to create the frozen abomination that threatened his friends. *Come on, show me how to beat you,* he thought, desperate to find something he could exploit.

Mal . . .

He brushed away the distraction, immersed in his own senses.

Mal . . . Mal . . .

He shook his head. *Whatever you are, go away.*

Mal . . . Mal . . . MAL!

Pain burst his concentration. Resurfacing in his body, Malcolm gasped like a swimmer coming up for air.

"Mal, look!" Valentine pointed at the battlefield, verging on panic. "We've got to help them."

He saw it now. The Watchers and the Ember Guard were hard-pressed, holding the line but slowly retreating as more and more waves of Skrim joined the fight. There must have been a thousand now! Still foggy, Malcolm shook his head.

"But we're supposed to—"

"We're supposed to save lives, and that includes theirs! Come on, you *know* we can do our part after."

A Watcher went down, overwhelmed by a cluster of Skrim. Then another fell, and the line of defenders began to bow. *But if we don't do our part, will that cost even more lives?* Malcolm stared, caught between two impossible decisions.

"Mal, come on!"

What do I do?

CHAPTER 44

Captain Armel swung with fury. Blazing red, the massive iron warhammer *whooshed* through the air and shattered an attacking Skrim's leg. The monster crashed onto its back, flailing razor-sharp arms.

Armel leapt high, a spike extending from the top of his weapon. The Skrim's pincers glanced off his blazing armor as he landed on its torso. With a shout he drove the spike deep into its chest. The para-nexus sparked and died, and the creature fell to pieces.

In the second he took to catch his breath, another struck from behind. Armel gasped from the impact. Clinging to his weapon, he somersaulted to absorb the fall and catapulted back to his feet. Four Skrim surrounded him.

Setting his jaw, he spun the hammer. "Come and meet your doom."

They charged. Armel's world became a blur of ice and iron and pain and rage. Over and over he swung, pulverizing every block of ice that came within reach. His side ached like a rib had cracked—howling, he pushed it out of his mind and swung again.

A corner of his mind registered different movement nearby.

As he slid narrowly between two ice claws, he turned to see an unarmored man covering his flank. Shirtless, black hair flying, he swung a claymore like someone born with a sword in his hand.

Armel almost called out his gratitude . . . until the man turned.

"What are *you* doing here?" he demanded, whirling his hammer to deflect an attack.

"I may not be Chronauri, but I can still swing a sword," Tyrathorn called.

"You have no place on this battlefield!"

"I will do my part, Captain!" Tyrathorn cleaved the head off a Skrim and ducked under its counterattack. "I will help stop what I created, or die trying."

The next wave of Skrim arrived. Despite the hatred burning through his veins, Armel chose to stand beside his former prince. It still wasn't enough.

A crushing blow knocked the captain onto his back, dazed. A thud followed as Tyrathorn hit the ground beside him. His hammer had flown away somewhere, and now half a dozen Skrim loomed overhead. Mastering his fear, Armel refused to close his eyes. He muttered a prayer as icy weapons poised to strike.

Two blurs rushed between them. Flashes of light and pops like thunder burst in the air around them, and then the blurs were gone. All six Skrim fell to pieces.

Armel blinked. *What in Eternity . . . ?*

Tyrathorn leapt to his feet. Staring after the blurs, he cheered and pumped his fists in the air.

Agape, the captain watched as twin waves of destruction raced down the battle line. His eye could barely track the

Gilberts as they moved through the Skrim raining fire and lightning. Everywhere they passed, the ice monsters burst into melting chunks, leaving their hosts free.

Before he knew it, the first waves had been vanquished. The twins turned and moved toward a place between Armel's force and the next waves of Skrim. Even now, he knew those unnatural creatures were out there somewhere in the distance, approaching. He stared after the twins, hoping desperately that they had found a solution.

THE twins skidded to a halt as energy arced and burst around them. Malcolm grinned at his sister. It felt good, getting his hands dirty.

"Good thing you saw what was happening," he said as their bodies slowed back to normal. "Thanks for getting me to move."

Valentine nodded, studying the Everwatch army. "They don't waste time."

The soldiers had already carried the rescued Skrim hosts to the crest behind them. In mere moments, they re-formed the battle line and prepared to fight again.

Despite their impressive discipline, Malcolm couldn't help shaking his head. "That was, what, three waves? We destroyed a thousand at most."

"And I'll bet each wave gets bigger." Valentine gestured behind her. "They can't do this forever."

"The captain was right. We need something big and we need it now."

"I have an idea for my part. Did you find anything?"

Malcolm shrugged, feeling helpless. "I saw how a para-nexus works, but how do I break five thousand of them at once? I need *one* thing that can take them all out." He stared through the forest, anxiety building in his chest. "Who knew these tiny little machines would be such—"

He cut off, the solution exploding in his mind. *If I can pull that off . . .*

"Be right back," he said, then sprinted toward the Captain.

Armel met him halfway. "We're grateful for the—"

"In a hurry, sorry," Malcolm said. "Can I borrow your hammer?"

The captain hesitated, reluctant. It was obvious how much he loved that weapon. After a brief pause, though, he handed it over.

"Thanks. Now, does anyone fight with silver weapons?"

"Silver alone would make a poor weapon, I think."

"How about copper?"

Armel pondered, then called over his shoulder. "Hetepheres!"

A dark-haired woman broke from the ranks, saluting the captain as she approached. For an instant she stared at Malcolm in wonder before resuming her soldier's discipline.

"Your backup weapon, please," Armel said.

Without hesitation, the woman drew a beautiful sickle-like blade from a sheath on her back. It gleamed reddish brown. Captain Armel nodded to her in gratitude before handing it to Malcolm.

"Thank you, Hetepheres. It will go toward a good cause."

The woman's face fell a fraction before she caught herself. "Of course, sir," she said, and returned to her place.

"Use it wisely," the captain said to Malcolm. "Hetepheres comes from ancient Egypt, and that is her last artifact from home."

Malcolm nodded, trying not to feel guilty for what he was

about to do to such a priceless item. The history geek inside him practically screamed.

"I promise."

He returned to his sister, a borrowed weapon in each hand.

"I hope you're ready," she said, staring through the trees. "Here they come."

Once more, a wave of Skrim appeared in the distance. By the ripples in the timeline, Malcolm knew their guess had been right—this wave *was* bigger. And the twins had less than a minute to defend their people. He let the hammer's head thunk onto the ground, handle pointing up.

"Put us in a bubble of fast Time, please?"

A *shift* brushed his senses as Valentine obliged. Focused on his work, he barely noticed them moving more quickly than the world outside.

He held the copper scythe by its handle. Wrapping the blade in a sheathe of Time, he willed the copper molecules to move faster . . . faster . . . *faster,* cranking up the metal's internal temperature until the blade glowed. Waves of heat rippled off the shiny surface.

"Mal, what are you doing?"

"What's that word for a metal that can be stretched into a wire?"

"Ductile."

"Right. When Clive talked about electromagnets, he said copper was ductile. Don't ask me how I remember it now."

The blade began to droop, soft as butter. Malcolm set its tip on the end of the hammer's handle. As he willed those molecules to slow, the tip cooled, allowing copper to bond with iron. *There. Now, move!*

Malcolm began to wind the blade around the hammer's handle, each revolution stretching the blade into a thick, glowing wire. It formed a spiral covering the handle from end to end. When the entire blade was spent, he dropped the ancient handle and hit the warhammer with a blast of cold. In seconds it was comfortable to touch.

"You're not serious," Valentine said. By her expression, she understood what he intended.

"Is it any crazier than what you have planned?"

She shrugged. "Count of three, then?"

Suddenly it was all too real. Hefting the warhammer, Malcolm faced the horde running in slow motion from the south—thousands of them. A sliver of doubt wedged into his heart.

"If this doesn't work . . ." he began.

"It will. We get one shot, and it'll work." They shared a last look, then she counted down. "Three . . . two . . . one . . . now!"

Valentine dropped the bubble and absorbed a massive flow of energy. Malcolm opened himself fully to Time, letting it race into him.

Once again the earth shook, the Skrim coming so close that he could see their hosts trapped inside. So close that their jagged hands raised high, ready to strike.

"Ready?" he called.

"Do it!"

Malcolm called down the most colossal lightning strike the town had ever seen, bolts of such terrifying power that the sky appeared to rip apart. His body became an open conduit. As Time poured through him, he stretched out with his will, and each lightning bolt obeyed his call.

He caught them as they fell, channeling their power into the iron hammer and its copper coil. A colossal charge built inside the weapon until it could bear no more.

In his hands, the hammer and coil had become a giant electromagnet. Aiming his makeshift device toward the enemy, Malcolm released the surge of power and pushed it toward the Skrim in one massive electromagnetic pulse.

Each para-nexus was an incredible machine . . . but still just a machine with components like any other. As the pulse swept over the southern hills, it passed through each and every para-nexus, frying internal components and causing catastrophic failures.

All at once, thousands of tiny doomsday devices shut down. The Skrim stopped dead.

Which meant the people inside them would die even faster. Either they would be crushed as the monsters fell, or they would freeze and suffocate in minutes. The twins had known that. So it was Valentine's job to get them all out at once.

A split second after Malcolm's pulse, Valentine released her own power in a dazzling display. It burst into millions of hair-thin threads, the barest slivers of Time. As they heated the air around them to exactly ninety-eight degrees, the threads scattered toward the Skrim as fast as supersonic bullets.

In the blink of an eye, the ice monsters were cut to ribbons by swarms of tiny fire blades, hot enough to melt ice but not burn human flesh. The threads followed in the wake of Malcolm's pulse, freeing every host from their frozen tombs. In unison they dropped to the ground, unconscious but alive.

A great silence fell over the forest. All was still, like the calm after a storm. The twins sagged against each other, panting and exhausted.

"It's over," Valentine said. She choked on a single sob. "I almost didn't believe . . ."

Malcolm wrapped his arm around her shoulder. "I know. Me, too." He placed a hand on his heart. "For you, Clive."

Behind them, the quiet was broken by a single, whooping cheer. The twins turned to see Tyrathorn sprinting, grinning from ear to ear, arms wide open until he held them in a crushing bear hug.

The army of Everwatch did not follow. Instead, they waited for their captain's lead—and they did not have to wait long.

Armel pumped his fist toward the sky. "*VICTORY!*"

Ember Guard and Watcher alike burst into raucous cheers, stomping their feet and clanging their weapons. As they filled the air with sounds of celebration, Tyrathorn stopped shouting long enough to clap the twins on the shoulders.

"You have accomplished the impossible yet again. I am proud to call you my friends."

The twins returned his embrace. Though the day had become one for celebration, there was something Malcolm needed to say.

"I'm sorry, Thorn. We didn't save everything, and I just wish . . ."

Tyrathorn's smile was tinged with sadness. "I will miss my gifts, but I consider their loss a part of my penance. After everything the Black Tempest did, I am blessed just to be alive. So I will return to Everwatch a prisoner, and maybe, one day, they will be able to forgive me."

"When they see the man you are, Thorn, they'll want to," Valentine said.

"Yes," Malcolm said. "Eventually they'll see what we do."

Small but strong hands suddenly seized Malcolm and

whipped him around. He barely had time to recognize Asha before she kissed him long and hard. Then his hands were clutching her waist, pulling her closer. The softness of her lips and the scent of cinnamon filled his senses for an eternal moment.

When they parted, their little group had been surrounded by the celebrating mass of warriors. Captain Armel congratulated them, even looking at Tyrathorn with something less than hatred. The twins thanked him profusely for believing them, and for coming to help.

Something stirred at the edge of Malcolm's perception. He stopped short, looking to Valentine for confirmation. Her eyes found his, filled with the same alarm. The feeling had come from the direction of the Skrim. *Oh, no. Please, no more.*

Clutching Asha's hand, Malcolm followed Valentine until they passed through the masses. With a clear view of the shattered forest, they could see clearly what was happening.

The people were waking up.

One by one they came shakily to their feet, nervously taking in the sight of a battle-scarred forest and a band of armed warriors. Men and women, young and old, wardrobes from jeans to cocktail dresses, even a few faces Malcolm recognized from around town.

"They're afraid," Valentine said. "We have to let them know they're safe."

Malcolm shared a glance with Captain Armel. He bowed, acknowledging the unspoken request, and began handing out orders to his troops. Laying down weapons and shedding armor, they dispersed into the crowd to welcome people back from the brink.

Valentine found a shivering preteen girl and wrapped her in a warm, comforting hug. Malcolm and Asha approached a man with faded clothing and a scraggly gray beard. Knees wobbling, he just managed to stand as they reached him.

"Hey, you're okay," Malcolm said, gently taking his arm. "We're here to help."

"Oh, thank ya kindly," the man said. "Much obliged."

"What's your name?"

"They call me Bottle Joe." He examined Malcolm and Asha with keen eyes. "You the ones saved Ol' Joe from that nasty cold?"

They smiled, and Malcolm nodded.

Joe squeezed his hand. "Then, young sir and miss, you got a friend for life!"

As they helped their new friend find his way home, as Malcolm watched his new allies lend aid to the people of Emmett's Bluff, he allowed himself finally to relax. To savor, not so much the victory, but the feeling of safety that came with it.

He repeated it to himself again.

Everyone was safe.

THEY heard the celebrating from over the ridge.

Awash in relief, Fred and Winter clutched each other tightly. He could feel her trembling. Now that the threat had passed, he found himself wondering how to help his friend pick up the pieces of her life. Whatever it took, he would be there.

But right now, there was something else he had to do.

"Be back in a few," he said, untangling from Winter.

Her eyes narrowed. "Where are you going?"

"Chill, girl, I just gotta take a leak."

He ducked through a hole in the wall and sprinted into the forest. When the feeling had seized him, he knew it wouldn't go away until he saw for himself. He had to be sure.

So he followed the trail of destruction left by Asha's battle. He passed by burning craters, scorched and broken trees, half of a double-bladed sword, until finally he found it.

The patch of ground where snow had melted and the earth underneath was deeply scarred. *Must be where Asha killed her.* Except, where was the Frost Hammer?

Instead of a body, he found a faint trail in the snow. Fred trekked deeper into the forest for half a mile, following the trail until it came abruptly to a stop.

Where it ended, Charlotte Corday lay back against a fallen log, gasping for every breath. Fred felt a flash of pity. It was easy to see why Asha had presumed her dead. Burned and broken, she seemed to be clinging to life through spite alone.

Corday must have heard him approaching and tried to defend herself. Somehow she'd carried the other half of her weapon, only now it lay just beyond her grasp. She reached for it, trembling in desperation as her fingers brushed the handle.

She gave up as he stood over her. Sagging, she fixed him with pleading, bloodshot eyes.

"Pl . . . please help me," she said, her voice like the crumbling of dried leaves. "H-h-help me g-go away. Won't both-th-th-er anymore. Pleeeease."

Fred knelt and rested his hand on her shoulder. "Are you suffering?"

The sound she made was almost a laugh. Her chest heaved in protest.

"Sssoooo much pain. Sssssoooo tired of raaaage. Of b-b-battle. Want onnnnly to disssssap-p-pear. Please h-help?"

Fred studied her for a long moment. When he finally spoke, his tone had softened.

"My friends Mal and Val, they're the best of us. They're just so good through an' through. Know what I mean?"

Corday nodded.

"I should be more like them. They're so good, they make me wanna be better. Right now they'd tell me to be kind. To believe you could change." He smiled down at her. "And they'd want you to have a second chance."

Corday's lips cracked a smile, eyes full of hope. "Th-th-thank y—"

"Thing is, though, we *are* different." He stared up at the trees in thought. "In lots of ways. Their family's normal, I'm a rich kid who mostly lives alone. They got these crazy powers, I'm just an average bro. But the one way we're totally different? They believe in mercy, and I believe in protecting them no matter what. I believe in doing things they won't do—can't do—to keep them safe. Because the world needs them. So, really, the biggest mistake you ever made?" His eyes dropped back to Corday, brimming with cold fury. "You threatened my friends."

Panic filled Corday's eyes. Without another word, Fred moved his hand from her shoulder to her throat and squeezed.

CHAPTER 45

*D*on't ask me how it happened. I don't a hundred percent understand it, either. But when a future version of you shows up and tells you all manner of bad things are about to happen, you listen. More than that, you do what it takes to make it right.

I had a secret project. Y'all saw pieces of it, but I didn't want to say nothing 'til I got it to work. Had an idea for a single-use Time travel device. Preprogram a day and a place, and if there's an emergency, press the button and off you go. Like an escape hatch. For the life of me, though, I couldn't make the thing work. Got about halfway and hit a wall.

Then our friends from Everwatch showed up. I got a look at their nexus and the little "Beacon" hidden inside, and . . . I recognized my design. Somehow, at some point in the timeline, my design got back to 'em and they managed to finish it. So, as anyone would, I used the Beacon as a reference to finish my prototype. Yeah, I know—crazy, full circle time travel stuff right there.

Anyway, that's where Future Me comes in. One day I'm in my lab, and suddenly he pops outta nowhere. Turns out my Beacon prototype worked, and he used it to come back and warn me. Things were gonna go real bad, but with the two of us working together, we might just buy our friends a chance.

By the time y'all see this, it will already have happened. I'll be gone, and if you're reading this now, I hope it means we made a difference. I hope you sent that evil woman packing. Only scary thing is I'll never know. Future Me didn't see beyond the point where he jumped away and traveled back to help me. So I'll just have to have faith in you, which now that I think about it, ain't too hard.

Future Me and I, we'll help as much as we can. Then it'll be my turn to go back, so you're gonna see me disappear in a flash. Don't worry. It means I've gone back to Past Me, so I can tell him what's coming and help him save our friends. Then it'll be his turn to travel back and help the next Clive.

From what Future Me says, I won't get long to say goodbye. If I didn't get to say it then, I'm sorry. But I'm saying it now—I love you all. You're as much family as any blood could be, and then some. Keep being the heroes you are. One day, I just know it, you're gonna save the world.

Truly,

Clive Jessop

Oh, and one more thing. Someone's gotta take my half-made Beacon design back to Everwatch's early days. Slip it in some scientist's mailbox and let 'em finish what I started. From what I saw, the Ember Guard ends up making pretty good use of it. Please and thank you.

OVER the next week, news spread like wildfire. People had watched their loved ones transform into giant ice monsters, wreak havoc, and run off into the hills, only to stagger back hours later. Videos on YouTube were racking up millions of views.

The victims remembered little. What they did remember was waking up to a band of warriors who seemed to have stepped out of legend. Over and over, they shared the incredible tale with reporters around the world, even with people on the street who'd traveled to see Emmett's Bluff. Once again, their town was Home of the Strange.

The one thing they remembered most clearly, though, was the one thing they would never tell the world. The one thing they had promised not to reveal, except maybe in private whispers to loved ones. The memory of teenage twins at the head of that legendary army, shining like the sun, reaching through Time and space to set them free.

Those twins stood now in Clive's laboratory, along with everyone they loved. Together they read the letter he had left for them. Together they said goodbye to their friend, sharing stories of how the great Clive Jessop had touched their lives.

Valentine had bonded with Clive over gadgetry. She stood hand in hand with John, who talked of late nights spent in this very building with his old friend, working together to create the wondrous gadgets that had helped them survive. He vowed to continue that work—which would be possible now that Clive had left him the auto shop in his will.

Malcolm had first come to know Clive through Walter. He shared memories of listening to their stories while old records played. Asha hadn't known Clive well, but spoke of her admiration for his spirit, and for what he'd done to protect his friends.

Though Oma Grace could have spoken for hours, she chose to say only a little for now. She was proud of her friend, and it was plain how much she would miss him.

Fred and Winter offered their goodbyes, managing to stay

serious for most of it. But they wouldn't be Fred and Winter if their arguments didn't make everyone laugh.

Neil Gilbert was there, too. He hadn't known Clive well, but he owed the man a debt for the lives he had given back to them. At his side, Callie de la Vega echoed his gratitude.

Malcolm couldn't take his eyes off the diamond engagement ring glittering on Callie's finger. It was surreal, knowing that their family would have a new member.

If their father had fallen for a lesser person, the thought might have filled him with dread. Fortunately, Callie was *not* a lesser person, but a wonderful one. She had brought so much joy back to Neil's life, and ever since the twins' battle, she had dedicated herself to supporting them. Malcolm, and even Valentine now, looked forward to having her in their lives.

Speaking last, Tyrathorn echoed his sister's sentiments. Captain Armel stood beside him, a silent observer. Only he remained—the Ember Guard had returned home the day after the battle. Amazingly, the captain had agreed to give Tyrathorn longer before going back. Now, though, it was his turn to say goodbye.

One by one, Tyrathorn worked his way around the circle of friends, offering best wishes. When he came to the twins, he clapped them on the shoulders in his customary way, like they were old comrades.

"My friends, it has been an honor," he said. "Thank you for helping me remember who I am. One day, I hope, we shall meet again."

"Thank *you*, Thorn," Malcolm said.

"Your training saved our lives, and a lot of others." Valentine hugged him. "Whatever they call you back home, here you'll always be a hero."

Tyrathorn smiled, eyes glistening. Before tears fell and he embarrassed himself, he turned to his sister.

"Ashandara," he said, "are you certain of your decision?"

Asha nodded. "There are two new Chronauri here that need looking after," she said. "I will stay and watch over them."

Malcolm was thrilled—no matter how often she spoke those words, they never got old.

When the request had been relayed to King Jerrik and Queen Meliora, amazingly they had agreed—on a temporary basis, anyway. New Sixth-*sev* Chronauri were unheard of, after all. Everwatch would need an emissary to stay in contact with them.

Of course, an emissary of such importance should have a rank to match. Not only was Asha now a full Ember Guard, but the first Second-*sev* Chronauri to be a High Protector.

There was even a place here ready for her—Walter's house had sat dark and quiet for far too long. It needed new life.

"I will miss you, sister," Tyrathorn said as they embraced. "Thank you for believing in me. One day, I hope I will bring honor to Garris's memory."

"Our people will see who you really are, Thorn," Asha said. "I know it."

They pulled apart and Tyrathorn turned to the captain. "Shall we?"

Armel nodded. He stepped forward to shake everyone's hand in farewell, ending with the twins. "Should you ever need anything, you have only to ask and we will be there. You have allies now. All of Everwatch is at your back."

"That means a lot," Malcolm said. "And if Everwatch needs anything, you know where to find us."

"Thank you, Captain," Valentine added. "For everything."

With that, Tyrathorn and Captain Armel stepped to the center of the room, where they'd cleared a space to jump home. Facing Armel, Tyrathorn held up his hands.

Armel reached for the shackles at his belt. Then his eyes met Tyrathorn's and something passed between them. An understanding, or maybe the beginnings of a truce. Whatever it was, the captain paused, then left the shackles on his belt. With a grateful smile, Tyrathorn lowered his hands.

Captain Armel drew a small, squarish device from his belt pouch. Flipping up the cover, he tapped a series of buttons. A blue light flashed, indicating that it was ready to recall them home.

"Until next time, my friends," Tyrathorn called.

Captain Armel saluted and pressed the button. Behind them a blue vortex burst to life, sending a rush of chilled air through the room. The vortex grew, expanding to meet the device's call, and began to wrap around the two men.

When they had disappeared halfway into the dazzling blue light, Winter broke into a sprint. Running full force at the vortex, she leapt at Tyrathorn. Her arms and legs locked around him as if her life depended on it.

"Surprise!" she shouted.

The last things Malcolm saw were the shock on Tyrathorn's face and the glee on Winter's. Before anyone could react, the vortex closed and winked out of existence. They stood gaping at each other.

Fred broke the stunned silence. "Okay, okay, okay, what in holy—"

A familiar feeling washed over Malcolm. "Everyone move!"

"You heard him—back away!" Valentine commanded, clearly having felt it, too.

As their family retreated, they stood back-to-back, absorbing Time and preparing for whatever might be about to happen.

"What is it?" Asha called.

"Something's coming," Malcolm said.

Shift.

With a bright red flash, a small portal opened above their round meeting table. A wooden box the size of a microwave dropped through, and the portal disappeared.

The group regarded each other, puzzled and wary after what they'd just been through. Gingerly they approached the box, with the nervous air of rabbits ready to bolt at the first sign of trouble.

The wood was old, that much became obvious as they drew closer. The real surprise, though—names were carved into the side, matching every person standing in the room at this very moment. They eyed each other, uncertain.

Finally, Malcolm could stand it no longer. "Only one way to find out."

While everyone gathered around, he found the seams and pulled. The wood fell away to reveal another box inside, this one made of beautifully carved metals—silver and gold and copper and more that he couldn't identify.

Malcolm studied the intricate clockwork lock, hoping the mystery sender had thought to include a key. As his fingers traced it, the box beeped and light pulsed from deep inside. He stepped back, hoping nothing would explode.

Instead the lid bloomed open to reveal an inner machine spinning to life. As it clicked and whirred, hundreds of multi-colored glass beads rose into the air, swirling around each other. Bright lights shone through them from inside the box, and before everyone's eyes, a hologram appeared.

Winter grinned at them. Dressed in garb that Malcolm recognized from Everwatch, she appeared older than when they'd seen her minutes before. This Winter could easily be in her mid-twenties. That devilish grin was still the same.

"What's up, guys?" the hologram said. "I'm betting you've all got silly looks on your faces. Am I right?"

She was.

"Thought so. Wish I could see that—I'd make fun of you *so* hard. Especially you, Fred, you big dummy." She chuckled, then turned serious. "I'm sorry for the way I left. Really. Should have done it right, been a grown-up, said goodbye. I wish I had. But I saw them leaving and suddenly I just couldn't stand it anymore. I couldn't stand the thought of going back to my broken house and my broken life." She paused, gathering her thoughts. "But . . . I'm happy here. I've been happy here for a few years now. I remember once, back in Emmett's Bluff, Thorn told me Everwatch could fix people who thought they were beyond repair. That was me, and he was right. I want to see you all so much, but Everwatch is my home now. I love it more every day."

Malcolm's heart warmed for Winter. After the tragedies she'd suffered, it was good to see his friend so at peace. That, he realized now, was the difference in her eyes.

"Anyway," Winter said, "this message will self-destruct in five seconds. Better run."

Someone behind Malcolm gasped and he heard footsteps. Just as he was about to run, Winter threw back her head and laughed.

"Okay, I know I got some of you! Suckers."

"I'm gonna cross Time just to choke that girl," Fred said, though he smiled from ear to ear. Of course he would miss his best friend, but it was obvious he saw it, too. All he had wanted was for her to be happy.

"One more thing, and it's kinda serious," Winter said. "Malcolm, Valentine, the king and queen urge you to search for the Chrona and learn everything you can from her. They don't know how to find her anymore, but they're hoping another Sixth-*sev* can. And you need to do it fast because . . . well, they think something may be coming."

Malcolm stiffened.

"They're not sure why, but something's different and they're worried," Winter continued. "Since they started, they've had a huge range of years they could travel to, even thousands of years into your future. But now they can't jump nearly that far. Something is blocking them, and they don't know what or why, or even how. So you've got to get crackin' and learn how to be Sixth-*sev*."

She paused, and that familiar grin reappeared. "That's all for now. We'll see each other again, don't worry. Someone's gotta keep you guys cool, even if I have to do it across history." She waved and her smile grew warmer. "I love you guys. Take care."

The lights faded and Winter's hologram disappeared.

"Wow," Valentine said.

"Yeah." Fred shook his head. "Glad they're treatin' her right."

"What could be happening?" Asha said. "I've never heard of us being inhibited like that."

Malcolm squeezed her hand with affection. *Always focused on the fight. That's my girl.* "Don't know, but I guess we'll start looking for the Chrona. No clue how to do that either, though."

"We do need her," Valentine agreed. "I still feel kinda clueless about what we can really do. And if she knows what's happening to the timeline, maybe we can get ahead of it."

"In the meantime, you should continue training," Asha said.

Malcolm nodded. "Great idea. We'll start soon."

Asha cocked her head. "Soon?"

With a grin, she released his hand and went to the bag she always kept within reach now. After their fight in the ballroom, she had determined never to be caught unprepared again. Drawing her *qamas,* she moved toward the door.

"No time like the present."

The twins exchanged a knowing smile. Maybe they *should* start again. After all, who knew what the future held? Whatever it threw at them, though, they would face it together. And they would be ready.

"Okay," Valentine said. "Let's get to work."

CHAPTER 46

In a pitch-dark room, a red light flashed.

Over and over again it pulsed, insistent. Finally, the room's lone occupant reached out and touched the light. With a soft beep, it became a solid glow.

"I'm here, sir," she said.

"Your report is late again," a man said. His deep voice rumbled through her chest.

"I apologize. The mission has been . . . more intricate than I anticipated."

"Shall we send another?"

"No!" She paused, reining herself in. "No, sir, I have it in hand."

"That remains to be seen."

She warred within herself, wanting desperately to ask. Needing to understand. But if she said the words—if she revealed her doubts—would it ruin everything?

"Sir, I—" she cut off. Then, before her courage failed, she pushed forward. "I've spent time with them now. They seem so different than I expected. Is it possible that . . . could we somehow be wrong about them?"

She braced herself.

"They are convincing," the voice said. "But do not be fooled. The Gilbert twins will one day rain destruction on the timeline. Their very names will mean suffering and death. You have seen this for yourself. It is a future that you, and you alone, have been sent to prevent." He paused, letting the words sink in. "Have you reconsidered, Calypso? Shall we send another?"

The red light flared, bathing the woman in its angry glow. Though she knew her master couldn't see it, Callie de la Vega stood straighter, her face becoming a stone mask.

"No, sir." She paused, gathering the courage to say it. "You have my word. By the next time we speak, the Gilbert twins will be dead at my hand."

ACKNOWLEDGMENTS

These aren't your normal, everyday acknowledgments. Why? Because you'll find buried treasure at the end. So just stick with me for a few paragraphs.

First and foremost, I owe a huge debt of gratitude to my family. I've said before that Mom and Dad always let me dream. It's true, and a huge reason why you're reading this today. Hopefully it'll be why you read my books for many years to come.

Eternal thanks go to North Star Editions for giving my work a new home. I'm ridiculously excited to see where we go next. Thanks to TJ da Roza, my editing guru, for giving this book the bird's-eye view and helping it grow into something better.

To author friends who helped along the way, whether it was a beta read or just an encouraging word, thanks for always being there. From the very first day I announced the publication of *The Year of Lightning*, the writing community has welcomed me with open arms. It's such an awesome team to be a part of, and I'll do my best to pay it forward to the next wave of new authors.

Music plays a huge part in my writing process. So, once again, it's fitting that I thank some of the artists that helped me along the way: Lindsey Stirling, whose music gave heart and power to Asha Corvonian; James Newton Howard, whose soundtrack to *The Village* helped me write Malcolm's first kiss; Ryan Miller, whose soundtrack to *Safety Not Guaranteed* gave Asha new life at a crucial moment; and Henry Jackman, whose soundtrack to *X-Men: First Class* helped me find Tyrathorn's earnest strength and helped Valentine finally break through that wall.

Last but never least, thanks to YOU for being a part of this awesome adventure. If you want to drop me a line and talk about books or time travel or anything cool, my e-mail is RyanDaltonWrites@gmail.com. You can find me on Twitter @iRyanDalton and Facebook at www.facebook.com/ryandaltonwrites. There's also my website, www.ryandaltonwrites.com.

If you're a reader, keep reading. A writer, keep writing. A dreamer, keep dreaming. Dreams have power, and there's no telling where yours might take you.

Oh, by the way, the real treasure was inside you all along. It's friendship.

Or lasagna.

Or something.

RYAN DALTON either wears a cape and fights crime abroad, or writes about it from his red captain's chair at home. Perhaps he's a superhero that's trained with the world's finest heroes, or he's a lifelong geek who sings well and makes a decent dish of spaghetti. It's also plausible that he's been plotting to take over the world since he was ten, or that he's since been writing novels to stir the heart and spark the imagination. Either way, he lives in an invisible spaceship that's currently hovering above Phoenix, Arizona.